# The Secrets Raspberries Keep

A Novel By

**Amber R. Gilpin**

AMBER R. GILPIN

# The Secrets Raspberries Keep

For now we see through a glass, darkly; but then face to face: now I know in part; but then shall I know even as also I am known.

1 Corinthians 13:12

# The Secrets Raspberries Keep

*A Novel by*
**Amber Gilpin**

© 2026 Amber Gilpin

# Dedication

**To Rebecca, Willow, Melayne, Hunter, and Levi—**
May you grow up unburdened by what came before you, bold in your truth and rooted in love.
You are the reason the story changes here, the reason old patterns were not carried forward.
This is for you—so you'll know where we come from, and how far love can reach.
**To the women who came before me and the ones who walked beside me—**
Thank you for surviving, for carrying faith and fire, and for reminding me that healing is never meant to be done alone.
**And to the men who gave more than they took—**
who stood without dimming our light and showed me that gentleness can be its own kind of power.
Thank you for teaching me that not all hands hurt.
*This story is ours. Thorns and all.*

# Content Advisory

The story that follows does not shy away from the hard things. It walks through grief, memory, and the quiet wreckage some traumas leave behind. Like the raspberries in Mamaw's thicket, tender in places, thorned in others, it asks to be approached with care.

**Please read and proceed at your own discretion.**

Within these pages, you may encounter:

- Sexual assault and rape
- Grooming, coercion, and manipulation
- Domestic and emotional abuse
- Suicidal thoughts and self-harm ideation
- Substance abuse, overdose, and addiction
- Post-partum depression and complicated grief
- Discovery of human remains, murder, and cold-case investigation
- Death of family members, funerals, and intergenerational trauma

These subjects are handled with respect and authenticity, but some scenes may feel heavy or unsettling. If you find yourself overwhelmed, you are not weak for stepping away. Skip ahead. Set the book down. Breathe. Ask for help if you need it. Your well-being matters more than any chapter.

**You are not alone.**

- National Sexual Assault Hotline (RAINN): 800-656-HOPE (4673)
- Suicide & Crisis Lifeline (U.S.): 988 (call, text, or chat)
- National Domestic Violence Hotline: 800-799-SAFE (7233)
- If you are outside the United States, please consult local resources.

Take whatever time and tenderness you need.

When you're ready, Jenny's story will still be here, waiting in the shade, just past the thicket.

# Chapter 1



*Journal Entry– May 5, 1974*

*Sometimes I think the woods know our secrets before we ever speak them. As a girl, I used to run barefoot past the raspberry thicket along the edge of the field, thinking it marked the edge of the world. But the older I get, the more I believe some places aren't meant to be crossed until we're ready. God gives us thorns not just to guard the fruit, but to make sure we're brave enough to reach for it.*

*-Ruth*

As children, my sister and I wandered the woods behind our grandmother's house, chasing secret treasures and escaping the sweltering Tennessee sun. In the shade, our imaginations took flight. We built castles from branches, dug trenches with our hands, and claimed our kingdoms with flags that Mamaw had sewn from pieces of fabric scraps. We followed deer paths as deep into the woods as we dared. The braver we grew, the deeper we went, until we reached a place where the undergrowth grew thick, and the raspberry briars wove a living wall across the path. We could go no farther.

What treasures lie beyond those brambles? We imagined a hidden realm we called the Kingdom of the Does, a secret place where sleek does and speckled fawns ruled, far from buck antlers and shotgun blasts. We were certain that one day, we too would rule our own world.

By the end of tenth grade, I no longer wandered those woods. Life had grown busier. Basketball practice, grades, and the pressure to make my parents proud filled my days. My sister Sheryl was about to graduate as the valedictorian of her class. We didn't talk like we used to. Once, she had been my secret keeper, but time has a way of changing those things. Sheryl had grown tall like Daddy but looked so much like Momma with long auburn hair that glinted red in the sunlight and soft brown eyes that always seemed to see right through me. She dressed for the part of an aspiring lawyer, but with her own flair. She was always wearing bright colors, sharp lines, and her favorite blue jeans that she swore she could wear to a courtroom if they'd let her. Her hands were delicate, her nails always neatly filed, not meant for calluses or manual work. Long gone were the days of being valiant female knights in the castles we built. Now, Sheryl was in love with a boy, ready to graduate top of her class, and go to college to pursue her dream of becoming a lawyer. She wanted nothing more than to escape this town; a degree was her ticket out.

The boyfriend, Tommy, didn't bother me. Around here, folks would call him a good ol' boy—into hunting, fishing, and tearing up the backroads in his Jeep. Honestly, I thought he was good for Sheryl. He kept her heart tethered to the mountains. She had her sights set on becoming a big-time lawyer in D.C., which felt like a whole other world to me. I didn't want her to leave. She was part of this place, a part of me. I wanted her to succeed, sure. But I wanted her to do it here, where we belonged. *Why couldn't she be Tennessee's best lawyer?*

But Sheryl still had castles to build. And I knew, deep down, that she'd make a difference in this world. Part of me swelled with pride just thinking about it. But a bigger part felt afraid, afraid of losing her, and maybe even more afraid of being left behind. Of never quite measuring up. How could I ever make Momma and Daddy proud when I couldn't shine brightly like Sheryl?

I still remember the last basketball game of our season that year. Our school hosted the county championship, and it was the final day of the tournament. Our team had fought hard, practiced all year, and we were ready. We had played teams from all over our little county, and we just knew that we were going to take home the tournament trophy. More importantly, we knew that if we won, we would be headed for regionals and then on. We took great pride in our team. *There was no way we wouldn't win,* I had thought. My stomach was dancing with butterflies, and as I looked out the locker room door, I saw my Momma and Daddy sitting in the stands where they always did.

They never missed a game, no matter how busy they were; they made the time to be there. Looking back on it, that was more important to me than any championship ever could be. At the time, though, my younger self only knew that if my team won that trophy, then I would have been a part of something big, something worth celebrating. It didn't take long to realize that would not be the case. The team we were playing was tough. They were bigger, they were faster, and they had trained harder. We could barely keep up, but we tried. Then, after half-time, our point guard broke her ankle, and it was all over but the crying, as we say. And crying, we did. Our hearts were broken, and we had been humbled.

The worst part was the car ride home. My parents tried to comfort me.

"It's okay, kiddo," Daddy said. "You can't win them all."

"No matter how good you are," Momma added, "there's always someone better. That just gives you something to reach for."

I know now they meant well. But all I could think about was Sheryl—always ahead, always better. I'd be chasing her shadow forever. When we got home, I told them I needed a walk. They nodded, and I headed down the dirt road to Mamaw's. She loved me unconditionally, and her hugs had a way of making me feel as though all was right in the world. But that day, she wasn't home. So, I cried alone on the steps of her porch.

As I sat in silence, my gaze drifted toward the woods where my sister and I had once spent endless days, laughing, exploring, and losing ourselves in the magic of childhood. *How long had it been since we last set foot beneath those trees?* I couldn't remember. But something about them called to me that day, a quiet pull I couldn't ignore. I rose, wiped the tears from my cheeks, and stepped toward the familiar tree line.

There, just beyond the edge, I spotted one of the old deer trails we used to follow with bare, eager feet, our voices echoing with laughter and the silly marching songs we made up on the spot. But that day, there was no laughter. There was only a storm of frustration pushing me onward. My legs ached from the game, but I didn't care. I was built like Momma, short and strong, with an athletic frame and a temper to match when pushed hard enough. Sweat clung to my tanned skin and my unruly hair, pulled into a loose ponytail, stuck to the back of my neck as I trudged toward the woods. As I walked, the path narrowed. The trees pressed in tighter, and the air grew thick within the brambles and undergrowth. A familiar wall of raspberry briars loomed ahead, those same thorny vines that had turned us back time and again. *But not today*, I had thought.

The briars scratched and clung to me, tearing at my jersey and biting into my sweaty skin, but I kept going. Halfway through, I hesitated. Doubt crept in, but anger burned brighter. I clenched my jaw and pushed forward, determined to break through. And then, finally, I emerged. The underbrush thinned, though the trees remained close and cast long, eerie shadows. Still, I felt something like pride flicker in my chest. I'd done it! I'd gone farther than we ever had as children. I had crossed into what we once called the Kingdom of the Does.

A laugh escaped me at the memory of that silly name; how magical and distant this place had once seemed. But the sound died quickly on my lips. Something caught my eye, a shape on the ground, just barely visible. *No... it couldn't be.* My feet moved on their own, cautious but steady. With each step, a sick certainty grew in my gut. And when I was close enough, no more than five feet away, I knew. A human skull lay half-buried in the earth, staring back at me with empty sockets.

The woods, once filled with joy and the songs of childhood, now rang with a different sound: my own scream, raw and echoing in the hush of the trees.

# Chapter 2



*Journal Entry– September 27, 1993*

*A child's laughter carries like birdsong through these hills. Sheryl has Jenny chasing fireflies again, and I pray they never grow too old for that kind of wonder. The world will try to take it from them soon enough. I keep Psalm 91 close these days: "He shall cover thee with His feathers, and under His wings shalt thou trust." I ask God to keep them safe under His wings-wherever they may wander.*

*-Ruth*

My memory splinters around the moment Daddy reached me. One blink, I was staring at ribs laced in moss; the next, he was there, boots sinking into leaf-rot, his breath a prayer between clenched teeth. He said later my scream carried clear across the holler, ricocheting off the ridgeline like a warning shot. He half-dragged, half-guided me down the deer path and onto Mamaw's porch, but it plays in my head like a lamp-light flicker, too dim to last, too bright to forget. My whole body rattled, knees knocking like pine boards while questions buzzed louder than the first cicada of summer. *Who was she? How long had she lain in that green grave? Could bone be a lie?* No, the truth was right there in the dirt, staring up through eye sockets the color of river mud.

Flesh was long gone, but hair—rich and dark, nearly the shade of my own, snaked through the briars, as if the forest itself refused to let her go. I didn't notice Daddy jog back to the house for the telephone. I only felt the porch boards quake beneath his boots when he returned. He pressed a sweating glass of water into my palm, but I never drank it. Just wept again, deeper this time, my sobs buried in the tobacco-sweet scent of his work shirt. The woods around us fell preacher-quiet. No jaybird fuss, no squirrel chatter, just the creak of the porch swing and the sound of my breath catching like a prayer that didn't know where to land.

When the sirens finally split the hush, their wail sounded foreign in our end-of-the-road world. No police ever came this far unless called for. I kept seeing that hair, how it still looked brush-smooth, as if she'd risen early to set it right before vanishing. Maybe that was why it haunted me: it made her feel near, like a girl I might've sat beside in school, a girl with lungs and laughter, not a nameless tangle of bones beneath raspberry thorns.

An officer stepped onto the porch, boots quiet on the old boards.

"Evening, hon," he said, voice low as creek water. "I need to ask you a few things. Feel up to talking?"

I managed a nod.

"Let's start simple. Your full name?"

"Jenny Ann Thompson," I answered, sharper than I meant. Then, because folks around here don't warm to strangers without an introduction, I added, "And you are…?"

A hint of amusement ghosted across his face. "Fair enough. Shaffer Jordan, ma'am. Just made my way down from West Virginia, still learning who's who." He tipped his hat, the gesture halfway between apology and promise.

I nodded again, unsure of what to say. My eyes trailed up the hill to where they were putting caution tape around the woods. My mind began to wander off again about the girl I had seen lying up there. When I heard Officer Jordan say, "Miss, excuse me, Jenny," I turned to face him. "Sorry," I said weakly.

He smiled a very kind smile again, "It's okay. I know this must be tough on you. Honestly, I am a little nervous myself. This is my first case. So, how about we get through this together, huh? Just tell me about what happened to get you to that spot in the woods today, okay."

I told Officer Jordan everything I could, how the game ended in a thumping loss, how fury carried me straight into the briars. The Kingdom-of-the-Does part, I kept to myself; I needed him to treat me like a witness, not a fanciful child. By the time I finished, my throat was raw, my muscles trembling the way a plucked banjo string hums long after the note is struck.

Sergeant Pete Serogia arrived while I was catching my breath. He was a long, lean cedar of a man, hair already salting at the temples, eyes the color of green bottle glass buried in red clay. Folks in Pedoux knew Pete. He and Daddy chased the same fly balls in Little League and shipped out together when the recruiter promised the Navy would show them the world.

Pete strode up the porch steps and tipped his hat.

"Howdy, Abe."

Daddy met his handshake. "Pete."

They moved to the edge of the house, voices low, heads dipping in slow disbelief while dusk pressed in around the eaves like a gathering storm.

Pete turned to me. "Take Miss Jenny home. She needs to rest. If we need anything else, you know we'll be in touch." He gave me a reassuring squeeze on the shoulder. It helped. I believed Pete would find out what happened to the woman in the woods. He had to.

As Daddy prepared to take me home, my grandparents pulled in.

Mamaw looked scared. I wanted to run to her, but my legs wouldn't move. As Pete and Officer Jordan explained the situation, I watched the color drain from Mamaw's face. She clutched Daddy's arm and said, "Take me inside, baby."

She passed by me, taking my hand briefly. I wanted to cry again.

Mamaw Ruth was the gentlest soul I knew. I could already picture her sinking to her knees by the old iron bed, whispering prayers that threaded through the floorboards, pleading for the unknown woman, for her people, and for justice to rise as surely as dawn. Her prayers lingered, like the scent of wild honeysuckle long after the bloom.

Papaw Harlan, usually all grin and porch-banter, stood marble-still while the deputies spoke. Sergeant Pete caught the tremor in his jaw and murmured that he'd come back later for the formal questions. Papaw shuffled past me without a word, shock bleaching the sun from his face.

The weeks that followed crawled like a copperhead through dead leaves, slow, silent, and unsettling. I woke slick with sweat, chased from sleep by dreams of empty eye-sockets and rasping leaves. Questions gnawed at me until my ribs felt hollow: *Who was she? How long had the forest kept her? What darkness pinned her there?* The police circled back, questioning me, Daddy, Momma, Sheryl, even Mamaw and Papaw, but every interview felt like pushing water uphill. Answers stayed buried, and the holler settled into a hush thick enough to taste, as if the pines themselves were keeping the secret.

Some of the answers to my questions came one sleepless night as I stood outside my parents' bedroom door, listening.

"Did you know her?" Momma asked.

"No," Daddy replied. "But I remember her missing posters. I was in fourth or fifth grade then."

My Momma wasn't raised here as a child. Her family had traveled around and didn't settle in this area until she was a junior in high school, so she wouldn't have known the girl.

"So sad, just seventeen years old. Why, that is still a baby. Did Pete tell you what happened to her?" asked Momma.

"He said that she had been hit in the back of the head and that she had been strangled, but she's been out there so long they aren't sure exactly what the cause of death is," Daddy replied.

I remember hearing those words and immediately feeling sick. *Who would do such a thing?* I knocked on the door and went in. They immediately stopped discussing it. "What do you need, Peanut?" my daddy said.

Daddy was a solid man, broad-chested and square-jawed, with a weathered face that spoke of years spent under the sun. His hands were big and rough, the kind that knew their way around a toolbox but gentle enough to tend to a little girl's skinned knee. He was drawing tobacco smoke from his pipe, his voice low and steady to match. People in town said he didn't say much, but when he did, you listened. He was strong in that quiet way that made you feel safe without needing to explain why. And when he called me "Peanut," all the walls I'd built inside myself seemed to soften.

"I just can't sleep," I told them.

My momma was a small woman, barely five feet tall, but she carried herself like someone twice her size. Her auburn hair was always braided down her back, neat and deliberate. Her dark eyes could slice through an excuse like a hot knife through butter, yet if you looked close enough, there was love there. The kind you had to earn. The kind you had to understand to recognize.

Momma was never the affectionate type. Stern, yes. Practical to a fault. She didn't waste words on comfort or softness, but we never doubted she loved us. When she smiled, really smiled, it was like watching winter break. Just for a moment, you could almost see the girl she'd been before the world turned hard.

She gave me one of those smiles then—faint, worn at the edges, but full of something like sympathy—and gestured for me to come closer. She wore her favorite nightgown, the same one she'd worn for as long as I could remember. Something about it made the room feel steadier. She wrapped her arms around me, something she hadn't done since I was small, and whispered that everything would be all right.

I wanted to believe her. God, I wanted to.

But I couldn't.

The world wasn't safe anymore. My innocence had cracked clean through, and no amount of love could patch it back together.

# Chapter 3



*Journal Entry– April 29, 2005*

*There are some aches only the Lord knows about. I see shadows in Jenny's eyes sometimes, things too heavy for a child to carry. I don't know what she's seen or what burdens she's shouldering, but I pray over her every night. I trust that God sees what I cannot, and that He will cover her in mercy.*

*-Ruth*

Time marched on, and the woman found in the woods that day faded from everyone's minds, except mine. I still dreamed of her, lying there as the forest floor pulled up over her like a blanket of moss and leaves. I'd wake in cold sweats, heart racing, tears in my eyes. I still had so many unanswered questions. I still wanted to know all the secrets those raspberries had kept over the years. Just knowing that the body had been lying there the whole time while Sheryl and I played pretend. We imagined all the ways we would conquer the world and how we would be women who made a difference. And the whole time, a woman whose life had been taken too soon lay just yards away. It made me sick to think about. *What if we had been brave and pushed through the raspberries sooner? Would they have been able to find more evidence? Could they have brought justice to her sooner?* I would never know.

Over time, I learned more from the news. Her name was Andrea Campbell, and she was from the neighboring town, Wallens. It was so small it made Pedoux feel like a city, and Pedoux was barely more than a dot on the map. Our biggest claim to fame was the old drive-in movie theater that drew crowds from neighboring counties. On weekends or during big premieres, the field would fill with cars and voices. By the next morning, the town would be quiet again, slow-paced and sleepy, where people waved as they passed and nothing bad ever seemed to happen. Or so I used to think.

After that day in the woods, I knew better. That truth lingered, never quite at the front of my mind, but never far behind. It sat just beneath the surface, waiting to rear its ugly head.

I remember going to the park with my family a few months later. Daddy and I were tossing a softball while Momma and Sheryl made sandwiches at the picnic table. He lobbed a throw, and the ball skipped off my glove and into the brush. I chased after it, reaching through the tangle, and a branch snagged my shirt, just like the raspberry briars had.

In that instant, the memory slammed into me. How carefree I'd been just a moment before, laughing, playing, smiling. Then guilt settled in. *How could I enjoy myself when Andrea's story remained unfinished? When no one had been held accountable?* I realized then that life would never feel quite the same again. There would always be shadows. Always the knowledge that the world isn't always safe, that darkness can wait just beyond the edge of your happiest days.

Sheryl had been accepted into Georgetown University, her dream school, since she was thirteen. She used to walk around the house quoting Ruth Bader Ginsburg and scribbling mock Supreme Court opinions in the margins of her notebooks. She said D.C. was where things happened, where the real change-makers lived, and she wanted to be one of them. When the acceptance letter came with a full-ride scholarship, Momma cried, and Daddy walked around grinning for a week straight. They told everyone who would listen that their oldest was going to be a lawyer, maybe even work for the Justice Department or argue a case before the Supreme Court someday. I was proud of her, too, although I missed her more than I'd cared to admit. Even though she wasn't there with me, I still felt the pressure to live up to her example. I wanted to make my family proud, but I was starting to realize I wanted them to be proud of me, not some faded imitation of my sister. I didn't want to be lost in Sheryl's shadow my whole life.

I could no longer bring myself to do the things I once loved. No more nature hikes, no more horseback rides, no more sleepovers with friends. I didn't feel safe in other people's homes, rooms that once felt familiar now felt full of shadows. I started looking at everyone differently, like I was waiting for someone to slip, to reveal something they'd buried. I questioned how guilty everyone around me might be, how much they might know and never say.

The friends I'd once laughed with now felt like strangers. I couldn't connect with them, no matter how hard I tried. I even walked away from basketball that year. I'd made the team, showed up for tryouts, and laced up my sneakers like I used to, but the memories crept in anyway. Even the feel of the jersey sticking to my sweaty skin conjured up the image of those empty eye sockets, watching. I tried to stay distracted, but the weight of it all made it impossible to carry on like nothing had happened. The girls on the team didn't want to hear about the things that haunted me any more than I could keep choking them down on my own. I needed space. I needed stillness. I wanted to move forward, but how could I, when so many unanswered questions still lurked in the corners of my mind like cobwebs left too long undisturbed?

That was the year I found archery, or maybe it found me. I'd followed Daddy out to his old tool shed to help him dig out the snake for the kitchen drain. The place smelled of rust and oil, the wood swollen from decades of humidity and memory. Hanging behind the door was a bow I'd never seen before, layered in dust and time. I lifted it down gently, like it might crumble in my hands, and pulled back an imaginary string. The real one had long since vanished. I aimed down the length of my arm and loosed an arrow in my mind.

"Your Papaw bought that for me when I was about your age," Daddy said, his voice soft, clouded with old summers. "I used to shoot at hay bales for hours. Got real good, too. Your Uncle Dale and I would toss up empty cans and try to hit 'em before they hit the ground. We thought we were something."

The next day, when I got home from school, the bow was waiting for me in my bedroom—new string, polished limbs, a neat row of arrows laid across my bed like an offering. I dragged it outside and hauled a hay bale from the barn. From the moment I gripped the bow, it felt like it belonged to me. Like it had been waiting.

Day after day, I stood under the wide sky and loosed arrows until my arms throbbed and my shoulders trembled. It wasn't like basketball. There was no roar of the crowd, no huddle of teammates shouting encouragement. But it filled something in me that had gone hollow. It was quiet. Focused. Steady. And in that stillness, I found something close to peace.

Archery became a ritual, almost meditative. I'd clear my mind as I notched the arrow, inhaling slowly, feeling the rise and fall of my breath. I'd focus, aim, and release. The wind whispered against the fletching, the arrow hissed through the air, and then, thwack, the sharp, satisfying sound of impact. That rhythm, that repetition, calmed the turmoil inside me. It gave me something to hold onto when anxiety clawed its way up my throat.

Looking back, I'm not sure I realized it then, but archery gave me more than peace. It gave me a sense of control. A sense of safety. My arms had grown stronger from practice, lean and precise. The faint lines left by the bowstring on my forearm were like badges I wore with quiet pride. I may not have been tall or graceful, but my body was solid and capable. Just like the girls in the stories Sheryl and I used to dream up, only real. With a bow in my hands, I didn't feel small or powerless anymore. I felt like I could protect myself if I needed to, and I needed that. Because no matter how much I tried to hide it, or how tough I pretended to be, the truth was, I had been scared, terrified.

I had never been so close to death as I was that day in the woods. It rattled something deep inside me, shook me to my core. From that moment on, I wasn't the same. It altered the way I saw the world and myself. Looking back, I can see how it shifted the entire course of my life.

With Sheryl gone, the house felt emptier than ever. I thought, maybe now that it was just the three of us, Momma and Daddy would draw closer, that they might reach for me in all of the turmoil and change. But somehow, the opposite happened. They drifted further away, especially Momma.

Now, with the benefit of time, I understand more than I did then. Momma was carrying more than I could imagine back then. Her past was catching up with her. Her own mother had died around that time, a woman she barely knew. Shortly after Momma was born, her mother left her on her Granny's doorstep and disappeared. A few weeks later, her father, my Grandpa Cliff, came back for her. He was in the Air Force, and from then on, Momma bounced from base to base, traveling across the country with Grandpa and his new wife.

I never met that wife. Grandpa Cliff was fiery and impulsive, leaving behind a trail of ex-wives. The only one I ever knew was his last, Nana Florence. She was wild and wonderful, the kind of person who filled a room with laughter. Momma used to say that if Florence had raised her, her childhood might have been a happier story, but that wasn't how things turned out.

Instead, she was raised by Grandpa's second wife, a woman named Eileen, who was cruel and cold. Once I was older, Momma told me stories of how Eileen starved her for days, letting her drink only water, treating her more like a burden than a child. When Grandpa was home, Eileen would play the part of the doting wife and stepmother, all smiles and sweetness. He never saw the truth until the divorce, when Momma finally told him everything. She said he was devastated, that the guilt sat heavy on him for the rest of his life.

After the divorce, they moved to Tennessee, where Grandpa's roots were. There, he married again, his third wife, Angie, and had a set of twins. Grandpa retired soon after, determined to be a better father the second time around.

It was around then that Momma met Daddy. They didn't wait long. They ran off and got married. I know she loved him, but in my heart, I believe she wasn't just running to him. She was running from something. From her pain. From her past. She became Jean Ann Thompson and tried to leave that other life behind.

But when her mother died, that door swung back open. And no matter how tightly she had tried to close it, Momma had no choice but to face everything she'd spent years trying to forget. Momma drifted farther from us once her own mother passed. She wasn't unkind, just remote, gliding through the house on antidepressants and nerve pills, tending chores with the vacant steadiness of a wind-up doll. Daddy, heartsick and devoted, fixed his whole world on mending hers. Whatever attention he had for me got folded into that mission and tucked away.

The rooms filled with an uneasy hush. Without Sheryl, the house felt cavernous. I wrote her letters after school, spilling worries I couldn't voice aloud. I pictured her striding across some sun-bright campus, forgetting small-town shadows while I sank deeper into them. I never expected an answer; the writing itself was the splint that held my heart together.

At sixteen, I didn't have names for half the storms inside me— rage, grief, raw loneliness. I quit basketball and, with it, my circle of friends; they drifted off like leaves once the season changed. Shame clamped my mouth shut. I skipped visits to Mamaw and Papaw; the old place only reminded me of what had broken. Even their marriage felt different now, two people sharing a porch but staring in opposite directions ever since the woods surrendered that skeleton. Whether they sensed the chill between them, I couldn't say, but I felt it. Finding that body stretched a long, cold shadow over all of us, and none of our lamps seemed bright enough to chase it away.

# Chapter 4



*Journal Entry– August 9, 2005*

*"There's a hollowness that settles in a house right before something breaks. I remember the first time I knew one of my babies was hurting and didn't know how to help. The Lord gives us discernment, but it doesn't make the waiting any easier. I've learned to pray in silence, to trust that God sees what we cannot."*

*-Ruth*

It didn't take long before I started falling in with the wrong crowd. I began spending time with kids who, like me, were trying to carry around too much sadness without anyone to help hold it. Some came from broken homes. Others had parents lost to addiction, or they bore scars from traumas of their own. Being with them made me feel a little less ashamed of how much my life had begun to unravel. In a crowd of people who felt like they had no one, we had each other.

The trouble was, we were all navigating the darkness without a flashlight. So, most of our choices were as messy and misguided as we were. My taste in music changed. My clothes changed. My hair changed. My parents noticed, but they chalked it up to "just a phase," never realizing it was a silent cry for help. Sure, every kid goes through phases, but this was something different. I know now there were signs. But back then, it felt like no one saw them. No one saw me.

So, I started smoking. I drank. I went to parties. I made choices I knew weren't smart, but at least I was somewhere I felt like I belonged. Around people who wanted me around. And that was enough to keep me in that cycle.

One wrong turn landed me at a party Lonnie Casey was throwing. Marie, his little sister, was still at my side in those days, same as always. We'd known each other since spelling tests and monkey bars, but it was grief that made us kin: her folks burned alive when a drunk driver clipped their Buick on Christmas Eve. From that night on, she swore she'd never drink and drive, and she drove that vow into me like a nail. No matter how wild the evening got, we kept our keys pocketed like crosses.

Losing her parents forced Marie to grow up overnight; finding the girl in the woods had the same effect on me. We'd drifted in those years when girls begin to change shape and direction. I was chasing basketball stats and GPA scores while she was learning how to live with ghosts. But grief drew us back together, two satellites wobbling around the same dark star.

So, we drank too much in her aunt's sagging farmhouse, telling ourselves it was safe because Aunt Julie was off at some boyfriend's trailer, blitzed on pain pills and warm beer. She'd told Lonnie he could have people over, so long as he "kept the place tidy." At sixteen, I thought that made her cool, thought freedom tasted like malt liquor and bad music. Only later did I understand: Julie wasn't a gatekeeper. She was a warning in flesh and bone, the kind you don't recognize until it's too late.

Sometime in the early morning hours, I stumbled upstairs to Marie's room. She said she would be up right behind me, but I was too drunk to care. I collapsed onto the bed, pulled a blanket over me, and drifted into a restless sleep. I don't know how long it was before the door creaked open again. I scooted over, expecting Marie. But then I felt large hands grab my waist and turn me over. It was Lonnie.

I tried to say something, to push him away, but he clamped his hand over my mouth.

"Relax," he whispered. "It's fine."

I thrashed against him, tried to scream, but he shoved my face into the blanket and yanked my pants down like I was nothing. My mind splintered. *What do I do? What do I do?* I couldn't move. My limbs were ice and stone all at once. I was terrified, more afraid than I had ever been in my life. I couldn't breathe right, couldn't think, couldn't get my body to obey me.

He leaned in close, the heat of his breath crawling down my neck.

"You know you want this," he murmured. "I see the way you look at me. Let me teach you how to be a woman."

I didn't want this. *Did I?*

No.

No. I didn't.

I was just a girl trying to survive the day. Just a girl who had laughed at the wrong joke, worn the wrong jeans, drank the wrong thing.

I could only cry.

And then the most horrifying thought rose up like bile in my throat: *This is how you end up dead in the woods.*

So I stopped fighting.

I didn't give in, but I didn't fight back either.

I went still, silent, the way small animals do when they know they've already been caught. I lay there limp, the weight of him pressing into me like a stone slab, like I was being buried alive. My tears slid down the sides of my face into the fabric beneath me. He saw them. I *know* he did. And I think, God help me, I think he liked it that way.

When it was over, he left the room without a word, like nothing had happened. Like I was nothing at all.

I crawled to the bathroom on hands and knees, the floor tilting under me. I turned the faucet until the pipes howled and scrubbed until my skin burned raw. The water wouldn't get hot enough. I could still *feel* him. My stomach turned, and I threw up everything I had—cheap vodka, shame, bile. I scrubbed again until the mirror fogged over and my reflection blurred into something I didn't recognize.

I didn't close my eyes that night. Not once. I couldn't.

I lay there in the dark, replaying everything again and again. My body no longer felt like mine. It was foreign, ruined, something used and discarded. I kept thinking, *This is what it feels like when your soul comes unstitched.*

If I could've shed my skin, stepped out of it like a snake, and left it there on the floor, I would've. I would've done anything to get out of the body that betrayed me. But I was trapped, flesh and bone wrapped tight around the ruin of what used to be me. My body wasn't my home anymore. It was a prison. And there was no key.

Morning light crawled across Marie's hallway like something guilty. I crept downstairs and phoned Momma. She pulled up quicker than I expected, engine idling like a held breath. All the way home, she kept her eyes on the road, hands white-knuckled on the wheel. Not a single question, only that thick, humming silence that felt louder than words. I've spent years wondering if she already knew.

After that, I walked through school as if a stain bloomed across my skin for everyone to read. I told myself I'd invited it, smiled wrong, laughed too loud, let him think I was game. But even while the shame chewed at me, I knew the truth. I hadn't said yes, I hadn't been ready, and no part of me had wanted any of it.

I spent countless hours steeped in self-hatred and disgust. Lonnie's words echoed through my mind until they became my own. *You know you want this.* Maybe I did something to make him think that. Maybe

I smiled too much. Maybe I shouldn't have worn that shirt. I twisted every detail until the blame curled back into me like a hook. I was the one at fault. It had to be me.

Most evenings, I'd drag out the new target Daddy bought me, a foam block with a bullseye printed dead center like a wound waiting to be reopened. I'd set it up at the edge of the yard, where the grass grew thin and the woods pressed in like they were watching. Then I'd notch an arrow, draw back the string, and let it fly.

Each shot was like aiming at a version of myself I couldn't stand to look at anymore.

I craved the pain, the slap of the string across my arm, the way it left raised welts like warnings. My shoulders burned, my muscles shook, but the thing gnawing at my center stilled, just for a moment. The silence after each release felt holy. Final. The thud of the arrow sinking deep into the target echoed like a heartbeat I didn't want to feel.

Sometimes, I wondered what it would be like to aim a little lower. A little closer.

But I never did. I just kept shooting.

Not to feel better, just to feel *anything* besides what was already eating me alive.

Life spun out like a hurricane with no eye. You'd think I'd never cross Marie's threshold again, yet she still felt like the only tether I had. So I kept returning, skirting Lonnie when I could. He talked to me like it was any other Tuesday with a voice butter-smooth, gaze lingering just long enough to chill the bone. Pretending nothing had happened became its own strange refuge; acknowledging it felt like standing in the open during a thunderstorm, waiting for the next strike.

Then one day, he followed me into the bathroom. He didn't ask. He didn't stop. And I didn't fight. I wish I had. But by then, I had already begun to believe my voice didn't matter, that saying no wouldn't change anything. That somehow, this was just what I deserved. That moment blurred into the next, and soon it became a pattern. I stopped counting how many times.

Lonnie would treat me like a stranger around others, cold and dismissive. But when we were alone, he whispered soft, flattering things, words I had longed to hear from someone, anyone. For a time, I clung to those words like they meant something. Like they made what was happening less awful. I told myself I was wanted, maybe even loved. But deep down, I was just trying to fill a void no one else seemed to notice. I was starving for affection, for security, for something steady in a world that kept spinning out of control.

Now I know what it was.

It was rape. Over and over again.

And the worst part? He made it sound *sweet.* Said things like "You're so special," and "You know you want this," but only ever during the act—when I couldn't move, couldn't breathe, couldn't scream. His voice dripped with tenderness while his hands forced me still. I wasn't making love. I was being taken. Stripped of choice. Stripped of voice.

I wasn't consenting. I was surviving.

What he did to me wasn't just violence; it was **grooming**, **coercion**, **manipulation**—all wrapped in soft words meant to confuse me, to keep me quiet. There was no relationship, no dating, no chance to say no. He didn't need to threaten me outright because my fear did all the work for him. He created the silence he fed on, the kind that rots you from the inside out.

I didn't recognize the monster because I was too busy blaming myself for letting it in. It was too raw to understand how the trauma was warping everything inside me. The way I saw myself. The way I measured love. The way I equated safety with stillness and obedience. He conditioned me to disappear on command. To go silent and still. And each time he walked away like nothing had happened, I hated myself a little more for letting it happen again.

He wasn't giving me love; he was reinforcing my silence.

He wasn't showing affection; he was cultivating my shame.

He wasn't powerful; he just knew how to make me feel powerless.

And for a long time, it worked.

Because when your body becomes a battlefield, you stop believing it's a place you're allowed to live in.

Those moments, horrific and confusing, became the fabric of my everyday life. I didn't realize it then, but I was losing pieces of myself one by one, numbing just to get through the days. What he did shaped me, not because I chose it, but because trauma has a way of burrowing deep, of changing the way a person walks through the world. And for a long time, I walked with my head down, carrying secrets no one could see.

In all the letters I wrote to Sheryl, I never mentioned Lonnie. I never wrote about the drinking, the parties, or the nights I couldn't sleep. I only told her that I was sad. Lonely. She was worried. I could sense it in the tone of her replies, even in the few she managed to send back. And when she finally came home, she noticed. She noticed the weight I'd lost, the way my clothes hung looser, the dark circles under my eyes. One evening at dinner, she said something about it, softly, but clearly, directed at Momma and Daddy. I remember feeling betrayed, like she had tried to expose me. But deep down, I also felt a flicker of warmth; someone had seen me. Someone had noticed I was sinking.

Daddy asked if I was okay. I reassured him I was, and that was the end of it. No questions, no pressing. Just silence.

Now, I know they loved me. I believe they always did. But at the time, their love was buried beneath their own struggles, their own wounds and distractions. I couldn't see that then. All I could see was that no one had reached for me. Not in the way I needed. And so I drifted through that season of my life like a ship set loose with no compass, with no direction, no anchor, just a vast, aching blue stretching endlessly ahead.

Those next few years passed in a blur. The drinking. The partying. The sex. I felt unmoored, like something had cut the rope holding me steady, and I was left to drift through days that bled into nights. And somehow, no one seemed to notice. Perhaps it was because I maintained good grades. School had always come easy to me, or maybe no one was really looking.

Only Sheryl saw me. Truly saw me. And now, I wonder if it wasn't because she was struggling too, just in a different way. After all, we shared the same roots. The same mother and father. The same grandparents, whose house didn't feel like a refuge anymore. Maybe she had her own pain to carry, and starting over somewhere new had been her way of surviving.

As graduation crept closer, all I felt was a hollow kind of dread. I'd been accepted to a few good schools, the kind folks brag about, but I couldn't bring myself to feel anything about it. I knew my indifference let my parents down, but by then, I was too worn out to carry that guilt, too. They made me feel like an afterthought, and somewhere along the way, I started treating myself the same.

When the day finally arrived, I walked across that stage more confused than I had ever been. The cap and gown didn't feel like a triumph. They felt like a costume, a performance. I smiled for the pictures, clutched my diploma, and wondered quietly: *What now?*

After the ceremony, we went out to eat at a local restaurant. Sheryl was there, dressed up and glowing, with a new boyfriend in tow. Tommy was long gone. He had never been the kind to leave the mountains. Coal dust ran in his veins, and like many boys from around here, he ended up in the mines.

Her new guy, Luke, worked construction. Like Daddy, he was a contractor, and the two of them dove into the topic across the dinner table, swapping stories about rising lumber costs and new tools they couldn't wait to get their hands on. Sheryl told us they met while a crew was replacing the sidewalk in front of her dorm. According to her, it was love at first sight. She looked at him with that same starlit gaze she used to save for dreams of D.C. and courtrooms.

I couldn't help but be happy for her. He seemed like a decent man—steady, soft-spoken, the kind of quiet that didn't need to prove anything. But only time would tell. He was built like the work he did: broad-shouldered, sun-bronzed, with hands rough from years of gripping lumber and swinging a hammer. He wore worn jeans, scuffed boots, and what was probably the nicest button-up shirt he owned.

He looked like someone you'd want beside you in a storm.

His hair was sandy brown and tousled, like he'd just taken off his hard hat, and his eyes had that calm kind of blue that made people feel safe without knowing why. He and Sheryl looked good together, like maybe he was the anchor she needed, and she was the spark that might keep him from drifting too far into silence.

Watching them, I couldn't help but think, just maybe, she'd found something solid in a world that rarely offered guarantees.

Midway through dinner, while we were still clinking glasses and passing around dessert, they dropped their big announcement. They were getting married.

I caught Daddy's face as the words settled over the table. His jaw tensed. Strike one: Luke hadn't asked for his blessing. That didn't matter much to me, but I could tell it did to Daddy. Still, Sheryl was grown, and it was her choice. As long as she was happy and Luke treated her well, I could support that.

After dinner, while Daddy muttered something about "stealing the spotlight," I came over and said, "It's okay, Daddy; I'm happy for her."

Then I turned to Sheryl and her new beau, with a half-smile and said, "But Luke, if you ever hurt my sister, you might just find yourself buried in the woods."

No one laughed but Sheryl and me.

That's the thing about trauma. It twists your sense of humor until dark things sound like jokes. And sometimes, that's the only way you know you're still capable of laughing at all.

Daddy grabbed Luke by the arm and said, "Let's talk, young man." His voice was calm, but a weight lay behind it. The kind of weight that said this isn't just small talk. As they stepped away, Sheryl turned to me, her eyes already scanning the room like she was checking to make sure no one was listening.

"Good," she said, "I wanted to talk to you anyway."

I looked at her, raising an eyebrow. "What's up?"

She lowered her voice. "Don't tell Momma and Daddy, but… Luke and I have been living together already. We have a spare room, and I talked to him. He's okay with it. So… would you want to come stay with us for the summer? Just get out of here for a while? I think it might do you some good."

I didn't even think; I just threw my arms around her. I nearly knocked her off balance with how tightly I hugged her. She had no idea what she was offering, not really. But I did, and I wasn't going to let it slip through my fingers.

"I'll take that as a yes," she laughed, squeezing me back.

"Of course it's a yes," I said, pulling away just enough to look at her. "You're a lifesaver, Sher. For real."

The fog in my mind lifted just enough for me to breathe.

# Chapter 5



*Journal Entry– May 30, 2008*

*Jenny left this morning. She's gone to Sheryl's for the summer. I cried once the car pulled out of the drive. Not because I think she's leaving forever, but because I see the ache in her trying so hard to be brave. Lord, I ask You, plant peace in her spirit and let her know she is never truly alone.*

*-Ruth*

Before I knew it, my bags were packed and I was standing on the porch of the house that had raised me, whispering goodbye to the only life I'd ever known. The wood groaned under my feet like it, too, felt the twinge of parting. Luke had gone back to work not long after graduation, but Sheryl lingered a while longer, and that stretch of days—quiet, fleeting—settled in my memory.

Each evening, we gathered around the old dinner table, the one with knife marks in the wood and a sun-faded runner down the middle. It had been too long since we'd sat like that, shoulder to shoulder, grace said with bowed heads, the clatter of forks punctuating laughter. Stories spilled easy, and even Momma, usually tight-lipped and tired, found herself smiling more than not. She let slip tales from her girlhood, bits of her past we'd never been trusted with before, like secrets passed down from a ghost who finally decided to speak.

At night, Sheryl would crawl into bed beside me just like we used to. We whispered and giggled into the dark, falling asleep mid-conversation like we had as kids. For a few nights, it felt like nothing had ever changed. But when the weekend rolled around and it was time to leave, that old heaviness settled in again.

I hugged Momma tight, then Daddy, and climbed into Sheryl's little Toyota Camry, the same one Daddy had given her for her sixteenth birthday. My own vehicle, Papaw's old Nissan truck, had been left behind. It needed work, and my parents didn't think it was safe for the long drive. So I left it, and home, tucked away behind me.

As we rumbled down the drive, I caught one last glimpse in the side mirror, Momma and Daddy standing shoulder to shoulder on the porch, still as statues beneath the porch light's dying glow. I hadn't expected the hitch in my breath, the way grief rose sudden and sharp like a splinter working its way to the surface. It was just the summer, I kept telling myself that, but something in the air felt heavier than goodbye. The trees whispered like they knew I wouldn't come back the same. Maybe none of us would. That moment, quiet and ordinary as it seemed, folded shut like the last page of a worn-out book.

Sheryl and Luke lived in a quaint little suburb just outside of D.C., close to her school and her job, neat and quiet like something out of a brochure. She said it was a good neighborhood, full of trees and walking trails, with parks on every corner and a lake not far from their street. She remembered how much I used to love being outside, getting lost in the woods for hours, barefoot in the dirt, wild and free.

I hadn't done anything like that in years. But the way she spoke about those places stirred something in me—a faint pull, a memory half-buried. A long-forgotten pull toward the kind of peace that only comes from the hush of trees and the steadiness of the ground beneath your feet.

When we finally arrived, their home looked like it had been plucked from a storybook. A cozy stone-and-siding cottage with a gabled roof, a red brick chimney, and a sunroom porch enclosed with windows that caught the afternoon light just right. Tall, leafy trees framed the yard, casting cool shade and making everything feel tucked in and safe. Sheryl explained that Luke had bought it as a fixer-upper, hoping to flip it and put the profit toward a bigger house when they started their family.

I smiled and nodded, but part of me suddenly became cold.

The thought of Sheryl starting a family that didn't include me stung. I was happy for her, truly, but part of me felt left behind, like she was crossing into a life I couldn't follow. I looked at her and realized that she was no longer just my sister. She would soon be someone's wife, someone's mother. If I had known then what I know now, I wouldn't have lost her. I was gaining something. Luke might not have been family by blood, but from that summer on, he would become my brother. And that house, that moment, felt like the start of something new.

I spent the first week or so exploring all the places Sheryl had told me about. I found a few little shops I liked, cozy spots that made fresh bread and the kind of coffee that made you want to sit and stay awhile. I wandered trails that twisted through quiet parks and found comfort in the stillness beside the lake. With each passing day, I felt something in me begin to loosen. It was like learning how to breathe again, like remembering who I used to be before everything got so heavy.

One afternoon, I was sitting at a picnic table in a park not far from Sheryl's house, enjoying the soft rustle of the trees overhead. I opened a book I'd brought from home. It was a worn guide on Tennessee's local fauna I'd taken from Daddy's shelf, with his permission. As I flipped it open, an envelope slipped out from between the pages and landed in my lap. Written on the outside in Daddy's handwriting were the words:

*"I hope you're enjoying your time with your sister. I miss you back home, but have fun, Peanut. Here's a little money. Do something nice for yourself.*

*Love, Dad."*

Inside was $200.

My eyes burned with tears. I hugged the envelope to my chest and blinked up at the sky. I missed him more than I had realized, and Momma too.

After finishing my coffee, I headed to a thrift store I'd spotted a few days earlier. I walked through the aisles with slow steps, running my fingers across racks of fabric in colors I hadn't worn in years. For too long, my wardrobe had been black hoodies and the same tired boots, like I was trying to disappear into myself. But now, something inside me wanted change. Something softer. Brighter.

I left the shop with a few new outfits, light colors and breezy fabric, and a pair of simple sandals. On the way home, I stopped by the grocery store and picked up the ingredients for chicken parmesan, Sheryl's favorite. It felt good to plan a surprise for them, to do something thoughtful. They had taken me in without hesitation. I wanted to show them how grateful I was.

Cooking had always been my comfort zone. In the kitchen, I felt steady—confident. It was one of the few places where my hands didn't shake, where I could create something from scratch and know exactly how it would turn out. There was peace in that kind of control. Food had always been my way of saying *I love you*, a quiet language of care I didn't have to put into words.

When Sheryl and Luke walked through the door and saw the table set, their faces lit up with surprise. I could tell they hadn't expected it. The fridge wasn't empty when I arrived, but it hadn't exactly been stocked either, and from the stack of takeout containers in the bin, I could tell that had become their routine. I didn't mind. They were busy. Luke worked long hours, and Sheryl was juggling school and a part-time job. They were building something. I just wanted to give them one less thing to worry about.

As we sat around their small table, plates full and laughter easy, I felt a pang of homesickness. Back home, dinner at the table wasn't just a habit; it was sacred. A daily ritual of clinking silverware and sharing stories. For a moment, I missed it deeply.

As we finished our meal, I told them I wanted to look for a summer job.

Sheryl smiled brightly. "That's great to hear. Actually… there's a little place right beside my work that's hiring, and I think you'd love it."

She told me about the greenhouse and garden center next to the dental office where she worked at the front desk. The way she described it made it sound like something out of a dream full of sunlight, plants, dirt under your nails, and the smell of flowers everywhere. She offered to give me a ride the next morning so I could apply. It sounded fantastic. But deep down, I didn't let myself get too excited. I had no experience with that kind of work. I figured there was no way they'd hire someone like me.

Still… a tiny spark of hope flickered anyway.

The next morning, I rode into town with Sheryl. As we pulled up to her office, I glanced across the street at the Meadow Spring Garden Center. A hand-painted sign sat on the sidewalk just outside the door: Now Hiring.

My stomach fluttered with nerves. I'd never really applied for a job before, not like this. Back home, I'd worked a short stint at the local grocery store, but Ted, the owner, had known our family forever. There'd been no application, no interview. He just handed me an apron and told me where the time clock was.

This was different. This felt real.

"Now or never," I mumbled to myself as I grabbed my bag and stepped out of the car.

"Good luck!" Sheryl called, giving me a quick wave before disappearing into her office building.

I crossed the street slowly, my heart pounding in my ears. The bell above the door jingled softly as I stepped inside, and I was immediately greeted by a wave of earthy warmth. The scent of soil, herbs, and fresh blooms wrapped around me like a hug, and something inside my being eased. It smelled like home.

The space was alive with color, green fronds spilling from shelves, tiny pots of succulents lining the windowsills, and hanging baskets swaying gently from hooks in the ceiling. Before I could take a second breath, a beaded curtain rattled at the back, and out stepped a woman who looked as though she'd wandered straight out of an Appalachian folktale.

Her hair was black as coal at midnight, but streaked with threads of silver, like lightning carved through a storm sky and was braided neatly over one shoulder. A wide straw hat shaded her sun-kissed skin, and a tangle of garden tools peeked from the bulging pockets of her well-worn apron. She wore a faded tie-dye shirt, khaki shorts that hit just above the knee, and wire-rimmed glasses that hung from a beaded chain around her neck. She looked like the kind of person who'd spent her life coaxing things into bloom.

She gave me a warm smile, one that reached all the way up to her eyes, and I felt my nerves soften.

"Well, hello there, honey," she said, her voice soft and sun-weathered. "What can I help you with today?"

I swallowed and returned the smile. "Yes, ma'am. I'm here to ask about the job opening."

The woman chuckled kindly and motioned me toward the counter. "Well, you're in the right place. I'm Marigold, but most folks just call me Mari. This is my little slice of heaven. You ever worked with plants before, sweetheart?"

I tucked a strand of hair behind my ear, feeling the nerves bubble back up. "Not officially. I mean, I've helped my Mamaw with her garden back home. Tomatoes, beans, and some flowers. I've always loved being outside, in the dirt. It's… peaceful."

Mari gave a thoughtful nod, leaning on the counter with one elbow. "Peaceful is a good word for it. Gardening's a lot like healing. It's slow, patient, and messy before it's beautiful. Where are you from? I can tell it's not from around here."

"No ma'am," I said, soft but steady. "I'm from Tennessee. I'm staying with my sister for the summer. I needed a change of scenery. I'm just… trying to get my feet under me again."

Mari studied me for a moment, then smiled gently. "I like honesty. And I like people who aren't afraid of a little dirt and hard work."

She turned and grabbed a small clipboard from behind the register. "Well, I'll need you to fill out a little application, Formality and all, but truth be told, I've been hoping someone would walk through that door who looked like they needed this place as much as it needs them."

I blinked; not sure I'd heard her right. "Wait… are you saying I got the job?"

Mari grinned. "I'm saying I've got a good feeling about you, and I've learned to trust my instincts. You seem like someone who's ready to grow. You'd be surprised how much these plants can teach you a little about that," she chuckled.

A laugh bubbled out of me, half-relief, half-shock. "Thank you. Really. You won't regret it."

Mari handed me the clipboard and winked. "I already don't."

# Chapter 6



*Journal Entry– July 12, 2007*

*There's a strength in silence. I learned that the year my mother died. It was the first time I prayed out loud in an empty room and felt like someone heard me. I hope Jenny and Sheryl find that kind of quiet strength. Life isn't always kind, but our roots can still run deep in the Lord.*

*-Ruth*

I showed up that first morning wound tight as a spool of thread, nerves humming just beneath my skin, caught somewhere between hope and dread. Mari met me at the door with that same warm smile she'd worn the day we first crossed paths, like she'd been expecting me all along. Without so much as a pause, she took me under her wing and started walking me through the garden center, naming the plants like old friends and speaking in a voice that calmed the trembling place inside me.

My first task was repotting thyme that had outgrown its starter trays. Mari showed me how to mix the potting soil just right for herbs, explaining each step as if she were passing down a secret recipe. By the end of the day, I was beat, but it was the good kind of tired. The kind that sinks into your bones and leaves you full of pride. I had already learned so much, and I couldn't wait to come back the next morning.

That evening, I came home with dirt-stained hands and a genuine smile on my face. Luke was in the kitchen, grabbing a drink when he spotted me.

"Well, hey there, working gal," he said in that easygoing voice of his. "How was day one?"

"Hey, Luke! It was great, but I'm exhausted," I laughed.

"Well, come on out back," he said, motioning toward the porch. "I'm about to fire up the grill and make burgers. You can tell me all about it."

"Since when can you cook?" I teased.

He chuckled. "I can't. I can grill."

Outside, he popped open a beer and checked the heat on the grill. "Looks like we're ready to go," he said, laying the patties onto the grates. The sizzle of meat hitting flame and the scent of smoke and charred meat curled into the humid air. It smelled like summer. I sat nearby, content.

I remember thinking how normal it all felt. We had become friends recently, but genuinely. Maybe it was the way we bonded over wedding planning fatigue. Sheryl had decided Luke and I needed to be involved in every little decision, from the font choices for the invitations to the merits of birdseed versus rice.

Luke didn't care. "As long as we're married," he'd say. "Could be in the middle of the drugstore parking lot for all I care." And me? I had no clue what I was doing. I'd never dreamed of weddings, not my own, not Sheryl's.

Still, there we were, offering opinions on table runners and place settings. The only thing I felt any true excitement about was when she asked what flowers would look best. On that, at least, I had an opinion.

I'm sure Sheryl missed Momma during all of it. This was the kind of thing a daughter did with her mother. The kind of thing Momma used to love. But now? It was always the same answer: "Whatever you want.

Whatever you think is best. Just tell me what to do."

Looking back, that must've been heartbreaking for Sheryl. She had poured so much of herself into this wedding. She was scrimping, saving, and crafting everything by hand. A corner of my room had become a storage closet for DIY centerpieces and thrifted decorations.

And yet, despite everything, she kept smiling. She kept hoping. And I admired that, more than I let on at the time.

Over the next few weeks, Mari taught me a great deal, not just about plants, but about life as well. She had an easy way about her that simultaneously put me at ease and made me envious. What I wouldn't give to feel so comfortable in my own skin. Mari loved herself, forgave herself, and shared herself effortlessly. She inspired me in so many ways. Those days in her little shop really helped heal a part of my soul.

As I worked, the smell of damp soil clung to the back of my throat as I crouched near the greenhouse tables, gently teasing tangled roots from a flat of lavender. Mari had told me to talk to the plants. "A little encouragement goes a long way," she'd said with a wink, and I found myself whispering to the little plants as I worked. "Easy now, little one. Stretch your toes," I murmured, guiding a tender shoot into its new clay pot.

The sun filtered through the slatted windows above, casting lines of golden light across my forearms, warm and steady. I hadn't checked my phone in hours. I hadn't thought about home. The quiet was just quiet, neither heavy nor lonely. Just… still. And in that stillness, I felt something begin to root inside me, too.

I could finally see who I wanted to be. At the beginning of summer, I had no idea what I wanted out of life. I had no idea what career I wanted or who I hoped to become. But now I knew, I wanted to be happy. And having my hands in the dirt, helping those tiny plants reach for the sun, encouraging them to take root and grow, brought me joy. Seeing the smile on a customer's face when they pressed their noses against the delicate petals and inhaled made my day. I found peace here, and I knew one day I wanted a shop like Mari's of my very own.

Luke, Sheryl, and I settled into our own easy rhythm. We all worked during the day, then spent the warm summer evenings out back, grilling supper and swapping stories. Sheryl would talk about her plans for the future— the wedding, bright-eyed and full of ambition, while I helped Luke work on the house. He was teaching me how to install tile, and I found I liked it. I'd always enjoyed building things. Daddy had taught me early—how to read a tape measure, wire a light switch, square up a porch. He never had a son, so I was his help. And I was eager to learn, not just because I liked using my hands, but because working beside him meant I had his full attention.

To be fair, Sheryl liked creating things too, just not with grout under her nails.  She preferred arranging centerpieces and selecting paint swatches, and honestly, she excelled at it. Their little house was really coming together, inside and out. I had no doubt it would fetch a pretty penny when they were ready to sell.

Little did I know that time would come sooner than later.  Sheryl came home one day in tears.

"What's wrong?" I asked.

"Where's Luke?" she said.

"He's not made it in yet. Sheryl, what's wrong?" I demanded.

She looked like she didn't want to say, but the weight of her secret was crushing her; I could tell. So she reached into her purse and pulled out a pregnancy test. I looked down and saw that it was positive. She just began to sob.

"Don't cry, Sheryl. I thought you wanted a baby," I tried to console her.

"Don't you see?" she said, "We aren't even married yet.  We aren't ready. The house isn't done! I can't spend more money on a wedding. I'll need to save for the baby."

I hadn't taken all of it into account before—the job, the pregnancy, the distance from home. No wonder she was so overwhelmed. Just then, Luke walked through the door and saw Sheryl sobbing. I caught the flash of fear that crossed his face before he rushed to her side. And that was the moment I knew, this man really *was* the right one for my sister.

Sure, Momma and Daddy might frown on them living together or having a baby before getting married, but none of that mattered to me. What mattered was how he looked at her, how he didn't hesitate. This man *loved* her. I saw it clear as day. And more than that, I knew he would do right by her and by their child.

I told them I'd give them some privacy and stepped out the front door, the screen creaking shut behind me. I needed air and space to let the weight of Sheryl's news settle. A walk would do me good. I headed toward the park, thinking a short hike might give them time to process the emotions of their new discovery without me hovering nearby.

At the edge of the park, I spotted a trail I hadn't taken before. A weathered wooden sign marked the entrance:

**Ridge Path — 0.5 miles to Whisper Falls.**

That sounded perfect, just long enough to clear my head.

As I started down the trail, I let my thoughts wander back to Sheryl and the baby. A baby. My sister was going to be a mother. The idea filled me with a strange mix of joy and dread. I was happy for her, truly. It was a scary thought, too. There were so many unknowns when it came to bringing a child into this world. It felt like risky business. Still, I loved children, and I already knew I would love this baby, no matter what.

I had been deep in thought, so I hadn't noticed that the trail narrowed as I walked, the tall grass brushing my calves, the trees leaning in closer with every step. Sunlight filtered in dappled beams through the canopy above, but the shadows deepened around me. Suddenly, I noticed how tightly the forest was pressing in.

It hit me all at once, the rising panic, the shortness of breath, the choking pressure curling up beneath my sternum, sharp and suffocating. The woods were too quiet. Too familiar. My vision blurred at the edges, and a cold, clammy sweat broke out along the back of my neck. My heart pounded in my ears. I couldn't breathe. I couldn't move.

Then a voice, calm but unexpected, broke through the spiraling fog.

"Excuse me, miss, are you okay?"

I turned, startled, and saw a man standing just a few feet behind me, one hand outstretched, concern written across his face. But I didn't see his kindness. I saw danger. I bolted.

I shoved past him without a word, adrenaline coursing through me like fire, and ran back down the trail, faster than I thought I could. I didn't look back. I couldn't. My only thought was to get away.

Maybe he meant well. Maybe he really was just trying to help. I probably looked like a mess—pale, sweaty, shaking in the middle of the path. *But how could I know that? How could I trust that?*

Andrea might have thought she was meeting a helpful stranger, too. She ended up dead in the woods, buried and forgotten until I stumbled across her bones. No name. No justice. No one to stop it from happening. No… I couldn't assume kindness. Not anymore. Because what I did know, what I would never forget, was that the world isn't the safe place I once believed it was.

I made it back home to find Luke and Sheryl still sitting on the couch, deep in conversation. I told them I loved them and slipped off to bed without much else. The adrenaline still pulsed beneath my skin. The walk home had helped me settle a little, but my heart was still racing, and all I wanted was to lie down and hope the spinning in my head would stop.

As I stared up at the ceiling, thoughts of Andrea crept back in. I hadn't let myself think about that day in quite some time. Life had thrown so much at me since that day in the woods that she had quietly slipped into the background, tucked away behind newer traumas. But tonight, she was front and center again.

I found myself wondering if there had ever been any new developments in her case. *Were they still working on it? Had anything surfaced in all these years?* I hadn't heard a thing, but that wasn't surprising. No one in my family, or in town for that matter, ever brought it up. It had become taboo, a shadow draped over our picture-perfect storybook town that everyone preferred to ignore. We all knew better, of course, but it was easier to pretend. Silence made the pretending possible.

I made a mental note to look it up in the morning, just to see if anything had changed. But right then, I didn't have the energy. I just needed rest.

Sleep came in fits and starts. That night, I dreamed I was back in the woods, only this time, I wasn't alone. The air was thick, buzzing with flies, and the trees pressed in close, like they were trying to keep me there. A man in all black trailed behind me—tall, silent, with a wide-brimmed hat that cast his face in shadow. I never saw his eyes, but I didn't need to. I *knew* if I stumbled, he would kill me.

I tore through the underbrush, branches clawing at my arms, thorns catching my clothes. The ground shifted beneath me, slick with rot. Just as I reached the old raspberry thicket, the one from childhood, I saw something buried there, a hand. Pale. Still. Sticking out from the bramble like it was reaching for help. I screamed, but no sound came. The man reached for me, his fingers grazing the back of my neck.

And then I woke up, gasping. Drenched in sweat, heart thudding in my ears, the ghost of that outstretched hand still flickering behind my eyes.

It was still early, earlier than I needed to be awake. But there was no going back to sleep now. So I reached for my phone and searched for her name: Andrea Campbell, missing from Tennessee.

There wasn't much.

A few old articles from when she first disappeared. Another, dated a year after I'd found her, marked the anniversary. It included a short quote from a detective saying the case was still open and that any tips should be directed to the sheriff's office.

The last article hit hardest. It officially labeled her murder a cold case. There were no suspects. No viable leads. No next steps, just waiting. Waiting for someone to come forward. Waiting for a miracle.

My whole body tensed as I stared at the screen. The not knowing was unbearable, and I wasn't even her family. I couldn't imagine the hole they must have lived with every day. The silence. The unanswered questions.

Andrea deserved better than that.

The house was quiet when I made my coffee and slipped out the door. I walked to work in the early morning light, hoping the fresh air might help clear the lingering fog in my mind. I met Mari on the sidewalk just as she was turning the key in the lock.

"Good morning, sunshine," she said warmly. "You're here early."

I managed a half-hearted smile and returned the greeting, "Good morning."

Mari paused, her eyes softening. She could always tell when something was off. It wasn't just that she was observant; though she was, it was like she could feel my emotions before I even spoke to them.

I followed her into the shop, the familiar scent of soil and flowers washing over me like a balm. We started setting up for the day, and to my surprise, Mari rolled up her sleeves and began helping with my morning duties.

"You don't have to do that," I said, trying to protest. "This is my job."

She just smiled and kept working. "I know. I just felt like I needed the company today."

I didn't push it. It wasn't long before the words started pouring out of me.

First, I told her about the dream, then about Andrea, the hike yesterday, the man in the woods, everything but Lonnie. That part of my past was still too heavy to touch. Too tangled in shame and silence. I wasn't ready yet. Like my town back home, it just felt easier to pretend it hadn't happened than to face the weight of what it meant.

Mari listened without interruption, her hands busy mixing soil and compost in her slow, steady rhythm. She never pushed. Never judged. Just let me speak, let me be heard.

When I finally stopped, my voice hoarse, I looked down at my dirt-smeared hands and whispered, "I'm ashamed of myself... for being so scared."

Mari paused, as she always did, taking a moment to consider her words with quiet intention. Then she said, "Dreams like that... they're not just bad memories trying to scare you. They're your soul's way of telling you there's something you still need to face. Doesn't mean you're broken. Just means you're still healing."

I didn't respond. I couldn't. So she kept going.

"Fear's tricky, honey. It'll whisper that it's keeping you safe, when really, it's keeping you stuck. But you know what's braver than not being afraid?"

I looked at her, eyes searching.

"Choosing to live anyway. To keep planting things. To keep loving people. To keep walking through the woods, even when you know what might be hiding there."

She tapped her fingers gently on the rim of the clay pot between us.

"Andrea's story matters, Jenny. So does yours. You don't owe silence to anybody, not even the ghosts that hover at the edge of your breath. If speaking her name lets you breathe easier, then speak it. I'm here to listen for as long as the Lord keeps me on His green earth."

I believed her.

I loved this woman, and without a shadow of doubt, I knew she loved me, too. It shone in the way she gave, expecting nothing back, pouring light as naturally as sunlight through greenhouse glass. One day, I told myself, I'd learn to love like that, to hand someone else a lantern the way she'd handed one to me.

Side by side in the potting shed, words spilled out of me like water finding a crack in stone. I spoke of home, of Momma receding behind pill bottles and closed doors, of how small and unseen I felt inside walls that once rang with laughter. Mari kept her hands busy but her heart wide open, never flinching when the hard parts surfaced.

She'd been right that first morning: I did need this place-earth under my nails, the steady hush of growing things, her quiet faith in me. And standing there among trays of basil and flats of marigolds, I dared to wonder if the garden needed me just as much, soil and soul, each healing the other.

# Chapter 7



*Journal Entry– November 21, 1981*

*Your first time in the saddle isn't about learning how to ride. It's about learning how to trust yourself, the horse, and the path ahead. I still remember my first ride through the trails with my sister squealing behind me. That's when I knew, freedom often starts with a single step outside your fear.*

*-Ruth*

When I arrived home that evening, Luke was outside by the sawhorses, knee-deep in another house project. He looked up from sanding a piece of trim and waved.

"Hey, kiddo," he said. "How are ya? I didn't get a chance to talk to you yesterday, with… everything. Are you alright? You looked pretty upset when you came in. I hope you're not stressed about the baby just because Sheryl is."

I shook my head, walking up the drive. "No, not at all. I'm happy for you both, honestly. I know Sheryl's emotional, but I also know she'll be okay. She's tough."

Luke let out a long breath and set the sander down. "Yeah, she is. But I'm scared too, if I'm being honest. Damned scared."

I smiled. "I think you're supposed to be."

He laughed, wiping the sweat from his brow. "Yeah, I guess you're right. So, what was bothering you last night, if it wasn't that? Anything I can help with?"

I didn't pour my heart out to Luke the way I had with Mari. Some truths still felt too tender, too raw, but I did tell him about the man in the woods and the panic that had gripped me. Something about talking with Mari had cracked the door open, just enough to let a little more out. I told Luke how the woods had always been my refuge, how losing that sense of safety felt like losing a part of myself. I mentioned my bow, left back home, and how I missed the focus it gave me—the release. I told him I wished I had some way to burn off the anxiety that kept blindsiding me, creeping up when I least expected it.

Luke nodded, leaning against the edge of the workbench. "Yeah… I get that. After yesterday's news, I've been feeling it too, like the walls are closing in. Could use a little stress relief myself."

He paused, then looked at me with a grin. "Do you work tomorrow?"

I shook my head. "Nope. Got the day off."

"Good. Me too," he said, nodding to himself. "I'm gonna take you somewhere. Show you what I used to do when I was younger, something that always cleared my head. I think it'll do us both some good."

I raised an eyebrow, intrigued. "And what exactly do you have in mind?"

He just smiled and shook his head. "Nope. It's a surprise."

I tried to pry it out of him, teasing and guessing, but he wouldn't budge. Still, I trusted Luke, and his excitement was contagious. By the time I went to bed that night, the anxiety had softened, replaced by a flicker of something I hadn't felt in a while.

Anticipation.

Maybe tomorrow would hold something good. Maybe, just maybe, I'd find a new piece of myself waiting at the end of whatever path Luke had planned.

The next day, Luke told me to wear my jeans and boots, as I'd need them. He wrapped Sheryl in a big hug and kissed her forehead before turning to me with a grin.

"You two have fun," she said, following us to the porch. "Be safe!"

As I climbed into Luke's truck, I glanced over. "Alright, are you going to tell me where we're going now?"

"Nope," he said, his smile widening. "You'll see soon enough, kiddo."

We drove toward the edge of town, then turned onto a winding back road, and then another, until the pavement gave way to gravel.

"I didn't even know y'all had gravel roads this close to D.C.," I joked, raising an eyebrow.

Luke chuckled. "Just a few, if you know where to look."

Just then, a wide wooden sign appeared ahead, stretched across the dusty road like a banner: **Circle C Stables.**

My breath caught. "No way…"

"Excited now?" he asked, glancing over at me.

"Oh my goodness, yes! I haven't ridden in years," I said, already feeling my heart lift. "My friend Kasey used to have horses. I rode with her all the time, but… we stopped being friends a long time ago."

The words tasted bittersweet. That girl, the one who rode bareback at sunset and laughed without thinking, felt like someone I used to know in another life. Kasey and I had been inseparable once, but after I found the body in the woods, everything changed. I pulled away from everyone, even the people who loved me. Kasey tried to reach out at first, but I couldn't find the words for what I was feeling, and eventually, she stopped asking. I didn't blame her. I didn't know how to be a friend back then. I didn't know how to be *anything*.

It was hard to reconcile who I had been with the version of myself I was slowly rediscovering that summer.

It had been exactly what both Luke and I needed.

The moment I stepped into the barn, the warm, earthy scent of hay, horse sweat, and leather hit me like a memory I didn't know I'd been missing. The rhythmic swish of tails, the sound of hooves shifting in straw, the soft, curious nickers. It all felt like coming home to a part of myself I had buried.

I was paired with a big, painted Tennessee Walking Horse named Jasper. As I brushed him down, my hand trailing through his thick mane. I leaned into the quiet between us and said softly, "Thank you, Luke."

But he shook his head. "No, thank you. Having you here this summer has helped Sheryl more than you know. She's been homesick, though she'd never admit it. And she's carried guilt about leaving you behind. Just having you close has made a world of difference. Not to mention all the work you have helped do around the house."

I smiled and kept brushing Jasper's side. "It's been no trouble at all. I've really enjoyed it. Honestly… I didn't realize how much I missed out on by not having a big brother."

Luke laughed. "Well, you're stuck with me now, kiddo."

We left the barn walking side by side as the late afternoon sun cast long shadows behind us. Luke stopped to talk to Sam, the stable owner, and told him we'd be back again. I really hoped we would.

Once we were back in the truck, engine humming and dust kicking up behind us, Luke cleared his throat.

"So," he said, tapping the steering wheel, "I need your help with something. But you can't tell Sheryl. Can you keep a secret?"

I raised an eyebrow, suspicion in my voice. "Depends on the secret."

He grinned. "I've got an idea… and if you're in, I think it's going to be good. Really good."

Once he told me what he had in mind, I couldn't stop smiling.

I was all in.

The following week, Luke and I scrambled around the backyard like a couple of caffeinated squirrels. We were draping fabric, hanging string lights from the old trees, placing folding chairs, and trying to make sense of our slightly insane mission: throw together a surprise wedding in less than twelve hours.

Mari was there too, clipping stems and arranging flowers like a woodland enchantress. She had been thrilled to help. "This is my kind of magic," she said, fluffing peonies with a knowing smile.

"Have you heard from your mom and dad? Are they in town? What about the minister?" Luke asked, wide-eyed as he patted his pocket for the tenth time, making sure the wedding bands were still there. Gone was his usual calm. He was practically vibrating with nerves, his voice pitched an octave higher than usual.

"Calm down," I said, wiping my forehead. "Momma and Daddy are checked into the hotel. Mamaw Ruth had wanted to come, but Papaw Harlan wasn't feeling up to the drive. She promised she'd say a prayer at sunset, though. She said love ought to travel on the wind.

The preacher just called. He'll be here in five minutes. I spoke to Sheryl's coworker, and she's got her chained to her desk with paperwork for at least two more hours. You've got time. Now finish hanging those lights, and for heaven's sake, go take a shower. You stink."

He half-laughed, half-sighed. "You're a lifesaver, you know that?"

I smirked. "I won't let you forget it either."

By some miracle, as the sun began to set, everything was in place. The yard had transformed into a glowing dream—soft lights twinkling in the trees, flowers adorning every surface, and the smell of summer heavy in the air. Luke rushed off to shower, and I slipped into the dress I'd bought the day before. It was a vintage mauve lace gown from my favorite thrift store in town. There hadn't been time for Sheryl to pick out some godawful bridesmaid dress, and thank God for small miracles.

When Sheryl got home, she looked exhausted, dropping her bag by the door.

"What are you all dressed up for?" she asked, eyeing me suspiciously.

"You have a date or something? You'd better tell me all about it later. I'm whipped."

I laughed. "Oh yeah, but first, before you get too comfortable, try this on. The lady from the bridal shop called. She said this gown just came in, and it fits every detail you asked for. She needs to know ASAP if it works, though, because she's going on vacation and wants time to alter it if needed."

It was a total lie Luke and I had cooked up, but she didn't seem to question it. She was too tired or too trusting, I wasn't sure. She groaned. "Ugh, fine. But it better not take long."

"I promise," I said.

The dress fit like it had been sewn for her. Of course it did. Her hair was already pulled back into a simple coiffure, her makeup soft and glowing. She never went to work in anything less. She was stunning.

"Turn around," I said, and gently placed the veil on her head. "Look how beautiful you are, Sheryl." I meant every word.

She blushed, eyes sparkling.

"Come stand in the hallway so I can see you in better light," I added.

She followed me into the hallway, where the back door opened into the yard. "Oh, did you hear that?" I said, pretending to look surprised. "Luke must be home. Quick, out back before he sees you! You know it's bad luck for the groom to see the bride in her dress before the wedding."

I didn't believe in the silly superstition, but I was sure Sheryl did.

She gasped, giggling. "You're right! Okay, okay, go, go!"

The door swung open, and she stepped outside, then froze.

Her mouth fell open as she took in the backyard transformed into a fairy-tale wedding. Strings of lights twinkled overhead, wildflowers lined the aisle, and guests, just a handful of them, stood scattered among the chairs. There was Luke's mother, our parents, Sheryl's best friend from high school, a few work and college friends, and Mari, who said she would stay and help if she could. She had traded out of her typical tie-dye shirt for a long-beaded amethyst gown and looked quite ethereal standing by the large oak in the back, where the punch bowl and a simple, elegant cake sat.

Sheryl turned to me, her eyes wide and glistening. "How?"

I placed the bouquet into her hands, one Mari had crafted with wild roses and lavender, and picked up my own smaller one.

"Don't worry about how," I said softly. "Go marry that man and ask questions later."

She nodded, blinking back tears. "Thank you," she mouthed.

I reached for the train of her dress and helped guide her down the steps. As she began her walk down the aisle. At the end of stood Luke, his eyes locked on hers, a mix of nerves and joy on his face. I watched my sister walk toward him, every step a promise, every breath a beginning. I took my place beside her, heart full. And just like that, I watched Sheryl step into her next chapter as Mrs. Thompson-Whitaker.

The wedding was wonderful. After the ceremony, everyone laughed, smiled, and danced beneath the twinkling lights. Sheryl beamed the entire evening. We had been worried she'd be upset that we had spoiled all her big plans, but in the end, she was just happy to have married her best friend.

When the night came to a close, I rode back to the hotel with Momma and Daddy so the newlyweds could have the house to themselves. Sitting between them again made me realize just how much I'd missed them and how much I missed home. I was so glad they'd come; I was grateful for every minute we had together.

The ride was quiet with the kind of silence that felt full rather than empty. Daddy drove with one hand on the wheel, humming low to some old country song on the radio, and Momma sat beside him, arms folded but relaxed, her eyes soft in the glow of the passing streetlights. For a moment, it felt like I was little again, safe in the backseat, no need to explain anything to anyone.

Momma was in good spirits, even if she still seemed a little skeptical about the rushed nuptials. She asked more than once that evening why they'd felt the need to hurry. I just smiled and shrugged. I wasn't about to be the one to spill the newly married couple's secrets.

The next morning, the three of us returned to Sheryl and Luke's house for breakfast. I had already promised Luke I'd house-sit while he took his bride on a short honeymoon. They couldn't afford much, but Luke was determined to make the time special. I agreed without hesitation. They needed that time for just the two of them. Soon enough, there would be no more "just Sheryl and Luke." A new little life would join the picture and shift all of their focus.

Momma and Daddy headed back to Tennessee that evening, and I hated seeing them go. I had missed them so much more than I realized. I promised I'd come home for a weekend visit soon. Sheryl spent the rest of the evening packing, making sure every last item was ready. I hadn't seen her that giddy in years. They were planning to drive up the New England coast and stop wherever the road took them. Nothing was set in stone; they were simply chasing an adventure together.

That kind of spontaneity wasn't natural for Sheryl. She usually needed every detail outlined in advance, but watching her lean into the unknown like that told me just how much she trusted her new husband.

The next morning, as they loaded their suitcases into the rental car, Luke paused and held out his truck keys to me. I blinked in surprise.

"Take care of it while I'm gone, kiddo," he said, grinning. "Just in case you need to go somewhere and don't feel like walking. Work's close, but the grocery store's not."

I smiled as I took the keys. "Maybe you can go for another ride," he said. "You remember how to get to the stables?"

"If I don't, I've got GPS, old man," I said, waving my phone at him. He laughed.

"Don't hesitate to call if you need anything," he said, his voice softening.

Sheryl, true to form, fussed over me. She pointed out the list of emergency contacts she had posted on the fridge—numbers, addresses, instructions, all in neat handwriting. I rolled my eyes.

"I'm not a kid," I reminded her.

"No," she said, pulling me into a hug and ruffling my hair. "But you'll always be my baby sister."

Luke kissed the top of my head, and with one final wave, they were off. I stood in the driveway watching them drive down the street, then looked down at the keys in my hand and smiled.

I had to work that evening. I had promised Mari I'd help unload a shipment of exotic plants she'd been excitedly awaiting all week. But tomorrow was my day off, and I already knew what I'd be doing with it.

I was going back to the stables.

# Chapter 8



*Journal Entry– July 21, 1983*


*Not every apple in the orchard turns out sweet. Some grow misshapen. Some rot from the inside long before the skin shows a blemish. But others, others shine with the kind of light only God can give. I pray that I learn how to tell the difference. Not just in fruit, but in people.*


*-Ruth*


I found my way back to the stables and was greeted by the stout man Luke had introduced me to before, Sam, the owner and manager. I reminded him that I'd come with Luke a while back, and recognition sparked in his eyes.

A grin spread across his face. "Well, I'll be. Luke's a good one. Known him since he was just a boy. Fine young man, that one. Always had a good head on his shoulders."

"I think so too," I said, smiling. "He and my sister just got married."

Sam beamed. "That's a great thing to hear. Though I doubt you came all the way out here just to tell me that. So… you ready for another ride?"

"Yes, sir," I replied. "Is Jasper available?" He had been the big walking horse I'd ridden last time.

"Ah, sorry," Sam said, shaking his head. "He's off with the farrier getting new shoes. But my favorite gal's here today. She's my own personal Cadillac, but I could make an exception, just this once."

"Are you sure you don't mind?" I asked, hesitant.

"No, ma'am. She'll take good care of you. Come on."

Sam led me into a smaller barn tucked off to the side of the main stable that housed Jasper. It was where he kept his personal gear and horses. We walked through the structure and out into a fenced-in lot behind it. That's when I saw her.

She was the most beautiful horse I'd ever laid eyes on, a Rocky Mountain Saddle Horse with a rich, dark chocolate coat that shimmered like satin. Her flaxen mane and tail, pale as sunlight, danced in the breeze as she pranced toward us, graceful and spirited.

"She's stunning," I breathed.

Sam chuckled, giving the mare a gentle pat. "Hey there, Miss Starshine," he murmured, nuzzling her nose.

I must've given him a curious look because he shrugged and said, "Daughters."

I laughed. That tracked. Sheryl and I used to name every pet we had with something dramatic and regal, as if we were bestowing titles on the nobles in our imaginary kingdom. I smiled at the memory of us defending our lop-eared bunny, Lady Eleanor Hightower, Duchess of Meadow Downs, with sticks like swords.

Sam helped me saddle Starshine and pointed toward a distant stand of apple trees beyond the fence line.

"She loves it over there," he said. "If you bring back a good one, she can have it as a treat, after you cool her down and brush her off, of course."

"Deal," I grinned.

Starshine was a fantastic ride. Her gait was smooth and rhythmic, and though she had spirit, there was a gentle steadiness in the way she moved. I could tell she'd been well-trained, likely to be able to handle Sam's daughters. She responded to even the subtlest shift in my posture, her ears flicking back and forth attentively.

We slipped into an easy rhythm as we made our way toward the orchard. Sunlight pressed gently against my shoulders, and the only sounds were the soft rustle of leaves and the distant call of a bird hidden in the trees. With each step, I felt myself begin to unwind, like I was finally breathing in air I didn't have to fight for.

Then I heard hooves behind us, thundering at first, then slowing as they drew near.

"Hey, Sam!" a voice called out. "Oh… you're not Sam."

"Nope," I said, turning with a smile. "Definitely not Sam."

The rider laughed, slowing his horse to match our pace. "Saw Starshine and figured she had to be with him. He must really like you if he let you take his girl out."

"I don't see how he could. We barely know each other," I said with a shrug. "But he's fond of my brother-in-law, so maybe that's why. Either way, I'm grateful. She's incredible."

"That she is," the rider agreed, patting his horse's neck. "I'm Dalton, by the way. What's your name, if you don't mind me asking?"

"Jenny," I said, brushing an unruly strand of hair behind my ear.

There was something familiar in his Southern drawl, a softness that reminded me of home, even though it felt out of place this far north.

He looked to be in his early twenties and had a farmer's tan. I could tell from the pale skin that peeked from beneath his shirt collar, but his arms and face were bronzed from the sun. He had deep green eyes, a handsome face, and a tousled mop of sun-kissed hair that looked like it had never met a comb. I blushed at the thought of running my fingers through it.

He must've noticed because he flashed me a grin, mischievous and charming.

"Mind if Copper and I join you on the ride to the orchard?"

"I guess not," I said, suddenly feeling shy.

Dalton rode a buckskin Quarter Horse, strong and calm. He told me they did calf roping together, and it showed. There was an effortless trust between them, the kind born only from time and shared experience.

When we returned to the stables, I realized I had genuinely enjoyed Dalton's company. He had a playful energy that made conversation easy. After dismounting, I started unsaddling Starshine, but Dalton offered to help.

"No thanks," I said with a small smile. "I've got it. I actually enjoy this part."

I brushed Starshine down slowly, savoring the quiet connection, checking her hooves like I had been taught. When I finished, I rewarded her with the apple I'd picked, and she crunched it happily before trotting off into her paddock.

On my way to settle up with Sam, I passed Dalton leading Copper back toward the larger barn across from the arena, the one where I figured they hosted barrel racing and roping events. I waved.

"You're coming back soon, I hope?" he called after me.

I grinned. "As soon as I can!"

"Good! Maybe we can ride together again."

I shrugged and laughed. "We'll see."

He flashed another one of those crooked smiles, and I thought about it all the way back to the house.

That night, brushing my teeth before bed, I caught my reflection in the mirror and hesitated.

*Was he really interested in me? Or was he just being nice?*

It had been a long time since I'd allowed myself to think about a guy that way. Lonnie had ruined that for me. But something about Dalton made me feel… ready. Or like I could be.

Then I looked at myself, my wild hair, my strong, athletic build. I wasn't what the world called beautiful. I wasn't a size two. I had curves, sure, but I had never seen myself as someone who could catch a guy's eye, especially not someone like Dalton.

*I remember thinking he was out of my league.*

Still, I went back to the stables two more times that week. And each time, Dalton rode with me.

He told me he worked there part-time. He cleaned stalls, exercised horses, and maintained the tack room in exchange for boarding Copper. He said he couldn't afford it otherwise. I liked hearing about the care that went into keeping the place running. There was something grounding about it. Honest work. Simple rhythms. It reminded me of home.

On my last visit before Luke and Sheryl were due to return, I told Dalton that I wasn't sure when I'd be back.

"Luke'll need his truck again, and it's too far to walk," I explained.

A flicker of disappointment crossed his face, but then he brightened.

"Well," he said, "how 'bout this, if you've got a free day and I'm not working my main job, I'll come pick you up. No problem."

"Really? That would be great."

We exchanged numbers before I left. And as I walked back to the truck, I felt a tiny spark in my chest. Hope.

That next morning, Sheryl and Luke returned. They looked so happy, tired, too, but in a good way. The kind of tiredness that comes after a long day in the sun, when your skin feels warm and your bones hum with quiet exhaustion. Their smiles were soft, peaceful, like they'd been floating on a cloud for days. I hadn't realized how much I'd missed them until I saw them again.

They greeted me with big hugs and handed me a small velvet box. Inside was a delicate necklace Sheryl had picked up in Boston. It was a fine gold chain with a tiny charm shaped like a compass rose; its center set with a single pale blue stone. On the back was a small engraving: Find your way. The words curled into me like a fist..

"I saw it and thought of you," Sheryl said softly.

"I love it," I whispered, and I meant it.

I told them I'd kept busy while they were gone. I'd been working at the greenhouse and had painted the bedroom I was staying in. They hadn't asked me to; I just needed something to do. One night, when I couldn't sleep, I picked up a brush and started.

I've always had the tendency to stay busy. Still do. Even now, after everything I've learned, some habits are hard to unlearn. Back then, sitting still felt dangerous, like drowning. If I wasn't moving, wasn't working, the thoughts would come in waves, crashing one after the other until I couldn't breathe. So I painted.

And they appreciated it. Especially Luke.

"Thanks for everything, kiddo," he said. "Did you get a chance to ride?"

"I did," I said, my voice lighting up. "Sam even let me take his horse out."

"No way, not Starshine?" Luke grinned. "Man, I'd love to have that horse. She's a real beaut."

"Isn't she, though? And she rides like nothing else."

"Well, that's it. I'm officially jealous. But I'm glad you had a good time."

"Oh, I did," I said, then hesitated. "And I think… I may have met someone."

"Oh really?" Luke raised an eyebrow, playful suspicion in his voice.

Sheryl perked up instantly. "Excuse me, I'm the sister. I'm supposed to get the boy gossip, not him," she said, pointing at Luke with mock indignation.

"Yes, but I'm the brother. I have to screen these boys," he countered, smirking.

My heart warmed at the exchange. I hadn't known it then, but Luke had once had a sister of his own. She was eight years older, lost in a car wreck coming home from prom when he was just nine. He told me years later that marrying Sheryl had given all that love a place to go again. I could never replace the sister he lost, but in his eyes, I became family. Truth be told, if you didn't know better, you might've sworn Luke and I were the siblings, not Sheryl and me.

I told them about Dalton, how I'd met him at the stables, how he'd offered to give me rides out there now that they were back, and I'd be without a vehicle.

I wasn't asking permission. I was eighteen. They knew that. Still, they cautioned me to be careful. I hadn't known him for long, and they were right, of course. But I was trying hard not to live in fear anymore. That kind of fear had already taken so much from me.

We ordered takeout that night since none of us felt like cooking. As we ate around the small kitchen table, Sheryl and Luke exchanged a glance. I knew something was coming.

"So," Luke began, "we've been talking. We want to go ahead and finish getting the house ready to sell. We need more space before the baby comes."

I nodded slowly. I understood. It made sense. But it still stung. This place had started to feel like a soft landing.

"We're looking at three-bedroom houses," Sheryl added quickly. "That way, there's a nursery and a guest room. One you'd be welcome to, if you wanted to come with us."

Her words warmed me, but I knew I wouldn't. I wouldn't follow them to the next house, not this time. I needed to find my own space, to stand on my own, in whatever way I could.

"Thank you," I said. I wouldn't tell them yet, but I'd begin looking for my own place too.

"So," Luke grinned, "you up for helping me get this place ready to list?

It's gonna be extra work, but I'll pay you since it'll take away from your hours at the greenhouse."

"Of course I'll help," I said. "I'll ask Mari if I can cut back a little while we finish everything."

I tried not to show how that made me feel, like the ground was shifting under me again. I knew life was just a series of changes, but that didn't mean I liked them. Not then.

That night, I lay in bed thinking about what came next. Would I stay here? Go back home? I had a job I loved. I loved the stables, the lake, the quiet trails. And I had just met Dalton.

Maybe… I could find a roommate. Or a small place of my own. So many thoughts had run through my head. I pulled out my phone and, without thinking, messaged him.

"Are you up?"

Ding. Instant reply.

"Hey, pretty girl. Of course. I was hoping you'd message."

We texted late into the night. It quieted my mind, gave me something else to hold onto besides the chaos of change. Looking back, I realize that's how love starts to feel like a drug. Not the pure, true kind, but the kind that numbs. That soothes the ache for a little while. But I wouldn't know that for a long time.

The next morning, as I was heading out for work, Sheryl stopped me at the door. She pressed a small canister into my hand.

"Pepper spray," she said matter-of-factly. "I know you're going to start dating. This isn't a small town like back home, where I knew all the boys you talked to. So… just keep it with you. Please."

It was probably a good thing I hadn't had this when I panicked on the hiking trail. I might've maced some poor man who only meant to help. But Sheryl was right, it might just save me one day.

A strange thought crept in: *what if Andrea had had pepper spray? Would it have made a difference? Would she still be alive?*

And for the first time, I wondered how much that day in the woods had affected Sheryl, too. *How had it changed her?* I'd been so busy trying to survive my own pain that I'd never stopped to consider hers.

The thought lingered in my mind as I headed into work, the pepper spray swinging from my keychain and my new necklace resting just below my collarbone. Mari noticed both not long after I walked through the door.

She reached out gently, her thumb brushing across the compass charm as I held it up for her to see. A soft smile touched her lips, and she gave my cheek a gentle pat. I saw the fine lines around her eyes when she smiled, delicate, lived-in wrinkles that held stories I'd never know. And just like that, a wave of longing washed over me. I thought of my Mamaw and how much I missed her.

*I need to email her when I get home*, I reminded myself. Email had become her favorite way to talk since she'd gotten her new computer, and she'd fuss if too many days passed without a message from me.

Later, while we worked side by side repotting a tray of lemon balm, I took a deep breath and told Mari about Luke and Sheryl's plans. About the house going up for sale. About needing to cut back my hours and find a place of my own.

She didn't miss a beat. "Well, of course, sweetheart," she said without hesitation. "You tell me what hours you need, and I'll make it work."

"Thank you," I murmured, grateful, but also a little unsteady. The words spilled out before I could stop them. "I guess I'm just… nervous. Everything's changing so fast."

Mari dusted the soil from her palms and looked at me with those warm, weathered eyes that always seemed to know more than they let on.

"Well, honey," she said gently, "that's the thing about life. Sometimes, we've got to let go of good things to make room for the right ones."

She paused for a moment, her gaze drifting around the greenhouse.

"Seasons change, whether we're ready or not. But just like the garden, you don't lose what you planted. You carry it with you. In your hands. In your heart. What you've grown here…" she gestured to the tables of plants around us, "it's part of you now. And it'll keep blooming, even in the next place you grow."

Mari always had a way of saying just what I needed, even if I didn't understand it fully in the moment. I listened to her then, but I understand her words so much more now.

The rest of the day passed in quiet rhythm. We talked about the saplings I was trimming and the subtle change in the air. Fall was creeping in, just barely, but it was there. You could feel it in the breeze, see it in the way the light hit the glass just a little differently. The end of summer was coming.

By the end of my shift, I felt lighter.

I walked home with a smile on my face, the compass charm bouncing softly against my chest. I was still scared, yes, but beneath the fear was something else. I was beginning to feel excited about the future, about finding my own place. I couldn't remember the last time change felt this welcome. I was starting to see it for what it really was.

An adventure.

# Chapter 9

*Journal Entry– September 6, 2008*

*There's a kind of sorrow that comes with packing up a house. Not because of what's lost, but because of what gets left behind, things no one else would notice. The hum of a screen door. The way the morning sun slants across a kitchen floor. The dent in a wall from a boy's wild childhood. We don't just leave rooms; we leave versions of ourselves tucked in the corners.*

*And sometimes, the heaviest boxes are the ones no one can see. The quiet shames. The old regrets. The dreams we gave up to survive.*

*But I've learned, over time, that even a heart that's been bruised can still bloom. Even a worn housewife can be a wellspring of strength. The world may not always see us, but our children do. Our grandchildren do. And in their eyes, we are more than the battles we've fought; we are the roots that keep on holding.*

*-Ruth*

That lighthearted feeling didn't last long. When I got home, Sheryl was on the phone with Momma and Daddy. "Yes, she just walked in," I heard her say. "Jenny, come here. Momma and Daddy want to talk to us both."

I walked over, and she put them on speaker.

Daddy's familiar voice came through, warm but serious. "Well, girls, we've got some news."

There was a pause. "Mamaw and Papaw have sold the farm. They'll be moving soon."

He went on to explain that Mamaw and Papaw had decided it was time to downsize and move into town. Momma and Daddy were already helping them pack, but they wanted to know if we'd come down in two weeks to help with the move.

Of course, we agreed.

After we hung up, Sheryl looked over at me and said, "It'll be good for us to go. Luke and I need to tell Momma and Daddy about the baby anyway. We'd rather do it in person."

Any calm I had felt from earlier vanished. I wasn't sure why the news hit me so hard, but maybe it was just more change, piling on. But it shook me.

That farm had been more than just land. Their house had been my second home. The woods behind it had been our sanctuary, where Sheryl and I built forts and chased deer trails, where our imaginations had run wild in the Kingdom of the Does.

Those woods held my best memories… and my worst.

For a long time after finding Andrea, I couldn't think about the forest without seeing her body again, those bones tangled in leaves. But lately, time had softened the image. Now, when I thought of her, I saw the missing posters. The photo of her smiling. The articles with her name and age. Slowly, she'd become more than what I'd seen that day. She'd become real.

Still, hearing that the farm was being sold felt like losing an anchor I didn't know I'd been holding onto. It was the last piece of what once was, of a childhood I'd already lost more of than I ever wanted to.

And now… what would that holler become?

*Who would move into the house where my Mamaw hung quilts out to dry and Papaw fed his dogs every morning without fail? Who would become Momma and Daddy's neighbors now?*

I stared out the window for a long time, pondering questions I couldn't answer. Everything was changing, and it felt like the bones of the world were rearranging themselves beneath me—quiet, slow, and merciless.

I told Sheryl I needed a walk and stepped outside. The air was heavy with that strange stillness that comes just before dusk. I felt unmoored, like I had no bearings, no compass, just the little charm around my neck, the one Luke and Sheryl gave me. I held it in my hand, gripping the cool metal as if it could tether me to the present.

I took a deep breath, pulled out my phone, and called Dalton.

He answered on the second ring.

"Hey," I said, trying to sound lighter than I felt. "Are you free?"

He was. He said he could meet me at the park. As I walked into town, the sun dipped lower on the horizon, casting long shadows over the pavement. When I reached the parking lot, his beat-up Ford Ranger was already waiting.

It wasn't much to look at with rust along the fender, a crooked bumper, but I didn't care. I climbed in.

"You shouldn't be out walking this late," he said as I buckled my seatbelt. "It's too dangerous."

There was concern in his voice, and I appreciated it. It felt nice to have someone worry about me.

As we drove, I told him about the last two days, about the farm being sold, about all the changes I wasn't ready for. He listened quietly, his eyes on the road, nodding every now and then. He didn't interrupt. He didn't try to fix it. He just let me talk.

He turned down winding backroads I didn't recognize, roads that seemed to slip deeper and deeper into stillness. Eventually, we came to a wide pull-off by the river. No cars. No noise but the rushing water and the hum of summer cicadas.

"Come on," he said, parking the truck. "I want to show you one of my favorite spots."

He reached for my hand, and I let him take it. He led me down a narrow path to the riverbank, where the water had deposited a patch of pale sand. The moon was rising, silver and bright, casting its glow across the rippling current. We sat side by side, tossing small stones into the water, watching the ripples dance away.

I talked more than I expected to. About home. About the woods. About the weight of missing the way things used to be. I wasn't sure why I felt so open with Dalton. Maybe it was the way he listened. Maybe it was the pressure building inside me, needing somewhere to go. He was there, and I was full to overflowing.

After a while, the silence stretched between us. Then he leaned over and kissed me.

It was sudden, deep, and sure, but not rough. My heart pounded, surprised and uncertain. I didn't pull away.

Still, I felt nervous. I glanced at my phone. It was nearly eleven. I told him I needed to let Sheryl know I was okay.

He nodded, and I stepped a few feet away to call her. She didn't answer, so I sent a text instead.

***I'll be home late. With a friend. Have a ride. Don't worry. Love, J.***

When I came back, he was sitting in the sand, watching the moonlight shimmer across the water. I sat down beside him. He slipped his arm around me, and before I could think twice, I let myself lean back.

I gave in.

I let him take me there, into a moment that felt quiet and heady and far away from everything else. But even as it happened, a part of me drifted.

I liked Dalton. I really did. But I wasn't ready for that. I didn't know how to say no, and somewhere deep down, I feared that if I did, he wouldn't want me anymore. At eighteen, I still believed that a woman's value came from how much a man wanted her.

I know now how wrong that was. A woman's worth doesn't come from desire. It comes from God. She is precious because she exists. Because she was made to be cherished, not used. I didn't understand that then. I only knew what life had taught me.

I thought of Lonnie. The only other person I'd ever been with. My stomach turned.

I lay there, my back pressed into the cool sand, the moonlight threading through the trees overhead. I felt… separate from myself. Like I was watching it all happen from somewhere far away.

When it was over, Dalton whispered soft things against my skin. He hadn't hurt me. He hadn't forced me. It wasn't like Lonnie.

But still… I felt ashamed.

Not because of Dalton, but because I had abandoned something inside myself, I hadn't even known I was supposed to protect.

*This wasn't who I wanted to be.*

He drove me home after, and we didn't talk much. The silence sat thick between us, broken only by the roar of the truck engine and the occasional crunch of gravel under the tires. I stared out the window, trying to anchor myself, but I still felt uneasy in my own skin. I tried to play it off by smiling faintly, tucking my hair behind my ear like nothing had shifted inside me. I didn't want Dalton to know how I really felt. I didn't want him to think I was overthinking it, or worse, that I regretted it.

I liked him. I wanted to like him. I was still in disbelief that someone like him had even noticed me.

When we pulled up to the house, I reached for the door handle, eager to escape the weight in the cab. But before I could open it, Dalton grabbed my wrist, not hard, but firm enough that I noticed.

"What, no kiss?" he said with a smile.

I leaned over to give him a quick kiss on the lips with a smile that didn't quite meet my eyes. "Call me tomorrow, okay?" he said, still holding my wrist a second too long.

I nodded. "Sure, goodnight," I said softly, slipping away and closing the door behind me. I didn't turn back.

Inside, the house was dark and still. I crept to my room, careful not to wake anyone. I kicked off my shoes, crawled into bed, and lay there in the dark, staring at the ceiling.

Ding.

My phone buzzed against the nightstand. A message from Dalton lit up the screen.

**Already can't wait to see you again. Tonight was great.**

I stared at it for a long time. *Had it been?* I didn't know what I was supposed to feel. Flattered? Special? Happy? Instead, all I felt was hollow.

A message from earlier lit up right after.

**Be careful and have fun. There's food in the fridge if you're hungry when you get home. —S.**

I should have been hungry. I hadn't eaten all day. But I couldn't bring myself to go to the kitchen. My stomach turned at the thought.

I lay there for a long time, still in my clothes, still wearing the necklace Sheryl had given me. I clutched the tiny compass charm between my fingers, searching for a direction, any direction.

And when the tears came, slow at first, then heavy and hot, I didn't fight them. I cried myself to sleep that night. And when the numbness finally crept in to replace the ache, I welcomed it.

Over the next two weeks, I stayed busy helping Luke finish the house.

At the pace we were working, we figured we'd have the house ready to list just after we got back from helping my grandparents move. With every fixture we replaced and every nail I hammered, it felt like I was sealing up part of a chapter I hadn't been ready to close.

That reminder hit me hard. I still hadn't figured out where I was going next. I needed to start seriously looking for a place of my own.

Dalton and I rode together a few times, but something between us had shifted. The conversation didn't flow like it had before. He'd talk about the horses, his job, and I'd nod along, distracted by thoughts I didn't want to share. Being with him started to feel like walking through water, possible, but slower, heavier than it should have been

Our relationship was… progressing. Whether I was ready for that, I still wasn't sure. Dalton pushed for more intimacy, and too often, I gave in, even when I didn't feel ready. He wasn't like Lonnie; he didn't scare me, but I kept wishing he'd show the same interest in me without expecting something physical in return.

The night before, I rode back to Tennessee with Sheryl and Luke, and Dalton came to pick me up. We didn't go to the stables this time. Instead, he offered to drive me around town, said we could look for places to rent. I'd already circled a few listings in the classifieds, but I was hoping we might stumble across a crooked **For Rent** sign tucked behind some overgrown hedges or pass a porch with a hand-painted notice in the window, someone looking for a quiet tenant or a half-decent roommate. Since Dalton knew the area better than I did, I rode along with him.

We talked about small things, music, work, half-remembered stories from our childhoods, but even when his words were light, there was something heavy threading through them, like rust under paint. His stories about his father were vague, clipped at the edges. He mentioned his mama leaving when he was little and how it had just been him and his dad ever since. I asked, just once, about the bruises I'd seen on his arm. He laughed, said they were from breaking in a stubborn gelding. But there was something in the way he said it—too fast, too practiced—that settled wrong in my gut.

Like a house with fresh siding nailed over rotten boards, something wasn't right.

And deep down, I already knew it.

At one point, he casually suggested we get a place together.

"Wouldn't have to worry about roommates that way," he said. "We could split everything. Be easier on both of us."

He wasn't wrong. Financially, it made sense. But emotionally? It was too soon. I wasn't ready, not for that kind of commitment, not with so many questions still hanging between us.

I sidestepped the suggestion, changed the subject. I could feel the shift in his mood after that. He didn't push, but he didn't smile much either.

As we drove back to the house, I stared out the window, discouraged. Everything we'd looked at was either too expensive or already taken. When we pulled into the driveway, we sat there for a few quiet minutes.

"I wish you weren't leaving," he said finally.

"I know," I replied. "But it won't be long."

"Can't your sister and Luke just go without you?" he asked.

I shook my head. "No. I promised I'd help. Plus, I miss Momma and Daddy, and my grandparents. I want to see them."

He looked out the windshield, jaw tight. "Yeah, but… won't you miss me?"

"Sure, I will," I said, offering a small smile. "But I'll be back soon. I still need to find a place to live, and Mari's counting on me. She has a large shipment of aquatic plants arriving for the greenhouse expansion. She needs the help."

He huffed and leaned back in the seat. "Alright… but you better call. I'll be missing you, ya know."

I gave him a quick kiss and opened the door. "I will."

As I stepped toward the house, my heart felt split down the middle. Part of me cared for Dalton, maybe more than I wanted to admit. But another part longed for home. For peace. For a hug from my Mamaw.

The drive back home stretched long and slow, like the road itself wasn't quite ready to let me go. I was eager to see my family, to fall back into something familiar, but the thought of leaving the farm gnawed at me. That place had become more than a quiet patch of land; it had been my refuge, my reset. Saying goodbye felt like peeling off a layer of skin. I was caught somewhere between the comfort of going home and the sting of parting with a chapter that still held me, equal parts restless and raw. I was returning to something deeply rooted in me while also preparing to let it go.

As soon as we pulled into the driveway, I didn't even unpack. I walked straight to my Mamaw's house.

When she opened the door, her face lit up with one of those kind smiles I had missed more than I realized, and then I really noticed how much she had aged. Her features were softer now, more lined, and her posture had changed just a little. But her spirit, that steady warmth that had anchored so much of my childhood, was still there.

She pulled me into her arms, and the second she did, the floodgates opened. I broke down completely. I let out all the sorrow, all the anxiety, stress, and shame I'd been carrying. She didn't flinch. She didn't pull away. She just held me, steady and sure, the way only she could. She let me cry it all out, her arms a refuge I hadn't even realized I'd needed so badly.

When I finally pulled back, her hands, those same hands that had bandaged my cuts, baked me cookies, mended my clothes, cupped my face gently.

"I know, baby," she whispered. "I know."

At the time, I figured Mamaw was simply easing my sorrow over losing the farm. Now I suspect she saw the deeper ache, the way life was stretching me thin, testing my legs the same way a river tests its banks. She understood how lonely it felt to lean on God when your prayers echoed back unanswered, how hard it was to find out who you're meant to be in a world where too many men feel taller only when they've cut a woman down.

There are good men—Daddy, Luke, Sergeant Pete—but for every one of them, it seems there's a fistful more who'd sooner grind a woman into dust than lift her up.

Mamaw knew that truth like scripture. She'd stared this world in the eye and still met it with grace, humor, and iron-spined resolve. When she wrapped her arms around me that day and refused to let go, I realized she could feel the lesson seeping into my bones. The same hard lesson she'd learned long before: stand firm, keep your faith, and never let a man's shadow dim your own light.

After my visit with Mamaw and Papaw, I walked back to Momma and Daddy's house. I couldn't begin to count how many times my feet had made that trip. Ever since I was big enough to walk, I'd padded down that red dirt road to my grandparents' house like it was part of my daily routine. The thought of someone else living in their home turned my stomach. I pushed the thought aside as I climbed the steps and opened the door.

I walked in on a conversation between Sheryl, Luke, and my parents. Just in time to hear Momma say, "Oh, so that's why the hasty wedding."

It didn't need to be said out loud, so of course, Momma said it. She didn't mean it to be rude; that was just her way. But I still saw the flicker of hurt in Sheryl's eyes. I knew then that she had told them about the baby.

So I spoke up. "I think it's great news. I can't wait to have a niece or nephew to spoil."

That did the trick. I saw Momma's face soften into a smile at the thought. She loved babies, and it had been a long time since there had been the pitter-patter of little feet across the floors of their home.

That night, we gathered around the scarred wood table, a deck of dog-eared cards shuffling between us. Laughter braided with the occasional tear, grief, and joy shared the same breath, which somehow made the old kitchen feel more alive than it had in years.

Later, I slipped beneath my childhood quilt, the scent of cedar still clinging to the cotton, and sleep folded me tight. I hadn't rested that soundly since before the body in the woods.

Dawn slipped in peach-pale through the curtains, and I coaxed my old truck to life, the engine rattling like loose prayer beads. She was no beauty, but she was mine, and the hum of her tires on the backroads sounded like freedom.

At Mamaw and Papaw's, I set to boxing up the odds and ends around her computer desk. Between the stationery and a jar of mismatched buttons, I found an old photo album wedged behind the monitor. Pressed between its pages, carefully, like a rose tucked between hymnbook leaves, was a brittle newspaper clipping: a marriage announcement I'd never seen before.

It was yellowed and fragile, the edges curled like it had been read a thousand times. There, in the grainy black-and-white photograph, stood a much younger version of my grandparents. Mamaw, with her dark brown hair swept up in soft curls, wore a simple dress that hugged her petite frame, and those unmistakable blue eyes sparkled with mischief. She had always been feisty, the kind of woman who could hold her own in any conversation and make you laugh until your sides ached. Even now, with her hair turned silver and her figure softened by time, she still wore her cotton gowns and an apron tied around her waist like armor—ready to bake, garden, or wrangle grandchildren.

Papaw stood beside her in the photo, tall and lean in a suit that didn't quite fit his long limbs, his grin full of the kind of charm Mamaw used to say could talk a preacher into lying. He'd worked at the sawmill all my life, but to us, he was the man who could fix anything. He built us dollhouses and wooden swords, handed out ice cream and soda like it was treasure, and always had a practical joke up his sleeve. He could be stern when it mattered, but he loved Sheryl and me deeply.

Across the top of the clipping, the headline read:

**Miss Ruth Hollis Weds Mr. Harlan Thompson – October 12, 1958**

That photo, that tiny announcement in brittle newsprint, reminded me of the love story that had quietly shaped so much of my childhood. It wasn't flashy or perfect, but it endured.

We spent the next few days packing up the rest of Mamaw and Papaw's belongings and helping them settle into their new house in town. It was modest, a single-story home with a tiny porch, flower beds that hadn't yet bloomed, and beige siding that looked like every other house on the street. It was practical, close to the little grocery store, just a few minutes from their family doctor, and easier to maintain. I understood why they chose it, but still, it didn't feel like home. It lacked the creak of worn floorboards, the familiar scent of Papaw's aftershave in the bathroom, or the faint trail of flour dust in Mamaw's kitchen after baking biscuits from scratch. There were no forts behind the couch. No hiding spots for Christmas gifts. No flowers blooming just beyond the porch swing.

This new place wasn't stitched together with memories. It was just a house. Clean, convenient, unfamiliar. But if this was where they wanted to be, then I would support them.

I drove back to the farm after dropping off a load of kitchen necessities for Momma to put away. The gravel popped beneath the tires like it always had, and the wind carried the scent of honeysuckle from somewhere deep in the woods. As I pulled into the drive, a deer stepped from the tree line. Her coat was sleek and copper in the golden dusk. She stood still, her ears alert, eyes locked on mine. For a moment, it was like time folded in on itself. She was beautiful, wild, and haunting.

But instead of awe, a shiver danced down my spine. The weight of memory came rushing in. There was a whirlwind of recollection and emotion—laughter in the holler, secrets in the trees, bones beneath the brambles. I took a deep breath, turned away, and made my way into the house.

Inside, Mamaw was crouched by a bookshelf, placing her paperbacks in a cardboard box. I reached down to help and spotted a worn stack of diet and weight-loss books. Glossy covers from the '80s and '90s, each promising transformation.

My breath caught.

I had never noticed them before, not really. But now they felt like artifacts of something quiet and tragic. My Mamaw, the woman who had wrapped me in warmth, whose hugs smelled like cinnamon and cedar, had once believed she wasn't enough. That she had to shrink to be worthy.

She had not seen herself through my eyes.

In her mirror, she must've seen flaws, softness where the world said there shouldn't be, wrinkles that love had etched into her skin, numbers on a scale that told her lies. But when I looked at her, I saw strength. I saw kindness. I saw the woman who stitched quilts by hand, who kept a garden full of blooms even in dry summers, who held generations together with the quiet glue of devotion.

She had always been more than enough. She may have thought she was imperfect. But to me, she was exceptional.

I stepped outside to ask Daddy for help loading Mamaw's books into the bed of my truck. He'd been cleaning out the old shed where Papaw kept the lawnmower, and I spotted him hauling out a weathered, dust-covered box. He cracked it open, and I caught a glimpse of what was inside: empty whiskey bottles, rattling faintly with each step he took.

I glanced at him, confused. He didn't meet my eyes.

"I'll tell you later," he muttered.

I just nodded.

He followed me inside and helped me stack the boxes near the front door. One sat off to the side, and as Daddy went to pick it up, Mamaw stopped him.

"Put that one in the front of Jenny's truck," she said, her voice soft but certain. "Those are for her and Sheryl to keep."

I smiled, touched. "You don't have to do that, Mamaw."

But she knew how much we loved to read, and how much those worn and dog-eared books meant to us. They weren't just stories; they were pieces of her. Memories in paper form. Daddy carefully placed the box in the passenger seat before I headed off with the last load of the evening.

By the time I made it back to Momma and Daddy's, I was bone-tired. My legs ached, my arms were sore from lifting, and my mind was foggy from the weight of the day. I flopped onto the bed and reached for my phone. Twelve unread messages from Dalton. Two missed calls.

I sighed.

***I'm sorry***, I texted. ***I'm exhausted. I'll call you in the morning.***

I didn't have the energy to deal with him just then. I figured he'd be annoyed, but he knew how much I had on my plate.

That night, sleep clambered over me like ivy on an old brick wall, steadily, insistently, and with no intention of letting go. In my dreams, the woods were darker than usual, the sky hanging low like a lid pressed tight. I walked alone down a narrow path, the trees pressing in, their limbs creaking with secrets. I came to the raspberry thicket again, but this time the berries were blackened, shriveled on their stems, the thorns curling like claws.

Something called to me from beyond them.

And then I saw her.

Andrea.

Not bones. Not memory.

Her.

She lay half-curled in the brush, pale and still, her once-beautiful hair snarled in the thorned canes, as if the raspberries had grown around her, unwilling to let her go. Her limbs were splayed in unnatural angles, arms and legs twisted like roots clawing for purchase in the earth. The thorns wrapped tight around her wrists and ankles, cradling her in a cruel embrace, each barb a tiny dagger drawing beads of blood that glistened darkly in the shadows. She didn't look like a girl who had vanished, she looked like something the forest had grown.

But her eyes… her eyes found mine.

They didn't blink.

She began to move, her lips parting, her mouth forming a soundless plea. I could feel her desperation, the words fighting to rise from her throat, but no voice came. She tried again. Still, nothing. Just the eerie rustle of the leaves around us.

Then the ground began to stir.

From beneath the soil, bones began to rise.

Not fast. Not loud. Just steady. One by one, they pushed up through the earth like roots growing in reverse, small hands, delicate ribcages, broken teeth, collarbones wrapped in phantom vines.

Dozens of them.

Then hundreds.

They surrounded Andrea like a crown of silence.

Every bone was a girl who'd disappeared.

Every fragment, a woman who'd been told to stay quiet.

Every splintered piece, a secret never spoken aloud.

The forest swelled with the weight of all that loss. Of all that silencing.

And I just stood there, unable to move. Unable to run. The roots curled around my feet, anchoring me in the moment. Andrea's gaze never left mine. Her mouth kept moving, silent and urgent. Begging me to listen. To remember.

And I did.

Even after I woke, gasping for breath and slick with sweat, I remembered.

Her eyes.

The thorns.

The bones rising from the ground.

And the weight of what had never been said.

I turned on the lamp, breath catching in my throat, as if I'd surfaced too quickly from deep water. *What was that?*

Maybe being back at Mamaw and Papaw's had stirred something in me, unearthed old feelings I hadn't fully faced. But I knew, deep down, that the dream wasn't just about Andrea. It was about all of us. The ones who carry our pain quietly. The ones who survive what should never have touched us.

Our stories are different, but the hurt is the same. Passed down. Layered. Inherited like old furniture or family recipes. That dream lay heavily on me, like the fog that settles thick over the river just before dawn.

I lay there in the stillness, too afraid to fall asleep again. So I waited for the light, hoping that morning might loosen the grip of the night.

When it finally did, I got up and checked my phone to find a message that was blinking on my lock screen:

**I guess you don't miss me so much after all.**

I stared at it for a moment, caught between confusion and frustration. Dalton knew I was busy. Still, guilt crept in like a shadow under the door. I didn't want to make him feel unwanted, so I typed out an apology, promised I'd message more now that things were winding down. He didn't reply right away, which was unusual for him. *Maybe he was more upset than I thought.*

I headed into the kitchen, poured myself a cup of coffee. The house was quiet in that soft early morning way, sunlight just beginning to spill across the linoleum floor. Daddy walked in, handed me a silver thermos, and said, "Here, pour that in. You're welcome to ride with me this morning. Your momma's staying here to finish up some things, and your sister and Luke already headed out. Let's get the rest moved before this rain starts."

I climbed into his old Chevy, the leather seats warm from the sun. As we drove down the familiar winding road toward the new house, my thoughts drifted back to the box of liquor bottles; the image nagged at me.

"So… where did all those whiskey bottles come from?" I asked, my voice quiet. "Mamaw and Papaw don't drink."

Daddy exhaled hard through his nose, keeping his eyes on the road. "Not now," he said. "But your Papaw sure did. When I was a boy, he drank like a fish. Mean ol' cuss, too. Cared more about whiskey, gambling, and chasing women than he ever did about being home. And when he was home, when he was drunk…" His jaw tightened. "Me and Dale were his favorite targets."

His words knocked the air from my lungs. I turned to look at him, stunned.

I had never seen Papaw act out of the way. Sure, he had a temper. I'd seen him cuss a rusty tractor or throw a wrench when things didn't go right, but never toward us. Never toward Mamaw.

Daddy shook his head, eyes still distant. "He beat Dale so bad one night, your Mamaw had finally had enough. Threw him out. Told him to go back to his momma's house, that she wasn't putting up with it anymore."

He paused, like the next part hurt worse than the last.

"After a time, he changed. Started going to church with her. Got saved. Put the bottle down for good, and become a better man. But it was too late for me and Dale. We were already gone. I joined the Navy, Dale the Marines. We just needed to get away from him. Far away."

The silence between us grew thick.

"I came back because I love my momma," he added quietly. "Wanted to make sure she was taken care of, no matter what. But Dale? He never moved back. Never forgave him. I talk to him a few times a year, but I don't think he's spoken to Papaw in over a decade."

I sat in silence, trying to reconcile the stories I'd grown up hearing with this new version of Papaw. The man who fed stray dogs in the holler. The man who carved wooden toys for us. The man who always saved the last bite of dessert for Mamaw.

It was hard to imagine him as the monster Daddy described, but I believed him all the same. Some truths settle in slowly, like dust in sunlight. They are visible only when the light hits just right. I had always seen Papaw as a quiet strength, a steady hand, but then I began to see him as layered. Human. Flawed. Changed. That didn't erase the good, but it complicated the picture.

I didn't know then what I do now, but as the truck rumbled toward town and the clouds thickened above us, I knew this much: family is stitched from stories, some beautiful, some broken. And even when the pages don't all make sense, you keep reading. You keep turning the page.

In my own journey of self-discovery, I was beginning to uncover hard truths about the people I loved. If I could offer them grace for their imperfections and love them just the same, then maybe, just maybe, I could learn to do the same for myself.

# Chapter 10



*Journal Entry– June 21, 1987*

*There was a time I thought love meant enduring, no matter the weight. I told myself God would bless my faithfulness if I just held on tighter. But even the strongest rope frays when it's pulled too long in one direction. Harlan used to come home with liquor on his breath and words in his mouth that he couldn't take back. And well, I stayed. I stayed longer than I should've, longer than my heart could bear.*
*But when he finally laid not hands, but fists on Dale, I knew love wasn't meant to make martyrs out of mothers. That night, I packed Harlan's bag and told the Lord I was walking by faith, not fear. And Harlan, he didn't change right away, but he changed.*
*And maybe that's the miracle, when grace gives a man enough time to reckon with himself. I still love him, but I've learned love has to stand beside truth if it's going to last.*

*-Ruth*

We didn't talk much on the ride back from Mamaw and Papaw's new house. The truck bed was empty now. The last of their things had been unloaded, but the weight of what Daddy had told me still pressed heavily against my mind. I'd always known Papaw could be sharp-tongued and stubborn, but I hadn't known the whole story. Not until Daddy said it out loud, voice low and far away, like he was telling me something he'd tried hard not to remember.

It was the kind of truth that changed things, not just how you saw someone, but how you saw the ones who came after them. Daddy had grown up in that house, but he'd made sure we didn't deal with the same demons he had. He never raised his voice unless he had to, never raised a hand at all. Just steady, patient, a man who carried his pain quietly, so his kids didn't have to. And now that I knew, I could see it. The difference was deliberate.

Thank God he had been different.

That night, I sat on the porch long after the others had gone to bed, listening to the sounds of the night, the distant hoot of an owl, the creak of tree branches, the soft hum of crickets. The stars blinked overhead, quiet and steady, and I found myself thinking about how much people carry in silence. How many wounds are hidden behind gentle hands and easy smiles? I kept thinking about Mamaw, how she stayed all those years with Papaw, even through the drinking, even when the meanness must've shown through more than once. I didn't understand it when I was younger, and part of me still doesn't. Maybe it was her faith that anchored her, the vows she made, not just to Papaw, but to God. She believed in loving people through their brokenness. Maybe she hoped he would change, or maybe she believed that enduring it was her cross to bear. But even the strongest faith has a limit. And when he went too far, that was it. Loving someone doesn't mean letting them break you. Mamaw might've stayed longer than she should've, but she left when it counted most. Maybe that's its own kind of strength. If she hadn't finally put her foot down, Papaw might've never changed. But because she did, because she stood her ground and wrapped herself in faith and grace, Papaw had to find his own way back to God before he could ever find his way back to her.

The next morning, Sheryl knocked on my door with her sunglasses already on and a familiar edge in her voice. "Ride into town with me? I need to pick something up from the pharmacy, and I'm thinking about picking up a brochure from that realtor next to the bakery."

She said it like it wasn't a big deal, but I knew her well enough to hear what she wasn't saying. She was thinking ahead. Past the house that wouldn't be hers much longer. Past summer. Past the safe little bubble we'd built since the wedding. She was already halfway out the door in her mind, making plans for the next chapter.

We pulled out of the driveway into the morning heat, cicadas singing their scratchy song from the treetops. The tires hummed low against the packed earth, and sunlight flickered through the leaves like little fireflies. I stared out the window, still half-lost in yesterday's conversation with Daddy, still thinking about the past and how it shaped everything that came after.

We stopped at the pharmacy first, just a quick pick up for pre-natal vitamins and ibuprofen. While Sheryl paid, I drifted toward the endcap near the checkout, where the local papers were stacked beside peanut brittle and denture cream.

**Cold Case: 36 Years, No Answers**, the front page read, with Andrea Campbell's photo just below the fold, by S. Jordan. The name stirred something in me, familiar like a song you half-remember, like a scent on someone else's coat.

Sheryl glanced over my shoulder. "I can't believe they're still running stories on that."

I didn't answer. My throat had gone dry.

The tile under my feet turned to moss. The fluorescent lights hummed like bees in a thistle patch—constant, busy, and just a little too close. I was sixteen again, stumbling through the woods, arms scratched raw from briars, lungs burning from the screams. The paper crinkled in my hand before I even realized I'd picked it up.

Sheryl touched my elbow. "Jen."

I blinked hard. The moment slipped like water through a crack, gone but not forgotten. I folded the paper and set it back down.

We stepped out of the pharmacy, my hands still trembling. We hadn't meant to run into anyone. We were just running errands. But life in a small town never really gives you that luxury. I saw them, Momma's two younger sisters, Cindy and Mindy, leaning against the railing in front of the Dollar Saver like they owned the sidewalk…. Their arms were crossed, expressions already half-curled into smug little grins. It was like they'd been waiting for someone to look down on.

They hadn't changed. Still dressing a decade too young, still teasing their hair too high, still full of the kind of bitterness that grows in people who never got what they thought they deserved. They were only a few years older than Sheryl, and somehow still stuck in the same circles, the same stories, the same stale gossip that had fueled them since high school.

"Well, would you look at that," one of them said, Cindy, maybe, I could never tell them apart. "Didn't know we were too distant to be invited to a family wedding."

Sheryl didn't blink. She just eased her sunglasses higher on her nose and smiled with that smooth, tight grace she'd perfected over the years. "It was just a small thing. Nothing personal. Figured a drive to D.C. might be a bit much for y'all." She stretched the word out slow, syrupy, like honey sliding off a spoon.

My jaw nearly dropped. I'd never seen her like that before—so calm, so sweet, it could've been served at breakfast with biscuits.

The other sister raised an eyebrow. "Oh, well, we heard it was all a little… rushed."

Cindy, or Mindy, leaned in, voice dipped in fake concern. "Had to hurry and tie that man down before he got away, huh?"

Then, with a wicked glint, the other added, "Or maybe they're in the family way?"

Their laughter rang out sharp and hollow, bouncing off the concrete like a slap. I felt my fists clench. All I wanted was to throw something back at them, something mean and cutting that would wipe the smugness right off their faces.

But Mari's voice rose in my mind like a steady tide. *Don't give your peace away just because someone else is empty.*

So I held my tongue. Swallowed the sting. Lifted my chin.

Sheryl just kept walking, heels clicking neatly and deliberately on the sidewalk. I followed beside her, the echo of our steps louder than anything those two could've said. And as we passed the bakery, I realized something: Grace didn't always look soft. Sometimes it looked like steel in your spine and silence in the face of cruelty. Sheryl had both, and I was learning.

I asked Sheryl how that didn't drive her nuts, how she could walk away from all that pettiness without letting it get under her skin. She just shrugged and said, "I'm already winning. I have Luke. I have love. I have a wonderful family. And I have a great sister." She nudged me with her elbow and grinned. "They're just stuck with each other." We both laughed, the kind of laugh that shakes off the last of someone else's bitterness.

Those two girls really were nothing like Momma. They had the same blood, sure, but none of her quiet strength. Where Momma gave, they took. Where she held her tongue, they ran theirs. I think Grandpa Cliff knew it, too. In all his guilt over how his wife had treated Momma growing up, he'd spoiled the younger two to death. And it showed. They'd grown up being handed things instead of earning them, praised instead of guided, and their entitlement clung to them like perfume too thick to wash off. Honestly, I don't think he even liked them. Anytime we were all together, you could see the annoyance written all over his face. Just the sound of their voices made his eyes twitch. He'd grit his teeth, drum his fingers on the arm of his chair, and stare out the window like he was trying to will himself somewhere else entirely. Maybe spoiling them was just his way of making up for something he couldn't fix, but it never seemed to bring anyone peace, least of all him.

I'd had a good day with Sheryl, aside from our brief run-in with those two. After the pharmacy, we stopped for ice cream, letting the cold sweetness melt the last of the tension from our mouths. She'd grabbed the brochure from outside the realtor's office and tucked it under her arm. Then we took the long way home, coasting down familiar backroads framed in fields of goldenrod and Queen Anne's lace. The windows were down, warm wind in our hair. It felt like we'd slipped into a memory, two sisters, carefree for a little while.

We waved at folks we hadn't seen in years. People who still stopped what they were doing just to smile and lift a hand. They'd say, "There go Abe and Jean's girls," like we'd never left. That's the way of a small town, where who you are is always tethered to who you come from.

Sheryl looked out across a hayfield glowing in the low afternoon sun. "I think I'd like to raise my baby here," she said quietly, almost to herself. "He deserves to have a home where he can run barefoot, catch lightning bugs, and know what silence sounds like. I want him to feel how still the world can be, before it starts pulling at him."

"You already know it's a boy?" I asked with a small smile.

"Well, no," she said, laughing a little. "It's just a feeling. Luke thinks it's a girl, but what does he know?"

"Doesn't he want a son?" I asked, though deep down I couldn't think it mattered either way, at least not to me.

"Actually, no. He wants a daughter," she said, softer now. "I think it's because of his sister… Alana."

Her voice caught just slightly, and I knew not to push. It explained a lot, including the gentle way Luke touched her belly and the long silences he sometimes fell into when the subject of children came up.

His grief was stitched quiet and tight into the fabric of his love.

"He'll be a great dad," I said, my voice sure.

"Yeah," she replied, eyes shining. "It's part of what I love most about him."

The tires rolled slowly over the familiar curve of the drive, the dust rising in little puffs behind us. Fireflies had just started to blink along the fenceline. Tomorrow evening, we'd be heading back to Virginia. Luke and Sheryl wanted to get the house listed and had to return to their jobs.

Dalton had messaged already. **Can't wait to see you**, he'd said. But the words felt distant now, like they belonged to a different life, one I wasn't quite ready to step back into.

As soon as we stepped into the house, we knew something was wrong. The air inside was heavier than the humid dusk outside. Momma sat on the edge of the couch, hands folded tight in her lap, her knuckles pale. Luke leaned against the doorframe, arms crossed, head lowered. Daddy stood up slowly, the way someone does when they've got something hard to say.

"Sit down, kiddo," he said, voice low.

My heart slipped into my stomach. I pulled out a kitchen chair, every muscle tight.

Momma stood and walked closer, her voice shaky but clear. "I'm sorry, sweetie… your friend Marie passed away today. They found her in her driveway, in the car. They think she overdosed."

The world stopped moving. My mind rejected the words at first. Then a memory hit me so hard it knocked the air from my lungs—Marie, standing on the fire tower that night, belting "I Fall to Pieces" into the dark like she was born for the Opry. We passed a bottle of warm, cheap wine between us, our legs swinging over the edge, the whole county spread out below. She swore up and down she was gonna leave Pedoux someday.

"Sing my way outta here," she'd said, letting out a laugh that shook her shoulders.

I told her I believed her.

And I meant it.

We were two girls teetering between recklessness and hope. God, she was magic, before the darkness swallowed her. Before we drifted. Before I left.

And then I cried. Not loud or dramatic, just an aching kind of weeping that came from someplace deep, where childhood memories and old wounds live tangled together. I cried for Marie, for the pieces of her no one had saved, and for all the versions of us that would never make it home.

# Chapter 11


*Journal Entry– January 22, 1993*

*The past never stays buried. It waits, quietly, in the corners of memory, like dust under a rug. But God sees it all, even the hidden things. I've learned that healing doesn't mean forgetting. It means being brave enough to face what hurts you... and choosing not to let it define your future.*

*-Ruth*

I lay in bed that night, tears soaking the edge of my pillow. I was crying for Marie, for her life, for her death, for the way it ended. To die alone in a car… my heart broke at the thought. I couldn't stop wondering if it had been on purpose. Maybe it was an accident. Maybe she was just trying to numb the pain for one more night. But either way, it was terrible. We were so young. Marie had spiraled, that much was clear. No guidance. No hand steady enough to pull her back. Guilt sank into me like an anchor dropped in still water. I had left. I had saved myself. *But had I left her behind? Had she been completely alone because I wasn't there?*

And what if I had stayed? Would I have been in that car with her, chasing the same high, running from the same ghosts? Would my family be the ones sitting in shock? I couldn't stop the thought from creeping in. It made me feel hollow. Then my mind drifted, like it always seemed to, back to Andrea. The woods. The body. The silence that followed. How many questions went unanswered? How many pieces of pain had I tucked away just to keep going?

Everything felt like a tangle of roots, twisted and buried. Marie and Andrea. The girl I used to be and the one trying so hard to move forward. One thread pulled another. Nothing stood alone.

A soft knock broke the quiet, and Daddy stepped into the room, his presence filling it with warmth and sadness all at once. He sat on the edge of my bed and reached out, gently stroking my hair, just like he used to when I was little and afraid of storms.

"I love you, kiddo," he said, voice thick. "I'm sorry."

That was all. But somehow, it said everything. I could hear the weight in his words. He wasn't just sorry about Marie. He was sorry for all of it. For the pain I'd carried, the things he hadn't seen soon enough. The parts of me I'd had to piece back together on my own. He stood up slowly, tucking the blanket around my shoulders, and kissed the top of my head.

"Goodnight, Daddy. I love you too," I whispered, my voice barely steady.

As he stepped out, Sheryl crept in, barefoot, wrapped in the same old comforter she used to drag around when we were kids. She didn't say a word, just lifted the corner of the covers and slid in beside me. Her arms wrapped around me, warm and familiar, and I let myself break.

She held me like she used to when the world got too big, like only a sister can. And I cried, cried until the sobs softened and sleep finally found me.

When I woke the next morning, she was gone. I was alone, and I felt it deeply, like the echo of something once whole that had slipped just out of reach.

As I sat there in bed, still feeling hollow and unsure, my phone buzzed on the nightstand. It was Dalton. I didn't want to answer. My chest felt too tight and my thoughts too heavy. But I knew if I didn't pick up, he'd just keep calling, probably more and more irritated each time.

I held the phone to my ear. "Hello," I said, the word barely more than a whisper, laced with grief I couldn't hide.

He had taken my tone personally. "Well, hello to you, too," he said, sarcastically. "Aren't you excited you get to see me today?"

"Sorry, Dalton," I said softly. "I'm just… not feeling great."

He sighed. "What now?"

That tone, sharp and impatient, cut deeper than he probably realized. Or maybe he did realize it and just didn't care. He used to sound concerned when I was upset, warm, and attentive. Lately, though, it has always felt like I was doing something wrong just by having feelings at all.

"My childhood best friend passed away yesterday," I said. "I'm having a hard time with it. She was like a sister to me."

"Oh. Bummer," he said flatly. "Well, I'll cheer you up when you get home."

I stared at the ceiling. The disconnect between us was a canyon. "Dalton… I'm not coming home today," I said. "I'm staying for her funeral. I need to be here."

There was a long silence on the line.

"Damn, Jenny. It's been a week," he snapped. "How long are you gonna be gone? Don't you miss me?"

I had missed him, but hearing his voice now made me question why. Why had I ever felt so drawn to someone who could make my pain feel like an inconvenience?

"Of course I miss you," I said, even though part of me didn't anymore. "But I need to do this. I'll be home soon. I promise."

Another pause. Then a grudging, "Okay, I guess."

"Hey, listen, I've got to go," I said quickly. "I think I hear Momma calling me."

She wasn't. But I couldn't stand another second on the phone. The lie felt like a betrayal, but not to him. It felt like I was betraying myself for needing to lie to escape the guilt he was piling on me.

I didn't have the language for it then, not for what was happening. No one talked about emotional manipulation or gaslighting. Back then, people didn't use words like "toxic" or "coercive control." We just whispered to ourselves that something didn't feel right and tried to carry on. Abuse doesn't always leave bruises. Sometimes it leaves confusion, doubt, and shame. And in towns like ours, most people kept their darkness behind closed doors. You didn't air your dirty laundry. You smiled in pictures. You held your tongue. And if you were hurt, you told yourself maybe it was your fault, maybe you were too sensitive. Women were raised to endure, to rationalize, to keep things quiet, because speaking out too often meant being blamed or disbelieved.

I didn't know it yet, but the guilt I felt wasn't mine to carry. And the love I thought I had… it was already unraveling.

The next few days passed in a blur. Sheryl and Luke packed up and returned to Virginia, though Sheryl offered to stay behind with me. I told her to go. She had a new life now, one that needed tending, and I didn't want to be the reason she put it on hold. I hadn't even thought about how I'd get back to Virginia when the time came. Part of me assumed Daddy would drive me, though I hated the thought of asking. It felt selfish to need anything more from him just then.

I stood in front of the mirror, dressed in black, my arms limp at my sides. The fabric clung to me like grief. I hadn't worn anything like it since I'd left, but it reminded me too much of a time when my entire wardrobe looked like this. My depression had been woven into everything I owned, like my clothes were crying out for someone to see the shadows behind my eyes. Most people didn't, but Sheryl did. Even through my letters, she knew.

That thought made me reach for the necklace she'd given me, the tiny charm warm from where it rested against my skin. I held it there, fingers curled around it like an anchor. I was so grateful to have her. She had always been a lighthouse for me, even when I resented her glow. She reminded me where the shore was, where I was safe.

Whatever jealousy I once carried for her was melting away. I could feel it fading each time I looked at her and felt pride instead of bitterness. As I began learning to love myself, I found more room to love others, especially her. There was no room for resentment in healing.

But I couldn't stop thinking about Marie. How she never got to feel that kind of peace. How the darkness swallowed her whole before she ever saw the light. She'd been dealt such a cruel hand, born into chaos with no one to steady her. I wondered what her life would have been like if she'd had someone like Sheryl? A sister to pull her back when she was drifting too far?

And then it hit me like a punch to the gut.

She did have a sibling…Lonnie.

My breath caught in my throat, and the color drained from my face. I was going to see him tonight. I was certain of it. And I wasn't ready.

The room started to spin, and I staggered back, grabbing the edge of the desk. My stomach turned. I barely made it to the trash can before I heaved, bile burning in my throat.

I was not prepared for this.

I barely slept. The hours between then and the funeral passed in a blur—hushed voices, stiff clothes, the silence holding me together by threads. When the time came, I climbed into the car beside Momma and Daddy, the weight of dread settled heavy on me.

The funeral was held at the only funeral home in town, a squat brick building that hadn't changed since I was a kid. When Momma, Daddy, and I pulled in, I was surprised by how empty the parking lot looked. I had expected a crowd. Marie had known so many people, but grief doesn't always bring them out, especially when addiction is involved. People find ways to justify staying away.

Inside, the air was heavy with the scent of lilies and stale coffee. I recognized classmates I hadn't seen since graduation, older folks from around town, and a few faces from the darker corners of my past. Daddy paused outside the door to talk to Pete, who hovered near the service in his officer's uniform. He had made it to the Chief of police now. I glanced around and spotted some of the kids Marie and I used to party with. None of them looked like they'd fared much better than she had. A girl named Tan caught my eye, someone I'd always liked. She had bounced through foster homes like a pinball, never landing long enough to feel safe. That night, her hair was tangled and unbrushed, her black jeans torn, and her band tee hacked into a crop top. Her eyes were glassy, pupils like pinholes. She probably thought no one noticed, but when you've lived that life, you can always tell. The numbness gives people away.

I didn't approach them. That wasn't my world anymore, and I wasn't going to get pulled back into it. But I didn't carry hard feelings either. I nodded, offered a quiet wave, and said a silent prayer. I prayed they'd find the light before it was too late, before they ended up where Marie was now.

I stepped toward the casket and looked down at my friend. Her skin was pale and waxy. She looked older than she should have, like life had carved too many lines before her time. I didn't know if it was the drugs or death that had done it, but either way, it had stolen her youth. Her life. She had once been so bright, so full of fire. Her voice was made for something greater. I used to think God had dipped her throat in honey just so the angels could learn how to sing. I'd always been a little jealous of that.

I hoped she was singing now, somewhere beyond all of this. But the truth was, I didn't know if she was saved. We had never talked about God. Never talked about grace or salvation or eternity. And that shamed me. I'd hidden my faith back then, afraid of being mocked or misunderstood. I could've shared my light. Maybe she would've found a different path. Now I'd never know.

Then I heard a voice behind me.

"I didn't expect to see you here, kitten."

I froze. Lonnie.

He was the only one who ever called me that. I felt my stomach knot and forced myself to turn around. This was Marie's funeral, I reminded myself. I could get through this.

"Of course I'm here," I said, voice steady. "I loved Marie."

He nodded slowly. "She loved you, too. Even after you left, she said you were one of the only good things she ever had. She was proud of you, you know. Proud that you got out."

His words landed hard—sharp, sudden, and breath-stealing. I wasn't expecting kindness from him, not after everything.

"I'm really sorry," I said. "For your loss."

It felt strange, offering him sympathy. If the world made sense, he'd have been the one apologizing to me.

I asked, "Where's your aunt?"

He jerked his chin toward the front of the room. His aunt stood there in heels too high, voice too loud, laughing with the funeral director like she was trying to charm her way into a discount.

"She's probably hoping for a payment plan," he muttered. "We'll be paying this off for a decade."

"I hadn't thought about that," I admitted. "You don't think about those things when you're young."

Lonnie looked… different. Grounded. Sober. And it stopped me cold. I'd never seen him look so clear-eyed. He was still handsome in a rough sort of way, but it didn't matter. I knew what was behind that face. And even so, there we were, talking like acquaintances, maybe even like old friends.

It felt surreal. How could I stand there beside someone who had hurt me so deeply, talking as though nothing had ever happened? I used to think I was broken for doing that, for not screaming or running the other way. But now I know, it wasn't brokenness. It was survival. That's how trauma works. It teaches you to smile through your fear, to maintain the peace at all costs. It teaches you to prioritize safety over truth, especially when the truth is too heavy to carry in the moment.

I hadn't come to confront Lonnie. I had come to say goodbye to Marie. But standing there, I realized I was also saying goodbye to a version of myself, the one who still needed Lonnie to acknowledge the pain he caused. Because maybe I didn't need that anymore. Maybe I was enough without his apology.

I took one last look at Marie and whispered, "I'm sorry." Then I turned and walked away.

I found Daddy still talking to Pete, who lit up the moment he saw me. He pulled me into one of his signature bear hugs, warm and familiar, the kind you don't realize you've missed until you're in it.

"I've missed you, kiddo," he said, pulling back just enough to get a good look at me. "Let me see you… Yup, still a little punk." His grin stretched wide as he pulled me back in and kissed the top of my head.

Pete was one of the only men I ever let get away with that. He had been like an uncle to me growing up, always around, always kind, always steady.

"Well, you're looking old," I teased, and he laughed, that same deep, weathered laugh I'd always known.

"Touche, kiddo. You got me," he said with a grin.

We said our goodbyes, exchanged hugs and love, and made our way back around the building. We found Momma by the ashtray stand, her cigarette burning low between her fingers. I always wished she'd quit. I wished Daddy would, too. Sheryl and I had fussed at them about it for years, but they were from a world where everybody smoked, and they hadn't fully let that part go. Maybe they would now, I thought. With a grandbaby on the way, maybe they'd think a little harder about how long they wanted to stick around.

"I'm ready to go," I told them both, my voice firm.

There was nothing left for me there. Marie was gone. She wasn't coming back, and I wasn't going to keep looking back either. I'd mourn her, and I'd carry her memory, but I couldn't carry the weight of that world anymore.

It was time to move forward.

We made it back home just as the sun dipped low behind the trees. I went straight to my room and stripped out of those dark funeral clothes, like I was peeling off a piece of my past. I balled them up and tossed them into the trash. For a second, I thought maybe I should donate them, let someone else get use from them. But to me, those clothes were heavy. They were stitched with grief, soaked in old pain, lined with the ghosts of who I used to be. It felt almost superstitious, but I didn't want to pass that weight on to anybody else. Maybe it was foolish. Still, it felt good to throw them away. Like shutting a door.

I slipped into my lavender nightgown, soft and familiar, and reached for my brush to braid my hair the way Momma used to when I was little. That's when I saw it, the box of books Mamaw had given Sheryl and me, still sitting in the chair by my desk. I'd completely forgotten about it in the chaos of the last few days.

I thought about waiting until Sheryl and I were together again to go through them. But then I figured, what would be the point in dragging them all the way to Virginia just for her to box them up again when they moved back? So I pulled the heavy box over to my bed, sat cross-legged on the quilt, and lifted the lid.

The scent of old pages rose to meet me—warm, dusty, and familiar, like the hush of a rainy afternoon spent indoors. A flood of memories stirred as I sifted through the box. There were a few of Mamaw's worn devotionals, their spines creased, and their pages softened by years of prayers and pencil marks in the margins. Next came the cookbooks, filled with handwritten notes and recipe cards stained with grease and smudged with flour. And then the mysteries, the same ones she used to read aloud to Sheryl and me, her voice low and steady as we sat cross-legged on the living room floor, hanging on every word. We'd beg her to keep going, even when the sun slipped behind the hills and the room grew dark around us.

Beneath them all, tucked like an afterthought, was something that hadn't been mentioned at all.

A journal.

# Chapter 12

*Journal Entry– November 3, 1970*

*There are some hurts that don't bruise the skin but leave you aching just the same. The kind you carry like a stone in your apron pocket-heavy and silent. I've learned to go about my days with a smile while my prayers get longer at night. Some things you hand over to the Lord not once, but every single morning. I used to think love meant everything would feel easy. But I know now that real love, the kind that lasts, has calloused hands and tear-stained cheeks.*

*I don't know what tomorrow holds. But I do know this: I want my children to see a mother who stood firm in faith. A woman who stayed soft, even in a world that gave her reasons to harden. I want them to know that strength doesn't always look loud; it sometimes looks like folding laundry and whispering, "Lord, help me," under your breath.*

*-Ruth*

I stood there, holding the old leather journal in my hands. The cover was soft and worn, its edges scuffed and faded with time. I could see that the pages had begun to yellow, and when I brought the book closer, the scent of age, dust, ink, and timeworn paper rose up to meet me. I knew, even before I opened it, that it had belonged to my Mamaw. She had kept journals for as long as I could remember. There were several, tucked into nooks around her house, filled with neat cursive and verses copied from Scripture.

I hesitated. It didn't feel like something Mamaw meant to include, more like it slipped in by mistake, tucked away in the shuffle of sorting and goodbyes. But there it was, resting in my hands like a question I didn't know I needed to ask. I held it tight against me, like a memory you don't dare let slip, and for a moment, I swore I felt her there with me. Not just in memory, but in spirit—quiet, steady, close. Maybe it was faith or maybe just grief, but finding it that night felt like more than a coincidence.

I felt a twinge of guilt, but my fingers moved on their own. I cracked it open anyway.

I saw the first date written in ink on the inside page: December 12, 1960.

My breath caught. Mamaw would've only been twenty-one then, not much older than I was at the time. I began to read.

*"Today, I sat on the edge of the bed and counted my blessings, even as the morning sickness rolled through me like waves. I told Harlan, and his eyes went wide with both joy and fear. We're going to have a baby. I still can't quite believe it. I feel too young, too uncertain, but I pray the Lord will guide us. I want to be strong, for the child, for him. For myself."*

I stopped. My eyes lingered on the ink, faded just slightly, as if the years had softened the weight of the words. I felt like I was trespassing, peering into a version of Mamaw I had never known, young, newlywed, unsure.

For a moment, I debated whether to keep reading. Was this meant for my eyes? Was I invading her privacy? But the longing to understand outweighed the guilt. There was so much I didn't know about my family's past, so much that had shaped my daddy, my Mamaw, and Papaw. Their lives had shaped my own. Their history was the soil I'd grown from. And with every word I read, I felt like I was uncovering pieces of myself.

I read the first two entries and felt a shift in my perspective. I had always seen her simply as "Mamaw", the apron-wearing, flower-planting, biscuit-baking version of her. But in those pages, she was more than that. She was a woman. Young. Afraid. Full of hope and doubt. She wasn't so different from me.

What struck me most was how often she leaned on her faith, even in moments of fear. She didn't have all the answers. She didn't know how things would turn out. But she trusted the Lord to carry her through, and I knew, deep down, I needed to do the same.

I laid the journal on the nightstand and drifted off to sleep, its weight still lingering in my hands like a silent prayer. I knew I'd return to it the next day. I had to; there was more I needed to understand.

When I woke early from a fitful sleep, the sky still streaked with gray, I reached over, turned on my bedside lamp, and picked up the journal again. This time, I flipped deeper into the pages, past the early days of new love and morning sickness.

What I read stopped me cold.

*"He came home late again. I could smell the whiskey before he ever spoke. I tried not to cry, but I did. I cried quietly, facing the wall, hoping he wouldn't see. It's not just the drinking, it's the weight of it all. The silence. The loneliness. I married for love, but some nights I feel like I'm living with a ghost. I keep praying he'll come back to me, the man I thought I married. I don't know how much longer I can carry this alone."*

I pressed the book to my chest, my throat tightening. It tore at my heart to know Mamaw had felt so broken, so abandoned inside her own home. I had never realized the weight she'd been carrying, all while smiling for us, baking pies, sewing quilts, telling bedtime stories like nothing in the world had ever gone wrong.

And Papaw... I'd never seen him in that light. Not once. I didn't know if I'd been ignorant or if he'd truly changed that much. I hoped, God, I hoped, it was the latter because Mamaw deserved a love that cherished her. A love that wrapped its arms around her, not one that made her cry quietly in the dark.

Reading those words felt like looking into a mirror that reflected not just her pain, but mine too. It made me question everything I thought I knew about the people who raised us, but it also made me admire her more than I ever had before. She hadn't just survived. She had endured. And through it all, she had still given love, given grace, given herself.

I stayed curled in bed for hours, completely pulled into Mamaw's past. Her words reached across time, wrapping around me like the soft blanket she used to drape over the couch.

As I neared the final pages, I came across an entry dated November 1961. The ink was darker here, the handwriting a little shakier, as if the emotions had spilled faster than the pen could keep up.

*"The baby finally went down just after midnight. His little fists unclenched as I rocked him in the dark, and I watched his lashes flutter like leaves settling after a storm. I should've felt peace in that moment, should've felt joy, but instead, a sorrow rooted itself deep, heavier than sleep, harder to shake.*

*I caught Harlan with another woman last week. I didn't mean to. I wasn't looking. I'd run into town to fetch diapers and was coming back around the side of the church when I saw them. He didn't see me. I couldn't move. It was like my soul had been knocked clean out of me.*

*He came home that night like nothing had happened. Kissed me on the cheek. Held the baby. Asked what was for supper. And I said nothing. I've held it in, like breath underwater.*

*I keep praying. I don't know what else to do. I pray for our marriage, for the boy we brought into this world, for the man I promised my life to. I pray God reminds him of whom he used to be.*

*Some days I want to scream. Other days, I just want to disappear. But most days, I just hold my baby, and I pray. I pray because I made a vow. Because*

*I believe people can come home to themselves. And because even now, even with my heart cracked wide open, I still love him."*

By the end of the entry, tears streamed down my face. Oh, how I felt that pain with her, like it had passed straight through the page into me. The thought of her hurting in such a quiet, hidden way tore at my soul. I couldn't stop the anger that welled up inside me toward my Papaw. I knew he had changed. I'd only ever known the softer version of him, but knowing he had once been so selfish stirred something deep in me. Hadn't he seen the damage he'd done to her? Or worse, had he simply not cared?

I reminded myself that times were different then, that divorce wasn't seen as a real option, not for women like Mamaw. Society had taught her to bear, to carry her pain without complaint, to persevere no matter the cost. I was grateful her prayers had made their way through, that she had my daddy, and she had us girls. A part of me still wished with all my heart that Papaw had truly seen her and how precious she was, like a rare jewel, carved by God's own hand.

I couldn't read anymore. My heart was too heavy, and I didn't want to keep feeding the anger rising in me, not when Mamaw had clearly long since chosen forgiveness. Still, I knew I'd never see Papaw the same way again. I wasn't sure I ever really knew him, not fully.

But time has a way of sharpening our vision. Looking back, I can see more clearly now: the man I knew wasn't separate from the man he had been. He had carried his own burdens, walked through his own fire, and somewhere along the way, he had changed. Just as Mamaw had. Just as I had been changing. His path had forged him into the man I loved, but knowing the truth had left a stain on that love, faint but permanent. And as my own path wound closer to theirs, braided with each truth I uncovered, I could feel it reshaping me too.

I just didn't know yet whether to welcome that change or grieve it.

My parents hadn't bothered me in my room that day. I'm sure they were giving me space to grieve, to sort through everything in my own time. Grieving is a lonely process. No matter how you love someone, you can't grieve for them. All you can do is stand nearby and watch as the storm rips through their heart and soul, helpless to stop it. Grief is like a tornado that way. You can't predict its path, and when it hits, it changes everything. It leaves behind a silence that echoes and scars that never quite fade. The most anyone can do is help you rebuild when it's over. But even then, the land is never the same, and neither is your heart.

When I finally emerged from my room that afternoon, the scent of fried chicken filled the air. I followed the aroma into the kitchen, where Momma was at the stove. I blinked for a second because, at that moment, I almost saw Mamaw there. Her sleeves were rolled up, stirring gravy with patience. I knew there would be biscuits in the oven and sliced tomatoes on the table. I knew it without needing to ask. Even though Momma hadn't always said I love you out loud, she said it in her own way. That day, she said it by making my favorite meal. And as I have grown older, I have learned to cherish those quiet I love yous most of all.

That evening, as we sat around the dinner table, a noiseless weight hung in the room. It felt almost disrespectful to fill the silence with small talk or forced smiles. So we didn't. We just sat there, letting the comfort of each other's presence speak for itself.

I was the one to speak first, my voice barely cutting through the stillness. "Daddy, can you give me a ride back to Virginia this weekend? I need to get back to work. I feel guilty for leaving Mari for so long."

"Don't worry," he said, his voice soft. "We'll make sure you get there, pumpkin."

"Thank you," I replied, and we all went back to eating quietly.

When I finished, I gathered the plates and took them to the kitchen to wash, just like I used to. Momma told me I didn't have to, but the rhythm of it felt grounding. Familiar. Like muscle memory wrapped in warmth.

Later, I lay on my bed, staring at the journal on the nightstand. I couldn't bring myself to pick it up again. My mind was already full, too full to carry someone else's memories on top of my own.

Just then, my phone dinged. It was a message from Mari. She'd sent a photo of a newspaper ad for a small studio apartment. I smiled, grateful she'd thought of me.

For a moment, I had expected it to be Dalton. He'd been messaging me all day. I had replied, but my words had been short and tired. I didn't have the energy to give more.

I was reminded of something Mamaw used to say: "You can't pour from an empty cup." And right then, my cup was bone-dry. I needed someone who could pour into me for once, but I also knew better than to ask. Everyone was fighting to hold onto their own peace.

So I turned to the only place I knew I could find rest. I prayed. I asked the Lord for comfort and clarity, for discernment and peace. And by the time I whispered amen, my eyes were heavy, and I welcomed sleep like an old friend.

The weekend slipped in fast, trailing a hush of sorrow behind it. I hated to leave, but I had responsibilities. And I missed Sheryl, Luke, and Mari deeply, like an old song I couldn't stop humming under my breath.

But there was something I noticed then, something quiet but telling. I didn't miss Dalton, not in the same way. That truth landed soft at first, easy to ignore, but it should've struck harder. It was a sign I wasn't ready to see: things with him weren't what I'd once hoped they would be.

I found Daddy in the den. "You ready to go?" I asked.

He stood up. "Come here first," he said, walking out the front door. I followed him, confused.

He climbed into my old truck and turned the key. It started right up.

"What are you doing?" I asked, surprised. "Aren't we taking your truck?"

"Nope," he said with a grin. "You're taking yours. I've been working on it. It's more reliable now. I don't like the idea of you walking around at night in the city. So now, you don't have to."

My breath caught, and I flung my arms around his neck. "Oh, thank you, Daddy," I said, tears burning in my eyes.

That old truck had always been a symbol of independence for me. I raced back inside to grab my bag and came out just as Momma stepped onto the porch, the screen door clapping shut behind her. I wrapped her in my arms and held on longer than I meant to.

"You better call the second you make it, young lady," she said. "I'll be worried sick."

She turned to Daddy. "Are you sure that thing's safe, Abe?"

"Of course it is," he said with a smile. "I fixed it, didn't I?"

She shook her head, but her lips twitched. I loved seeing them like that, picking at each other in the kind of intimacy only time can build.

After one more round of hugs, I climbed into my truck and buckled in. I looked in the rearview mirror, tossed my arm out the window to wave goodbye, and headed down the road.

I took the scenic route out of town, the one that wound near the water. Fireflies danced above the lake's still surface, and bullfrogs croaked from the banks. The air was thick with magnolia and memory. I hadn't even left yet, and already, home was calling me back.

As I drove, I passed a small campground. A hand-painted sign out front read: Campers for sale and rent. A phone number hung below in faded black ink. I slowed for just a second. A thought crossed my mind, but I kept driving.

The truck pointed north. Toward Sheryl. Toward work. Toward the life I was trying to build. But somewhere along the way, that old feeling crept in, the one I'd had after graduation.

*What am I doing with my life? What do I really want?* I still didn't know.

In retrospect, I realize you're never truly sure what you're doing, or what you want out of life. Not completely. Because those things shift as we do. We grow. We hurt. We heal. We change.

Life isn't stagnant. It's seasonal.

And maybe that's the point. Maybe we're not meant to have it all figured out. Maybe we're just meant to keep moving, to keep learning, to keep embracing change, one season at a time.

# Chapter 13

*Journal Entry– January 21, 1995*

*There are seasons in a woman's life when she starts to see things more clearly, not because her vision sharpens, but because her heart gets quiet enough to listen.*
*I remember being young and believing I could carry the world on my back if it meant someone might love me for it. I thought love was something you earned with patience, with softness, with staying. But I know better now. The longer you try to be someone's shelter when they won't even come in out of the storm, the more soaked and cold you'll become.*
*I hope my granddaughters learn this sooner than I did:*
*That home isn't always a place.*
*That being needed isn't the same as being cherished.*
*And that sometimes, the strongest thing you can do is let go of the weight you were never meant to hold.*

*-Ruth*

I arrived back at Sheryl's the following morning, just before sunrise. I drove through the night, and I was exhausted. Before I even got out of my truck, I texted Momma and Daddy to let them know I'd made it safely. Then I slipped quietly into the house, turning the doorknob slowly so I wouldn't wake anyone, and crept into my room. I collapsed onto the bed, needing to rest before my shift that evening.

I was excited to see Mari again. Oh, how I had missed her peaceful, reassuring presence.

As I lay there, I realized something had shifted. Things didn't feel quite the same as they had before I left. I already missed home, not just the people, but the place. The Tennessee air felt easier to breathe. I couldn't hear the crickets singing their lonesome song outside my window here. I sighed, feeling lost.

When I woke, I could hear Sheryl and Luke's voices drifting through the house. I checked my phone, and it was already past noon. I had to get ready for work, but at least having my truck with me now would cut down on the commute. I stepped into the kitchen and was greeted with a big hug from Sheryl.

"How are you holding up, kiddo?" Luke asked.

"Oh, I'm making it," I replied. "I was nervous about driving that far alone, but it was an easy trip."

"I'm glad," he said. "Your sister was worried about you making it by yourself."

I smiled at her. I knew that feeling. I would always worry about my sister, too.

I walked to the cupboard and poured myself some cereal. "So what are you two doing home? I figured you'd be at work."

Sheryl smiled and pulled a small piece of paper from her pocketbook. "We just got back from the OB-GYN," she said.

She handed me the ultrasound photo. I held it in my hand, and suddenly, it all felt real. My sister was going to be a mother. And somehow, I already loved that little baby more than I thought I could.

When I handed the picture back, my eyes were burning with unexpected emotion. Sheryl must have noticed.

"The doctor said the baby's doing great. He's got a strong heartbeat," she said, smiling.

"She," Luke interjected, and I laughed.

"Maybe you're both right," I teased. "Maybe it's twins."

The look of horror that flashed across both their faces made me laugh even harder.

"It's not funny!" Sheryl said. "I'm nervous enough about one. Plus, I don't want to be as big as a house."

Her comment made me think of all those weight-loss books Mamaw had been boxing up to take with her. It's strange how much a woman's weight seems tied to her worth, how she sees herself, how others see her. Like extra pounds somehow means she's less precious than before. It's a sad and exhausting way of thinking.

Sure, being healthy matters, but there are so many battles a woman faces that affect her weight: childbirth, hormones, or, in Mamaw's case, a thyroid condition. But to me, I would have loved Mamaw, or Sheryl, at ninety-five pounds or three hundred. And I know every woman has people in their life who feel the same.

"Oh hush, motherhood will make you even more beautiful," Luke said, his voice low and sincere.

That was exactly what Sheryl needed to hear, and I could feel the tenderness between them settle like morning light on dew. It was the kind of moment that didn't need an audience. I quietly picked up my bowl of cereal and slipped away to my room, giving them space to be alone. They deserved it. Every couple should have the chance to grow their love without someone else hovering in the corners. I needed to figure out where I was going to stay, soon.

As I got ready for work, I emerged once more into the soft light of the kitchen. I hugged Sheryl and gave her all my love. Luke had already left to grab a few last things from the hardware store. He was finishing up the small details around the house before the realtor came the next day to photograph everything and list it.

"Grab a coat," Sheryl called after me as I reached for the doorknob. "It's getting cold out there. Fall is definitely on its way."

She was right. A definite chill had crept into the air, sharp and whispering, like the early hush before a storm. The year was turning over again, and September unfolded like an old photograph, sepia-toned and filled with things I hadn't yet faced. That realization pulled my thoughts toward the calendar. My birthday was less than a month away. October first, I'd be nineteen. Nineteen.

And when I thought back on the girl I had been just a year before, it was hard to believe she was me. So much had happened. So much had changed. I had changed. And still, I wasn't sure of the road ahead, but at least I had started to figure out the roads I didn't want to walk. Sometimes, that was just as important.

When I got to work and saw Mari's face, glowing and familiar behind the counter, something inside me exhaled. My shoulders softened, and I smiled a real smile, one that changes your whole face. I walked straight to her and pulled her into a hug.

"Oh, how I've missed you," I whispered.

"I've missed you too, my girl." She pulled back and cupped my arms. "How was your trip home? I was so sorry to hear about your friend."

I told her everything, about Marie, about how different it felt to be home, how the place had been calling me louder than I knew. I told her how I hadn't even told Dalton I was back yet because I was still so unsure about everything. About him. About us.

As I spoke, I noticed the subtle shift in Mari's face. Her brow creased, a rare expression for someone whose laugh lines were more practiced than worry. Most of the marks on her face were soft and sun-warmed, like petals folded from years of kindness. But now, a line of concern settled between her eyes.

She paused, then placed a hand gently on mine.

"Jenny," she said, her voice a hush of wind through dry leaves, "sometimes love isn't love. It's control dressed up in flowers and empty promises. It doesn't matter how someone acts when they're at their best. What matters is how they treat you when life is hard. If you find yourself always walking on eggshells, it's not your fault you're barefoot. It's his fault for throwing them on the floor in the first place."

Her words settled into the hollow I carried like a second shadow, the part of me I pretended wasn't there.

But I just nodded and brushed them off with a soft smile. I wasn't ready to unpack all of that, not yet. There was shame in the truth I carried, like his behavior had smudged something meant to be untouched in me. Like if I admitted he wasn't good to me, I was somehow less good, too.

Now, I know better. That's just another trick in a manipulator's handbook to make you believe the hurt is your burden to bear. But back then, I was still sorting through the fog, trying to find myself in the middle of someone else's storm.

I had missed working side by side with Mari. I had missed the feeling of soil slipping between my fingers, the rich scent of earth and blossoms mingling in the air, the gentle hush of sprinklers sweeping across rows of thirsty stems. There was something sacred about this place, a kind of quiet the world outside couldn't reach.

It was a haven. A stillness wrapped in green.

I heard the front bell jingle, and Mari stepped away to greet the customers. She came alive out there, glowing as she shared her passion with anyone willing to listen. It was her gift, no doubt. Not just the way she spoke about plants like old friends, or how she knew the perfect soil mix for every bloom, but the way she saw people.

That was her true calling.

She had a way of knowing exactly what someone needed, even when they didn't. Sometimes, she sent folks away without a single thing in hand. Like the time she told a flustered young man, "Your wife doesn't need flowers. She needs your attention." Or the sweet older lady trying to coax azaleas into stubborn soil. Mari gently explained that azaleas need acidic soil and soft shade, and that some yards, no matter how full of love, simply weren't built for them.

It wasn't just about plants. It never had been. Mari cared about people.

That made it all the more curious that she had no family of her own, no husband, no children. Just herself and this little shop, nestled between concrete and quiet. And somehow, that seemed enough for her.

If she longed for anything else, she never said.

After work, I sent Dalton a message to let him know I'd made it back. He was quick to respond, eager to see me. He said he'd stop by after his shift at the warehouse.

I'll admit it, despite all the questions circling in my head about his temper and the quiet bruising of his words, I still wanted to see him. I had missed being held. Missed the illusion of being wanted. That kind of closeness could feel like a drug, sweet and numbing and easy to confuse with love. When the world spun too fast, there was a certain relief in curling into someone's arms and pretending it didn't. So when he showed up that night, I let myself sink into him like a tired swimmer into warm water, too weary to fight the current.

In the weeks that followed, I slipped back into a rhythm of work during the day, evenings wrapped in Dalton's arms, trying to believe they were a safe place. The house had gone on the market, and with that, the looming question of where I'd go next. I started searching again, halfheartedly at first, and then Mari sent me a listing. It had already been taken, but the landlord, a kind woman with a soft voice and warm laugh, said she'd have another unit available soon. She took my name and number, saying anyone Mari trusted with her plants was someone she'd trust with her keys.

I called Mari the moment I hung up. She was thrilled. "One less thing to weigh you down," she said, and she was right. I hadn't yet told Sheryl or Luke that I didn't plan to move with them, but I knew I'd have to soon. Next, I called Dalton, expecting him to share my excitement. I thought he'd be proud of me, maybe even relieved that I was finding my own footing. Instead, he sounded hurt. Distant.

"I thought we were talking about getting a place together," he said flatly.

I tried to explain that I just needed something of my own for now, a place where I could breathe and think clearly. But the air between us thickened. His silence turned cold, and the celebration I'd imagined wilted before it ever had the chance to bloom.

It stung. It always did when he pulled away like that, when disappointment hung heavier than it should. More and more, I found myself walking on invisible eggshells, careful with every word, every choice, unsure of what might set him off next.

After a few moments of awkward silence, he said, "Well, what are you doing this weekend?"

"I've got to help Mari with a big order we just got in," I told him, knowing he wouldn't be thrilled to hear it.

"You're working again this weekend?" he asked, a sharpness in his voice he didn't try to hide.

"Yeah, Mari needs help with the order. I told her I would."

He acted as if I'd betrayed him.

"It's not like you need to be there every minute," he said.

I opened my mouth to explain, but why should I have to?

That was the first time I hadn't answered right away. The first time I let the silence stretch.

And yet, we agreed to meet that evening.

Dalton insisted on picking me up. He didn't like it when I drove myself, said it "took away from our time together," but I'd started to see it for what it really was: control wrapped in concern. He needed to be needed. And if I were independent, if I didn't rely on him, where would that leave him?

When he pulled into the driveway that night, he rolled the window down and gave me a smile. Not his real one, the one that used to make me blush, but a tired, fractured version of it.

"I'm sorry for how I acted earlier," he said as I got in. "I was into it with my Pops again. I shouldn't have taken it out on you."

I nodded, murmured something like, "It's okay," even though it wasn't.

That's how it always went. He'd lash out, apologize, promise he was just stressed, tired, or overwhelmed. And for a while, I'd believe him. I wanted to believe him.

But his words were starting to feel like borrowed lines from a script I'd heard before. He could never seem to hold onto his temper long enough to keep from bruising me, not with his fists, but with frustration, with silence, with blame.

And still, part of me held onto the idea that he could be better. That maybe if I just loved him right, if I gave enough, softened enough, he'd find the version of himself he buried under all that rage. I thought maybe I could save him from it if he'd just let me.

What I didn't understand then was that love doesn't fix what someone refuses to face. That control isn't care. And that when someone chips away at your spirit piece by piece, even if they call it love, even if they whisper apologies into your hair afterward, it's still harm.

I wasn't ready to name it. Not yet. But it pressed along the edges of me, a longing woven into the lining of who I was. And one day, I knew that ache would demand more of me. It would ask me to either keep shrinking to contain it, or finally let it break me open and set me free. But for now, I just wanted to feel wanted. Needed. Loved.

It would take me years to understand that longing can become its own kind of prison. That aching to be needed, when you don't even feel whole, is its own quiet form of abuse. And it wasn't fair, not to him, not to me. I should've walked away. It would've been the most honest thing I could have done.

But just like he wasn't ready to face his anger, I wasn't ready to face my own reflection. I couldn't look straight at the parts of me that were still cracked and bleeding. I was trying to fix what I already knew was broken, but I was doing it blindfolded, stumbling forward with my eyes closed, convincing myself that love could light the way.

We were lying in the bed of his truck, our bodies still twined together, the metal beneath us cooling as the night settled in. I traced lazy patterns along his chest, and somewhere between a sigh and silence, I told him I'd really like to go camping for my birthday.

"Oh yeah, that would be fun," he said, then asked, "When is your birthday?"

The question caught me off guard. *How could he not know?*

What sort of love were we building if he didn't even know something as simple as that? I had memorized his birthday without even trying, but I guess mine had never come up. Still, I didn't scold him. He was asking now, and I told myself that counted for something.

"It's October first," I said softly.

"Jen, that's just two weeks away. Why didn't you say something sooner?" There was a spark in his voice, a flicker of concern that felt real.

He ran his thumb slowly down the back of my arm, and I shivered. "Well, camping we will go," he murmured. "If that's what you want, then that's what we'll do."

I smiled and curled deeper into his embrace, letting the moment warm me. Moments like that were nice, gentle. They made me believe he could be the person I hoped for. And as long as those soft hours outweighed the sharp ones, I stayed hopeful.

Hope, I'd later learn, can be both a comfort and a chain.

We fell asleep there in each other's arms, resting until the dew settled over us like a veil. I woke chilled, skin damp with morning, and Dalton wrapped his coat around me before opening the truck door so I could climb inside. The drive home passed in peaceful quiet, the kind that pretends nothing is wrong.

But as the sky lightened and the world stirred awake, I knew I couldn't put it off much longer. I'd have to tell Sheryl that I wasn't moving with them. I hoped she wouldn't take it personally. The truth was, I would've preferred it, being close to them, wrapped in the safety of family. But something in me whispered that it was time, time to give them their space. Time to stand on my own two feet. Time to test whether I could float, or if I'd sink.

I just hoped I was ready to find out.

# Chapter 14

*Journal Entry– September 12, 1980*

*I once knew a woman who forgot her favorite color.*
*She had been bright once, so full of her own thoughts and ideas she could*
*barely sleep at night. She had dreams about wildflowers in the front yard,*
*painting the kitchen yellow, and writing poems on the backs of receipts. But*
*then she married a man who only ever asked her what was for supper and if*
*she could quiet down a little when she laughed too loud.*
*Slowly, her voice got softer. Her shoulders sloped more. Her questions, fewer.*
*She stopped wearing red lipstick because he didn't like how it looked. She*
*stopped dancing barefoot in the kitchen.*
*By the time she remembered herself, years had passed. Her hands were worn.*
*Her eyes, tired.*
*But one day, while folding laundry, she looked up at the window and*
*whispered, "Green. My favorite color is green."*
*And just like that, she started coming back.*

*-Ruth*

I told Sheryl and Luke the next day about finding a rental. They were surprised, and I could see the disappointment flicker in both of their eyes. But underneath that was love, so deep and steady it caught me off guard. And that love, it was good for my soul.

Still, I knew I was making the right decision. They needed space to build the kind of life that was only possible in the quiet moments between two people in love, figuring out how their rhythms aligned, learning the little things that made the other worth choosing again and again. They deserved that, especially with a new life soon on the way.

The thought of them raising the baby without me nearby tightened something inside me and gave me pause. They had plans to buy a house closer to Momma and Daddy, to settle down somewhere with roots deep in the hills. Luke wanted Sheryl surrounded by the people who knew her best, and I think he needed that comfort too, whether he'd ever say it out loud or not.

He didn't talk much about his family, but over time, I'd pieced it together. His sister had been his person, the one who understood him when no one else did. After she died, his mother all but disappeared into her martinis and her perfect furniture, living like no one else in the world mattered. His father was a hotshot marketing executive with a jaw like stone and expectations to match. Luke had once told me, "He wanted a replica. I gave him a carpenter."

Choosing a blue-collar life had been his rebellion, and his punishment. His father had all but cut him off; the only resemblance of a relationship they kept was for his father's pride. I think that's why Luke clung to us the way he did. We saw him for who he really was, and we loved him all the better because of it.

Truth be told, Luke was made for the country, for front porches and slow mornings and calloused hands. He was the kind of man who didn't see the point in rushing, who understood that in East Tennessee, the roads twist and rise and fall, and the only way to drive them right is to take your time.

Thinking of those backroads tugged at my heartstrings like a song I hadn't heard in years but still knew by heart. My life had carried me to Virginia, but my soul? It still lived in the hills of Tennessee. I knew I'd find my way back one day, back to where the air felt softer, and the land seemed to understand me without asking.

But for now, I was just learning how to stand on my own. I had a job that was mine. A relationship I was still trying to make sense of. And soon, a place to call my own. It wasn't home, *not yet*, but it was something. And I needed to prove to myself that I could build something, even if it wasn't meant to last.

After I shared the news about the rental, I told Sheryl and Luke I wanted to go camping for my birthday and asked if they'd come along. Sheryl lit up at the idea. We'd always loved curling up in our tent at night, whispering stories under flashlight beams. We'd giggle until our sides hurt while Momma and Daddy fished along the bank, the fire crackling steadily and low well into the night.

But Luke had grown more protective since she became pregnant. "I think we should sit this one out, Sheryl," he said gently. "We can go after you have the baby. I don't want to take any chances. Besides, let's let the kids enjoy camping without us cramping their style."

She didn't argue. That's how I knew she really loved him. Anyone else, she would've fought tooth and nail to do what she wanted, but not with Luke.

"Did you say cramping our style?" I teased. "Sheesh, you really are turning into an old man."

We all laughed, and the tension from the discussion about the apartment faded like smoke on the breeze.

My birthday came quicker than I expected, and early that morning, the landlord called, just like she'd promised. The rental would be ready the following week, and we could meet on Monday to go over the lease and deposit. I was thrilled. Something steady. Something mine.

It was a Saturday, and we were all home, so I shared the news.

"I'm proud of you," Sheryl said, pulling me into a hug. "Even though

I'll miss you, I understand. You need to stand on your own. I felt the same way once."

"Thank you," I said, holding onto her warmth.

I hadn't really thought of Sheryl feeling that way, like she had something to prove. But of course she had. She worked herself to the bone in school. She wasn't just pushing for herself, but for Momma and Daddy, too. Like me, she had also wanted to make them proud.

I found myself wishing we hadn't drifted apart. If we'd shared more of our fears and private hopes, maybe we would've made the road easier for each other. There wasn't anything she could face that I wouldn't stand behind her, and I knew she'd do the same for me. But some truths only come with time, with distance, when you realize it was never a competition. And if it were, you were always on the same team.

That afternoon, I set my backpack and pillow by the door. Sheryl helped me pack sandwiches and snacks into a cooler for the trip.

"Now, I know you're camping for your birthday," she said, "but when you get back, we're having dinner to celebrate."

"I promise," I said.

Momma and Daddy called too, both wishing me a happy birthday, both saying they had a gift waiting for me when I came home. A pang of guilt settled in my stomach. I hadn't told them I was planning to stay longer. They thought I was only there for the summer, and summer had already slipped by. But I couldn't bring myself to say it. Not on my birthday. So, I just thanked them and promised to call when I got back from the trip.

By the time I hung up, Dalton was outside, leaning on the horn. I grabbed my things and shouted, "Love you, Sher!" as I walked out the door.

"I hope you remembered the tent," I called with a smile as I climbed into the truck.

"Of course I did," he said. "Are you excited?"

I really was. It had been so long since I'd gone camping. I was ready to sit by the water, to read, to breathe. I wished I'd brought my fishing poles from home, but a good book was tucked in my bag, and for now, that would be enough.

We set up the tent and built a fire near the lake. It was beautiful, still, and quiet. Cattails swayed along the shore. Fish broke the surface now and then in silver flashes. The lake didn't allow motors; if you couldn't paddle it, you couldn't put it in. I liked that. I thought maybe I'd save up for a canoe of my own.

Dalton gathered firewood while I read, and when he returned, we unpacked the cooler and ate our sandwiches by the flames. He cracked open a beer from his cooler and offered me one.

I shook my head. "No thanks. I just want to relax, not party tonight."

"Suit yourself," he said, already opening another.

We sat for a while, my head on his shoulder. He talked about work and Copper, his horse, and how they'd been training for the roping competitions at the stables this fall.

I told him I missed riding. "I want to go again soon."

"You know I'll go with you anytime," he said.

"Maybe you can show me how to rope," I suggested. I smiled. "I've never done that before."

He shrugged. "I don't know. It takes a lot of practice." There was something sharp in his voice, so I let it go. Maybe it was just his thing. I didn't want to step on it.

So I changed the subject. "Oh, I forgot to tell you. The woman with the apartment called this morning. I can go sign the lease Monday."

I tried to sound light, hopeful. "I think having my own space will help me breathe. I'm excited to build something for myself."

His mood shifted fast, faster than it ever did when he was sober. He went silent, then said, "So what, you're happy to live without me now?"

I took a breath. "That's not what I said. I just need to feel like I'm making my own choices. That doesn't mean I don't want you in my life."

He stared into the fire. "I just don't think you appreciate me anymore. I hoped you'd see everything I do for you, especially after this trip, but you're always pulling away. It's always about you and your problems."

"I'm not pulling away," I said. "I'm just trying to figure myself out."

"It's been worse since you went back home," he snapped. "You keep shutting me out."

I could see it in his eyes. They were glassy and simmering. He was nearly drunk. I knew I shouldn't argue. But sometimes, I was my Momma's child, and I couldn't let a man talk down to me.

"I'm not shutting you out, but I can't keep making myself small just to make you feel big," I said harshly.

It was the wrong thing to say. I knew it the moment it left my lips.

His face changed. A flash of hurt, then rage. Like a wounded animal cornered, he struck back, but this time not with his words. His hand cracked across my face. I felt the sting, then heat, then the slow trickle of blood in my mouth.

It happened so fast I couldn't even move. I sat there, stunned. And just like that, the moment passed. His face twisted in regret, but it didn't matter. Some things you can't come back from. No amount of apologies could make it okay.

I stood and walked toward the tent.

He followed. "Jenny…" his voice pleaded.

I turned, hand outstretched. "Stay back."

I grabbed my backpack and pillow and started walking toward the road.

"Jenny, please," he called behind me. "Don't go. I'm sorry. It won't happen again."

He grabbed my wrist. I was ready that time. I turned and sprayed the mace Sheryl had given me straight into his face.

He screamed, "You psycho bitch! What's wrong with you?!"

There it was again. The real him.

That's right, I thought.  I'm the bitch now.  In that moment, I remembered something my Momma once said: "Sometimes, being a bitch is all a woman has to hold onto in this world."

Back then, I didn't understand, but I was learning. It wasn't about being cruel, or cold, or mean. It was about surviving in a world that calls you difficult the second you say no. That calls you selfish for wanting space. That calls you ungrateful for drawing a line.

They call you a bitch when you don't fold.

So maybe being a bitch just means you stood your ground when no one else would stand with you.

Maybe it means you finally said no and meant it.

I pulled out my phone and called Luke. He didn't answer, so I sent a text: ***Please come get me***. I dropped a pin with my location.

He replied almost instantly. **On my way**.

By the time I reached the road, my legs were trembling, but I kept walking. The dark woods pressed in on either side, quiet and thick, but my anger burned hotter than my fear. If someone had tried to drag me off into the trees that night, they'd have had a fight on their hands.

Looking back, I know how reckless that was. But anger makes you bold in all the wrong ways. It took me years to understand that acting from rage rarely leads to peace. Even now, I have to remind myself of that truth because the world doesn't always make it easy to stay soft.

Thankfully, Luke didn't take long. I saw his headlights curve around the bend, fast and sharp, not like him at all. Luke never rushed, unless someone he loved was waiting on the other end. When he pulled up, he didn't even put the truck in park before jumping out. The second he saw my face, he froze.

"What happened?" he asked, voice low and tight.

"I don't want to talk about it," I said, and I meant it.

I saw the fire in his eyes. And it scared me, not for myself, but for anyone who might be on the receiving end of it.

"Tell me where he is, Jenny," he demanded, his jaw locked.

"No, Luke," I whispered. "Please… just take me home."

I climbed into the passenger seat and leaned my head against the window. He stood there long enough for me to question what he was about to do, but then something in him softened. He climbed in the truck, let out a long breath, and reached over and patted my knee. "I'm sorry, Sis. Let's go home." And we rode in silence with nothing but the hum of the tires and the sound of my breath fogging the glass.

When we made it back to the house, we found Sheryl pacing the floor. Luke walked in first, and I could already hear her voice: "Is she okay?"

"I'm fine," I said as I came through the door.

Her eyes locked onto my busted lip and the swelling around my eye. I could already feel it growing sore, and I prayed it wouldn't be bruised too badly by morning.

"What happened?" she asked, her voice tight with fear and anger.

"I'll tell you what happened," Luke snapped. "That little bastard put his hands on her."

Sheryl turned to me. "Is that true?"

I just nodded. Tears welled in my eyes, and I fought to keep them from falling.

"I don't want to talk about it tonight, okay?" I said softly. I just wanted a shower, a quiet room, and a night to pretend none of this had happened.

I expected to cry myself to sleep that night, but I didn't. I just felt finished. I was done. Maybe because I'd already known, deep down, that this relationship was coming to an end. I wasn't blindsided by heartbreak; I was steadied by the truth I'd been trying not to face. If anything, I was angry that he would do such a thing, but I couldn't say I was surprised, not really.

His dad had beaten him, and I often wondered if that's why his mother had left, to keep from becoming his father's punching bag. Dalton was only repeating what he had learned about anger and power, about control. That didn't make it okay. I wasn't making excuses for him. He was a grown man, capable of making different choices. He had every opportunity to be better.

But I understood where he came from. And I also understood this: I wasn't going to let where he came from destroy where I was going.

After that night, one thing became clear. I was going home to Tennessee. The decision settled in my soul like a stone, heavy but certain. Once I admitted it to myself, I thought of Mari. She was the only reason I still felt tethered to this place, the only part of it that still felt good and grounding, but I knew she'd understand. Mari saw the worn places in a person, the ones they thought they'd hidden well.

I would tell her tomorrow, along with the lady who'd been kind and offered me the rental.

Part of me felt like I'd failed, like I was so close to building something for myself, only to watch it slip through my fingers. I had almost carved out a life here, piece by piece, but none of it felt steady anymore. The foundation was cracked.

As I drifted off to sleep, I remembered the faded sign outside the lake campground back home, the one advertising campers for sale and rent. I made a mental note to call them. Maybe a small camper in the hills was exactly what I needed, a soft place to land and finally catch my breath. I was done pretending I could keep living the way I had been. Something had to change, and I was ready.

The next morning, I opened the greenhouse door with a lump in my throat. The familiar scent of damp earth and rosemary embraced me in a familiar warmth, but instead of comfort, it left a weight I didn't know how to carry. Mari looked up from a row of ferns she was tending, her hands buried in soil, sleeves rolled to her elbows.

"Morning, sugar," she said, her voice as easy as ever.

I managed a small smile. "Hey."

She took a longer look at me then, her eyes softening as they landed on my busted lip and the bruising that had started to bloom under my eye.

"What's happened, honey? And what's on your heart?" she asked, wiping her hands on her apron as she walked toward me.

I let out a shaky breath I hadn't realized I was holding. "I came to tell you… I'm moving back home…to Tennessee." I paused, then added, "And I need to tell you what happened with Dalton." I hadn't told Sheryl or Luke the whole story yet, and part of me was afraid they'd see it as weakness or worse, blame me for letting things go too far, but I knew Mari wouldn't see it that way.

She didn't flinch. She just nodded slowly, folding her arms like she was getting ready to cradle a truth too heavy to drop.

"I knew something had shifted," she said quietly. "You've had a burden in your eyes lately."

"I feel like I'm giving up," I admitted, my voice cracking more than I wanted it to. "I almost had something here. A place. A life. And I let it all fall apart."

Mari stepped closer and laid a warm hand on my arm. "Oh, honey. You're not giving up, you're choosing yourself. That's not weakness. There's a world of difference between quitting and knowing when it's time to go."

I nodded, blinking back tears. "I just didn't want to disappoint you."

Mari gave me a soft, knowing smile. "There's not a thing you could do that would make me stop loving you. People don't come into our lives to keep us rooted in place. We love each other, so we can grow, and sometimes that means putting down roots somewhere new."

She reached up and brushed a bit of dirt from my shoulder, just like she'd done a hundred times before. "You're my girl, Jenny. No matter where you plant yourself."

Mari had given me more than a job; she'd given me room to begin again. And now, she was giving me permission to let go.

Before I left, she pressed a small tin of herbal salve into my hand. "For your lip," she said. "And for whatever else needs healing."

Then she looked me in the eye and added, "And one more thing, sugar. Don't carry Dalton with you. Not in your thoughts, not in your guilt, not in the quiet moments when you start to wonder what might've been. Some people come into our lives to show us what we'll never accept again. Let that be his purpose, and leave the rest behind."

She sent me home for the day with a hug and a blessing, and I walked out feeling, finally, a little more like myself.

It's funny how, in some of our most broken moments, when we're still gathering the shards and piecing ourselves back together, we feel more whole than we ever did before the breaking. Like, somehow, the version rebuilt from the ruin is closer to who we were always meant to be.

# Chapter 15

*Journal Entry– April 15, 1976*

*Some things don't bloom where they're planted, not because the soil is bad,*
*but because it's not their soil.*
*I learned that the hard way. Tried to force myself to thrive in places that*
*didn't make space for all I was. Smiled through silent dinners. Made myself*
*small so others could stretch. That's not living—that's withering.*

*-Ruth*

Over the next few days, I quietly made plans to return home. I was going to miss Mari more than I could say. Her steady presence had become a kind of shelter for me, soft and grounding, like cool earth beneath bare feet after a long, hard climb. I promised I'd come visit often and told her she had to see Tennessee sometime soon. She smiled and said she'd like that, that maybe it was time she got away for a bit. I hoped she meant it, truly. I hoped she'd let herself rest.

When I called Momma and Daddy to tell them I'd be home that weekend, I could hear the smile in Daddy's voice, and the quiet breath Momma let out before answering told me more than words could. They hadn't expected me to stay away forever, but they hadn't pushed either.

They just listened. No questions about why I was coming back. No picking at wounds I wasn't ready to name. Just love. Just welcome. That quiet acceptance—no pressure, no judgment—meant everything. It loosened something tight inside me, something I hadn't realized I'd been clenching for months.

I'd be going back to my old bedroom for a while, but not for good. I still planned to find my own place, somewhere small and mine. I needed to know I could build a life on my own terms, and this time, I meant to do it differently. I wasn't chasing their approval anymore. I was chasing something steadier: the belief that I could belong in my own skin.

If I could go back and talk to the girl I was then, I'd tell her this: You don't have to carry it all by yourself. You don't have to be the strong one all the time. It's okay to ask for help. It's okay to rest. It's okay to stop bracing for hurt and just let love in when it comes. The grace you give to others? You deserve that, too.

Being with Momma and Daddy again would be a kind of healing I hadn't known I needed. The older I got, the more I saw them not just as parents, but as people—flawed, tired, trying, loving the best they knew how. I'd taken so much for granted when I was younger, the way children always do. I wished I'd learned sooner to treasure the quiet things: the hum of Daddy's voice as he tinkered in the garage, the faint sound of Momma closing cabinet doors in the kitchen late at night, the way her footsteps paused outside my door like she wanted to knock but didn't. I used to think I was on the outside looking in, but the truth was, their world had always made room for me. I just hadn't known how to step back into it.

But there's no reverse in life. No going back to do it better. We can only go forward, carrying the lessons we gather, one tender truth at a time. And that's what I was doing then.

At that moment, the lesson I was learning, slowly and painfully, was that it's okay to not be okay. It's okay to admit the cracks in your spirit, to pause and breathe and say, "I need time." Healing starts with that kind of honesty.

And I was going home to Tennessee to do just that.

Because somewhere between the hush of the mountain creeks and the whispering of the pines, I knew the land would remember me. I knew the hoot owls would sing me to sleep, and the wind that rustled the sassafras would carry back pieces of myself I thought I'd lost.

All I had to do was answer the call.

My bags were loaded up in the truck, and I was ready to hit the road. Sheryl and Luke stood in the driveway.

"We sure are gonna miss you, kiddo," Luke said.

"Yes, we are," Sheryl added. "But we won't be far behind. We're coming down to look at some houses for sale next weekend."

"I'm gonna miss y'all too," I told them, and I meant it. "I love you, Sher. And you, too, Luke."

They both wrapped me in tight hugs and stood back to watch as I climbed into the truck, ready to drive back home.

But before I left, I had one more stop to make.

I pulled into a parking spot in front of the greenhouse, heart thudding. I couldn't leave without telling Mari goodbye. I was already trying to hold back tears when I opened the door.

She knew why I was there the moment she saw me. Without a word, she peeled off her gloves and walked straight toward me, pulling me into her warm, steady embrace.

When she finally let me go, she reached up and unpinned the marigold brooch she always wore on her apron.

"You remind me of marigolds, you know," she said. "Bold. Bright. Not afraid to bloom even when the season turns cold. I wore this brooch after my mama passed. It made me feel like I was carrying her with me, even when I didn't feel strong."

She paused, then pinned it gently to the strap of my bag.

"Let it remind you that healing doesn't mean forgetting. And moving on doesn't mean leaving anyone behind. The women who've loved you, they're still with you. In your spine. In your voice. In your fight. Just like I'll be."

She pulled me in again, holding me close. She smelled of damp earth, lavender oil, and something warm like sunshine on old wood.

"And one more thing," she whispered near my ear, "don't you ever shrink to fit back into places you've outgrown. If something doesn't make room for all of you, your strength, your softness, your scars, it's not meant for you."

I hadn't realized how much I needed someone to believe in me, until she did.

With tears in my eyes, I opened the greenhouse door, and as I walked back to the truck, the marigold brooch caught a sliver of sunlight, glowing like a promise.

I buckled in and pulled back onto the road. The old radio crackled to life as I rolled the window down, letting in the crisp autumn breeze that had finally settled in for good. Leaves whispered across the pavement like secrets, and the wind, for once, felt like a friend instead of something I had to brace against.

On my way out of town, I passed the turnoff to the stables. Dalton's truck was just pulling onto the lane, and for a brief moment, our eyes met. He caught a glimpse of me as I drove by.

I hadn't spoken to him since that night. He'd called and texted, left message after message. Apologized over and over. But I wouldn't be swayed. He had crossed a line that couldn't be uncrossed.

I glanced once in the rearview mirror and watched his truck fade behind me, swallowed by dust and distance. Then I turned my face back toward the sun.

I was leaving him behind.

We were on different paths now, and I didn't flinch at the thought. I was moving forward. He wasn't coming with me. And that was okay.

There was a time I couldn't have said that. Back then, the hurt was still too raw, the anger thrumming just beneath my skin. But things had shifted. With distance came clarity, and with clarity, a kind of peace. I don't know where he is now, or who he's trying to be, but I hope he's doing better. I hope he's learned to let go of the weight he carried, the way I had to learn to release my own. The pain. The blame. The bitterness. If I hadn't, I would've become the very thing that hurt me. And I refuse to live that way.

"The drive crackled beneath my tires as I rolled in just after midnight. The porch light was still glowing, and to my surprise, they were both waiting up. Daddy met me before I'd even cut the engine, and when he pulled me into his arms, it felt like the weight of the world slid right off my shoulders. Momma stood just behind him in her housecoat, smiling through the screen door.

"I saved you a plate," she said softly, like no time had passed at all.

I wrapped her in a hug next, breathing in the scent of home—fabric softener, wood smoke, and something warm on the stove. The comfort of it all settled around me like a well-worn quilt: soft, familiar, and sure.

And in that quiet moment, I knew, I had made the right decision.

The following day, I found my bow was still where I'd left it—tucked behind the old pantry door, string slightly frayed, limbs gathering dust.

I turned it over in my hands, remembering the way it used to feel— solid, steady, like something I could trust.

That evening, I walked out to the field behind the house with a half-empty quiver and more weight on my heart than I knew what to do with.

The first shot missed wide.

The second hit closer.

By the third, my shoulders loosened, breath fell into rhythm, and something inside me released, a small, fierce thing that had been hiding for too long.

I wasn't aiming to hit the mark; I was aiming to find myself again.

Something had shifted in me that day, just enough to make room for hope. And not long after, life began to gather at the edges, like spring pooling beneath the frost.

Sheryl had been true to her word. She and Luke came down the following weekend to look at houses, and it didn't take long before they found one that felt like a real possibility. That evening, after supper, we were all gathered around the old oak dining table, the one Daddy had built with his own hands back when Sheryl was still in diapers. It was scarred and worn in places, stained from years of Sunday dinners, forgotten homework, and hot casserole dishes set down without a trivet. But it was ours. And with everyone seated around it again, it felt like the heart of the house had started beating once more.

The air was thick with the smell of fried chicken and collard greens, the kind that lingers in your clothes and hair long after the meal is over. The overhead light buzzed faintly, casting a warm yellow glow across the table, catching on the Mason jars full of sweet tea and the mismatched plates that had served us for generations. Sheryl sat beside Luke, one hand on her belly, the other curled around her glass. Her eyes sparkled the way they always did when she had something to say and couldn't wait to say it.

"I think we found it," she announced, a grin breaking across her face. "The house. Our forever home."

All heads turned toward her. "It's over in Wallens," Sheryl continued, her voice practically dancing with excitement. "It's a two-story farmhouse, white with green shutters and one of those wraparound porches like in the movies. It has three bedrooms and ten acres of land. So there will be room for the baby to run and play someday. It needs some work, but nothing Luke can't handle."

Luke chuckled softly, brushing a hand over his jaw. "I already told her I wouldn't mind fixing up another place. Kinda got used to it."

Daddy nodded with a small smile. "Sounds like a good place to raise a family."

"It does," Momma added, folding her napkin and resting it beside her plate. "Sounds like you'll be putting down roots."

That quiet sentence hung in the air for a moment, but not in a bad way. There was something shifting, a new chapter beginning, not just for Sheryl, but for all of us.

Luke turned to Daddy. "You know, I gotta say, Jenny here was a real help fixing up the place in Virginia. She learned fast. Helped me tile the kitchen, patch drywall, and even laid the pavers out back. Couldn't have done it without her."

Daddy looked over at me with raised eyebrows and a proud smile tugging at the corners of his mouth. "That so?"

I shrugged, a little embarrassed but grateful. "I enjoy working with my hands. I miss working with Mari, honestly. Being at the greenhouse gave me something steady, something that felt like mine."

Daddy tapped his fingers against the rim of his tea glass, thoughtful. "Well, I've been tossing around the idea of expanding the business. Thought maybe I'd add some landscaping work, but I'd need help. Someone with a good eye and work ethic." He looked at me directly then. "If you're up for it, I'd pay you to help me out. Wouldn't be flowers in clay pots, but it's honest work. Think about it?"

I felt something stir in me, something that wasn't dread or uncertainty, but possibility. I looked around the table. At Sheryl, glowing beside Luke. At Daddy, still full of quiet strength, and Momma with her steadfast way.

"Yeah," I said, feeling the truth of it in my bones. "I'll think about it." But in my heart, I already knew the answer.

# Chapter 16



*Journal Entry– September 14, 2003*

*Rivers have long memories. They remember every fall, every baptism, every body laid beneath their banks. I've seen the way they wind through a place like veins through flesh, carrying the past, whether we want them to or not. The land dries out, but the river never forgets.*

*-Ruth*

Early the next morning, I told Daddy I wanted to take him up on his job offer. I was ready to carve out my own path, even if it meant calloused hands and aching muscles. I knew it wouldn't be easy, but I didn't need easy. I needed forward. The money would help me start saving for a place of my own, sure, but more than that, I needed purpose. Something steady. Something that asked me to show up every day and keep going, one step at a time, just like Daddy always said. If I kept at it, maybe I'd end up somewhere that felt like mine.

When I told him, he looked more than proud. He looked pleased, genuinely glad. We'd always worked well side by side, and I think he liked the idea of having me around. He had other men on his crew, but they were usually scattered across larger job sites while Daddy handled the smaller ones himself. Now that he was expanding into landscaping, he said he needed someone he could count on, someone to help with mulching, clearing flower beds, and getting yards prepped before the first hard frost. When winter settled in, there'd still be work—splitting firewood, hauling loads, maybe even a few small construction jobs if I needed the extra money.

I promised myself I'd work extra hard. Daddy's offer wasn't just a paycheck, it was trust. By believing in me, he'd put salve on a part of my heart I didn't even know was still bleeding.

"This evening we'll get you a toolbox together," he said, sipping his coffee. "You can keep it in the back of your truck for jobs, just in case you're out there working without me."

I lit up. "Thank you, Daddy. I can't wait to get back to work. I need to keep my mind and hands busy."

Then, out of nowhere, he said quietly, "So… you gonna tell me what happened to that lip and eye? I could still see the bruising through the makeup, Peanut. Figured you'd tell me when you were ready, but I had to ask."

I froze. I'd been hoping they'd chalk it up to clumsiness, maybe a fall, maybe nothing. But no such luck. I'm sure he and Momma had whispered about it in bed those first few nights. It was almost gone now, barely visible without the makeup, but during that first week home, I'd done my best to hide it. Still, I should've known, the moment we were alone, Daddy would ask.

"It's nothing to worry about now," I said, trying to keep my voice steady. "It won't be a problem anymore."

He watched me for a second, then asked gently, "You want to talk about it?"

I shook my head.

He nodded and didn't press.

Looking back, there are still moments when I wish Daddy had pushed harder—demanded answers, pried the truth out of me no matter how tightly I tried to keep it buried. Sometimes I think maybe that's what I needed: someone to cut through the silence and drag the pain into the light.

Years later, when I finally worked up the nerve to ask him why he hadn't, his answer caught me off guard.

He said he trusted me. Trusted that I'd find my own way, that I'd make the choices I needed to make, even if they weren't always the right ones.

His words settled deep, filling a hollow I hadn't known was still aching, but they left a sting, too. I remember saying, soft but certain, "But I was still a kid." I didn't know which way was up. I needed someone to see past the surface, to step in when I didn't have the words. Because shame is a quiet drowning, and children don't always know how to reach for a hand that isn't already reaching for them. Sometimes, they need someone to cross the distance first.

But once I'd really listened, once I let his meaning sink in, I saw his silence through a different lens. It hadn't come from indifference or absence. It was love, shaped by the only tools he had. In his eyes, stepping back wasn't turning away. It was trusting me to find my footing. What I once took as distance, he meant as dignity. He believed in me, even when I didn't yet believe in myself.

Still, part of me wishes he and Momma had stepped in sooner. That they'd pierced the fog and pulled me back before I wandered too far. But I've come to understand: it wasn't apathy that held them still; it was uncertainty. Weariness. Maybe even hope that I'd right myself in time. They loved me in the only way they knew how, and I was too lost to see it then.

But in that quiet, imperfect love, something lasting took root. I see now how the Lord, my parents, and even the ache itself were part of the shaping. Every silence, every misstep, every tear I thought I cried alone. They were sharpening me. Not into something fragile, but into something steady. Not bitter, but deep.

I'm still becoming, but I'm no longer lost.

That truth settled into the air between us, and later that evening, Daddy took me out to the garage without saying much. He climbed up on an old stool and pulled down a weathered toolbox from the top shelf, said it had been his daddy's. Papaw had given it to him during the move. It was army-green and rusted in places, with three drawers and a top that unlatched with worn metal clasps. The sides were scuffed, the corners dented, and it was heavy in my hands like it had stories of its own. I loved it right away.

Daddy set it on the workbench and began dusting it off with an old shop rag.

"I know it's not much," he said, "but I thought you might like to have it. We'll see what all's in here and add anything else you might need."

He tugged open the top compartment, then pulled out the first drawer, rattling with old sockets and a few mismatched screws. But when he reached for the middle drawer, it stuck. He wiggled it a few times until it finally gave, sliding open with a groan.

Inside, lying flat and still, was a single piece of paper. It was yellowed with age, the edges curled, the print faded. Daddy picked it up carefully and unfolded it.

And there she was.

Andrea's face stared back at us.

It was an old missing poster from 1972. Her school photo, smiling, hopeful, young, sat at the center of the page, surrounded by the details that had once been plastered all over town.

I gasped. A flood of emotions hit me all at once: grief, fear, disbelief, and something deeper I couldn't name. "What in the world is that doing in there?" I asked, my voice barely above a whisper.

Daddy looked down at the paper, quiet for a long moment. "I remember when they handed these out everywhere," he said finally. "I was just a boy when she went missing. This must've been the toolbox

Papaw was using back then. He probably kept it in his truck, just like you'll keep it in yours."

The weight of that hit me harder than I expected. The past had never felt so close.

"Have you ever heard anything else about the case?" I asked. "Are they still working on it? Has Pete ever said anything?"

Daddy shook his head. "No, he's never said, and truth be told, I've never asked. It's awful, what happened. I hate to think what her family's been through, but I don't think they'll ever find answers now. It's been too long. It would take a miracle."

I hated hearing that, even if, deep down, part of me had started to believe it too. Still, I'd held on to hope. Hope that one day the case would be solved, that if justice ever came, maybe some piece of my own hurt would ease along with it.

Maybe that was just wishful thinking.

That night, lying in bed, I couldn't shake Andrea's face. The photograph—the one on that old, curling paper—clung to me like smoke, thin and inescapable. Familiar. Haunting. Long after I closed my eyes, she lingered, hovering at the edge of sleep like a memory that refused to fade.

Sleep came in torn sackcloth scraps that night. Each time I drifted under, I found myself standing on the splintered choir loft of the old Riverside Chapel, the one long swallowed by floodwater and creeping vine.

The river had receded just enough to leave the pews slick with mud, hymnals half-open like drowned birds. I could hear a lone piano key ringing, again and again, though no hands pressed it.

Moonlight poured through the broken rose window, glazing the water on the aisle until it looked like liquid pewter. I stepped in, and silt swirled around my bare feet, the current tugging at my hem like a child who didn't know how to ask.

Then I saw her, Andrea, kneeling in the chancel, waist-deep in the dark tide. Her hair floated around her face like river grass, her dress billowing as if it still wanted to breathe. She wasn't tangled in thorns this time; she was tethered by a rope of missing-person flyers, each one sodden, letters bleeding off the paper in long black rivulets.

I tried to speak, but the chapel air was thick and briny, filling my mouth with salt. She raised her eyes, blue, tidal, patient, and set a finger to her lips.

Behind her, stained-glass saints cracked under the weight of water-logged wood. With every distant thunder-rumble, another shard fell, plinking into the river that now lived inside the church.

Andrea dipped her hands beneath the surface and lifted something shining, a locket. She offered it out to me, and as the moonlight struck its face, I saw not a jewel, but a tiny skull etched in metal, jaw unhinged, as though mid-confession.

The single piano note shifted, became two, then three, an off-key lullaby echoing through the ruined pews. Andrea mouthed words I couldn't hear, but this time they weren't pleas. They were a hymn I hadn't heard in years, but knew deep in my bones:

*"And am I born to die?"*

Water rose to my chest. I reached for her, for the locket, for the song, anything solid, but the current swept the relic away, spun it through moon-shattered ripples, and Andrea with it. All that remained was the broken piano chord and the wet rustle of hymnbook pages turning themselves.

I woke with the taste of river silt on my tongue and the hymn still thudding in my ribs like a second heartbeat.

I reached for the old toolbox beside my bed and opened the top, needing to see something real, something solid. The poster was still folded inside the lid where I'd tucked it before. I ran my fingers along the edge of the paper and whispered, "I haven't forgotten you."

Because I hadn't.

And I wouldn't.

At first light, I woke heavy-limbed and hollow, the kind of drained that clings to you after a dream too vivid to shake. My head ached like I hadn't slept at all, and the weight of the night still pressed behind my eyes. I felt raw, like something had been peeled back inside me. Restless and unsteady, I needed something to quiet my mind. I needed the feel of dirt under my nails, the rhythm of work to drown out the echo of what I'd seen.

So, when Daddy gave me the day's task, I set straight to work. He had me clearing out an old flower bed behind a small cottage in town. The summer blooms had long since faded, and the beds were tangled with weeds, thick, stubborn things that had wrapped themselves tight around the roots of every surviving shrub. I got down on my knees, shoved my gloves on, and began pulling. With each weed I tore free, I felt something loosen inside me. Every tangle I dragged from the dirt was a small release. A knot unspooled. A breath exhaled.

It wasn't just yard work. It was therapy, a reckoning that moved through me like the turning of seasons—slow, certain, and long overdue.

There was something deeply symbolic about it, this work of uprooting what didn't belong. The weeds were everything that had tried to choke me: shame, fear, silence, control. They were the lies I'd been told. The pain I'd buried. The parts of me I didn't want to carry forward.

And the soil, rich, dark, waiting, was everything still possible.

It reminded me of the greenhouse, of Mari's soft encouragement as I'd whispered to lavender roots and nestled them into fresh pots. But this wasn't gentle. This was the hard part. The dirty part. The fight.

Before anything new could grow, the bad had to be ripped out by the root. The flower bed couldn't thrive unless someone did the work with hands in the dirt, sweat on the brow, refusing to let the wild things win.

So I kept pulling. Kept clearing.

And as the sun crept higher and the flower bed began to look more like a promise than a tangle of ruin. I wasn't healed, not yet. But I was making space. And maybe that was the beginning.

145

# Chapter 17



*Journal Entry– December 23, 1978*


*The first snow fell tonight—thin as lace, slow as forgiveness.*
*After supper, I stepped onto the porch and watched it hush the yard, laying its*
*small white hands over every rough place the year has left behind. How*
*strange that winter, the coldest season, carries the warmest promise: nothing*
*is too battered to be covered in mercy.*
*Tomorrow we'll walk to the Christmas Eve service by lantern light. The*
*Church will smell of cedar boughs and paraffin, and the children will stumble*
*through their lines about "no room in the inn." I never fault them for the*
*fumbles. They remind me that God trusts shaky voices to tell steady truths.*
*I think the real miracle of Bethlehem wasn't angels splitting the sky but*
*ordinary people making space where there was none, an overworked*
*innkeeper, a frightened girl, a carpenter who kept choosing love over pride.*
*It's easier to hang a No Vacancy sign over our hearts than to clear a corner*
*for grace. Yet the whole Gospel is one long invitation to move a few boxes*
*and let the Light come in.*
*If I have a prayer this Christmas, it is this:*
*that my children, and their children after them, will remember that holy*
*work.*
*That when the world feels crowded with grief and long roads, they will still*
*risk opening the door, still light a candle, still believe there is room enough for*

*weary travelers and newborn hope alike.*
*Snow keeps falling. The yard is nearly clean.*
*So is my heart.*

*-Ruth*

Day after day, Daddy kept his promise and kept my hands busy. I cleared out garden beds, hauled fallen limbs, and pruned the fruit trees to coax new life from them come spring. With every root I wrenched free, the noise in my head quieted. By nightfall, even the ghosts grew drowsy, and for once, sleep came so clean it felt like snowfall in an empty field. There were no restless nights, no tossing and turning from half-remembered dreams, just deep, steady rest that pulled me under like a warm tide.

One evening, as November waned and the air turned crisp with the promise of winter, Sheryl called. She told us the house had finally sold. They'd already put in an offer on the one they'd fallen in love with over in Wallens. She had half-expected it to be gone by now, but in a town as small as ours, homes didn't move like they did in the city. People wanted something polished, something turnkey. Not everyone could look at a worn-down porch or a sagging roof and see what it could become. It takes vision, and a kind of hope rooted in love, to look at chipped paint and overgrown grass and still see a home.

We were all excited about them coming home, and when moving day finally arrived, everyone pitched in. Daddy coordinated the trip with Pete, who brought his horse trailer to help haul everything back to Tennessee. The two of them drove up together and helped Luke pack every box and piece of furniture with steady hands and deliberate care, determined to bring Sheryl and Luke's life back home in one piece.

While they were on the road, Momma and I stayed behind. The house was quieter without the men around, and we used the time to make something special.  We painted the nursery in their new home soft shades of green and yellow, colors that felt like early spring and new beginnings.  Then we pulled the old crib from storage, the same one that had once held both Sheryl and me when we were babies.  As we assembled it, I could almost hear echoes of our past in the gentle creak of the wood.  We placed it carefully beneath the window, where the afternoon sun spilled in like honey across the floor.  It was our little surprise for them when they came home, to remind them that we were there to support them on this new and exciting journey.

By the time Christmas neared, they were all settled in, just as the first flakes of snow began to fall.  It felt good to have everyone under one roof again, to fill the house with laughter and life.  I was still living at home with Momma and Daddy, still saving for a place of my own. But instead of feeling restless or anxious to leave the house that had built me, I found myself sinking into its comfort, into the scent of Momma's cooking drifting from the kitchen, the steady crackle of the woodstove, the way warmth seemed to live in the walls.

Most evenings, we circled the kitchen table under the honey-gold lamp, a deck of cards shuffling between us while dusk stole the light early.  Shorter days trimmed the work hours, gifting us those slow pockets of time to laugh, sip cocoa, and let the dark press gently against the windows.

I've always loved winter. It feels like God's quiet way of reminding the world that it's okay to rest. The cold pushes us indoors, yes, but it also draws us closer to the fire, to each other.  It invites us to slow down, to breathe deeply, to find comfort not in the bustle of life but in its stillness. In the hush of snowfall and the warmth of hearth and home, there is peace.

As Christmas Day approached that year, mid-afternoon found me weaving through Main Street, chasing last-minute gifts for Momma and Daddy. The streets were dressed in garlands and string lights, and the air smelled faintly of pine and chimney smoke. While weaving through the bustle of holiday shoppers, I spotted a familiar face across the street, Lena-Grace, a friend from elementary school.

We had been close as children, but we drifted apart once my life started to unravel, and I slipped into a crowd she had no place in. Lena was never the type to party or drink. Still, she was never cruel about it either. Even in high school, when I walked the halls weighed down with quiet shame, she always offered a gentle smile and a soft "hello."

So when I saw her now, bundled up with a paper bag of wrapped gifts in her arms, and she smiled that same warm smile, something in me lifted.

I waved. "Lena! Hey!"

She looked up, and her eyes lit with recognition. "Jenny! It's good to see you."

I crossed the street, feeling lighter than I had in weeks, full of something close to cheer. "How are you?"

"I'm well," she said, eyes scanning me with quiet sincerity. "And I'm glad to see you look well, too."

"I am," I said, smiling. And I meant it. I had changed, not just on the outside, but in ways that mattered deeper. The black band tees and heavy eyeliner were gone. That day, I wore deep brown corduroy jeans and an earthy green shawl wrapped around my shoulders. I looked more like myself than I had in our high school years.

Lena looked much the same as she always had, simple but graceful. A long denim skirt, a cranberry-red blouse, and her blonde hair braided neatly down her back. Pale freckles dusted her cheeks like sifted flour, delicate and sun-kissed, as if summer had left its mark and never quite let go. There was something almost otherworldly about her beauty, like she belonged more to candlelight and old psalms than to the noise of the world. She was beautiful in a way I used to envy.

But standing there on that street corner, I didn't feel envy. I felt admiration. She was grounded, settled in her own skin. And somehow, just being near her made me feel steadier in mine.

Back then, I hadn't understood the source of that peace, but now I do. That kind of stillness only comes from God. From knowing you're loved by Him, made on purpose, with purpose. That your value isn't earned, it's given.

We chatted for a few more minutes, our words turning to white in the cold. Wrapping my shawl closer around me, "Well, I should probably finish this shopping if I want time to wrap everything," I said, grinning.

Lena laughed softly. "I should head on home, too. But if you're not busy tonight, we're having our Christmas play at church. You're welcome to come and sit with me. I know Papa would be happy to see you."

Her father had been the pastor of Willow Creek Assembly for as long as I could remember. We'd never attended regularly, but he, like Lena, had always been kind to me. He'd shake my hand when he saw me in town, ask about my grandparents, or just offer a few gentle words of encouragement. People respected him, and rightly so.

When Lena mentioned the Christmas play, something tugged loose in me, a memory of Mamaw's hand warm in mine, spirituals floating through candlelight, the peculiar safety that lives in a pew softened by years of Sunday sermons. I wasn't sure whether it was church I missed or Mamaw. Maybe both.

Her invitation stirred what I'd folded away with the winter quilts: a longing for hymns, candle, flame halos, and the kind of hush that feels like God's breath.

"I think I need that," I whispered, surprised by the certainty in my own voice.

"Well, I hope to see you there," she said, her smile bright as lamplight. We parted at the corner.

Packages bought and a paper cup of cocoa warming my hands, I headed home, eager to wrap the surprises I'd found for everyone. Watching someone's face light up over a well-chosen gift is the best kind of magic, the very reason Christmas is my favorite season.

When the last bow was tied, I slipped a velvety maroon dress from the closet, paired it with black flats, and braided my hair. As I stepped into the hallway, Momma looked up from the stove.

"Well, where are you off to all dressed up?"

"To church," I said. "Lena-Grace invited me to their Christmas play. It sounded nice."

"That was kind of her. Tell her and her daddy we said Merry Christmas."

"You could come with me." I offered the words softly.

She hesitated, eyes sweeping the kitchen. "I've got too much to do here, maybe next time."

"Okay. I'll be back after. Love you, Momma." I kissed her cheek, pulled my cloak close, and stepped into the brittle night air.

By the time I rattled into the church parking lot, darkness had settled, and the cold bit sharp as peppermint. Inside, the glow of stained-glass windows told me the pews were already filling. A flicker of nerves rose, but I climbed the steps and eased the door open, hoping not to interrupt.

Lena sat three rows back. She turned at the sound, a grin blooming across her face, and motioned me over.

"I was hoping you'd come," she whispered as I slid beside her. "Saved you a seat."

I let my breath out, the velvet of the dress smoothing beneath my palms, and I was ready for whatever soft mercy the night might lay at my feet.

The hum of conversation faded as the sanctuary lights dimmed. A hush fell across the pews, reverent and expectant, like the space between snowfall and silence. Then the stage curtain drew back, revealing a hand-built stable nestled beneath a paper sky full of stars.

The set was simple, wooden beams, a hay-strewn floor, soft lamplight flickering from stage-left, but something about it felt more real than pretend. Maybe it was the way the young girl playing the innkeeper's daughter stepped into the scene barefoot, a tattered book in hand. Or the way she paused before speaking, as if carrying more than just lines, something fragile and real, tucked somewhere deep.

She spoke of turning people away, of watching her father lock the doors and hang the *No Vacancy* sign, of hearing knocks that went unanswered in the night. Her voice trembled.

I leaned forward.

Then came Mary and Joseph, not polished or pageant-perfect, but weathered-looking, worn from travel. Mary couldn't have been much older than I was when I first lost myself. She didn't speak much. She just moved with a gentleness that rang through me like a bell struck soft. When she handed the innkeeper's daughter a scrap of cloth and said, *"For courage,"* I felt it like it was meant for me.

The story unfolded in vignettes, between songs and soft monologues. A shepherd spoke of losing his temper, of walking away too many times, of standing alone under cold stars, wondering if it was too late to start again. Then the angels came, not booming or blinding, but with voices like water over rocks. And he followed them. He *chose* to follow.

Later, when Mary laid the baby in the manger and stepped back, townspeople entered with candles, each one naming someone history had nearly forgotten. *Tamar. Hagar. The woman at the well.* Each name was a thread, mending the quiet with something older than scripture, soft and true.

A cradle sat empty at center-stage. One by one, they placed their candles inside it, until the light pooled like hope.

My throat tightened.

Then the shepherd returned. He stepped forward slowly, his eyes lowered, not toward the audience, but toward the cradle at center stage.

In his hands, he held the worn staff he'd carried throughout the play, but now, he set it down gently in the straw.

He didn't speak. He didn't need to.

Instead, he reached for a small bundle of cloth, a simple swaddling wrap, and held it close, like it meant something more than tradition. Like it was forgiveness, or grace, or a second chance.

That image stayed with me.

The lights warmed, casting the whole stage in a soft golden glow as the final hymn began. The voices rose around me, steady and full, and I just sat there, unable to sing. My hands rested in my lap; my breath caught in the hush between healing and hurt.

I thought of Papaw and the ways he'd changed. I thought of Marie and all the things left unsaid. I thought of myself, sitting there in a borrowed pew, wrapped in borrowed stillness, wondering if it was too late to come back to something I'd walked away from.

And in that moment, it wasn't a voice I heard but a feeling. A warmth I hadn't known I was missing until I felt it.

It said: *You're not too far gone. There's still room for you here.*

Lena placed her hand on top of mine and gave me a knowing smile. She didn't rise to sing with the others; she just sat there quietly beside me, so I wouldn't be alone in my awakening. It meant more than I could ever put into words.

She was like a beacon.

In that moment, something in me was rekindled. My faith, long dimmed, stirred gently back to life, and with it, an old friendship was made new again.

I squeezed her hand as tears slipped freely down my cheeks. And I knew, without doubt, that my life would never be the same.

I went home that night with my spirits high and told Momma and Daddy how wonderful the play had been. I said I'd like for them to come with me the next weekend, and they both agreed to try. I didn't press them. I just nodded, smiled, and told them goodnight.

Later, as I lay in bed, I found myself praying for them, something I hadn't done in years. I prayed for their health, their peace, for all the unspoken burdens I knew they carried. Then I prayed for myself, for strength, for clarity, for the courage to keep moving forward. The tears came quiet and steady, washing through the corners of my soul like rain in spring.

When I finally said amen, a deep peace settled over me, soft and sure. It lightened my heart and made my eyelids heavy.

The next morning, I awoke to snow. It blanketed the ground in a way we rarely saw so close to Christmas in East Tennessee. The holler lay quiet under the hush of white, and the stillness felt holy. As I wrapped my hands around a warm cup of coffee and gazed out the kitchen window, I felt something I hadn't in a long time.

Gratitude.

Despite the hardships, despite the heartbreak, I was still here. Still healing. Still blessed.

# Chapter 18

*Journal Entry– November 3, 1986*

*There's something sacred about claiming a space for yourself. Doesn't matter
if it's four walls or a corner of borrowed land; when you sweep the floors,
hang your quilt, and say a prayer over the door, it becomes yours.
The world won't always understand a woman wanting her own quiet, her
own peace. But sometimes peace is the bravest thing you can build.*

*-Ruth*

I went to church that next Sunday, slipping into a pew near the back
just as the music began. The sanctuary smelled faintly of faded
perfume and lemon polish, and something in me stilled. Afterward,
Lena and I walked over to the little diner downtown, where the coffee
was always a bit too strong, and the booths squeaked when you leaned
back. We sat across from each other, fingers wrapped around warm
mugs, and talked about grace and love, about the things we were praying
for, and the things we'd had to let go.

She told me how her mama had passed when she was barely thirteen.
Just her and her papa since then, holding each other up.

"I admire your faith," I said quietly. "After all that, to still believe the
way you do…"

Lena gave me a soft, steady smile. "We all have lessons to learn," she said. "That's the beautiful thing about grace. It don't hinge on whether we deserve it. It just *is*."

I nodded, her words settling in deep. I hadn't walked a straight road, and there were parts of me still tangled up in regret. But even so, I felt something sacred stirring in the quiet places, like maybe mercy had never been about earning it in the first place.

The weeks that followed passed with a rhythm that felt almost gentle. I worked, tucked away what little I could, and kept going back to church. Most Sundays, Lena and I shared coffee afterward, our conversations stretching between scripture and sorrow, between what had broken us and what might still heal. We always made room for laughter, small, sudden bursts of it that felt like sunlight slipping through stained glass. Sometimes it rose from old memories, sometimes from nothing at all. It didn't matter. What mattered was that it was there, steady as breath. Even in the heaviness, we found ways to smile. Not because the pain was gone, but because we'd learned how to carry it without letting it swallow us whole.

Every weekend, I asked Momma and Daddy if they'd like to come along. They always said, "Maybe next time," and I kept asking anyway.

Then one Sunday, Luke and Sheryl invited me to attend service with them over in Wallens. I said yes. I thought about asking Lena too, but I knew she'd want to be at her own church, holding space for her daddy like she always did.

It felt good, sitting beside my sister again. Sheryl didn't say much, just folded her hands neatly in her lap, one resting on the curve of her belly. In just a few more months, there'd be a new life to hold. They'd decided not to find out the baby's gender ahead of time, said they wanted to be surprised. Somehow, that felt fitting. Like maybe the best things in life weren't meant to be known too early.

"As long as it's healthy," she had said, and I couldn't agree more. I planned to spoil that baby rotten either way.

On my way home that afternoon, I took a detour by the lake and passed Cedar Hollow Campground. I hadn't expected anything to come of it, but one of the campers near the dock had a sign in the window: **For Sale or Rent**.

I pulled in and got out to take a closer look.

Old Man Turner was stacking wood nearby. He looked up and grinned. "Well, if it ain't Jenny girl. What brings you out this way? How's your daddy and 'em?"

"They're doing well," I said, smiling. "I was just wondering about this camper, how much you're asking for it."

He scratched his chin. "Bought it for my kids, but they don't come in anymore. I was gonna rent it, but if someone's serious about buying, I might be open."

"I'm interested," I said. "I've been thinking it's time I had a place of my own."

He gave me a look that was part amusement, part affection. "Well, Miss Jenny, I can hardly believe you're old enough to be talking about that. But I reckon we could work something out."

We talked terms. I told him what I'd saved working with Daddy, and he agreed to take that as a down payment, letting me pay off the rest within a year.

When I left the campground that day, a flicker of excitement rose up in me, real and steady, like kindling finally catching flame. The thought of something that was mine, truly mine, lit a warmth in my soul. The road ahead didn't seem so uncertain anymore. It felt open, like something I could walk toward with purpose.

When I got home that evening, I told Momma and Daddy the news. Momma only asked if I was sure, but I saw the worry gather in the creases around Daddy's eyes.

"I'll be alright," I said, trying to make my voice sound braver than it was. "I'll be close to you and Sheryl both. The campground's right on the county line."

"Shouldn't you wait 'til spring?" Daddy asked, his brow tightening. "It's awful cold out this time of year."

"No, Mr. Turner said there's heat in the camper," I told him. "He used to spend winter nights out there fishing, so it should be fine."

Daddy nodded, slow and thoughtful. "Well, if you're sure, then we'll help you any way we can," he said, offering that kind smile of his, worn at the edges but still strong.

"Thank you, Daddy," I said, wrapping my arms around him. His flannel shirt smelled like sawdust and fresh coffee—familiar, grounding things that made me feel safe.

Momma was already on her feet, moving through the kitchen like a quiet storm, opening cabinets and drawers, pulling out whatever she thought I might need: spare towels, a box of tea, an old cast-iron skillet with the handle worn smooth.

It wasn't like her to speak her feelings out loud. She folded them into actions, into casseroles and clean laundry and hot tea on hard days. Her love had always moved through her hands. It took me years to learn that language, but once I did, I realized she'd been saying "I love you" all along.

The following week, I packed up my belongings and began loading them into the bed of the truck. Momma had set aside a few boxes of necessities, pots and pans, extra linens, and added a couple of boxes of food to help get me started.

They followed me to the campground, and Daddy helped me unload everything while Momma stepped inside and started cleaning, unpacking dishes, and stocking the pantry with the food she'd brought.

Daddy moved through the space like a man on a mission, checking the outlets, testing the waterlines, and inspecting the decking around the camper. I stepped outside and smiled at his quiet concern. When he noticed me watching, I walked over, and he pulled me in under one arm.

We stood side by side, facing the lake in all its quiet stillness. The surface shimmered under a pale winter sun, and the trees across the water were bare and reaching.

"Well, one thing's for sure," he said with a smile. "You've got a great view, Peanut."

"Maybe I can talk you into fishing with me sometime," I said.

We hadn't gone fishing in years. Life had gotten busy, and the simple joys had slipped through the cracks. But I still remembered those summer evenings down by the water, Momma casting her Zebco 33, Daddy whittling while we waited, and the four of us laughing whether the fish bit or not.

Maybe we could find our way back to that again. I hoped so.

As we stood there, Mamaw and Papaw's old truck pulled into the gravel lot. Mamaw climbed out slowly, carrying a bag in one hand. She had brought me a new set of bath towels, cream, and black, soft as clouds. She'd done the same for Sheryl when she moved off to college. It was her way.

"Thank you," I told her, brushing my hand over the fabric. "I love them."

She took my hand in hers and gave it a gentle pat. "You're welcome, baby. You're never too old for Mamaw to spoil you a little."

Papaw gave me a big hug. "It's a nice place, Sugarfoot," he said. The old nickname warmed something inside me.

"I think so," I replied. "I've been telling Daddy we need to fish a little this year."

"That sounds like a great idea," he said, reaching for the rail to climb the stairs.

I watched him struggle, each step an effort. His hands were gripping the railing tighter than I remembered. Mamaw followed slowly behind him. They had both grown so frail. I wasn't sure how I hadn't seen it before. Maybe I hadn't wanted to.

Papaw asked for a chair once he made it to the top, worn out just from walking up the steps. He leaned against the doorframe for a moment, catching his breath, and I could see the way his shoulders sagged beneath his coat, like the years were pressing down heavier than they used to. It pressed into a quiet part of me I'd boarded up long ago, but the boards had begun to creak.

He'd always been the strong one, the steady one. The man who could haul fence posts through red clay and lift us grandkids up like we weighed nothing at all. But now, he looked smaller somehow. Slower. And it hit me all at once how quickly time was slipping.

Right then, I made a silent promise to myself. I'd make more time for them—not just in passing, not just at holidays, but real time. I'd sit with them, let the hours stretch soft and unhurried. I'd listen to the stories they still carried, the ones tucked into the corners of memory like brittle photographs. I wanted to learn from them while I still could. To gather up the pieces of who they were before they faded, before all that quiet wisdom vanished into the hush of the hills.

As the sun dipped low behind the trees, casting long shadows across the lake, we all said our goodbyes. I stood on the deck, wrapped in my favorite blanket, the wind tugging gently at the fringe as I waved them off. Their trucks rumbled down the gravel drive, tires crunching until the sound faded into quiet.

They went home without me.

I lingered a moment longer, watching the still water reflect the fading light. Then I stepped back inside the camper and looked around. A few boxes set waiting to be unpacked, but it already felt like mine. Not just a place to sleep, but a space I had worked for, saved for, claimed for myself. It wasn't much, but it was enough.

Later, I curled into bed beneath the quilt Mamaw had made years ago, the one with the faded blue stars and frayed edges that always reminded me of home. The camper creaked softly as it settled, the wind brushed against the windows, and the world outside grew still.

I opened my book, exhaled slowly, and let the warmth of the moment wrap around me.

I was home.

# Chapter 19



*Journal Entry– April 12, 1992*

*Spring slid in overnight, soft as a hymn hummed under breath. Dogwoods are opening their white hands again, and the whip-poor-wills have taken up their evening watch. I stood on the porch at dusk and felt the hush settle over the holler. The Lord keeps reminding me: new life never shows up loud; it steals in quiet and sets its roots while nobody's looking. I reckon that's how He means for hope to work, too.*

*-Ruth*

Sunlight crept over the camper's tin roof. With one hand wrapped around my mug, I thumbed Mari's number and waited for her familiar hello.

"Mari, guess what?" I said. "I've got a place of my own now, a little camper right on the water."

Her laugh drifted through the line, rich and steady as fresh-brewed coffee. "Well, sugar, that's the best news I've heard all week. You know I've missed your voice."

"Come visit," I urged. "There's a full-size bed, a bunk room, even a pull-out couch. Plenty of space if you don't mind close quarters."

She paused, thinking aloud. "Let me see if my new girl can mind the shop and remember to water the ferns. If she can, I'll steal a few days. Lord knows I haven't had a vacation since roses learned to climb."

"Deal," I said, already picturing her straw hat on my porch.

I'd taken the morning off and settled on the deck that overlooked the drawn-down lake. Winter's low waterline cut raw, red scars along the banks, proof of where the freshwater once filled every hollow. Cradling my mug, I breathed a prayer of thanks for the strange abundance crowding my life: family still breathing, friendships that felt like anchor ropes, faith tuned up and humming again, and now this patch of independence.

Coffee finished, I laced my boots for a stroll to the dock. The wooden steps dipped toward the bank, and I caught the rail, just as Papaw had done the day before. A dull ache cinched my chest. Time was tugging them away grain by grain, and I'd been too busy to notice the pile it stole.

I pulled my jacket tighter. *This afternoon,* I promised myself *I'll go visit Mamaw and Papaw. No more waiting for a better day that never comes.*

I strolled down to the dock just after sunrise. The marina was already humming with anglers hefting tackle boxes, easing coolers onto bass boats, slipping through the floating store for minnows and hot coffee. It was still cold enough to mist your breath, but around here, fishing wasn't a hobby; it was a calling. Crappie and bass were biting, so the faithful showed up before the light could finish its stretch across the water. I made a mental note to dig my rod, reels, and tackle box out of Daddy's shed soon. My line hadn't tasted lake water in far too long.

After waving to a few familiar faces, I headed back to the camper and spent the rest of the morning nestling the last of my belongings into cupboards and cubbies. With every framed photo and folded throw blanket, the place felt a touch more like mine.

By early afternoon, I'd slid on my boots again, bound for Mamaw and Papaw's new house in town. It still felt strange driving there instead of to their old place out by Momma and Daddy's. Some family from New York had purchased the property as a seasonal retreat, planning to hunt deer come November. The thought of strangers tracing fresh memories through rooms that once echoed with ours unsettled me, as if their laughter might chase our own down the hallways, turning our past into little more than shadows on the wall.

I shook off the notion and ran through a mental grocery list while pulling into my grandparents' driveway. Papaw stood on the porch, frowning at the doorknob, while Mamaw sat at the picnic table working on a word search. She looked up and waved, her smile as bright as ever.

"Hey, Pap," I called. "Need some help?"

He puffed out a breath. "I've locked us out of the house. Reckon I'm hunting the spare key, but can't recall where I stashed it."

Mamaw chimed in, patience twinkling in her eyes. "We've been looking, but he can't remember."

"I'll take a lap," I said.

Circling round back, I found the kitchen door standing ajar behind the screen. I slipped inside, walked through the living room, and unlatched the front door. Papaw's eyebrows shot up.

"Well, how'd you manage that, Sugarfoot?"

"The back door was wide open. You might want to keep an eye on it, Pap."

He chuckled, shaking his head. "Well, I'll be. Thank you, darlin'."

Mamaw rose slowly, word search in hand. I offered my arm, and together we eased up the ramp. Halfway to the door, a memory washed over me, Mamaw gripping my tiny fingers years ago, steadying me as I clambered up a slick riverbank. Now our roles were reversed, time looping on itself like the slow bend of the Tennessee. Grief flickered, but gratitude glowed warmer. In that brief silence between us, I felt both the ache of passing seasons and the blessing of still being here to share them.

Once we were inside, Papaw's shoulders sagged; being locked out had rattled him more than he cared to show. He hugged me, promised a proper visit later, and shuffled off for a nap. I sank into the couch while Mamaw settled into the same wing-back chair she'd claimed my whole life. She kept at her word search; I thumbed through the stack of seed catalogs and church bulletins on the coffee table. Now and then, she'd glance up to ask after Daddy, Momma, or Sheryl, or how my first night in the camper had gone. Mostly, though, we sat in that easy, companionable hush that only exists with someone whose mere presence makes you feel tended to and at peace.

When I look back now, years older and a little weather-worn myself, the first memories that rise to the surface are the bright ones, standing barefoot on a kitchen chair while Mamaw guided my hands through sugar and dough, her wedding ring catching the light as she worked beside me. Or watching Papaw tie fishing flies at his desk, the tiny jeweled feathers flashing beneath his lamp like bits of caught lightning. Those were the golden days, lit from within by childhood wonder.

But the memories I hold closest are the quieter ones—the slow, sacred afternoons that came later, long after the forts had fallen and hide-and-seek was a game we'd outgrown. We'd sit nearly wordless in their living room, the clock ticking like a heartbeat, Mamaw reading from her Bible with a pen tucked behind her ear, Papaw humming faintly from his recliner as he tapped the armrest in rhythm. The hush between us felt holy, like a prayer we didn't need to speak aloud.

I drank it in like a traveler at the edge of a dwindling well, grateful, watchful, knowing the water wouldn't last forever. And even then, some part of me understood: moments like that don't come again. So I stayed as long as I could, soaking up the stillness, determined to remember the way it felt to be loved in such a quiet, unwavering way.

Mamaw was nodding off, her word-search sliding into her lap. I kissed the crown of her silver hair.

"I love you, Mamaw. I'm running to the grocery, but I'll be back soon."

"Okay, baby. You be careful," she murmured, eyes half-lidded.

The market was only a few blocks away, so I grabbed a handful of essentials: coffee, flour, a new dish towel in a cheerful sunflower print. I told myself I'd make afternoons like this a habit, not a rarity.

Over the next few weeks, I fell into an easy rhythm of work, church, stopping by Mamaw and Papaw's, checking in on Sheryl, sharing pot roast with Momma and Daddy. Evenings alone were my quiet reward: bare feet on the deck rail, paperback in hand, spring creeping across the lake on a warm breeze.

One such evening, a small black Civic eased to a stop behind my camper. I didn't recognize the car at first, but when Mari stepped out, a smile rose unbidden to my face, wide and honest.

"How on earth did you find me?" I laughed, meeting her halfway. "I was starting to think you'd forgotten that visit."

"I called Sheryl," she said, eyes dancing. "Thought I'd surprise you."

I hoisted her suitcase from the trunk. "Let me get your bags."

"I've got one more thing," she called, reaching into the back seat.

Moments later, she ducked through my doorway carrying a glossy-leafed peace lily in a cobalt pot, white blooms just beginning to unfurl.

"Oh, Mari, it's beautiful."

She set it on the counter, smoothing the soil with her thumb. "A home needs a plant or two, and a peace lily means fresh beginnings that last."

I hugged her hard, grateful for the grace she always seemed to bring with her, roots and all.

I spent the next few days playing tour guide, determined to show Mari every ridge and back road that had stitched itself into my bones. First stop was Momma and Daddy's, where Mari charmed them both by praising Momma's sweet-tea ratio, "just the right caramel bite," and swapping garden tips with Daddy about fending off tomato hornworms. We drove into town to Mamaw and Papaw's new place, too, where

Papaw called her "ma'am" until she laughed and insisted he use her first name.

I pointed out the pasture fence Sheryl and I used to balance-walk, the diner where half the high school still meets after Friday games, and the weather-grayed sycamore that once held our tire swing. One night, I took her to my favorite restaurant, hot chicken so fiery it made us both tear up, and told her how I'd crossed paths with Lena-Grace downtown, how we'd swapped numbers like no time had passed. We talked about Sheryl's looming due date, about the new landscaping jobs I'd taken on, and how pushing a spade into fresh dirt felt like shaking hands with an old friend.

Mari nodded, eyes soft behind her round glasses.

"Everything's a loop, Jenny," she said, folding a napkin into neat quarters. "Plant, tend, prune, rest, then new growth. Our lives follow the same rhythm, the only difference is the roots are our own."

Having her beside me made the days shine brighter, but by the week's end, I could see the restlessness flickering behind her smile. The Tennessee hills suited her. She looked natural against that patchwork of green and clay, but her heartbeat kept tempo with city streets and greenhouse aisles. She missed the constant hum of customers, the stories traded over seed trays, the daily resurrection of wilted things.

So when she climbed into her rental car, hands smelling faintly of basil from our last walk-through Daddy's raised beds, I hugged her tightly and let her go. I didn't begrudge her the pull of home. Roots grow where they're planted, after all, but the gravel dust hadn't settled from her tires before I felt the hollow she left behind.

I turned back into the camper and tucked the peace lily onto the narrow windowsill. After drizzling a ribbon of water into the soil, I brushed one glossy leaf with my fingertip and whispered, "Settle in and bloom, little one. We'll put down roots together."

The next day, a storm was rolling in, and the camper walls creaked as the wind shifted off the water, rattling the aluminum seams like a sigh. I ate supper standing up, saltines and pimento cheese, then let the tiny television drone while I rinsed the plate in the single-basin sink. Static rolled, cleared, and the local anchor's voice steadied:

*"Breaking tonight: William 'Bill' Campbell, 75, the father of slain teenager Andrea Campbell, was discovered dead in his pickup near the launch ramp at Cedar Point. Investigators say Campbell had been drinking and are treating the death as an apparent suicide.*

*Andrea Campbell disappeared in 1972; her remains were found in 2005 on rural property in Pedoux. The homicide remains unsolved, and authorities stress the cold-case investigation is still active. Any tips regarding this case are welcome and needed."*

Dishwater sluiced through my fingers as the words sank in. Bill Campbell, a man who'd lived with silence longer than Andrea had lived at all, had driven to the edge of the lake and never come back.

Was it grief that pulled him there... or guilt?

If he had a hand in Andrea's death, *why leave her on our land? Did he know Papaw? Had they struck some backwoods bargain I'd never be told about?*

The questions flickered across the camper walls with the TV's blue light—there, gone, there again—until I snapped the set off and the silence roared. Thunder clapped outside.

Waves lapped the bank like a slow, relentless clock. Somewhere out on that black water, Bill Campbell had decided the lake could keep what the earth refused to bury. And I couldn't help but wonder: *how many more secrets would die before the truth finally came up for air?*

# Chapter 20



*Journal Entry– July 31, 1987*

*A baby can turn a house quiet with awe. The way everyone leans in to hear her breathe, the way time hushes itself around something so new.*
*But even the sweetest beginnings can stir up old ghosts.*
*Sometimes, holding new life in your arms brings back the things you thought you'd laid to rest. The hopes. The mistakes. The prayers you never said out loud.*
*God's mercy covers us, but memory has a long reach.*

*-Ruth*

The phone shrilled beside my pillow at three a.m., and my heart leapt like a cat under a rocking chair. I fumbled in the dark, hand trembling as I grabbed it.

Momma's voice crackled through the line like static from an old radio. "Jenny, Sheryl's water just broke. We're headed to the hospital."

"I'm on my way," I said, already throwing back the covers and swinging my legs out of bed.

Hard to believe the due date had snuck up this fast. One minute we were fussing over nursery decor, and the next, I was yanking on jeans, shrugging into my jacket, and hustling out the door. The night air hit me like a cold slap, but I didn't stop. The engine coughed and groaned before it finally caught, and I pointed the headlights down the drive, tires spitting dust behind me.

"Lord," I prayed aloud, "let the delivery be smooth. Keep my sister safe. Keep that baby safe." My voice caught in my throat. "Please, just let everything be okay."

Pedoux had the nearest hospital, nestled along the riverbank at the edge of town. Wallens was too small to have one of its own. From the outside, Pedoux's building looked more like an old brick schoolhouse than a place where lives began and ended. It wasn't built for emergencies, not really, but they could set a bone, take an x-ray, or deliver a baby when needed. There was no official labor and delivery ward, but the nurses were kind and knew how to make do.

Sheryl had planned to give birth at the larger hospital out in Millbranch, nearly an hour's drive away. But when her water broke, the contractions came fast and fierce, and there just wasn't time. So, in the pale gray hours of April 25th, under humming fluorescent lights and atop worn linoleum floors, a beautiful, healthy baby girl made her way into the world.

When I first laid eyes on her, I couldn't breathe. My heart sang with love.

She was swaddled in a white-and-pink blanket, nestled in Sheryl's arms like she had always belonged there. Luke stood beside them, his hand gently cupping the back of Sheryl's head as he stared down at their daughter with a look so full of love it could bring a grown man to his knees. That room, sterile and cold just a moment ago, was suddenly warm, wrapped in the hush that falls when something bigger than us enters the room.

I felt the tears come before I could stop them.

Suddenly, then and there, I knew that one day, I'd want this, too. Not just the baby or the swaddling blankets or the soft lullabies, but the grace. I wanted to soften with age, to build a life where a child could fall asleep knowing they were safe. I wanted to become the kind of woman who knew how to forgive, how to hold space for someone else's pain. I wanted to raise a child baptized in love, not fear.

"Have y'all picked out a name yet?" I asked, though I already suspected they had a list tucked away, one for boys and one for girls. They were the kind of people who liked to be surprised, who believed in letting the baby tell her own story.

Sheryl looked up at Luke. Her voice was soft, full of reverence. "Alana Kate. After Luke's sister."

His eyes welled up, and for a moment, it felt like even the walls were holding their breath. I didn't know much about the wound he carried where his sister once lived, but I hoped this was the beginning of something mending inside him. Something deep and quiet.

"Have you told your parents yet, Luke? Are they coming in?" Momma asked gently, her eyes lingering on the baby's face.

"I told my mother," Luke said, clearing his throat. "She said she'd try to visit soon, but I'll believe it when I see it. Hard to tear her away from the country club and her evening cocktails."

Momma let out a small sigh and reached over to touch Alana's little foot. "Well," she said softly, "you should at least send them a picture. They might not realize it now, but one day that photo will mean the world."

I caught something flicker in her expression, a warmth I hadn't seen in a long while. For just a second, I saw the old Momma, the one who laughed loud and kissed our foreheads when we cried. I'd missed her more than I could say. And maybe, just maybe, this baby girl would help bring some of that light back.

I hated what the medication had done to her, how it dulled her voice, flattened her spirit, kept her eyes downcast even in joy. I know some folks need those pills, and I don't judge them for it. Some people are fighting battles inside that we can't even see, and the medicine helps them stay afloat.

But oftentimes, it's used to avoid the work of healing. Real healing means staring your pain in the face, sorting through every broken shard, and figuring out how to rebuild. It ain't easy. It's messy, and it's painful, and it takes more strength than most people know.

But I had faith my Momma could do it. I prayed she'd find the courage to walk through the storm instead of just numbing herself to the thunder.

Daddy and Momma stayed a little while longer, but they needed to head back. There were chickens to feed and morning chores waiting. Luke had to run home too; in all the excitement, he'd left behind the hospital bag Sheryl had packed weeks ago. He was usually steady as a pond, unshakable even when things got loud, but that baby had rattled him good. I saw it in his hands, the way they trembled just a little when he touched her cheek.

"I'll stay," I offered, settling into the chair beside Sheryl's bed. "She can rest. I'll keep an eye on my beautiful girl."

Alana slept soundly in the bassinet, her tiny chest rising and falling like the hush of a lullaby. One hand had curled into a loose fist near her cheek, soft as a petal, and I couldn't stop staring. The room was still, wrapped in that thick hospital quiet, the kind that only settles in places where joy and grief have both left their mark, where life and death breathe through the same air, just a hallway apart.

I turned on the little wall-mounted TV, muted the volume, and leaned back into the stiff plastic chair. My body throbbed with exhaustion, shoulders tight, feet sore, but something in me felt softened, stretched wide open. I thought of Mamaw then, how she used to hum when she rocked us, how she always said that holding a baby was proof God still believed in second chances.

Alana stirred slightly, then went still again. I let my eyes close, just for a moment, and listened to the soft rhythm of her breathing. There in the half-light of that small hospital room, with spring pressing its green fingers against the windows, I felt the fragile weight of time. Of all that had come before, and all that might come next.

Then the screen shifted.

**"WANTED: Information on the following cold cases."**

I sat forward. The names scrolled across the bottom of the screen, and there it was.

Andrea Campbell.

A chill crept up my spine, cold and sudden as a snake sliding through tall grass. My stomach turned, and I looked back at Alana. So small. So helpless. So precious.

Something fierce bloomed inside me, something wild and maternal.

I would protect her. No matter what.

Whatever it took, I would make sure that what happened to Andrea never happened to her.

Luke returned not long after, the door swinging open with the familiar weight of someone who'd finally exhaled. Just behind him came Mamaw and Papaw.

Mamaw's hands were full—one cradling a neatly wrapped gift tied with a pink ribbon, the other gripping a helium balloon that bobbed along behind her, declaring *"It's a Girl!"* in shiny, cheerful letters.

I watched their eyes light up the moment they saw the tiny bundle swaddled in the bassinet. Mamaw went straight to the crib and, with a kind of reverent awe, gathered the baby into her arms. She held her like she was holding grace itself. Then she pressed her nose to Alana's cheek and inhaled deeply, the scent of newborn skin like a balm sinking into old bones.

Papaw stood a step behind, watching her. His eyes were wide, glassy with something that looked an awful lot like love.

After fifty years of marriage, their bond had moved far beyond butterflies and fresh-cut flowers. It was worn in, like an old river rock shaped by years, smoothed by the current.

And yet… watching Papaw look at Mamaw like that, so gentle, so full of wonder, it hurt.

Because I knew too much.

I knew the stories passed in hushed voices between siblings, words coated in caution, spoken only when they thought no one else could hear.  I knew the bruises that weren't talked about, the tightness in Daddy's voice when he remembered.  I knew what it was to walk on eggshells around those who are supposed to love you. I knew what kind of man could leave cracks in the people who once trusted him most.

So I watched him now and couldn't reconcile it, the tender gaze of a man in love with the history of a man who had once been cruel.

Had time softened him? Had shame carved something better into his bones? Or was it just a mask he wore now, long after the damage had been done?

I didn't know.

And truth be told, I wasn't sure I ever would.

Life had already taught me that people are rarely just one thing. Most carry shadows behind their smiles, offering only the parts they want you to see, wrapping themselves in performance, in penance, in pretense.

Was it manipulation? Regret? Redemption? Wishful thinking on their part, or self-protection on ours?

I didn't know.

And standing there in that small hospital room, with the scent of baby lotion lingering in the air and the weight of old ghosts pressing up against the windows, I wasn't even sure I wanted to.

# Chapter 21

*Journal Entry– May 17, 1981*

*We don't always see our greatest work while we're living it.*
*Sometimes it's not in the jobs we hold or the dreams we chase,*
*but in who our children become, and what they carry forward when we're*
*gone.*

*-Ruth*

Folks talk about birth like it's the end of something.

Like once the baby's out and breathing, the storm's passed.

But sometimes, the storm comes later, quiet and slow, like mold creeping under paint. And by the time you notice it, it's already settled into the bones.

That's how it was for Sheryl. The first few weeks were the usual whirlwind: sleepless nights, sore everything, and the awkward rhythm of a new life trying to find its footing. But beneath the exhaustion, something else had its grip on her, something darker. Each time Alana latched onto her breast, it was like a piece of Sheryl slipped away. Her skin paled, her smile dimmed, and her eyes, once so sharp and full of spark, took on a faraway look.

About a month in, I finally asked Luke, "Is Sheryl okay? She seems…

off. Like something's wrong."

He rubbed the back of his neck, his eyes tired. "I think she's just worn out. Adjusting's been hard. I'm working more now so she can stay home with the baby. I try to help when I can."

"I'll come stay with her some," I offered. "Give her a break, let her rest."

"Thanks, Sis," he said, his voice warm but heavy. "It's a big change. But she's worth it. They both are."

And Luke meant that. He was already a better daddy than most. He doted on his daughter, changed diapers without complaint, and rocked her to sleep as if it were second nature. He brought Sheryl tea, kissed her forehead, and folded the laundry without being asked. But even the best partner can't carry someone through a storm they don't see coming.

One quiet afternoon, I sat with Sheryl in their living room. Alana lay sleeping in the old wooden swing bassinet I'd found at the town swap meet. Sheryl stared blankly ahead, not even blinking.

"What's wrong?" I asked gently.

She sighed, the kind of sigh that felt older than her years. "I don't know," she said, her voice low. "Something's wrong with me. I know it. I shouldn't feel like this."

My stomach clenched, the question already burning. "What way, Sher? Tell me."

"I just feel so guilty," she whispered. "I've got a beautiful baby, a husband who loves me… and all I want to do is cry. I don't feel like myself. I feel… hollow."

"That sounds like postpartum depression," I told her softly. "It's nothing to be ashamed of. It happens, and it's treatable. You should talk to your doctor."

"I don't want medicine," she said quickly, panic flickering in her eyes. "You've seen what it's done to Momma. I don't want to end up numb. I want to feel like *me* again, not some dulled-down version."

I hadn't thought of that, and she wasn't wrong. The medication had stolen something from Momma, her sparkle, her sharpness, the part of her that once danced in the kitchen. But Sheryl needed help, even if it was just someone to talk to. I told her that. Told her counseling could help, that she didn't have to fix it all on her own.

She just nodded, but the weight in her eyes didn't lift.

That's when I knew I'd have to tell Luke. He needed to know. He could make the appointment. He could make her go.

"You know I'll watch Alana," I said. "Give you some time to rest. Or even a date night with Luke."

"I can't," she said, her voice breaking. "I'm breastfeeding."

"You can pump," I reminded her gently. "You don't have to do it all, Sheryl. It's okay to lean on us."

After that afternoon in the living room, something in me wouldn't sit still. I found myself going over to Sheryl's house more often, sometimes under the guise of returning a borrowed book or bringing over leftovers from Daddy's grill night, but really, I just wanted to keep an eye on her.

She never asked for help, not once. But that's the thing about strong women, we get so used to holding everything up ourselves that we forget we're allowed to let it fall for a minute.

Sometimes I'd come by and take Alana for a walk in her stroller, giving Sheryl the chance to nap or just sit in silence. Other times, I brought my laundry and did it at her house just so I'd have a reason to stay. I learned to read the look in her eyes, the way her smile didn't reach them, the way her voice sounded too light when she said she was "fine."

I didn't say anything to Momma directly, but she must've noticed too. Not long after, she started coming around more. At first, it was simply dropping off frozen casseroles, folding baby clothes while Sheryl nursed, sweeping the porch without being asked.

But the real change happened one Sunday morning when Momma

showed up on the porch in her church dress, purse clutched tight in her hands.

"You girls ready?" she asked like it was the most natural thing in the world.

Sheryl and I looked at each other, surprised, but we didn't question it. We just grabbed the diaper bag and buckled Alana into her carrier.

That morning, we sat side by side in a pew near the back, me, Sheryl, and Momma, with Alana asleep in the sling on her mama's chest. The music started, soft and familiar, and for a moment, it felt like I was a little girl again, holding Momma's hand while she sang softly beside me.

Something had changed. Not all at once, but slowly, like spring thawing out the frost. She started coming more regularly, every Sunday, in fact, and then she started staying after, chatting with the women who lingered in the vestibule. The ladies' group invited her to a Wednesday night Bible study, and to my surprise, she went.

It wasn't long before she was helping with potlucks, bringing sweet tea and deviled eggs just like she used to. She even read aloud from a devotional one morning when the pastor's wife was sick, her voice clear and calm like a still river. I hadn't heard that voice in years, not muted by medication or dulled by sorrow.

I saw it in Sheryl, too. She still had hard days, but they didn't drown her like before. With Momma around more and Luke pitching in every chance he got, she had space to breathe again. She started brushing her hair before I came over, even put on a little lipstick some days. She began to smile at Alana in a way that felt real, not like she was trying to convince herself she was okay.

One evening, I came by just before sunset. The porch smelled like rain and fresh laundry, and I found the four of them sitting out front, Momma rocking Alana in her lap, Sheryl leaning into Luke's shoulder, her eyes soft and peaceful.

I stepped up onto the porch, and without a word, Momma handed me the baby. I cradled her close, her tiny breaths warm against my collarbone, and eased down onto the old rocking chair beside them.

A moment later, Daddy stepped out of the house holding two mugs. He placed one gently into Momma's hands, his fingers brushing hers like it was a habit, not a show. She looked up at him, eyes soft with something I hadn't seen in an age, something solace and warm.

It was a tender moment, fleeting and fragile, and I found myself holding my breath just to make it last.

"I missed this," Sheryl said after a long silence, her eyes tracing the horizon. "Us."

"Me too," I said, swallowing around the lump in my throat.

Momma didn't say anything. She just reached out and took both our hands in hers, gave them a gentle squeeze. In the porchlight, I saw something flicker across her face.

It wasn't just hope. It was healing.

I realized then that maybe none of us had come through the fire untouched. But here we were, together, scorched but still standing, still holding on to each other.

And that had to count for something.

It didn't happen all at once. Healing never does. But one afternoon, while folding laundry in silence, Sheryl looked over at me and said, "I think I need to go back to work."

I glanced up, surprised. "Already?"

She nodded slowly. "Not full-time. Just a few shifts here and there. Maybe something behind a desk. I just… I need to feel like myself again. Like I'm still in here somewhere."

Her voice cracked on those last words, but there was a spark behind her eyes that hadn't been there before. It wasn't just about money or distraction. It was about reclaiming something she feared she'd lost.

A week later, she took a part-time clerical job at the hospital, filing charts and answering phones. It wasn't the courtroom she once dreamed of, but it was something. A place to begin again.

Momma started watching Alana during Sheryl's short shifts, and I pitched in whenever I could. And slowly, that heaviness began to lift. The dark circles beneath her eyes faded, her voice carried more steadiness, and her laugh, quiet at first, came back like a song you hadn't heard in years.

It wasn't long before Sheryl was taking on more hours, more responsibility. She told folks it was about the money, about building up savings and giving Alana everything she'd need. But I wasn't so sure.

Sheryl worked the way some folks pray, fierce, head down, and afraid to stop, as though stillness might let the sorrow creep up and bite. Swing shifts turned into doubles, doubles into weekends, until the hospital lights felt more like home than the soft glow of her own porch. From a distance, it looked like ambition; up close, it was a kind of mercy she gave herself. If her hands stayed busy, her mind couldn't circle the ruins of old dreams.

Long before babies and marriage, she'd sketched cathedrals in her imagination: mahogany benches, her voice ringing clear beneath a judge's gavel. She'd planned to argue truth into the world, to stamp a lawyer's seal on every letter of her name. But life is a crooked road. Somewhere between final exams and morning sickness, that bright future slid off the map, and she woke one day to find she was singing in a much smaller choir.

The sorrow wasn't loud, more like the slow drip of a leaking roof that finally warps the floorboards. She'd stand in her kitchen at midnight, baby monitor humming, and see not the miracle she'd grown, but the courtroom she never walked. The weight of "what if" can press a woman flatter than any stone wall.

I wanted her to borrow my eyes for a spell. I saw the grace in her, the way her child bloomed beneath her touch, the way Luke's shoulders relaxed when she walked into a room. She had built a life rich as river bottom soil, but all she could see were the weeds of unfulfilled plans. And so she kept running, charts to file, beds to change, letting the hum of fluorescent lights drown the chorus of regrets.

I prayed she'd wake soon to see what she'd made: a house warm with supper and lullabies, a husband who looks at her like sunrise, a child who thinks Mama is just another word for safe. One day, she'll step back and see that the cathedral was never lost. She'd simply built it out of flesh and love instead of brick and law books. May she walk its aisles before the years slip away like backwater under the bridge.

# Chapter 22

*Journal Entry– March 30, 2014*

*Time has a way of sneaking past the screen door when no one's looking. One day you're barefoot in the garden, and the next, your knees ache just walking to the mailbox.*
*The seasons don't wait for anyone. They roll on just tulips, tomatoes, then frost.*
*There's a heaviness that settles in the soul when you start measuring life in doctor's visits and grandchildren's birthdays. Not a sadness, exactly, just the knowing. Knowing that most things in this world are borrowed, and someday we'll give them all back.*
*Still, there's beauty in that. The borrowed days, the quiet afternoons with rain on the roof, those are the ones that matter most. They don't shout. They don't demand. But they stay with you.*
*So I keep writing them down. Not to remember everything, but to hold onto the way it felt for a little while. To sit still in a world that's always rushing on.*

*-Ruth*

I t's funny how, no matter how much things change, people just keep on living.

Doesn't matter the trauma, the depression, the damage. Doesn't matter if you're tired or afraid.

You just keep waking up, going through the motions some days, because most folks are too afraid of the alternative.

But there were times I understood the ones who stood at the edge and leapt into the black, bleak unknown, just to make it stop.

I thank God every day that love and faith kept me tethered to this world.

Had they not, I would've missed the giggles of baby Alana, wouldn't have seen her stumble barefoot across the porch, or heard the sweet sound of her saying my name like it was the only one that mattered.

I wouldn't have watched my Momma draw near to God, or seen my Daddy follow her there, because he'd follow her anywhere.

And I wouldn't have found the pieces of myself I hadn't known were missing.

Time has a strange way of slipping past when you aren't looking. The days stack up like old devotionals in the back pew, gathering dust until you realize how many Sundays have gone by.

One morning, I looked up, and Alana was starting kindergarten. And I couldn't tell you where the time had gone, only that it had.

The rain was beating down on the old camper's roof, steady and relentless, driving me indoors. The work Daddy and I had planned would have to wait for clearer skies. The camper had settled over time, like a cat curling into the blankets. I had made it mine. Every corner held a trace of me.

I ran my finger along the spines of my books tucked into the narrow shelf above the little couch, thinking I'd curl up with one and let the rain be my soundtrack. But just as I reached for a novel, my eyes caught on Mamaw's old journal, the one I'd kept close all this time. Something stirred.

The idea seized me, gentle, but firm. Maybe it was time I started one of my own.

I set the journal aside, meaning to take it back to Mamaw when I saw her later. I'd be heading into town anyway, bringing supper to her and Papaw. Momma had said Daddy was making chili that evening, told me to come by and eat first, then carry some over to them. It had become our rhythm. I still loved to cook and grilled often for myself, but most days, I ended up at Momma and Daddy's for supper, just to spend time with them. Sheryl and her little family came by sometimes, too, when she and Luke weren't working. On the nights they had late shifts, Momma kept baby Alana, and I'd often take her outside for a little adventure.

She loved feeding the chickens and watching the cattle out in the field, her laughter rising like birdsong in the evening air. We'd started keeping a garden out back, and her tiny hands were happiest in the dirt, rich with Tennessee clay and sand. I'd hand her little starts of cucumbers and squash, and she'd place them gently in the holes I dug, patting the soil with careful, deliberate joy.

Seeing the world through her eyes reminded me that there was still innocence in it. And I prayed, quietly and often, that she'd be able to hold onto that a little while longer.

After supper, I headed out to town with a Tupperware full of chili. I knocked on the door to my grandparents. I heard the familiar call of my Mamaw, "Come on in."

"You really should be keeping your door locked, Mamaw. You don't live in the middle of nowhere anymore. I could've been anyone," I reminded her…again.

"Oh, posh," she said, waving her hand. "Locked doors only keep honest people honest. Besides, I heard that old rattling truck of yours pull in the drive. I may be losing my hearing, but even I can hear that."

"I like my old rattling truck," I said, leaning down to kiss the top of her head and setting the bowl of chili on the table. "Momma and Daddy sent supper. Where's Pap?"

"He's layin' down.  He ain't feelin' too well," she said, and worry creased her brow. "His heart's givin' him trouble. He's got a doctor's appointment on Tuesday. I'm makin' him go. You know how stubborn he is."

I got a bowl out of the cabinet and began fixing Mamaw a helping of chili. "Well, you sit down and eat," I said.

Once she was settled, I slipped into the freezer and pulled out a bowl of butter pecan ice cream, still kept just for me. I sat down beside her at the table and smiled.

"How's your sister doing?" Mamaw asked. "We miss her. Don't get to see her near enough. Though we saw that baby girl the other day. I can't believe how big she's gotten."

"Oh, you know how Sher is.  She's always working.  But I'll tell her you asked about her and remind her to come visit soon."

"That'd be nice. I miss you both. I wish you were still little and under my feet," she said, her eyes drifting toward some quiet memory.

"Me too, Mam. Me too," I murmured, placing my hand over her fragile one.

While we ate, we talked about work and church.  They'd started attending a church out in town, closer to home. They liked it fine, but I could tell they missed the one they'd gone to my whole life. Mamaw's face lit up when she told me their old pastor had come to visit. I could see how much it lifted her spirit.

"Are you still keeping your journals?" I asked.

"I am, sweetie. Helps me keep track of things. I forget more and more these days, it seems."

"I think I'm gonna start one myself," I said. "Was planning to stop by the store after I leave here and pick one up."

"Don't bother with that," she said, rising slowly from her chair. She grabbed her walker and made her way to the desk by the window. Opening a drawer, she pulled out a leather-bound book, just like the ones she always used.

"I've got an extra one right here. You take it. When I pick up some more for myself, I'll grab you another. You'll have those pages filled before you know it."

She sat back down, opened the front cover, and pulled a pen from the drawer. With slow, careful handwriting, she began to write something on the inside.

When I stood to leave, she tucked the journal and pen into my hands.

Before I left, I slipped Mamaw's old journal quietly back onto the shelf above her desk, the same spot she always kept them. Right between the brown one with the frayed binding and the green one with the little flower on the spine.

She never mentioned it, and neither did I.

When I stood to leave, she tucked the journal and pen into my hands.

"You be careful, baby," she said, her voice soft. "I'll see you soon. And if the Lord takes me before then, I'll meet you in the sky."

It was something she'd always said. To others, it might've sounded morbid, but truth be told, that was just the Appalachian way, staring death square in the face and saying, I know you're coming, and that's alright.

The older I've gotten, the more I've come to look forward to just that—meeting her in the sky, arms wide and rejoicing.

"I love you, and tell Pap I love him too," I called as I waved goodbye.

She blew me a kiss, and I drove away, the rain still drizzling as I made my way home. I took the long way, winding down the backroads, savoring the slow, quiet miles. The kind of drive where you could breathe deeper.

When I finally made it home, I slipped off my boots and changed into something warm. I grabbed the journal and pen Mamaw had given me and crawled into bed. I flipped open the cover to the page she had written on.

It read:

*To my Jenny-girl,*
*Life's got a way of pulling you in all directions at once. Some days you'll feel*
*like you're holding the whole sky on your shoulders. When that happens,*
*write. Write it down, even the hard things. Especially the hard things.*
*This journal is yours now. May it hold your truths, your tears, your laughter,*
*and the pieces of your heart you're still learning to love.*
*And when the day comes that I ain't here to listen, know I'm still with you.*
*Write me letters if you need to. I'll hear them just fine.*
*Love always,*
*Mamaw Ruth*

With tears in my eyes, I turned the page and dated the top. May 1st, 2015.

*I don't know what I'm doing, not really.*
*Mamaw said to write when my heart was too full to speak. Maybe that's*
*where I am tonight, somewhere between full and silent.*
*The rain hasn't let up all day. It tapped the roof like a metronome, steady as*
*breath, and I thought of how time keeps marching even when you're standing*
*still. Alana's laugh still echoes in my ears from earlier with mud on her little*
*boots, dirt under her nails, proud as anything about the squash she "planted*
*all by herself." Lord, I hope this world is kinder to her than it has been to me.*
*I keep thinking about Mamaw's hands, how delicate they felt in mine, how*
*steady her voice was when she said, "If the Lord takes me before then, I'll*
*meet you in the sky."*
*She's preparing, and that thought stings like a bruise you forget until you*
*touch it. I'm not ready to live in a world without her.*
*Maybe this journal will help me make sense of things. Or maybe it'll just be*
*a place I can be honest without needing to make everything sound okay.*
*Either way, I'm here.*

*Trying.*
*Living.*
*Writing.*
*-Jenny*

# Chapter 23



*Journal Entry– August 2, 1971*

*The summer heat has us bubbling over like a berry pie fresh from the stove, thick and sweet. Harlan spent the day out front, helping the Miller boys from up the road piece together a doghouse for their new pup, his hammer ringing sure and steady as a church bell at noon. From the kitchen window, I could see those young'uns bracing the boards while he set each nail, sunlight glinting off every swing.*

*While he worked, I straightened his dresser drawers and came upon the prettiest surprise tucked beneath his stack of Sunday shirts: a silver locket, no larger than a thumbnail, cool and bright in my palm. No ribbon, no card, just waiting in the quiet like a secret keen to be told.*

*My first notion was to clasp it to my heart and wander off into a daydream, but a hidden gift deserves its own right moment. So I eased it back where it lay, smoothed the shirts, and shut the drawer softly. Some blessings bloom best in their own good time, the way night-blooming jasmine keeps its perfume for the dark.*

*Harlan will hand it over when he's of a mind to. Until then, I'll let that little glint rest and shine. Summer's still thick around us, and surprises, like peaches on the branch, sweeten deeper if you let them hang awhile.*

*-Ruth*

Summer rolled in with a fierce grip that year. By July, the sun beat down on the lake like a hammer on an anvil, and the humid air clung to my skin, soaking through my shirt until it felt like a second layer of flesh. Daddy and I had spent the day building a new deck for Mrs. Jenkins after some poor soul, high on dope, ran off the road and ripped the post right out from under her front porch.

Incidents like that seemed to happen more and more. Meth and heroin had laid claim to even our sleepy, little town. There wasn't a house untouched by it anymore. You could sit back and look around and see how addiction had crept in like kudzu, slow at first, then sudden and smothering. I shuddered to think how easily that could've been me. If I hadn't clawed my way out of that crowd, I might've been the girl nodding off behind the wheel, or worse. Thinking I was somehow above it would've been foolish. Addiction doesn't care who you are. It doesn't care if you're rich or poor, white or Black, Christian or pagan. It snakes its way in just the same, wrapping around the bones and refusing to let go. I thanked God every day He spared me that torment.

Dating was hard enough without all that hanging in the air. There are addicts worth loving, folks who deserve to be pulled from the depths. But those kinds of relationships take the kind of grit I no longer had to give. I'd spent too many years dragging myself out of my own darkness. I didn't have the strength to go spelunking into someone else's.

Lena-Grace, bless her heart, had taken it upon herself to find me a proper match, like it was her personal mission from the Lord. I reckon it helped keep her from dwelling too much on her own loneliness. She was still tending to her daddy, carrying a kind of guilt for daring to want a life beyond caregiving.

She introduced me to a boy from her church named Andrew. We went out a few times. He was kind, soft-spoken, always held the door, and asked about my day. Thoughtful in the way men rarely are when they're actually looking. But it didn't take long for me to see what Lena hadn't.

Andrew wasn't just searching for companionship. He was hiding.

He hadn't told a soul, not even his own kin, but it was clear as candlelight in a dark room: Andrew was gay. In a town like ours, coming out wasn't just hard; it was dangerous. The kind of truth that could get you run off a job, or whispered about at a prayer meeting.

He told me he loved God and didn't want to live in sin. I told him if he was looking for judgment, he wouldn't find it in me. I wasn't there to cast stones. I didn't even have a jury seat. I was cracked straight through, just in ways that didn't show.

We became fast friends after that. His secret stayed buried with me, tucked away like a love letter never mailed. It wasn't mine to tell.

One late afternoon after work, Andrew and Lena swung by, and we headed down to the lake. The air was thick with the kind of summer heat that clung to your skin like memory. I peeled off my oversized tee and dove straight in, the water cool and forgiving. They followed, laughing as they hit the surface, sending ripples across the stillness.

We splashed and floated, that rare kind of laughter rising up, the kind that pulls you back to childhood, before shame and sorrow learned your name.

That's when Andrew elbowed me gently and nodded toward the shore.

"Who's that guy?" he asked, voice low with mischief. "He keeps looking at you."

I turned, and there he was, a man working on a houseboat not far from shore. He was shirtless, hammer in hand, his skin golden and dripping with sweat. Hair the color of wheat with a hint of wild berry curled at the nape of his neck. He had the kind of look that made you pause, like he carried secrets and stories written in the scars of his knuckles. When his eyes met mine, something stilled inside me.

"He's handsome," Lena whispered.

"Yeah," Andrew breathed.

I glanced at Andrew, amused that Lena still hadn't picked up on what was plain to me. She lived in a world that was black and white, all straight lines and Sunday school answers.

"He is very handsome," I murmured, looking back at the stranger. He looked again, and this time, he smiled.

The spell broke when Andrew splashed me, and I lunged toward him, laughing. "I may drown you," I warned.

We spent the rest of that evening wrapped in laughter, our joy echoing across the lake.

The next day, I found myself drifting back toward the dock. I didn't see the man, and I shouldn't have cared, but something in me sagged with disappointment. It wasn't like I planned to talk to him. I just wanted to look. Maybe that would've been enough.

I walked to the little shop at the end of the pier, hoping for a cold cone to cut through the swelter. But as I pulled the door open, I bumped right into him.

This time, he wore a cut-off shirt, the sleeves gone but the story still written clear across his arms—roped with muscle, shaped by the steady rhythm of swinging a hammer day in and day out.

I knew that rhythm. Years of working alongside Daddy had carved strength into my own limbs. I wasn't some delicate thing meant for sitting pretty behind a desk. I was solid. Strong. And sometimes, in a world that praised softness above all, that made me feel like I'd missed the mark. Still, I longed to be wanted, to be seen. I wanted someone to look past the calluses and catch sight of the tender parts I rarely let show.

It's not that I wasn't pretty. I knew I was, in my own raw, untamed way. But I didn't fit the mold of beauty most men seemed to chase. My hair curled wild around my face, refusing to be tamed. My skin bore the sun's kiss, browned and freckled from long days spent shaping flower beds, hauling mulch, and mowing lawns beneath the Tennessee sky. I wasn't about to trade any of that for daintiness. I needed the weight of work in my hands. I liked watching the land shift and yield beneath my touch, proof that I'd left something better than I found it.

So when I looked up and saw him, really saw him, I never once considered he might be feeling the same things I did. My heart tripped. My pulse beat loudly in my ears. Something stirred in me, sharp and alive. Just his gaze made me acutely aware of just how much of a woman I was.

"Excuse me, darlin'," he drawled. His voice was deep, smooth as moonshine, but there was a lilt to it, drawn-out vowels that didn't belong to these hills. He was Southern, sure, but from farther down. His words didn't snap like the clipped speech of the Appalachians. They rolled slow, like molasses over biscuits.

"Oh, excuse me," I said, but didn't move.

He just stood there, smiling, like he had all the time in the world.

After a moment, I realized I was the one blocking the door. "Sorry," I added with a nervous laugh and stepped aside.

He passed by me, but then turned. "So… am I gonna see you swimming later?"

"Oh, well, I was actually planning to take my boat out fishing," I replied.

"Well, maybe I'll see you on the water," he said, raking a hand through his thick hair.

"I hope so," slipped out before I could catch it, and I felt crimson creeping up my throat.

He laughed and gave me a wink before heading back toward the construction site.

Lord help me. Summer love could make a woman foolish, no matter her age. Between the heat and that smile, I definitely needed that ice cream.

I stepped inside the store, heart still hammering, and prayed I wouldn't melt before the cone did.

Inside, the girls behind the counter were chattering about the hot guy. The older woman who ran the store, Martha, was standing behind the register, arms crossed, her tight silver curls pinned up in the same old clip she'd worn since I'd known her. She was all no-nonsense and sensible shoes, but her lipstick was always bright red, like she still had a little fight left in her.

"Now you girls don't be bothering Jesse," Martha said, her voice firm but amused. "He's got work to do. They've got that big houseboat to finish building before the end of summer."

"Where's he from?" asked the taller of the two girls behind the counter. "It's definitely not here. They don't make men like that here."

The other girl giggled.

I didn't say a word, but I listened closely as I grabbed a glass bottle of Coke and an ice cream sandwich from the freezer.

"He said somewhere in Georgia when I asked him," Martha replied, wiping her hands on a dishtowel.

"Maybe we need to go to Georgia," one of the girls joked, sending them both into a fit of laughter.

I thought to myself, *Why go to Georgia when he's right here?*, but kept that thought tucked away.

"Is that all you need?" the cashier asked.

"Just this and some crickets," I said.

I paid, grabbed a few dozen worms for fishing that evening, and started back toward my camper. As I passed the dock, the man I now knew as Jesse cast me a grin and a lazy wave. I returned it with a small one of my own and kept walking.

That evening, I untied my little johnboat from the tree out front. I'd bought it off Momma and Daddy's new neighbor, a transplant from up North who sold it for next to nothing, even though it was nearly brand new. Said he needed something bigger. Folks like him always did. Bigger house, bigger boat, bigger life. But that little johnboat suited me just fine.

I never wandered out into the open water. I liked to keep close to the edges, where the coves curled in like quiet pockets of time. That's where the fish bit best, and the world felt still enough to hear your own thoughts.

I drifted to my favorite fishing spot and tied off. The sun was dipping low, casting everything in gold and shadow. I hadn't been there long when I noticed movement around the bend, a kayak slipping through the water with ease. Jesse.

He raised his hand in greeting, that same easy smile lighting up his face. And just like before, something in me stirred.

Lord help me, I could not be around this man and stay sensible.

"What's biting?" he asked.

"Nothing yet, but I haven't been here long," I told him.

"Well, maybe you'll have some luck now that I'm here," he said, a glint of mischief in his eyes.

Raising an eyebrow, I replied, "I'm sure I didn't need any luck."

He let out a laugh, smooth as silk.

"So what brings a Georgia boy to Tennessee?" I asked.

"How do you know I'm from Georgia?" he drawled. "You checkin' up on me?"

"Ha, no. I overheard the girls in the store chatting about you today. You had them all out of sorts," I said.

He shook his head. "Mrs. Martha really could use some better help. Those girls are always gossiping about something every time I go in there."

"Well, you really can't blame them. You are something to talk about."

*Had I really just said that out loud?*

He just laughed again, melting me like butter.

"So, you know where I'm from. Can I at least know your name?"

I smiled. "Jenny. Jenny Thompson."

"Nice to officially meet you, Jenny Thompson. I'm Jesse Marlow," he said, taking off his hat and placing it over his heart in a grand, mock-southern gesture.

I laughed, and right then, I got my first bite of the evening.

We sat there long into the night, trading stories about our lives—where we came from, the folks who raised us, the work that filled our days. When I told him I worked in landscaping and construction with Daddy, he didn't blink. No surprise, no awkward pause. Just a quiet nod, like it made perfect sense.

Now I understand why. The kind of work a woman does doesn't make her less. It might roughen her hands or steady her stance, but it doesn't strip her of grace. It doesn't dim her tenderness or her worth. If anything, it proves both can exist side by side—softness and strength, grit and gentleness.

By the time I glanced at the clock, it was pushing two in the morning.

"I've got to be getting in," I said, reluctant. "I've got to be up early for work, and I'm sure you do too."

"I do," he said, "but this was worth it."

He paddled off toward his uncle's houseboat, where he was staying, and I headed back to my camper.

"I'll be seeing you soon, Jenny Thompson," he called into the night.

And I made my way to bed with a smile on my face, feeling like a girl in the middle of her own summer novel.

He kept me feeling like that all summer long, like I was something rare and worth holding on to. We spent most every evening together, our laughter drifting out over the water like smoke from a slow-burning fire. It didn't take long before I found myself wrapped in his arms, the kind of hold that makes you forget where the world ends and you begin. Jesse had this easy way about him, like he'd walked straight out of some half-sung country song, all slow smiles and sun-warmed hands. He didn't just charm his way into my heart… and my bed, he waltzed right in and made himself at home. And Lord help me, I let him.

By the time July was done blistering the skin off our backs, I was all but convinced he might be the one. The ache I'd carried inside me for years, that hollow space left behind by boys who took and never gave back, felt softer, quieter, when he was near. Jesse made me believe in something again, something that looked a lot like love.

One weekend, with both our jobs on pause and the sun high in a cloudless sky, we loaded up a cooler and took Jesse's uncle's pontoon out onto the lake. The boat creaked underfoot like an old front porch, and we spent the day skimming the water's surface, waterskiing and lounging in the golden stretch of afternoon. The kind of day that seeps into your bones and makes you forget the world ever held sorrow.

After one run on the skis, I hauled myself back up onto the deck, dripping and breathless. My arms burned in that good, worked-over kind of way. I reached for a towel and started to wrap it around my waist, the familiar instinct kicking in. Years of never quite feeling right in my own skin made me shrink without thinking. I wasn't the kind of woman men looked at twice on magazine racks or billboards. I had muscles in my arms and thighs that had never seen the inside of a thigh gap. I had stretch marks on my hips and freckles where the sun kissed me too long.

But before I could tuck the towel tight, Jesse reached out and caught my arm. "Just come here," he said, his voice low and steady.

I hesitated, flushing. "I'm not hiding," I lied, eyes darting toward the cooler, the lake, anywhere but him. "It's just... this ain't exactly a swimsuit calendar body."

He stepped closer, brushing a wet curl off my cheek with his knuckle. "Jenny," he said, "I see you. I see all of you, and what I see is beautiful. You look like a woman who works for what she has, a woman who's earned every scar and curve. Your body tells a story, one worth reading slowly."

His words wrapped around me like fresh linen off the line, warm and unexpected. I blinked back the heat gathering in my throat and let the towel drop.

With him, I could breathe easier. He made me feel like I wasn't just wanted but seen. And for a girl who'd spent years trying to disappear, that was a kind of magic I hadn't dared believe in.

Our beautiful day out came to a sobering end as we headed back into the channel. The sun was beginning its slow descent, casting long shadows across the water, but it wasn't the light that changed the mood; it was the flashing blue and red on the far side of the lake.

TWRA boats and the local sheriff's department were clustered together near the bend, their motors idling low. A dive team was out, combing the deep with grim precision. They were dragging the lake, searching for a man who'd gone overboard and never come back up.

It happened more often than folks liked to admit; at least a few times a year, someone met their end that way. The lake was beautiful, sure, but it was just as quick to take as it was to give. One wrong step, one slip, one beer too many, and it became a grave dressed in blue.

As we sat there watching with our breaths held, hoping they would recover the lost, one of the divers lifted something from the water. It glinted in the fading light, slick with lake water and grime. A small object, delicate despite its long submersion.

I don't know why it caught my eye, why it stirred something deep in the pit of my stomach, but it did. Maybe it was the way the driver held it up so carefully. Something about that moment felt old, heavy with history. And for the first time all summer, the lake didn't feel like a place of escape. It felt like a mirror, and the past was starting to show through the cracks.

Jesse and I were silent as we made our way in, and the light grew softer. The boats were still hard at work when we docked. I sent up a silent prayer that they'd find him, that they'd bring his body home. At this point, there was no saving the man, but at least his family might find a sliver of peace. Closure may not raise the dead, but it can ease the burden of not knowing.

That kind of loss clings like lichen on stone. Even joy, when you find it again, carries the scent of mourning.

As we tied off the boat and gathered our things, I kept glancing back across the water, where the flashing lights still pulsed like a warning. The air felt different, thick, heavy with the weight of mortality. The laughter from earlier seemed far away now, like it belonged to someone else.

Back at the camper, Jesse held me close for a long while, neither of us saying much. The night air pressed in around us, still and knowing. In the dark, with his arms around me and my head against his chest, I thought about how easily life could turn. How water, which gave so much life and comfort, could just as quickly take it away.

# Chapter 24



*Journal Entry– October 18, 1960*

*Couldn't sleep for the flutter in my belly, might be worry, might be more.*
*Counted the days twice and still came up short.*
*I told the Lord I'll face whatever He plants in me, relief if He says "not yet,"*
*courage if He says "now." Either way, I won't run. Roots don't run.*

*-Ruth*

The dawn broke sickly yellow, like bruised fruit left too long in the sun. I woke to cicadas rasping like rusty saws and to the hollowness of Jesse's absence. Outside, he and the crew were laying the last coats of paint on the houseboat they'd conjured from summer sweat and salvaged pine, nailing on trim like a coffin's final brass. Soon, that project would float away, and I wondered what shoreless job his uncle would stake him to next.

The sheriff's cruisers were gone, their strobing blues drowned by daylight, and the lake had already rearranged its face into placid innocence. No hint remained that it had swallowed a man whole only hours before. A chill threaded the air, autumn's first teeth, and I knew the dam keepers would soon bleed the water down, bearing whatever sins it had kept beneath its green tongue. The thought rolled my stomach. I lurched to the rail and emptied sour dread into the reeds below.

*I can't afford to be sick*, I told myself, wiping my mouth with the back of my hand.

That evening, we kept to the camper, the lantern between us burning low. When I asked Jesse what came after the houseboat, he merely shrugged. His life was measured in contracts he never signed; his uncle pointed, and Jesse went. I tried to imagine waking each day without a notion of where night might find me. Daddy had raised me on the promise of steady work, and I clung to that predictability like a raft.

By morning, my insides revolted again. Three days I lay captive to fatigue and nausea, drifting between nightmares and the camper roof's rainfall song. On the third afternoon, Sheryl arrived, hair pinned back tight against the lake wind, cradling a mason jar of homemade chicken soup still steaming through the lid.

"Daddy says you've been poorly," she scolded, settling onto the porch chair. I wrapped my nightshirt tighter, knees to chin, soup warming the tremor in my fingers.

Her eyes narrowed, slicing clean through me. "You sure it's a stomach bug?"

I swallowed broth. "What else would it be?"

"That's what I thought." She dug in her purse and laid a small white box on the table. The letters glared like gospel. "Take it."

My mind stuttered, *no, we'd been careful.* Except that one night the sky cracked with heat-lightning and caution melted...

Bile surged; I bolted to the rail again. When I returned, breathless, she only raised an eyebrow.

"I'll take it in the morning, if I'm still sick," I promised.

"Tomorrow, Jenny Ann." She kissed my hair, authority softened by worry, and left me with the storm rattling my ribs.

When I had to race to the bathroom the following morning as sickness rolled over me, I knew I could wait no longer. Moisture hazed the mirror, rendering my reflection ghost-thin, already half-vanished. Outside, bullfrogs traded baritone gossip while the lake tongued the shore in lazy, liquor-thick laps.

I unwrapped the test, laid it on the porcelain sink, and set my phone timer. Each second clicked loud as a hammer on bone. I braided prayers with bargains, counted heartbeats in my wrist. When the timer fell silent, the truth rose, two pink lines, bright as blood on snow.

My palm flew to the flat of my belly: warm, fragile, harboring more than just my own restless pulse. A wood thrush trilled in the sycamore, a note sharp with both warning and wonder.

*Tell him*, the bird sang. *Tell them all.*

First thing, I had to steady my lungs. I cracked the door and light flooded in; dawn laying bare Jesse's denim jacket draped across the back of a chair, laundry folded but never put away, fishing poles propped like forsaken crosses. I clutched the plastic wand until it cut crescents into my skin.

Grass slicked my feet as I stepped outside. Across the cove, the ring of hammers drifted from the houseboat. I followed the sound until I found Jesse's silhouette against the whitening sky.

It was time to break the water's surface and speak the name of what grew inside me.

I walked down to the water's edge where they had been working. I called out to him. Jesse turned and smiled, brush still dripping sage-green paint, and walked to meet me halfway across the makeshift plank. Up close, I could see freckles blooming on his nose where the sun had had its way all summer. I showed him the test without ceremony, the truth plain as a brand. The smile vanished, and he stared until the color leeched from his cheeks, then wiped his palms down his jeans as though they had suddenly begun to sweat.

"Reckon we ought to talk after quittin' time," he muttered, voice thin and polite as a stranger's. Before I could answer, he pivoted back to the boat, shoulders drawn in tight as folded wings.

That night he came to the camper, but instead of slipping off his boots and settling beside me, he lingered near the door, cap in hand, eyes sweeping anywhere but my face. I was nervous and began to fill the emptiness with conversation of cribs, Daddy still kept in the barn loft. Jesse nodded once, twice, all silent acknowledgments, and finally said he needed some air. The screen door clicked behind him. I waited until the stillness stitched itself shut behind him. He was gone.

Morning revealed his bunk stripped bare, the toolbox missing. His rust-red pickup wasn't in the gravel lot, and the near-finished houseboat tugged at its moorings like an orphan. I scanned the shoreline for his broad frame, nothing but strangers with paint on their sleeves. On the porch rail, his Georgia ball cap waited, brim cupped to catch the dew, a small, sorrow-soaked monument.

I laid a hand over my belly, listening to the solitary metronome of my own heart and wondering how two pulses might keep time in the hush he'd left behind.

By noon, the dam gates groaned open and the lake began its slow retreat, dragging secrets into the sun. I stood barefoot at the edge, minnows flickering from my shadow, and understood that Jesse, too, had ebbed away.

I thumbed through my contacts until Lena-Grace's name glowed on the screen, but I couldn't lift that purity into the tangle of my shame, not yet. Instead, I tapped Mari's number. When her warm voice answered, the words spilled out before I could catch them, fast and heavy.

"Sweet girl," she said, "a baby is always a blessing, arriving exactly when the Creator intends."

She urged me to call my sister, to circle myself with my people, and promised to visit soon. Her kindness usually lightened me, but this time her truth settled heavily in my soul. I sent Sheryl a single text, **Positive**, then crawled beneath the cover and wept. I couldn't tell whether the tears were for the child blooming inside me or for the man who had vanished, but they rose from a well that seemed without end.

Dusk found Sheryl on my porch, Luke and little Alana trailing behind. Luke led the girl to the shoreline, teaching her to skip stones. His flat rocks skated; Alana's plunked in delighted splashes. Their laughter rang up the bank like wind chimes.

Sheryl pulled a chair beside me. "You're going to be all right," she said softly. "Have you told Jesse?"

"I nodded, but the words tangled in my throat, raw and ragged.

"What did he say?"

"He's gone," I forced out, the syllables tasting like rust.

"Gone?" Her brow furrowed, confusion flickering beneath concern.

"He left. No explanation, no nothin'." My voice cracked. "Packed up and walked out."

"Oh, Jenny." She pulled me in tight, her shoulder a place I hadn't known I still needed. And just like that, the tears came again—hot, immediate, unstoppable. Proof that the well was deeper than I dared imagine, and it had cracked wide open, reminding me how much sorrow still waited beneath the surface, waiting for any excuse to rise.

I told myself through the sobs: *If the men in my life were going to drift like water, I'd become the mountain—quiet, steady, and unwilling to chase what wouldn't stay.*

By morning, the grief had settled into something dull and heavy, but I knew I had to work. Bills don't wait, and the world doesn't stop spinning just because your heart cracked a little more in the night.

I showed up early at Momma and Daddy's house to see what Daddy had lined up. He stepped onto the porch with his thermos in hand, the screen door groaning behind him like it had something to say.

"What are we doing today?" I asked, trying to sound upbeat.

He gathered me into a hug. "Not we, Peanut. You can't be doing this kind of work while you're expecting." He kissed the top of my head. "Your momma knows, so you might as well go on in and talk to her."

"How?" I began, but I already knew.

"Sheryl called last night. She was worried about you."

Anger flickered in my eyes, hurt and betrayal tangled together. How could Sheryl share my secret?

"It's all right," Daddy said, giving my arm a reassuring squeeze. We walked inside together.

We sat at the kitchen table while Momma poured coffee. Silence settled heavily between us until I finally blurted out what weighed on my heart. "What am I going to do for work? I have bills to pay, and now I've got even more responsibilities."

"Don't worry, Peanut," Daddy said. "I'm going to talk to Terry at the feed store. It'll just be temporary, until after the baby's born. Then you can come back to work with me."

It was all too much; I could only nod. Daddy kissed my forehead, wished us a good day, and headed out the door.

Momma touched my shoulder. "Go lie down in your old room and rest. There's nothing you can fix this minute. We'll figure it out."

"I'm sorry, Momma," I whispered as I walked down the hall.

She followed and sat on the edge of the bed while I slipped beneath the familiar quilt. Her voice softened. "You've nothing to apologize for, sweetheart. A baby is never a reason for shame. Life doesn't always unfold the way we planned, but that doesn't make it wrong. You are loved, and you are not alone. Daddy and I will walk every step with you. I already know you'll be a wonderful momma. Your heart has always had room enough for everyone."

Her words soothed the knot of worry coiled inside me. Momma didn't speak her love often, but when she did, it wrapped around me and held me tight. I closed my eyes and let the exhaustion pull me under. *I would be okay. We would be okay.*

When I finally surfaced from uneasy sleep, the sun was already staining the curtains a lazy, tea-colored yellow. Past noon. My stomach lurched, but my hand groped first for the phone on the nightstand.

I scrolled till I saw Jesse's name. The call rang five times before his voicemail cut in with that lazy drawl, "Leave it, I'll get back to ya." I waited through the beep, breath snagging.

"Jesse, it's me… Please call. I just… just need to hear your voice."

I hung up, stared at the ceiling, and dialed again. Straight to voicemail. A third time, and the phone kicked me out even quicker, as though the universe itself had grown impatient with my pleading.

***Could you at least talk to me? I don't expect you to stay***, I thumbed, the words wobbling in the message bubble. Hesitated. Sent.

The read receipt never came.

A dull ache uncoiled behind my ribs. I'd always known Jesse drifted like river fog. One job, one season, then gone, but some foolish part of me had still believed I could anchor him. Maybe it wasn't fair to try. If a woman could choose not to carry a child, a man, I suppose, could choose not to stay for one. That was its own sort of equality.

Fine then. The child would be mine alone, and I would stand steady as bedrock.

It wasn't the life I'd pictured. I'd wanted a husband laughing in the doorway, chickens scratching beneath a line of sun-bleached sheets, but I'd long since learned God's plans don't always match the sketches we keep folded in our pockets. All summer I'd skipped church, dizzy with new love; now the hollow where prayer belonged yawned wide and cold.

I pulled on jeans, slid behind the wheel, and drove to Mamaw's. Before the screen door slapped shut, her voice rolled through the house in low, rhythmic waves, "Father, lay Your hand on my people…" She'd felt the tremor in the spirit already.

She turned from her kneeler, eyes widening. "Oh, baby, what's wrong?"

Words spilled right there in the little hallway: the two pink lines, Jesse's vanishing truck, the fear that gnawed my sleep. She steered me to the kitchen table, the family's confessional booth since time immemorial.

"I knew something was wrong," she breathed, folding my hands into hers. "Been praying since dawn without knowing why, just knowing I would need the Lord's strength today."

She gathered me near, and her prayer poured over me like warm rain, soaking straight to the marrow. I thought of all the unseen blessings still sprouting from prayers spoken by mothers, grandmothers, and their mothers before, whose names were fading from headstones. Folks talk plenty about generational curses; they forget the blessings woven into time by women on their knees pleading with the Father.

Boot-steps thudded down the hall as she finished with a gentle, "In the precious name of Jesus." Papaw Harlan appeared, flannel sleeves rolled, eyes sharp as crows' wings.

"What's happened here?" he asked, voice gravelly from a lifetime of sawmill dust.

Mamaw glanced at me, and I nodded. Her jaw set. "Jenny's expecting, and that scoundrel boy lit out before dawn, too yellow to face what he's sown."

The truth stung, but I let it stand. Papaw's face flushed dark. He paced, fists opening and closing like traps.

"A real man don't turn tail when the harvest he planted starts sproutin'. I've seen what runnin' does, seen children grow up chasing ghosts because their daddy couldn't shoulder his own name. A man that leaves his blood behind ought to feel that shame every sunrise till judgment comes."

His breaths came quick, anger rattling inside him like loose nails in a coffee can.

"Harlan, hush now," Mamaw soothed. "Getting riled won't mend a thing."

He opened his mouth for another broadside, then clutched his chest. Color drained from his weather-beaten face. Mamaw lunged, catching his elbow as he sagged toward a chair.

"Jesus," she whispered, and the room held its breath. Her earlier prayer still hovered like a promise. She had been right; she would need the Lord's strength that day.

# Chapter 25



*Journal Entry– December 12, 1974*

*There are seasons when everything quiets at once, when the wind seems to hush its howling, and even the birds stop their singing. This week has felt like that. Not sad exactly, just... still. Like the world is holding its breath. Harlan's been working late again. Says they're shorthanded at the mill. I believe him, mostly. But sometimes I catch a look in his eyes, like he's somewhere else. Like he's carrying something I can't see.*

*-Ruth*

I dialed 911 as Mamaw wiped Papaw's brow and urged him to drink from her glass of water. I could hear her praying under her breath while I spoke to the dispatcher.

"They're on the way," I told her, hanging up, grateful they had moved into town and were closer to the hospital now.

I called Daddy to let him know what was happening, and within minutes, the ambulance pulled into the driveway. I drove Mamaw behind it, my tires barely keeping pace with my racing thoughts. The sirens wailed ahead of us, and Mamaw never stopped praying. I whispered my own silent plea, not just for Papaw, but for her too. Her face was pale, lips tight with fear, her strength flickering like a candle in a draft.

We arrived at the hospital in no time. Mamaw rushed through the sliding doors, faster than I'd seen her move in years. There was nothing left to do now but wait.

Daddy arrived shortly after, then Sheryl and Momma. We all sat in the waiting room, a silence so heavy it felt like it could be sliced clean through. Time stretched thin.

After what felt like forever, a doctor finally emerged.

"Mrs. Thompson?" he asked, and Mamaw rose quickly. "If you'd like to come with me…"

He led her into Papaw's room while the rest of us sat, hearts thudding, breath caught in our throats.

When Mamaw emerged, her shoulders bowed under a mixed weight of relief and exhaustion.

"He's had a heart attack," she murmured, voice steady, but the tremor in her hands told the rest. "They've got him stable. He'll need to stay a few days, but Lord willing, he'll be able to come home soon."

Relief flooded the waiting room, and we all let out a collective sigh. Daddy and Momma hurried off to gather a bag of clothes, toiletries, and Papaw's favorite pillow so Mamaw could keep vigil at his bedside. Sheryl and I lingered, uncertain of our next move, until we each wrapped Mamaw in a hug that felt both too small and somehow all we had to give.

Stepping outside, the late-afternoon light felt harsh after the hospital's muted glow. I could mend a broken fence or soothe a scraped knee, but I could not stitch a heart back together, hers or his, and that helplessness hurt worse than any wound I could see.

Sheryl said, "Come on, let's go get some ice cream."

So I climbed into her car, and we headed to the little drive-in just down the road. The place was done up like a vintage diner—chrome trim, checkered floors, and girls in pink-and-white 1950s uniforms skating out to the cars. Doo-wop music bopped from a speaker by the menu board.

It was the best spot around to get a cone, but it wasn't just the ice cream that pulled at something in us. When we were little, Papaw used to sneak us bowls of vanilla right before bedtime, always saying, "Don't tell your Mamaw," though she'd already be in the kitchen fixing sprinkles before we'd taken the first bite. It was their kind of mischief, sweet, small rule-breaking that made us feel like the most loved kids in the world.

Now, years later, we sat there in Sheryl's car, eating in companionable silence, still unsure of what to say. But the ice cream helped. Somehow it always had.

She was the first to break the stillness. "Have you decided what doctor you're going to see?"

"No… I really haven't gotten that far," I said. "Honestly, I think the news might've given Papaw a heart attack." I meant it only halfway as a joke, but the words stuck bitter in my throat. I couldn't shake the image of his face twisted in anger, how quickly it had come on. I remembered Daddy's quiet warning about how violent Papaw used to be when they were young. I'd struggled to picture that before, but that day, I'd seen a glimpse of it. The rage simmering under his skin. It chilled me.

"You did not give him a heart attack," Sheryl said firmly. "It's all those Cokes and snack cakes he sneaks behind Mamaw's back. That's what's done it."

"You're probably right." I gave a half-smile. "Still, I haven't really had the chance to think through what I'm going to do next. Daddy is supposed to talk to Terry down at the feed store, see if I can work there until after the baby comes. He doesn't think I should keep landscaping while I'm pregnant."

"He's right," she said. "There's no reason to be lazy, sure, but you don't need to be out there lifting heavy stuff and pushing yourself either."

"Ugh, I know he's right," I groaned. "But I might die of boredom working behind a counter."

Relief curled into a smile, and Sheryl caught it, her expression shifting to meet mine.

"Well, I know you're sad about Jesse, and I'm sorry for that," she said gently. "But I'm excited you're having a baby. Alana's going to need cousins, and I need a little niece or nephew to spoil."

"I don't think I'm ready," I admitted out loud for the first time.

"No one ever is," she said matter-of-factly, and I knew she was right. Even if I were married, with a house and a live-in maid, I still wouldn't feel ready. There was nothing left to do but trust God. I had to believe He knew what I needed, even if I didn't yet.

When I got back to my camper that night, Lena and Andrew were waiting on the steps.

"Were you not going to tell us?" Andrew asked, bold as ever.

I froze, unsure which thing he meant. The baby? Jesse leaving? Papaw's heart attack? Maybe all of it. The truth tangled inside me, and I didn't know where to start. So, I just began to bawl.

They rushed to me, ushering me inside, arms around my shoulders, no judgment in their touch. Once we were settled, I told them everything. The whole mess.

"I'm sorry, you guys," I said through hiccupped breaths. "I've been an awful friend. I got so caught up chasing love that I forgot how much I already had. I forgot how much I love you. How much I need you both."

Lena leaned in and held my face in her hands. "Jenny Ann, you don't have to earn our love by being perfect. We're your people. That means we stand by you, especially when things fall apart."

Andrew nodded, softer than I'd ever seen him. "You couldn't lose us if you tried."

I needed them desperately, more than I'd even realized. And now I knew: no relationship would ever be worth losing the ones who kept me grounded.

Some roots weren't meant to be pulled up, not even for love.

Papaw came home a week later, and we all pulled together to get him settled in. A hospital bed now sat in the corner of their little living room, alongside a recliner to help him stand. It was strange seeing the house rearranged that way, like the furniture itself had shifted to make room for something we weren't ready to accept.

We'd all agreed to take turns visiting and sitting with them for a while until Papaw was mended.

There wasn't anything good about what had happened, but if there was a silver lining, it was that the crisis had kept us so busy, so focused on helping, that Jesse's absence hadn't been able to drown me. The heartache was still there, a quiet, persistent ache, but it didn't crush me the way it might have. Life was moving forward whether I was ready or not, and I had bigger things to worry about just then, than a man who didn't have the courage to stay.

That following week, I started my first shift at the feed store. It wasn't bad. Each day, I saw familiar faces, some smiling, some grumpy, all carrying stories with them. Mr. Ford, who'd been Momma and Daddy's neighbor my whole life, came in one afternoon, after one of his cows refused to take her calf.

"Come on out and see her, Jenny," he said. "She's a little speckled beauty."

I told him I'd bring Alana by. She loved climbing the fence behind Daddy's land to moo at the cows like she was one of them.

The door chimed again. I looked past Mr. Ford, and there he was. Jesse's uncle. My stomach dropped.

"You alright, Miss Jenny?" Mr. Ford asked, concerned.

"I'm okay," I lied. "Just a little queasy."

He nodded knowingly. "Renee swore by ginger candies when she was carryin' our oldest, Tommy." He smiled kindly. I wasn't even showing yet, but of course, people in town were already talking. That's just life in a small place. Nothing remains secret for long, but I didn't care. I refused to feel ashamed for having loved someone, no matter how it ended.

After Mr. Ford left, Jesse's uncle stepped up to the counter. I could see something in his eyes, guilt, maybe. Or regret.

"Jenny," he said quietly, "how are you holding up?"

"I've been better," I replied honestly. "How's Jesse?"

"Honestly? I don't know. I just heard… about the baby. Is that why he left?"

"I guess so." I shrugged, but my throat tightened.

"I'm real sorry about that," he said. "He wasn't raised that way. But all that runnin'… it catches up with a man eventually. You gotta grow up sometime. I know it ain't much, but if you need anything, just tell me or the missus. We'll help however we can."

Tears burned in my eyes, but I just nodded. I rang up his order and handed him his change.

His words meant more than I expected them to. But still, I knew I wouldn't be calling in any favors. If Jesse didn't want to be part of this baby's life, then I'd be family enough for the both of us.

Weeks ticked by. Day in and day out, life settled into a new kind of normal.

I'd decided to see the same doctor Sheryl had used over in Millbranch. He was a kind older man with soft eyes and a voice that never rushed, the sort who made you feel safe just by being in the room. He told me everything would be all right, and somehow, I almost believed him.

He never asked where the baby's father was or looked at me like I ought to feel ashamed. I figured he'd seen his fair share of girls like me, young women left holding the weight of a decision made by two, or worse, those who'd never been given a choice to begin with. It was a sad truth, but truth all the same. The kind that settled deep in your bones, even when you tried not to let it.

A new rhythm began to shape my days. I worked at the feed store, then spent most evenings with Mamaw and Papaw. While she made sure he ate and bathed, I helped clean or kept her company. Sometimes, I'd curl up in my favorite chair and read, just being nearby in case they needed anything.

After finishing a baby book I'd borrowed from the library, I wandered over to Mamaw's bookshelf to find something else. My fingers drifted along the spines of her journals, row after row of them, each marked with dates. A quiet record of a well-witnessed life. I'd gotten more serious about keeping one of my own since I'd found out I was expecting. Writing helped settle the whirlwind inside me, made it all feel less chaotic.

As I traced my hand across Mamaw's journals, I noticed a gap. The years moved steadily along like fence posts lining a road, until suddenly, nothing. A piece of time was simply missing.

I paused. It wasn't the journal she had accidentally placed in the box for Sheryl and me. I'd already slipped that one back where it belonged, nestled among the other journals. No, this was different. The gap was from the spring of 1972, and it caught in my throat like a hitch in a song you know by heart.

I stared at the empty space, wondering. The silence of that absent year pressed against me like a held breath—still, tight, expectant. That was the year Andrea Campbell went missing.

The realization settled in with a slow, creeping chill. My fingers hovered over the blank space on the shelf as if the journal might suddenly materialize under my touch. I told myself it was probably just a coincidence, or maybe the notebook had been misplaced during the move. But the air in the room shifted the way it had that day in the woods, the way it always did when I remembered.

In that moment, I recalled the weight of those first few days after we found her, how even the air had felt changed, charged with something eerie and unfinished. The way the wind whispered through the trees, as if it carried secrets too heavy for any one person to hold. The way silence had crept into our home, into our conversations, into our very bodies.

I shook my head, pressing my palm flat against my belly, grounding myself in the now. I wouldn't let myself get pulled under again. Not into that shadow. Not with a baby on the way. There was too much light ahead to go chasing ghosts.

It had been nearly seven months since Papaw's heart attack, and he still spent most of his days propped up in bed. Even walking the short distance to the bathroom left him breathless. The family and I were still taking shifts, helping where we could and soaking up every last minute with the man we loved.

Even Daddy was spending more time by his side. Most days, he sat beside Papaw and read aloud from old western paperbacks with cracked spines and yellowed pages. It had been good for both of them. Watching Papaw slowly fade had leeched the anger and resentment from Daddy's heart. He wasn't holding onto the whiskey-scented beatings anymore. Instead, he clung to the man who once taught him to bait a hook, the man who bought him his first tool belt, the same belt that still hung on a pegboard in Daddy's garage like a worn-out relic of boyhood.

I was showing now, my belly rounding out beneath thick winter sweaters, and I was grateful not to be out pulling brush or hauling weeds that season. Instead, I spent my evenings clearing space in my little camper, making room for the baby on the way.

Like Sheryl and Luke, I had decided to wait until the birth to learn the baby's gender. There was something quietly reverent in that choice, something beautiful about letting the mystery grow alongside the baby. It wasn't about being old-fashioned or dramatic. It was about learning patience, about trusting that the biggest answers in life don't always come in advance. And honestly, I wanted that first cry to be followed by the first knowing. A moment unspoiled by planning or pink-and-blue onesies.

Momma and Daddy had tried to convince me to move back in with them for a while, but I'd been stubborn. Maybe even selfish. I wanted time with my baby, just us. A little space carved out for the two of us to begin something new, on our own terms. Still, I promised I'd stay with them for the first couple of weeks after the birth. Momma would be there to help, and Sheryl swore I'd be glad for the extra hands when the sleepless nights came. I believed them.

One evening after work, I was folding tiny baby blankets and tucking them into the little bunk room in my camper when the phone rang. The ghosts I had refused to chase, it seemed, had decided to chase me instead.

I glanced at the screen. A number I didn't recognize. I figured it might be the doctor's office confirming my next appointment, so I answered.

"Hello, is this Jenny Thompson?" a man asked from the other end of the line.

"It is," I said cautiously.

"I know you may not remember me; we only met a few times. It's Shay- Shaffer Jordan. I used to be a cop in Pedoux. I worked the Andrea Campbell case."

A knot twisted in my gut. "I remember," I said softly, the image of him flickering in my memory. The young officer who'd asked me questions that day. Nervous. Gentle. Like he didn't quite know how to carry the weight of what he was investigating.

"Well… I was wondering if I could talk to you about that day in the woods," he said.

I sat down slowly, the phone pressing warm against my cheek. Part of me wanted to say no. I wasn't sure I could do this, drag myself back through that day, those emotions. Especially not now, with everything else hanging so delicately in place.

But the truth was, I still had questions. I still wanted justice for Andrea, even if I wasn't sure what that meant anymore.

The silence dragged on until he said gently, "Jenny?"

"Yeah," I breathed. "I can meet with you. The café on Main?"

"That's fine. I don't live in Pedoux anymore, but I'll be in town tomorrow. Could you meet then?"

"Yeah, I get lunch at noon," I told him.

"Okay. I'll see you then," he said.

"Okay," I replied and hung up.

I set the phone on the counter and pressed both palms to the cool laminate, waiting for my pulse to slow. Outside, dusk had already swallowed the campground. The wind off the lake rattled the roof, sounding like skeletal fingers drumming a warning.

A single lamp cast a honeyed pool of light across the bunk room. In it, the baby blankets lay folded like soft promises. I laid a hand over my belly and felt the faintest flutter, life stirring in the very place grief had once taken root.

Tomorrow, the past would sit across from me in a corner booth at the Main Street Café.

I clicked off the lamp, leaving only moonlight and resolve to guide me into the night.

# Chapter 26



*Journal Entry– March 13, 1974*

*The hardest nights are the ones when nothing actually happens, no slam of the screen door, no drunken shouting in the yard, only a hush so deep it rings in my ears like a warning bell. It's the not knowing that gnaws at a woman. What wind is gathering beyond the dark tree line? What shadow is stretching its hands toward her children?*
*I told the Lord I can face a storm if He'll just let me see its lightning first, but He seldom shows His cards. So I sit here mending socks by lamplight, heart beating like a trapped bird, praying over unnamed dangers. Maybe that's the test of faith: to step onto the porch at dawn, breathe the chill air, and trust that daylight will keep watch over whatever darkness would not speak its name.*

*-Ruth*

The bell above the café door chimed a timid announcement as I stepped into a wash of warm air laced with coffee, butter, and last night's fried catfish. Morning rain streaked the plate-glass windows, turning Main Street into a watercolor of red-brick storefronts and puddled asphalt. In a corner booth beneath a fading Coca-Cola clock, a man I recognized, though time had shifted his features. He waited with his left hand wrapped around a chipped mug, his right thumb drumming a nervous rhythm on a leather notebook. Shaffer Jordan.

He rose when I approached, and the years between us settled into sharp relief. His good looks were understated, weathered, not polished. Broader shoulders, faint crow's feet, quiet confidence that spoke of storms endured and lessons earned. Dark-brown hair, framed moss-green eyes alive with equal parts curiosity and apology. A shadow of stubble edged his jaw, and when he smiled a dimple eased angles that might have been too severe. I realized then that he must have been young when I found Andrea's body.

A slate-gray field jacket rested over a chambray shirt, sleeves rolled just high enough to show forearms freckled from miles spent in the sun. Nothing about him clamored for attention, yet a steady presence radiated from the sure way he stood, the attentive tilt of his head, the firm gentleness of his handshake. He wore authority and kindness like twin weights balanced perfectly in each palm.

I eased a hand over my belly, half habit, half reassurance, and slid into the booth opposite him. The cracked vinyl hissed, releasing trapped air and older memories. A server with her hair twisted into a sleek ponytail flashed a quick smile as she glided past with a tray of steaming biscuits.

"Jenny," Shaffer said, voice soft yet edged with relief, as though he hadn't been sure I'd come.

"Mr. Jordan, it's been a long time." My own voice quivered with nerves.

"Please, call me Shay."

His gaze dropped to my rounded middle, then back. "You look… well," he offered, carefully choosing a word that wouldn't trespass on deeper things.

"Healthy as I can be," I replied, folding clammy hands on the tabletop, pretending to study the laminated menu though I already knew what I wanted.

A heavy quiet stretched between us, one weighted by shared tragedy, until Shay cleared his throat and opened the notebook.

"Before we dive in," he began, "thank you for meeting me. I know this can't be easy."

"No, I wouldn't call it easy," I said, steadying my breath. "I've carried that day with me for almost a decade. Might as well see where it's leading. Are you still working the case after all this time?"

"Sort of," he admitted. "I'm not a cop anymore, decided the badge wasn't in my blood. I'm an investigative journalist now. But this case never let me go, so I kept track of it. I wanted to reach out sooner, but I hated the thought of dragging you back."

He hesitated, thumb worrying the notebook's edge. "I reached out because I remembered how much it shook you, Jenny, how you kept pressing for answers even when the adults tried to steer you away. Those same images are still burned into my mind, and I figured they must haunt you, too."

"Why now?" I asked, though part of me already knew because the weight of certain memories never lightens.

Shay's jaw tightened. "Because the case never stopped breathing, no matter how many fresh stories I chased. The evidence lab just flagged something new, and the moment I heard, I thought of you. I kept seeing you back then—sixteen, stubborn, shaking, but still insisting on the truth. I figured if the images still woke me up at night, they had to be visiting you, too."

"They do," I admitted, voice unsteady. "Some nights I dream I'm back in those woods, and the shadows won't stay still. Other nights it's just the smell of damp earth, but I wake up gasping all the same."

He nodded, relief flickering beneath his concern, as if my confession proved he wasn't alone in the haunting. "I didn't want to reopen old wounds," he said, "but I also couldn't keep this to myself. You deserved to know."

"Then let's see it," I whispered, bracing for whatever came next.

Shay flipped the notebook fully open. Inside, a photograph lay beneath a clear sleeve: a heart-shaped locket, tarnished, half its chain snapped like a broken promise, waiting to tell us what the night still wouldn't.

"This was recovered some months back," Shay said. "A volunteer dive team was searching for a drowning victim near the Old Wilson landing. They found this lodged under a fallen cypress log. Andrea's mother always said her daughter wore a locket, but we never found it back then."

A memory flashed, sunlight glinting off something small in a diver's hand on the lake that day with Jesse. The room tilted; color drained from my face.

"Jenny, you okay?" Shay asked, concern softening his voice.

I nodded just as the waitress reappeared. We placed minimal orders: coffee for him, water with lemon, and a house salad for me. Once she left, Shay continued.

"According to my source, Andrea's mom confirmed it looks like her daughter's. Whatever picture was inside is long gone, but there's an initial etched on the back. Her mom swears she never knew it was there, if the locket truly belonged to Andrea."

He hesitated, as if weighing what else to reveal.

"Back in '05, the coroner told us those raspberry canes worked like a natural fence," he said. "Thorns kept scavengers out, Andrea's bones and even bits of cloth stayed right where you found them."

I nodded, remembering the briars snagging my sleeves, the fruit bruised and bleeding sweet juice underfoot.

"Which means," Shay went on, tapping the image, "if this locket was hers, it should've been in that thicket with her. Somebody took it, or it was never there in the first place, before time and thorns locked everything down."

He paused, letting the implication settle. "That's why this little piece of metal matters so much."

Outside, a passing truck hurled water against the curb. The baby nudged beneath my ribs, a tiny drumbeat of future life, while the past coiled tighter around us.

"Tell me the rest," I said, steady as I could manage. The air between us felt thick as river silt, but I braced myself to wade in.

"An 'H' is etched on the back," Shay said, sliding the photo closer. "Because of that, the police leaned toward thinking the locket wasn't Andrea's. But I can't get past one obvious name…" he paused, "your grandfather's. Harlan."

A thick hush settled between us, heavy as the fog that rolled across the mountain.

"You can't believe…" I began, the word tangled in denial.

"I don't know what to believe," he admitted, voice careful. "But the thought won't let go. Back when we canvassed the town, a few folks mentioned your grandpa's younger days, said he was a man about town. Hard drinking, prone to stepping out on your Mamaw. They insisted he wasn't the man you probably know now."

Daddy's old warning thundered in my ears. I recalled certain journal entries I'd read of Mamaw's, half-phrases, midnight worries, committed to paper. Papaw Harlan had a past, no doubt. But Andrea had been only seventeen, and he would've been in his thirties.

The numbers alone sent a chill down my spine.

Shay watched me rub my arms as though I could wipe the gooseflesh away.

"Listen," he said, lowering his voice, "I'm not here to drag your family's name through the mud. I just can't ignore any thread, no matter how thin."

I nodded, swallowing the lump in my throat. "If you think an 'H' points to Papaw, you'll need more than an old rumor. The man can hardly walk now, and Mamaw still keeps his Bible on the nightstand."

"I understand," Shay said. "That's why I wanted to talk to you first. See if there's anything, letters, photographs, stories, you might remember that could help rule him out. Or in." He held my gaze a beat longer. "Either way, Andrea deserves the truth."

I traced a fingertip around the rim of my water glass, condensation pooling beneath. "I'll look," I said quietly. "But you have to promise me something."

"Name it."

"No blindsiding my family. They've carried enough."

"Scout's honor," he replied, hand to heart.

The waitress arrived with coffee refills; Shay shook his head, but I let her top off my water. As she left, he leaned forward. "If you're willing, I'd like to keep you in the loop. I'm filing a request for the dive team's full report, but small-town departments move slow. Could I text you if anything comes up?"

"Call or text anytime," I told him.

The corner of his mouth lifted. "And if you need anything, case-related or otherwise, you have my number now."

His sincerity wrapped around me like a knit shawl. "Thank you," I said, surprised by how much the offer steadied me. "I... I'm doing this alone." I rubbed the place where the baby rested within me.

*Why had I told him that?*

Shay's eyes darkened with understanding. "I'm sorry. You deserve better than that."

"Life moves the way it moves," I said with a shrug, though my voice betrayed a tremor. "Bills keep coming, babies keep growing."

He nodded, sliding the photo back into the notebook. "We'll find answers, Jenny. For Andrea, and for you."

Outside, under the café's striped awning, he hesitated. "Take care of yourself, and that little one. I'll be in touch soon."

"I'll be waiting."

Shay's footsteps faded down the sidewalk, swallowed by the hush that follows rain, and I found myself standing alone. The air still smelled of damp asphalt and coffee, but the rest of the street felt strangely hollow, like the whole town had crept inside me and was waiting for me to breathe again.

The baby fluttered inside me, a small insistence that the future was more than an idea; it was bones and heartbeat, skin knitting itself cell by cell. Yet all I could taste was the metallic tang of the past rising up like well water—cold, unbidden, impossible to push back down.

An H on a locket. Harlan.

I pictured Papaw in the hospital bed, breath rattling, hands that once swung a hammer now trembling just to lift a spoon. Could that same man have lured a seventeen-year-old into brambles and left her for the raspberries to guard? The idea crawled across my skin, leaving welts of doubt.

But memory is a trick mirror: tilt it one way, you see the grandfather who read us books and whittled whistles; tilt it another, and maybe, just maybe, you glimpse the parts that Mamaw kept silent. Harlan Thompson, age thirty-three, drunk on Saturday nights, fists more familiar with woodgrain bar tops than church pews. A man about town, folks said. A man the town chose to forget.

I reached into my purse for the truck keys, and the rain began again, soft, persistent. I stepped into it, letting the water bead on my hair, cooling the fever that had risen behind my eyes. Somewhere beyond those clouds lay a sun I couldn't yet see, but it was enough to know it was there. Shay's words echoed in my ears, a door to answers or to heartbreak, maybe both.

I climbed into the truck, the engine growling awake, wipers pushing aside the fresh sheen on the windshield. Heading home, I told myself I'd search for letters, photographs, anything that could clear or condemn the man whose blood runs in mine.

I lay awake long after midnight, sheets twisted at my ankles, sleep nowhere in sight. My mind ran circles around the same impossible thought: Papaw, the man who used to sneak extra chocolate into our milk, could he really be a killer? The memory of his anger the day he learned Jesse had left the baby and me flickered behind my eyes—brief, bright, unsettling.

On impulse, I reached for my phone and typed: *Are you awake?*

Shay answered almost at once: **Yeah, everything okay?**

*I'm fine,* I wrote back. *Just one question.*

**Shoot.**

*I heard a rumor years ago, but no one ever confirmed it. Was Andrea pregnant?*

Ticks of silence. Then: **She was. How come?**

*Trying to make sense of things,* I replied, only half the truth.

**I get it.** A pause. **You doing all right otherwise?**

*I will be. Sorry for texting so late.*

**Don't worry; I couldn't sleep either.**

**It was good seeing you today, even under the circumstances.**

*Yeah. Its nice knowing I'm not the only one who still carries Andrea with them,* I admitted.

The truth of it settled warm in my heart. Somehow, this man, practically a stranger, understood me better than people who'd known me since childhood.

**I was only twenty-one when you found her,** he texted back. **Never thought I'd face something like that in a small town. It's stayed with me.**

*Me too.*

A lull stretched. I thought he'd drifted off when another bubble popped up.

**I'm in town one more day. Planning to drive by Andrea's old house and the school, see it with fresh eyes. Want to ride along? Only if you're free.**

*I've got a prenatal appointment in Millbranch in the morning,* I wrote. *But I'm free afterward.*

**Perfect. My hotel's in Millbranch. I'll pick you up after your appointment, if you'll let me.**

*Sounds good,* I sent, surprised at how much I meant it.

Phone on the nightstand, I finally felt sleep pulling me in.

The next afternoon, I stepped out of Dr. Wheeler's office and spotted Shay idling near the curb in a charcoal-gray Ford Explorer, tires dusted red from back roads. He swung out as soon as he saw me, one hand sliding into the pocket of his jeans, the other lifting in an easy wave. Sunlight caught the flecks of gold in his eyes, and for a breath, I forgot the chill of the exam room.

He opened the passenger door, and his palm settled at the small of my back, steady, unhurried, as if guiding me was something he'd done a thousand times. The Explorer smelled faintly of sun-warmed leather and strong coffee. When the seat belt clicked across my belly, he eased the SUV onto the highway and asked, "How's everything with the baby?"

"All good," I said, smoothing the seatbelt. "Strong heartbeat, head down, running out of room."

We filled the first miles with catch-up talk, the kind of gentle inventory old acquaintances take when the years between them feel both thin and thick. I told him about my little camper by the lake, my temporary post at the feed store, how my hands itched to sink back into soil once the weather turned. He listened, nodding, as the landscape outside blurred through pines and empty corn fields.

"Labor's creeping closer every day," I admitted. "Can't lie, I'm nervous."

"You're strong," he reminded me, voice low and certain. "I saw that back then, and I see it now. You'll do great."

The words warmed me, though the knot in my stomach held tight. What I feared most was the vast, unknowable blank, pain I hadn't felt yet, days I couldn't picture. It was the same with Andrea's murder: not knowing who, or why, left too much room for shadows to sprawl.

Shay told me he'd moved to Grantham, just an hour and change from Pedoux, to chase reporting assignments, but the city left him restless. Born in a sliver of Eastridge, West Virginia, in a holler strung with honeysuckle and sagging mailboxes, he was never built for concrete. One day, he said, he hoped to trade traffic for tree frogs and start a family of his own.

"I get that," I said, watching the fields roll by. "Crowded streets make me itch. My camper's tiny, but the lake keeps its own kind of hush."

He smiled. "Quiet's worth more than square footage."

"Still," I added, palm drifting to my belly, "I'll need something bigger soon. Babies grow like weeds."

"Then we'll find you acres enough," he said, almost reflexively, as if it were already a shared plan. I glanced over; he kept his eyes on the road, but a faint dimple told me he meant the we as much as the acres.

Outside, a pair of crows lifted from a fence post, black wings slicing the late-day sun, and for a moment, the road felt like a narrow bridge between everything unknown behind us and everything possible ahead.

As we turned off the county blacktop and eased down the rutted drive, my pulse skittered like a rabbit in briars. Andrea's home place, or what was left of it, emerged from a tangle of sumac and pokeweed. A weather-scarred single-wide trailer crouched thirty yards back from the road. The yard lay in tangled ruin, weeds climbing a rusted swing set, an old wooden playhouse sagging sideways like it was bowing in grief. I wondered if Andrea had once crawled through its doorway, hair full of summer burrs, and whether she'd dreamed her own children might one day chase lightning bugs across this same patch of earth.

Shay slowed the Explorer to an idle. "I thought about asking her mother for an interview," he said, thumb tapping the wheel. "But part of me hates the idea of stirring it all up. Samantha, the younger sister, moved back in, caregiving full-time. Miss Campbell's got dementia now."

"You could still ask," I murmured. "The worst she can do is say no."

He tipped a silent nod. "Now, then?"

"No time like the present," I said, though my voice quavered.

He pulled onto the grass. An old powder-blue Buick sat listing on bald tires near the porch, paint peeling and rust spreading across the hood. It felt as if time had frozen the very day Andrea vanished, leaving everything to decay exactly where it stood.

We climbed out. Weeds slapped my shins, sticky with recent rain. Shay reached the porch first, but before he could knock, the screen door screeched open.

A woman leaned against the jamb, rail-thin and bottle-blonde, smoke curling from a Virginia Slim pinched between two trembling fingers. She looked to be pushing fifty, about Momma's age, but the years had ridden her hard. Creases radiated from her mouth, carved by decades of cigarettes and holding grief behind clenched teeth. A faded T-shirt hung two sizes too big over cut-off denim shorts that showed pale, brittle knees.

Her eyes, sharp and uncertain, flicked from Shay to me. "Can I help y'all?" she rasped, voice dry and cracked like a summer streambed.

Shay cleared his throat, softening his tone. "Ma'am, my name is Shaffer Jordan. I used to serve with the Pedoux Sheriff's Office. This is Jenny Thompson." He gestured gently toward me. "We're here because we're still looking for answers about your sister, Andrea."

# Chapter 27



*Journal Entry– August 28, 1972*

*Harlan's been off. Comes in late, won't say from where. Smells like creek mud and motor oil and something else I can't name.*
*He says he's tired. I say he's hiding.*
*Last night I found him out back, sitting in the shed with the light off, talking low like somebody was listening. I stood there a long time. He never knew I was there.*
*The boys are walking on eggshells. Dale never wants to come home, always at a friend's house. Abe wants to know if he's done something wrong.*
*I've weathered Harlan's bad spells. This feels like something else.*

*-Ruth*

"Jenny Thompson?" The woman drawled around a ribbon of blue smoke. "You're the one who found my sister, right?"

"I am," I said, the words small on my tongue, nothing else ready to follow.

"So you're the reason we finally got to bury a casket." She blew smoke toward the porch light. "Most days, Mama thinks Andrea's just visiting kin up in Breathitt County."

Her bitterness bit deep, but I held her gaze. "I'm sorry for what it dredged up," I managed. "But I never stopped wanting the truth."

Samantha stepped aside. "Come on in, then."

The screen door groaned shut behind us, and the living room opened like a time-locked box. Thin paneling, once honey-colored, had darkened to tobacco brown, seams buckled where summer heat had warped the walls. A single window, hazed with cooking grease and smoke, spilled a watery beam across shag carpet the color of dried moss, threadbare in every high-traffic path.

Furniture gathered in mismatched surrender: a sagging plaid sofa patched with duct tape, an avocado-green recliner draped in a chain-stitched afghan, a particle-board end table scabbed with mug rings. A floor fan ticked as it swung, stirring air that smelled of menthol smoke, fryer oil, and something faintly spoiled, bruised peaches or old liniment.

Along one wall rose a shrine of Andrea's school photos in dime-store frames, a brittle missing flyer pinned with a rusted thumbtack, news clippings yellowed and curling. Beneath them, a console TV served as a stand for a dusty porcelain lamp whose shade leaned drunkenly to one side.

In the kitchenette, linoleum tiles curled like dead leaves, and a harvest-gold fridge hummed off-key. An open bottle of generic cola and a sleeve of crackers rested beside a pill organizer marked MON through SUN.

The air itself felt heavy with grief condensed onto every surface like unshakable dust.

Shay cleared his throat, voice gentle but firm. "Ma'am, we believe there may be new information about Andrea's case."

Samantha tapped ash into a chipped saucer. "That's the same song those detectives sang when they came around askin' about some necklace. Mama swears it was Drea's, but I'm not convinced. Truth is, she just needs it to be. These days, she sees pieces of my sister everywhere."

"We understand," Shay said. "But if it is, it might point to the person who last saw your sister alive."

Her shoulders tightened. "Mama's having a good day. Don't ruin it."

"Would five minutes hurt?" I asked. "If she tires, we'll leave."

Samantha studied me, then ground the cigarette into a chipped saucer. "Fine, but keep your voices down. Loud noise scrambles her." She led us onto a narrow back porch, where Joyce Campbell sat in a faded green lawn chair, afghan tucked against the early-spring chill.

"Sammi, who's that come calling?" Joyce asked, her voice a paper-thin tremor.

"Folks askin' about Drea, Mama," Samantha answered.

Joyce's gaze drifted to me and pinned. "You're the gal found her in them nasty briars."

Samantha's eyes flew wide. The hairs along my arms stood up.

"Yes, ma'am," I whispered. "I'm sorry you lost her."

Joyce nodded, then spotted Shay's notebook. "More paperwork?"

"No, ma'am," he said gently. "We just want to talk with you."

Her fingers worried the frayed edge of the afghan while Samantha slipped inside. She returned with a dented cookie tin and set it on a TV tray between us.

"Cops gave this back after they closed the investigation," she said, lighting another cigarette. "Said it was everything pulled from Andrea's car."

She popped the lid. Inside lay a cracked hair comb, a key ring with a yellow plastic daisy, a dried-out tube of cherry lip balm, and a scarlet matchbook, Red Oak Tavern printed in white script.

Shay lifted the matchbook. "Did Andrea ever mention this place? The Red Oak Tavern's right off Route 89, isn't it?"

"Mama says Andrea wasn't much for bars," Samantha said. "She was headed to a study group the night her old Chevy conked out, halfway to town."

Joyce's eyes sharpened. "She called from the pay phone outside that tavern. Said a nice man stopped when her radiator hissed smoke and gave her a lift to make the call."

"Did she describe him?" I asked, voice tightening.

"Said he was older, real polite. Wouldn't take gas money," Joyce whispered, the memory scoring her throat.

Samantha exhaled smoke. "Deputies tried to trace him. Folks at the tavern claimed nothin' unusual, never saw Drea at all."

Shay scribbled. "Older man, polite, Route 89. Do you recall what time she phoned?"

"Close to seven," Joyce said after a moment. "My favorite program was comin' on. I muted the set to hear her."

Shay held up his phone. "May I photograph the matchbook? It could help us cross-reference."

"If it helps, do it," Samantha replied, her tone resigned.

"Did this happen right before she went missing?" I asked.

"Oh no," Samantha said. "That had to have happened a year or so before. Ain't that right, Mama?"

Joyce's fragile hand fluttered onto my wrist. "If you find my Andrea, you'll tell me, won't you?" Her voice slipped back to 1972, eyes wide with brand-new worry.

Something cinched tight inside me. Shay met my gaze, then knelt by Joyce's chair. "We'll do everything we can, Mrs. Campbell. That's a promise."

The box fan's slow click-click-click filled the porch. Samantha closed the tin and pulled it to her chest. "There's some Polaroids of hers out in the storage shed. When I get a chance, I'll dig 'em out."

Shay rose, tucking his notebook under one arm. "We'd appreciate it. Thank you both for your time." He handed her his card, and she tucked it into her cigarette pack with practiced ease, like it had always doubled as a wallet.

Joyce offered a faint, quavering smile, fragile as candlelight in a draft, as we stepped back into the heavy hush of the yard.

When we slid back into the Explorer, the doors thumped shut. Shay hadn't turned the ignition yet. We sat in the quiet, the porch light from the Campbells' house now a distant glow behind us. I stared out at the worn path unspooling in front of us, but my mind was still back inside that house, back on 1972.

"She never even went inside," I finally said. "That's what her mama said. She made a phone call and waited out front. So why keep the matchbook?"

Shay didn't answer right away. He reached into his jacket pocket and pulled out his phone, and looked at the photos he'd taken of her belongings, like they might reveal something new.

"Three matches left," he murmured. "Not a single mark inside. You'd think she'd toss it after using it, or never pick it up in the first place."

"Unless it meant something," I said. "But what? A matchbook from a place she never stepped into?"

"Maybe she took it without even thinking, just something to hold onto while she waited," he said.

"But to keep it?" I asked. "All that time? That's not random. That's… deliberate."

"Could've been a message," Shay said. "Or a warning. Or a memory." He glanced over at me. "You ever keep something you didn't want to explain?"

I nodded slowly. "Plenty."

He leaned back, tapping the steering wheel. "The police never gave it that kind of thought. They labeled her a runaway before the ink was dry on the report."

"That's what doesn't sit right with me," I said. "She was scared. You could feel it in her mama's voice. And nobody looked twice."

"They didn't want to," he said. "She was young. Female. Poor. Just another 'wild' girl who probably ran off with some boy. Easier to write her off than admit they might've missed something."

"Easier to let her disappear than dig into what happened."

He nodded. "Back then, a girl like Andrea didn't have much currency. Not with the police, not with the town. But she kept this." He held the photo up again. "It was like she was saving proof for someone. Maybe even for us."

I stared at it, heart twisting. "I could be nothing," I said.

"Or the only thing she dared hold onto," he said. "Something about it stayed with her, and if it stayed with her, it's going to stay with me."

We sat there a minute longer, the night closing in around us.

Shay glanced over, brow furrowed. "You okay?"

"I'm fine," I said, fastening my seat belt with hands that still trembled. "It's just… the more I learn about her, the more real she feels."

He started the engine, headlights cutting over ragweed and rusted lawn ornaments. "Yeah, I know what you mean. When we first found her, it was easy to separate the remains from a person's life. It was just bones on a table, paperwork to file. But when you sit across from the flesh she came from, when you hear the mother's voice…" He exhaled. "It's hard to reconcile the body with the girl who went to study groups with her friends."

We drove the winding highway in a hush. The sky had shifted to lavender dusk by the time we turned into the medical center parking lot, where my truck waited, lone and loyal beneath a buzzing streetlamp. As I reached for the door handle, Shay cut the ignition and stepped out too, pocketing his keys like he meant to hold onto the moment.

"I'm heading back to Grantham in the morning," he said. "But I'd like to see you again, if you're willing." Uncertainty clouded his voice, a subtle hitch I hadn't heard before.

I should have hesitated. We were bound by something macabre—a tangle of thorns, an old locket, decades of unanswered questions. And yet, the ache that had haunted me for years felt lighter in his company, like two people carrying the same stone had somehow made it half as heavy. The truth was, I wanted to keep that feeling a while longer.

"I'd like that," I said. My hands drifted to my belly, instinctive as prayer. "I'm not up for anything wild. These days, walking from the couch to the fridge wears me out," I added with a laugh that surprised me by sounding almost carefree.

"That's all right," he said, the tension in his shoulders loosening. "We'll figure something easy. Maybe coffee somewhere quiet, or I'll bring takeout to the lake."

The intimacy of that sent my head reeling. Before I could say anything, he said, "If you turn up anything, journals, photos, family stories, call or text. Day or night."

"Promise," I said, slipping into the cab. I shut the door and watched him in the mirror as he lingered beneath the lamp, hands shoved into pockets, face half-lit by warm glow. He stayed until my taillights vanished beyond the curve.

Driving home, I felt that strange fusion of steadiness and sparks, like standing barefoot on solid ground while a storm gathered just overhead. Somewhere between the past and whatever was coming next, something in me settled: We had been getting closer. Closer to the truth, closer to something that felt like hope.

I was drained from the day's adventure. The night pressed down, and sleep took me, but not kindly.

I stood in the briar patch again, moonlight bleaching the leaves bone-white. The raspberry canes grew taller than fence posts, thorns glinting like tiny knives. Every breeze made them rasp together, a sound halfway between prayer and warning.

Andrea was there, tangled in the center. No longer the scattered bones I'd found, but whole and heartbreakingly young, her dark hair matted against her cheeks. She cradled an infant swaddled in pale muslin. My infant. I knew it the way a body knows its pulse. The baby's fists worked the air, searching for a comfort it couldn't find.

"Andrea," I whispered, trying to step closer, but the briars tightened around my calves, snagging skin, drawing thin rivulets of blood that ran warm down to my ankles.

She lifted her eyes to mine, deep, accusing pools, and I saw that both she and the child were soaked in red. Crimson dripped from the infant's blanket, pattering onto leaves that hissed and curled at the touch.

I reached out. The thorns flexed, crawling up my arms like living barbed wire. Andrea held the baby forward, offering or pleading. I couldn't tell. Her lips moved, but the only sound was the pulse of my own heart hammering in my ears.

When I tried to speak, blood filled my mouth, metallic, suffocating. The canes surged, weaving a cage above us. Andrea's face blurred, dripping away like wet ink until only the baby remained, wailing in a voice far too old for such a small body.

I woke gasping, sheets twisted around me like vines, the echo of that cry still ringing in the dark.

There was no more rest for me that night. I turned on the bedside lamp and opened the journal Mamaw had given me, and began to write:

*Journal Entry— March 8, 2015*

*Couldn't make the dark leave me alone tonight. Closed my eyes and it pitched me straight back into the raspberry briars, Andrea whole, my baby bleeding, everything sharp and red. I woke with the taste of iron on my tongue and the sheets twisted like vines around my legs.*

*I keep seeing that matchbook in Shay's hand, the way its crimson cover looked almost new, like the years hadn't dared to touch it. One scrap of cardboard holding more truth than a foot-high stack of police reports. A stranger on Route 89, polite as Sunday shoes, hauling Andrea to a payphone. And somehow, that same road runs straight through my own family's history. How many stories can one small town bury before the ground starts spitting them back up?*

*Papaw's face stays with me—his soft, papery skin, the tremble in his hands. Nothing left of the man folks once whispered about. But the math won't quit: thirty-three and seventeen. What would those numbers have looked like side by side on Route 89 that summer night? I can't quite bring myself to believe it was him. Even knowing how he drank back then. There's no way you take a life and just live with yourself. Not unless something inside you already died first.*

*Andrea's daddy took his own.*

*Maybe that's something.*

*I don't know.*

*I keep wondering if Papaw let him bury her on our land, maybe he owed him something. A gambling debt, maybe. Or maybe it was guilt. I just don't know. I'll ask Shay about it tomorrow.*

*He said we're closer now. I want to believe him. When he stood under that parking-lot lamp, pockets full of unanswered questions, I felt steadier than I have in months. But dawn's creeping up, and the baby just shifted, a slow roll beneath my ribs, reminding me there's more at stake now than ghosts and old newspaper clippings.*

*I whispered a promise in that dream.*

*I don't know if I said it out loud or only in my head.*

*But I'll pen it here in ink:*

*Little one, we're going to find the truth,*

*and we'll stand on the right side of it,*

*even if the right side splits the earth beneath us.*

*Sleep's a lost cause. I'll sit with the lamp burning until the sun slips through the curtains.*

*Or until courage does.*

*-Jenny*

After my shift at the feed store, I headed straight to Mamaw and Papaw's. One step through the door, and I could feel the day's weight hanging in the room like humidity before a storm. Mamaw's face, usually quick with wit and wonder, looked worn thin, the corners of her eyes clouded by a tired glaze. Papaw slept in his recliner, chest rising in shallow waves, an afghan tugged up under his chin.

"Mamaw," I called softly, afraid any sudden noise might shatter what peace they had.

She poked her head around the kitchen doorway, gray wisps loose from her bun. "Jenny-baby, have you seen my glasses?" she asked, though the frames sat perched like a roosting bird on top of her head. I'd already reminded her twice that week; I managed a smile and tapped my own hair to show her.

"Oh," she breathed, half-laugh, half-sigh, sliding them down. "Mercy. This brain of mine's been boiled soft."

It hurt to see her like that, Mamaw, who could once shuck corn and recite half the New Testament without losing her rhythm. Lately, she lost sentences mid-stride, salted her soup twice if nobody caught her.

Still, she kept the wheels of this house turning: Papaw's pills sorted in jelly jars, the oxygen line untangled, his old gospel records spinning low so he could hum himself to sleep. She was determined to protect the life they'd built, even as it frayed in her hands.

"Mamaw," I ventured, "do you have any old photos of Daddy and Uncle Dale, when they were kids?"

Her eyes brightened. "Oh, land sakes, yes. Shoe boxes of 'em." She wiped her palms on her apron. "You want to look?"

"I do," I said, trying to keep my voice light. "Daddy doesn't have many. Thought I'd see what he looked like as a baby, before mine gets here."

The lie tasted chalky, but the truth might've split her heart clean in two. I prayed whatever I found in those photographs would quiet Shay's suspicions, prove the stranger on Route 89 was anyone but my Papaw Harlan.

Mamaw nodded toward the hallway. "You'll find the old photo boxes in the closet next to my desk. Haul out whatever you can. We'll dig 'til suppertime if we must."

I stepped into her bedroom and flipped on the lamp. Though the house was new, everything else felt transported straight from my childhood: the hand-pieced Lone Star quilt she'd stitched thirty years ago still spread over the same old iron bed; Papaw's well-worn Bible resting on the nightstand, a pair of reading glasses tucked inside like a bookmark.

Her writing desk sat beneath the window. A yellow sticky note clung to the corner—Sheryl's birthday scrawled in Mamaw's tidy script, my own right beside it, both phone numbers inked beneath. The sight struck me like a sledgehammer. It was a reminder that even the most familiar things had become something fragile she had to pin down.

I brushed aside last Sunday's Pedoux Herald and froze. There, half hidden beneath the paper, lay one of Mamaw's journals. Faded brown, spine neatly labeled in her looping hand:

Spring 1972

My pulse climbed into my throat. I eased into the chair and opened to a random page.

*Journal Entry — April 23, 1972*

*Harlan came in after midnight, boots muddy clear to the laces. Said the clutch went bad on Earl's truck, and he had to push it half a mile. I tried to laugh it off, but his hands were shaking so hard the coffee spilled before it reached his lips. Later, I found him shut in the utility room, shoulders hitching like a child who'd been whipped. I asked what hurt him so, and he just kept saying, "Can't fix what's broke, Ruthie," over and over.*

*He's been short-tempered all week, snapping at Dale for leaving the gate unlatched, snapping at Abe for chewing his pencil in church. I told myself it was another one of his straying spells. He always goes mean when he's guilty. Yet tonight felt different. Grief, not guilt.*

*Lord, whatever darkness has settled on my husband, shine Your lantern on it before it swallows the whole house.*

The ink wavered in places, as if her hand had trembled while she wrote. I closed the journal, palms damp, questions hammering louder than my heartbeat. If grief, not guilt, had rattled Papaw back then, what could have broken him so badly? And why had he never spoken of it?

I tucked the journal back beneath the paper, grabbed a few boxes of pictures, and carried them to the kitchen table.

"You had so many to choose from," I said, my voice quivering. "We can start with these."

I prayed harder than ever that I'd find a photo, something simple, something clear, that proved Papaw had been working in some other town that summer.

Something that proved it wasn't him.

One by one, I sifted through the years. Fourth of July cookouts, muddy boots on creek banks, birthday cakes glowing under dim kitchen lights. Dale and Daddy in Sunday ties. Mamaw breaking beans on the porch. Papaw, smiling faintly beside a fishing pole or oil-streaked toolbox.

Nothing strange. Nothing out of place.

No Red Oak Tavern. No strange cars. No bruised secrets hiding in the corners.

I let out a shaky breath I didn't know I'd been holding. Maybe, just maybe, Shay was wrong. Maybe the past wasn't about to crack open beneath my feet.

For the first time in weeks, I let myself believe that Papaw really had just been a man trying to keep his family afloat.

And that was enough to carry me into the next morning.

# Chapter 28



*Journal Entry– October 2, 1973*

*They say a woman don't break all at once. It's more like a slow leak in a place nobody thought to patch—drip by drip, day by day, until you're standing in a flood, wondering when the rain started.*
*It's the kind of breaking that don't make a sound, just a slow drowning in plain sight. You keep cooking supper, folding sheets, smiling for the pastor's wife, and all the while, the water's rising inside you.*

*-Ruth*

The next day, I wrestled with what to tell Shay. The photos hadn't revealed a thing to point toward Papaw being guilty. Just birthdays, creek banks, muddy boots, and faint smiles that belonged to simpler times. But that journal entry clung to me like a burr, nagging, needling.

Why had Mamaw dug out that particular notebook? What was she hoping to find buried back in 1972? Did she have her own questions she'd never dared ask out loud?

I didn't know what to think. So I decided to dig a little deeper before I told Shay about the journal. Still, I called him and told him I'd gone through the photos.

"I hope for everyone's sake it wasn't him," he said, his voice steady but edged with tension. "And that I'm wrong. But I'd really like to rule him out for good."

"Me too," I said. "Because I don't know what it would mean for my family if it were him. Either way, we need to find the truth."

"I've got another lead," he added. "Apparently, one of Andrea's friends remembers her mentioning a man she was seeing around that time, someone no one else ever met. I'd like to talk to her when I come back down. She's still in Wallens."

"When are you coming back?" I asked, trying not to sound too eager.

"A couple of weeks. I've got a project due, then I'll head back." There was a pause. "I was hoping I'd get to see you."

I thought I heard it, a nervous hope tangled in his words.

"I was hoping the same," I admitted, cheeks going warm.

The conversation drifted slow as river mist, swelling gently across the hours. We started with the easy things, the way fresh soil steams after a hard rain, how Mamaw's radio still crackles out old-time hymns even when no one's there to hear them, then slipped into hollows I don't often let anyone near. I told him how the house felt cavernous now, every hallway echoing with yesterday's footsteps, my grandparents moving careful as mourners, like they were afraid if they breathed too deep, the sorrow waiting in the wings might take it as an invitation.

Then I spoke the nightmare aloud, the one where Andrea's face stayed whole, my child's crib ran red, and the raspberries swallowed every sound but my own heartbeat. I hadn't planned to share it, but the words slid out, heavy and glistening, like fish pulled from deep water.

Shay listened without a word. When he finally spoke, his voice went rough at the edges. After his momma died, he packed up what she'd left— a cedar chest with an old chipped teacup, a worn Bible with notes in the margins, a lace-edged handkerchief, and a handful of family photos yellowed with time and followed the interstate till the mountains looked like home again. "Grief'll make a compass of you," he said, and something in him splintered on the syllables, the hurt still lodged like glass beneath skin. He said he'd laid the badge down for good the day the job stopped letting him sleep.

Hours slipped by, lantern-slow. Our voices settled into that porch-swing rhythm, while the crickets kept reckless time out in the pasture. Every so often, lightning bugs stitched gold thread through the dark, and I think that's what hope looks like when it's too tired to speak.

When the call finally ended, I lay down expecting the old terrors to crawl in beside me. But the night came soft, as if somebody drew a quilt over the stars. No screaming woods. No iron on my tongue. Only a dream: sunlight pouring through leaf-lace, raspberries blushing wild along a silvered fence, and a baby's laugh rolling across the air, bright and clean as linens snapping on a summer line. A hand, warm and certain, curled around mine. I woke to birdsong, still holding on.

I'd gone over to Momma and Daddy's the following weekend. Between long shifts at the feed store and evenings spent helping out at Mamaw and Papaw's, I hadn't made much time for family suppers. That night, though, Sheryl had taken the evening watch, which was rare. She buried herself in work most days, always needing something to keep her moving. But she'd brought Alana along with her, and I knew that alone would light Mamaw and Papaw up like Christmas morning. I just prayed they'd both live long enough to meet my baby. They'd always had a soft spot for children, maybe because they knew how short childhood could be.

Momma was frying up salmon patties and simmering soup beans, the scent warm and familiar, wrapping the kitchen in the kind of comfort only home cooking can offer. We gathered around the table like we used to, passing cornbread and sweet tea, laughter rising and falling in between bites.

As casually as I could manage, I asked, "You ever hear of the Red Oak

Tavern?"

Daddy's hand slowed mid-reach, his eyes narrowing, just slightly. "Not in years," he said. "Where'd you hear about that place?"

"Oh, just some old men at the store talking about it," I lied. The falsehood felt heavy. I hated how easily it rolled off my tongue, but I couldn't bear to hurt him with the truth. He was still nursing wounds from his own childhood, quietly healing from the bruises Papaw had left behind, even as he watched the same man shrink into frailty. Their relationship felt like it was stitched together with fishing line—thin, taut, and always threatening to snap.

"I only went a time or two, back before I shipped off," he said. "By the time I got home, it'd already shut down. But your Papaw? He spent many a night in that place. Him and his whole crew." His voice tightened, bitter like burnt coffee.

A lump rose in my throat, slow and thick.

"Was it just a bar, or…?" I let the question hang in the steam rising off the soup pot.

"It was a bar, sure, but they gambled in the back room. That's what kept him going back, I figure. He loved to show off at cards, was damn good at it, too. But it wasn't the games that ruined him. It was the whiskey. And the women."

He didn't say more, and I didn't press. Some truths bleed slower than others.

"Mamaw never talks about it," I said softly. "I don't know how she lived through that."

He shook his head. "Things were different back then. People didn't just leave. Divorce wasn't common, especially not around here. If she'd left him, folks wouldn't have blamed him; they'd have blamed her. Called her ungrateful, said she broke up her own home. Even when folks knew exactly the kind of man he was."

He sighed, wearied. "She should've left. Lord knows she had cause.

But I think she survived the only way she could, pretending it wasn't happening. Clinging to what she could control. The farther he pushed her away, the more she reached for the Lord. That's what saved her in the end. Her faith. Maybe him too, though not in the way folks like to think."

Looking back now, with eyes more open but less wide, I can see Daddy was right: in those days, whenever a woman left, folks decided she was the one who'd failed. They'd find some angle to pin the fault on her. Many places still play by those rules. A man might rip through a home like a storm, but tongues would wag that his wife must've nagged him, or his mama hadn't raised him firm enough, or some woman somewhere crossed him at the wrong moment.

Rarely did anyone allow that he might simply be wounded, and choosing to wound in return. Rarely did they admit that cruelty can be a decision all its own. Instead, the story always circled back, settling its weight on a woman's shoulders.

It isn't fair, wasn't then, isn't now, but that's the way the wheel keeps trying to turn.

Like everything else that happens along a person's journey, you can either let it drag you under, or you can rise in spite of it.

That's what makes women like my Mamaw and my Momma so strong. They kept going, no matter how many storms came one after the other.

They didn't just endure.

With every blow, their roots dug deeper. Their branches reached higher.

And the fruit they bore? It was all the sweeter for the struggle.

After supper, I caught myself wondering, if Papaw had spent so many nights at the Red Oak Tavern, had anyone ever seen him there with Andrea? Surely someone would've said something. But maybe not. In a place thick with smoke, drink, and dice, what was one more secret in a room already full of them?

That's the thing about seedy places: secrets cling to the walls like mildew. Affairs, abuse, debts, pills passed under tables. Folks look the other way when they've got their own dirt to cover.

Maybe someone *had* seen him with her. Maybe they just never spoke up. Had the sheriff's office ever really looked at my Papaw? I wasn't sure. And looking at him now—frail, breath wheezing through an oxygen tube—you'd never guess to ask.

I knew I'd have to talk to Shay about it. I couldn't hold it back much longer. I'd tell him about Mamaw's journal and Daddy's stories when he came back into town. He was due in the following weekend, and just the thought of it sent a ripple of nerves through me.

The baby must've felt it too, little limbs flipping like fish under the surface.

I laid a hand across my belly.

"Not much longer now," Momma said softly.

"Five weeks and counting," I smiled, though I could feel the exhaustion settling into my bones.

"Come on, I want to show you something," she said, and led me down the hall to my old room.

The bed had been made with fresh linens. A neat stack of baby blankets, diapers, and soft cotton gowns filled the little shelf beneath the window. A bassinet sat beside the bed, positioned just right so I could reach in without rising.

My eyes burned with sudden tears.

"I know you're not planning to move back in," Momma said gently, "but I thought we could have this ready. For those first couple of weeks… or anytime you feel like coming home. We don't want you thinking you have to do this alone."

She'd softened so much since Alana was born—gentler now, slower to scold, quicker to hug.

"That bassinet was yours," Daddy added from behind us, voice gruff with feeling.

"Your Grandpa Cliff bought it for us, believe it or not," Momma said, smiling at the memory.

"Thank you both," I whispered, voice cracking. The tears came easily then.

Pregnancy hormones were no joke. I'd always been the type to tear up at a sad movie or a heartfelt story, but then even Alana's cartoons had me crying. She'd catch me sometimes, her tiny fingers brushing the tears from my cheeks as she whispered, "Don't cry, Jenny." And somehow, that only made the tears come faster.

Friday rolled around before I knew it, and Shay was driving back into town. I couldn't tell if the fluttering in my stomach was from nerves about seeing him again, or from what we might learn when we met Andrea's old friend. He said he'd pick me up after work and asked if he could take me to dinner. I figured he either had something new to share or was hoping I did. The plan was to head back to Wallens the next day and keep digging.

I was just about to clock out when my phone buzzed. Daddy.

"Hey, Peanut," he said. "We're all heading over to Mamaw's this evening. She called and said she wanted everyone to come for supper. Said Papaw's had a good day, and she thinks it'd lift his spirits."

"Oh. Okay." My heart sank a little. I'd been looking forward to dinner with Shay, just the two of us. "I'll be there," I said, trying to keep the disappointment from showing in my voice.

As soon as I hung up, I called Shay. I hated the idea of canceling. But then a thought took root, maybe I didn't have to.

When he answered, I hesitated for half a breath, then said, "Hey, so… change of plans. My family's getting together at Mamaw and Papaw's tonight. Papaw's doing better, and Mamaw wants everybody there. I was gonna ask if… maybe you'd want to come with me? Meet the whole crew." I let out a nervous laugh. "No pressure, I know it's last minute."

He paused, then chuckled. "Meeting the family already? That's either a warning sign or a good omen."

"You brave enough?"

"I think I am," he said with a chuckle.

There was something in his voice that eased the weight I'd been carrying.

Maybe after seeing my family together in the intimate moments during family dinners, instead of just precinct interviews, he'd see how it just couldn't have been Papaw.

I headed home to change. The sun was just starting to dip, casting long golden streaks across the worn deck boards. I pulled on a soft, rose-colored blouse that cinched just above my belly and a long skirt that flowed gently over my hips. It was one of the few outfits I had that still made me feel pretty. I caught my reflection in the mirror and rested a hand on the swell of my stomach, full and round, ready to burst.

I remember thinking, I didn't know who I was trying to fool. There was no hiding it. No way Shay could look past the fact that I was carrying another man's child. A man who had found something in me he couldn't stomach, who walked away even while his blood grew inside me.

Still, I swiped on a little mascara, dabbed my lips with a soft-pink lipstick, and clipped in my favorite earrings, the little gold hoops Momma gave me for my seventeenth birthday. The ones that always made me feel just a little more like myself.

Just then, I heard tires crackling up the drive. A moment later, a knock on the door

I opened it and stepped aside. "I'm almost ready," I said. "Just trying to fish my flats out from under the bed. Not so easy with this thing in the way." I gave my belly a gentle pat and laughed.

"Here, let me help." He crouched without hesitation, reaching under the bed and pulling them out like it was the most natural thing in the world.

When he stood, shoes in hand, we were face to face in the narrow room. Close enough to feel the tension catch in the air between us.

"Thank you," I said softly, eyes locked with his.

"Do you need help putting them on?" he asked, his voice a little rough around the edges.

"I've got it," I said with a smile. "Slip-ons for me these days." I dropped them to the floor and slid my feet in, careful not to wobble.

As we stepped outside, he placed a gentle hand on the small of my back to steady me. "Be careful on that second step. It's loose."

"I know," I sighed. "I've been meaning to fix it. Just haven't gotten around to it."

"I'll fix it for you, if you'd like," he offered.

"I might just let you," I said as he held my elbow, guiding me down the porch steps like something delicate. Luckily, there were only three.

When we pulled up to Mamaw's, Shay came around and opened my door like a proper gentleman, something about the gesture so old-fashioned it caught me off guard in the best way. I stepped out, and he leaned in just enough that I could hear him over the creak of the porch swing in the distance.

"You look lovely, by the way," he said, voice low, sincere.

I didn't feel lovely. I felt swollen and stretched, foreign in my own skin. My ankles hurt, my dress clung too tight in all the wrong places, and I hadn't bothered with much makeup. But the way he said it, like it was a truth, not a courtesy, made something settle in me.

I smiled, small and unsure, heart tapping against my ribs. "Thanks," I said. "I'm still getting used to… all of it."

His eyes didn't drop to my belly. They stayed right on mine. "You're doing better than you think."

And somehow, I believed that might be true.

"Are you ready?" I asked instead.

"As I'll ever be," he said, grinning like he meant it.

The kitchen smelled like supper should—onions caramelizing in a cast-iron skillet, roast in the oven, the kind of scent that enveloped you like your favorite sweater. Mamaw had outdone herself.

Shay followed me in, a little quiet but polite as ever. He handed Mamaw a bouquet of daisies he'd picked up from the gas station down the road. She smiled, surprised and charmed.

I introduced him around, and we all gathered close, squeezing in chairs and pulling up extra stools.

Papaw surprised us all when he shuffled to the table on his own. The first time since the heart attack that he'd done that. "Don't fuss," he grumbled when Mamaw tried to help him with the chair. "I still know how to sit down."

Everyone chuckled, even Mamaw, though I caught her watching him closely out of the corner of her eye.

Just before we dug in, Mamaw folded her hands and nodded for the rest of us to do the same.

"Let's bow our heads," she said softly.

The room quieted. Chairs creaked. Even Alana stilled in her seat beside Sheryl, tiny hands pressed together like she'd practiced this her whole life.

"Lord," Mamaw began, her voice steady but worn at the edges, "we thank You for this food and the hands that prepared it. Thank You for this family, for the love that holds us together even when the world tries to pull us apart. We lift up Harlan tonight, give him strength and peace, Lord. And bless this house with gentleness in the days ahead. In Jesus' name, amen."

"Amen," we all echoed, some louder than others.

There was a moment of silence after that, not awkward but full, like the kind of hush that follows the last note of a hymn.

Shay sat beside me, answering Daddy's questions about his work and complimenting Mamaw's cooking so sincerely that she blushed and waved him off. Alana kept slipping him buttered beans from her plate and whispering that he looked like a cowboy. The room felt easy, full of forks clinking and stories passed like sweet tea.

Until Sheryl leaned forward and asked, "So, how'd y'all meet, anyway?"

I opened my mouth, but Shay beat me to it—too quick, too honest.

"I was a new officer in town," he said, smiling faintly. "I met Jenny the day she found Andrea's body."

The room stilled.

Forks stopped mid-air.

The air shifted like a door left open on a stormy night.

Even Mamaw, who had been reaching for the rolls, froze with her hand just hovering.

Papaw's expression didn't change, but something drained from him all at once. He pushed back from the table with a soft grunt.

"I think I need to lie down," he said. His voice was flat. Worn thin.

Mamaw was up in a second, helping him to his feet. "Of course, Harlan. Come on now." She looked at the rest of us, that tight smile she wore when things were coming undone behind the scenes. "Y'all keep eating. He's just tuckered out."

But nobody moved until they were down the hallway and out of earshot.

Shay looked at me, guilt rising fast behind his eyes. "I didn't mean…"

"It's okay," I said quietly. "He probably is tired. This is the first time he's even sat at the table since his heart attack."

The quiet lingered, thick as smoke, until Alana, bless her, asked for another roll and Daddy cleared his throat loud enough to startle the room back into motion.

But the warmth had shifted.

Something had cracked, even if none of us knew just how deep.

When he dropped me off at home, Shay apologized again.

"It's okay, really," I said, my voice soft. I explained how finding the body on our land had unsettled us all. How the endless questions from the police, from the neighbors, had worn us down. It felt like everyone expected us to hold the key to all the secrets and mysteries behind Andrea's death, when really, we'd been searching for the same answers as everyone else.

He didn't say what I knew he must've been thinking, that Papaw's reaction could have come from guilt. I don't know if he stayed quiet to spare my feelings or because he'd seen how frail Papaw had become, how thin Mamaw was stretching just trying to hold everything together. Either way, I appreciated the silence. It felt like kindness.

The next day, we headed back toward Wallens to meet Andrea's friend. Shay told me her name was Kim Satterfield, and she worked at the only diner the little town had. She'd agreed to talk to us on her lunch break.

We pulled into the cracked gravel lot of Tina's, a squat little cinderblock place with faded red letters flaking off the sign. It was the kind of joint where old men gathered each morning to sip bitter coffee and gossip like Baptist hens. Outside, a few plastic tables still sported ashtrays, chipped and stained with years of use. Time had barely brushed the place since its grand opening sometime in the '60s, and that's exactly how the people of Wallens liked it.

We slid into a corner booth, and when the waitress came by, we both asked for sweet tea and told her we were looking for Kim.

"I'll fetch her for ya, hun," the older waitress drawled with a wink, her hair teased and lacquered into a perfect silver dome.

Kim appeared a few minutes later, balancing two glasses in her sunspotted hands. She looked to be in her early fifties, but still clung to the trappings of her youth with heavy eyeliner, teased curls, and a bright red shirt that fit too tight and didn't quite hide the years.

"Would y'all mind movin' outside?" she asked, handing us our drinks.

"I'd like to smoke on my break while we talk."

We followed her out to a side patio shaded by a sun-faded red umbrella, where the kitchen staff sometimes took their lunch on fair-weather days.

"Thanks for meetin' with us, Kim," Shay said as we sat. "We just had a few questions."

"No problem," she said, lighting a cigarette with a flick of chipped pink nails. "Anything for Andrea and Joyce, bless her sweet soul."

"You mentioned Andrea had been seeing someone," I said, watching the smoke curl around her face.

"Yeah. She was real secretive about it," Kim nodded. "Plumb smitten, though. She'd sneak out to meet him, and I asked why she never brought him around. Figured he might've been married or somethin'. She got all riled up, told me not to insult her like that. Said he wasn't married, just that her daddy wouldn't approve. Said she was waitin' 'til she turned eighteen to let everyone meet him."

"So, she never introduced you to him?" Shay asked, trying to hide the discouragement in his voice.

"No," she said, dragging on her cigarette. "But I think he was a carpenter or something close. She said he worked with his hands. They used to meet down at Old Wilson Landing, all nice and tucked away. She even told me once they skinny dipped down there and nearly got caught by a passing squad car."

My stomach twisted. That was where the necklace had been found. *It had to be hers.*

Shay must've had the same thought. He pulled a photo from his notebook. "Was this Andrea's?" he asked. "It was recovered from the lake near that spot."

Kim took the photo and stared at it for a moment. "Sure looks like hers. She never took that thing off." She ran a thumb along the image like she could still feel the shape of it.

Shay handed her the second photo, the one of the locket's back, with the letter H etched into it.

"Any idea what the H stands for?" he asked. "We thought maybe it was the initial of the man she was seeing."

Kim shook her head. "I asked her about it once. It was the initial of someone she loved, alright. She had an old hound dog named Hank. I never looked inside, but I'd bet dollars to donuts that if you opened that locket, there'd be a picture of Hank's sad eyes in there," she said, smiling at the memory. "She loved that old mutt something fierce. He didn't last long after she was gone, grieved himself to death. I always said, if they'd taken him out looking for her, they'd have found her a lot sooner."

Something inside me uncoiled. The H wasn't for Harlan. It was for Hank. A wave of relief washed over me, chased by frustration. We were back to square one.

I told Shay as much once we thanked Kim and left her to finish her break.

"Well, we are and we aren't," he said, rubbing the back of his neck. "Now we know an officer nearly caught them at the lake. That's something. We know he probably wasn't married, though she could've lied. And we know he worked with his hands, possibly a carpenter."

"We should've asked about the old bar she called Joyce from," I said, kicking myself.

"Damn. You're right," he muttered. "Maybe she'll talk to us again once we've done some more digging."

It felt good, being included like this. We were uncovering something long buried, together. Our own quiet mission, determined to find what the police never had.

Back in 1972, the case had been cold before it ever got warm. Andrea's disappearance was chalked up to another runaway girl, and the file gathered dust. By the time I stumbled on her bones decades later, most of the leads were long dead or lost to memory. But something still whispered beneath it all. We just had to listen closely enough to hear it.

Shay eased his Ford beneath the live-oak limbs that crouched over my camper, headlights sweeping across the aluminum like moonlight on a pond. I asked him in for coffee, though what I really wanted was company that didn't need explaining. He nodded, ever quiet, and eased his way through the narrow door.

The place wasn't big, two steps from sink to sofa, another to the bedroom through a small door on the far wall. He lowered himself onto the faded plaid cushions while I fussed with the percolator. We both took it the same: cream, no sugar. Outside, katydids sawed at the night, their racket bleeding through thin paneled walls.

We talked shop at first, turning the facts of Andrea's case over and over, searching for something we might've missed. But the dam inside me was already groaning. That single truth Kim had given us, the H belonging to an old hound, not to Harlan, shook something loose. Relief rushed in so hard it tangled straight into grief. Grief for Papaw slipping away, for Mamaw unraveling thread by thread, for Andrea still waiting on justice in the cold red earth

My voice hitched; the coffee mug rattled in its saucer. Then the tears came slowly at first, then a flood I couldn't dam back if I tried. I saw the moment it hit Shay that I was coming apart; some men would've bolted for the door. He didn't. He set his cup aside and sat solid beside me, a steady harbor while I drowned.

"I'm sorry," I choked, wiping at my cheeks like I could scold the tears into stopping. "You didn't sign up for all this…"

"Hush now," he murmured, gentler than lullabies. No sermon, no fix-it words, just hush and presence.

Something inside me roared too loud for a room so small, so I slipped off the sofa, crossed the two worn boards to the bed, and buried my face in the pillow. I half-expected to hear the door click shut behind him. Instead, boots thudded to the floor, springs dipped, and his arms came around me, careful, reverent, like he was afraid I might shatter if held too hard.

I cried for Papaw's thinning pulse, for Mamaw stacking sticky notes against forgetfulness, for Andrea's bones in the woods, for the child in my belly who'd arrive fatherless into a world that sometimes let killers walk free. Shay said nothing; he didn't have to. He breathed slowly against the nape of my neck, the sure rhythm of a metronome telling my heartbeat to follow.

Sometime after midnight, exhaustion washed me clean. When dawn seeped through the gingham curtains, I woke wrapped in a patchwork quilt. Shay lay on top of it, one arm draped over my waist, boots still off, head nestled in my hair. The percolator sat cold on the stove. Everything else—case files, unanswered prayers, the fear of what came next, waited beyond that thin camper door.

But for the space of a breath, I just listened to him breathe and let myself believe steady might be enough.

# Chapter 29



*Journal Entry– February 20, 2015*

*I reckon there comes a time in every woman's life when she feels the weight of
all the stories that came before her and the stirrings of all the ones still left to
be written.*

*I remember when I first became a mother. I wasn't ready. Lord knows, I was
still learning how to be a daughter, a wife. But when that baby was placed in
my arms, all my fumbling made way for something fiercer. Something
rooted.*

*Babies don't ask for perfection. They ask for presence, for arms that don't let
go when the night gets long.*

*And grief, it doesn't wait for the right time. It comes when it comes. It can
walk hand in hand with joy, strange as that sounds. One breath in, one
breath out. A hello in the same hour as a goodbye.*

*That's the ache of living: to carry sorrow and sweetness in the same heart
and still wake up with enough love left for tomorrow.*

*-Ruth*

After that night, Shay and I settled into an easy rhythm. Even
with him back at work, we stayed close—calls, texts, little
check-ins that stitched our days together like patchwork. We

talked about everything: baby appointments and his looming deadlines, my odd cravings, and the nights neither of us could sleep. Nothing ever felt forced. Our conversations moved soft and steady, like the hush that settles over a holler after a summer storm.

Lena-Grace and I went shopping for the things I'd need to take to the hospital. I had less than a month left, and I'd bring a new life into this world. She was more excited than I was, and probably more prepared for it, too. Lena had always been the kind of woman who packed Band-Aids in her purse just in case, who remembered birthdays without a calendar, who helped in the church nursery like it was her calling.

I'd started going back to church with her, since Sheryl hadn't been going as often lately. She seemed to be working every weekend, chasing deadlines and pushing herself past the point of peace. I prayed she'd learn to rest before she burned herself out, like a candle left lit too long at both ends.

Lena kept filling the buggy with things I'd never have thought to buy on my own—tiny socks shaped like acorns, witch hazel wipes, nursing pads, a little nightgown printed with sleepy moons and stars. Things that whispered of comfort, of care.

"Thank you," I told her, shaking my head with a smile. "I swear, I'd have shown up with nothing but the clothes on my back."

She laughed, tossing a soft burp cloth into the cart. "You don't have to keep thanking me, Jenny. This is what friends do."

"I know," I said, my voice low with gratitude. "I just, I really do appreciate it."

Her eyes softened. "Andrew and I decided we're going to take turns checking on you and staying with you, just in case. Can't have you going into labor all alone."

A lump rose in my throat, grateful, not sad. "You guys are the best," I said, and I meant it with everything I had.

I didn't say it out loud, but her words lodged somewhere deep inside me. The thought of bringing this child into the world without anyone there had kept me up more nights than I'd ever admit. Not because I doubted I could do it. Lord knows I'd done harder things, but because I was tired. Tired of facing every mountain and storm on my own. Lena's kindness was like a quilt draped over all that fear, warm and unexpected.

My phone dinged then. It was a message from Shay. He'd sent a picture of a pacifier with a rubber moustache attached.

**Hear me out: Baby… but with authority,** he wrote.

I laughed out loud and turned the screen to show Lena. She laughed too, shaking her head. "So when do we get to meet this man who makes you smile like that?"

"Definitely soon," I said, cheeks warming.

"So… are y'all a thing?" she asked, without a lick of judgment in her voice.

"I don't know what we are," I admitted. "He makes me feel less sad. More safe. But I'm scared, you know? I haven't exactly had the best luck when it comes to men. Part of me's afraid to call it anything."

"I understand," she said gently. "But not all men are like the ones that hurt you. Look at your daddy. Look at mine. Look at Luke."

"I know," I said, sighing. Then I glanced over at her. "Enough about me. When are *you* gonna find your someone, Lena? It's okay to do something just for yourself, you know."

Her face flushed pink, and she tried to focus really hard on the baby thermometer she was pretending to read.

"Oh my goodness, you like someone!" I said, grinning. "You better tell me who!"

We spent the rest of the shopping trip talking about the new guitar player at church. He was handsome in a weathered, older-man kind of way, and that was just fine. Lena was an old soul. I prayed she'd find someone who saw her heart plain and true, someone who would love her in the quiet, steady way she deserved.

Because if anyone on God's green earth deserved the best, it was Lena-Grace.

After Lena and I had lunch at the café, I headed over to Mamaw and Papaw's house, carrying the soup of the day in a little to-go sack. Papaw must've really overexerted himself at dinner the other night. He hadn't gotten back up since, except to shuffle to the bathroom now and then. Mamaw had messaged earlier, asking if someone could bring supper by. She was just too worn down to cook after tending to Papaw all day. He'd been having a rough one.

When I got there, Mamaw was sitting at the kitchen table, folding towels with slow hands, looking bone tired. The kettle was still warm on the stove, but the burner had long since gone cold. Mamaw's tea sat untouched beside the folded towels, steeped too long, dark as molasses. That was the kind of tired she was, so tired even rest forgot where to find her.

"Let me do that," I said gently, finishing the stack she'd started. "You eat. I'll take some to Papaw."

"I was just about to…" she started, but I shook my head.

"No, really. Go ahead. I'll check on him."

She didn't argue.  I put the towels away in the drawer, picked up the little Styrofoam cup of soup, and carried it into the living room, where Papaw sat sunk into his recliner. He looked pale as a ghost, sweat dotting his brow like dew on morning grass.

"Hey, Pap. Let's eat," I said, settling beside him.

His eyes fluttered open, and he tried to smile.  I spooned the soup gently to his lips. His conversation was thin and ragged, coming in fits and starts like a faulty radio signal. His words tangled, lost in the quiet hum of the room. I could tell his body needed to rest.

"I'm going to put the rest in the fridge," I whispered after a few more bites. "You nap, okay? You can finish later when you wake up."

As I stood, he reached out and grabbed my wrist with surprising urgency. His grip was weak, trembling, but firm enough to stop me. His eyes locked onto mine, and for a moment, it felt like he was staring straight through me, into some place deeper than words.

"I'm sorry," he whispered. "I'm sorry about the baby."

My heart gave a little lurch.

"It's okay," I said, patting his hand softly. "You don't need to be sorry, Pap."

He closed his eyes and drifted off, the lines on his face softening as sleep took him. But the words stayed with me. Why would he apologize? It wasn't his fault Jesse had left. There was no reason for regret, not from him. Still, the sorrow in his voice lingered.

Watching him fade like that, I wondered what pieces of myself might one day weigh heavy on my own children. I wanted to believe I was breaking the cycle, but it's hard to be sure when you're still standing in the middle of it.

As I was saying my goodbyes to Mamaw, Daddy pulled into the driveway. He was coming to sit with them for a spell. I gave him a hug, passed along my love, and headed home for a shower. Exhaustion had started to press heavily on me, and my feet were swelling something fierce.

Spring rain began to fall just as I pulled onto the road, tapping softly against the windshield. The scent of honeysuckle drifted in through the cracked window, sweet and sharp, and somehow full of memory. It made my heart hurt and swell at the same time.

The rain kept falling, gentle but certain, like it knew something I didn't yet.

I was fresh out of the shower, pulling my shirt over my head, when I heard my phone buzzing on the counter. Three missed calls from Daddy.

That wasn't like him.

Dread curled in my gut as I picked up the phone and called him back.

"Jenny, we're at the hospital," he said, his voice thick and breaking. "Papaw's not gonna make it. They've called the family in to say our goodbyes. Come as soon as you can."

"Okay," I said, voice catching in my throat. I was already reaching for my jacket.

"Be careful in the rain, Peanut," he said softly. "Love you."

"I will. Love you more." I hung up and rushed out the door.

The rain had picked up, coming down harder now. I crossed my little porch and hurried toward the truck, my shoes slipping on the wet wood. As I stepped down onto the second step, the one I'd been meaning to fix for months, it gave out beneath me.

My feet flew out from under me. I went down hard, my head striking the edge of the step above. A sharp, blinding crack, and then nothing but rain on my face, cold and steady like mourning.

My hand flew to my belly.

And then the darkness took me.

I remembered nothing until I woke up in the hospital room the next day.

The lights were soft, the air heavy with the hush of waiting. Family and friends filled the space, quiet and worn. Sheryl sat in the corner holding Alana on her lap, reading from a children's book in a low, lulling voice. Luke stood at the window, arms crossed, staring out at the gray sky. Momma was beside my bed, her hands twisting a worn handkerchief until it looked like it might tear.

Lena was the first to notice I was awake.

"Jenny," she whispered. At the sound of her voice, all eyes turned to me.

My throat was dry, my head thick and slow. I didn't know where I was or how I'd ended up there. But then it all began to trickle back—the rain, the step, the fall.

"Papaw?" I asked first, voice hoarse.

No one answered.

And then my hand went instinctively to my belly, no longer stretched tight.

"My baby. Where's my baby?" I cried, panic flooding in all at once.

Momma rose quickly and took my hand in hers. "It's okay, Jenny. The baby is fine," she said, trying to calm me. "You hit your head hard and were unconscious. The doctors said your blood pressure dropped dangerously low, and they were afraid you weren't going to wake up. So they had to take her, just to be safe."

"She's a little early," Sheryl added gently, "so she's got to stay in the NICU for a while. But the doctors say she's healthy and strong. She's doing well."

"I want to see her," I said, eyes scanning the room. "Where's Daddy? Where's Mamaw? Is Papaw…?"

Sheryl met my gaze. "Daddy took Mamaw down to the cafeteria for coffee. They'll be back in just a minute."

Then she paused. Her voice softened. "Papaw's gone."

Grief surged through me, dark and sudden, like a bruise beneath the skin. He was gone.

This man who had loved me with his whole heart, who cradled me on the porch swing and passed down stories with cracked hands and tired eyes, this man I'd trusted all my life, and yet only recently realized I hadn't fully known. A man I once feared might have done something monstrous… was gone.

Grief tangled with guilt; sorrow laced with the bitter threads of understanding. In the end, what remained was the aching hush of loss.

He had taken his last breath just as my daughter took her first.

That's the way of things, I suppose.

One life closes its eyes, and another opens theirs. There's no such thing as all good or all bad, not in people, not in stories, not in the way life folds in on itself. Everything's tangled. Everything's layered. And with every ending, no matter how jagged, something new begins.

It hurts, but it holds, grief and grace twisted together like roots beneath the soil, unseen but steadying the ground we walk.

The door creaked open, and I turned, expecting to see Daddy, but it wasn't him.

Shay stepped inside, roses in hand, worry shadowing his eyes. He crossed the room and placed the flowers gently on the table beside me.

"How is she?" he asked, voice low, directed toward Momma.

"She just woke up. The doctor should be in soon," she said, brushing a hand across my blanket.

"I'll go let the nurse know she's awake," Luke added, giving my foot a gentle squeeze before slipping out the door. His face was taut with concern. He'd already lost one sister. I could see it in his eyes; he was terrified to lose another.

"How did I get here?" I asked, still trying to stitch the memory back together.

"I found you," Lena-Grace said from the corner of the room.

"I wasn't sure why, but the Lord kept nudging me to check on you. I'm so glad I listened. You nearly scared me to death, Jenny, seeing you lying there like that…"

"I'm glad you did," Shay said softly. "I'm sorry. I should've fixed that step the other day."

"It's not your fault," I murmured. "I should've fixed it months ago."

I swallowed hard. "I want to see my baby."

"You've had a C-section," Momma reminded me gently. "We've got to wait for the doctor to say when you can get up."

"As soon as he gives the word," Shay said, stepping closer, "I'll take you myself."

I nodded and let my eyes close, trying to block out the sterile light above me. I felt hollow, like something had been torn from me. Like some part of me was still missing.

I needed to see her. I needed to know she was real. That she was okay.

She. The word hit me.

I had a daughter.

The clock on the wall seemed to take a lifetime between each tick. Time dragged. I tried to distract myself with the conversation in the room, but the feeling lingered, something was missing. I needed to see my little girl. I needed to know she was okay. I wanted to feel her skin, see her fingers and toes.

The doctor arrived not long after, checking my head. I hadn't even realized it was bandaged until his fingers brushed the edge of the gauze. A dull ache pulsed through my skull. He said I was healing well and that my vitals were stable. Normally, a mother would be up and walking after a C-section by now, but because of the head injury, he didn't want to risk a fall.

"You can go down to the end of the hall to see your baby," he said gently, "but only by wheelchair."

"Thank you," I said, voice nearly a whisper. Tears burned but didn't fall.

A nurse soon arrived, the soft roll of the wheelchair echoing against the tile. I sat wrapped in a hospital blanket, arms aching for something they hadn't yet held. The overhead lights buzzed faintly. Somewhere down the corridor, a baby's cry broke the stillness. My breath hitched. Shay walked beside me the whole way, never letting go of my hand.

Momma and Lena followed closely behind. When we reached the viewing window of the nursery, I saw Mamaw and Daddy already standing there, still and reverent. Mamaw's hand rested in the crook of Daddy's arm.

The nurse wheeled me up beside them and gently locked the brakes.

"She's the second one on the right," she said, nodding toward the bassinets tucked under warm lamplight.

My eyes scanned quickly, but I already knew. There, swaddled in pink and white, with a tiny knitted cap sliding off one ear, was my baby. I felt it all at once: relief, wonder, grief, woven into something that stole my breath.

"She's doing well," the nurse said kindly. "Just needed a bit of monitoring, breathing and temperature mostly, but she's been strong from the start. If everything continues like this, she'll be in your room tomorrow morning."

I nodded, eyes locked on the rise and fall of her chest. Lena-Grace stepped up and rubbed my shoulder, her hand warm and steady.

The nurse glanced down at her chart. "Have you decided on a name?"

My voice was quiet, but sure. "Andrea Grace."

Lena-Grace's hand paused, then squeezed, and I squeezed back, letting her know the middle name was as much for her steadfast grace as for the miracle of second chances.

Shay stepped forward, reaching for my hand again. His grip was firm. Grounding.

The nurse smiled. "That's a beautiful name."

No one else spoke, but I felt it. The name lingered in the air, acknowledged, understood. Like a prayer spoken aloud.

Nobody had to say anything more. Andrea, gone but not forgotten. This wasn't just a name. It was a thread between past and present, between loss and life. We let the silence stretch. It didn't need filling.

Sunlight spilled gently across the hospital sheets the next morning when the nurse returned with the bassinet.

"She's all yours now, Mama," she said with a grin.

My heart pounded as she lifted the baby into my arms. The warmth of her tiny body seeped into me like spring rain into dry soil. My little Andrea Grace squirmed, her face scrunching, then settling into the crook of my arm.

I stared down at her, awe hollowing out a quiet space inside me.

"Hey there, sweet girl," I whispered, brushing her forehead with my lips. "I'm your Mama."

The room was still. Everyone else had gone home to rest, everyone but Shay. He didn't have to stay. But there he was, beside the bed, his eyes soft and glassy.

I didn't look up. I didn't need to. She was the part of me I hadn't even realized was missing, until now.

"I think she's got your eyes," Shay said quietly.

I smiled. "I think she's got all the strength of every woman who came before her."

# Chapter 30

*Journal Entry– May 7, 2015*

*There's a strange stillness in the house tonight. I can feel it in my bones, same way you feel a storm before it breaks. Harlan's boots aren't by the door no more. His humming ain't drifting in from the porch. I keep reaching for sounds that ain't there.*

*My boys carried him down the hill and laid him beneath the old oak tree behind the church. The same one where we said our vows all them years ago. I thought I'd feel more anger when this day came, but mostly I just feel tired. He wasn't always kind, Lord knows that. But he was mine. And grief doesn't measure itself by goodness. It just comes.*

*But God, in His strange timing, gave us a new baby this very week. A girl with my blood in her. I get confused too easily these days, but I know her name.*

*Andrea Grace.*

*A name like that feels like a thread, sewing old wounds shut with something softer.*

*-Ruth*

Baby Andrea and I left the hospital four days later. Our coming home was much like her birth, mingled with joy and sorrow, tethered in the strange way beginnings and endings so often are. That same day, we buried Papaw.

He was laid to rest in the little cemetery beside the church Mamaw had grown up in, with a spot already marked beside him, waiting for her. The idea of a patch of earth just sitting there, biding its time to claim her body too, unsettled me in a way I couldn't quite understand. It felt like death was already casting its shadow over her, even as she still drew breath.

I clung to my newborn while they lowered Papaw into the ground, afraid that if I let go of her for even a second, she might follow him down into the earth. In that moment, with the weight of grief pressing in and the warmth of new life in my arms, I understood just how fragile life really was. Precious. Fleeting.

We were surrounded by mourners—family, friends, old neighbors, folks who'd known him through the good and the bad. Even Uncle Dale came. I hadn't seen him since I was a little girl, but there he stood, shoulders slack, eyes brimming. Maybe now, with Papaw gone, he could bury the pain, too.

What struck me most that day was how death seems to sanitize memory. No one whispered about the drinking. No one mentioned the women. Daddy wasn't thinking about the shouting, the fists, the slammed doors in the middle of the night. No, we all spoke instead of the jokes Papaw used to tell, the way he picked his banjo on the porch, the late-night bowls of ice cream he'd sneak us when Mamaw wasn't looking.

Grief is complicated like that. I still don't know if it's a curse or a mercy that once someone's gone, we seem to shed their sins so easily. While they're alive, we hold their wrongs like stones in our pockets, but when judgment comes to call them home, we forgive them as easily as the Father. And I wonder… if we had offered that kind of grace while they were still here, might all our lives have been softer? Might our homes have been more peaceful? Might we have healed sooner?

After the funeral, Baby Andrea and I went home with Momma and Daddy. The house felt different now, like grief had settled into the corners, making the air thick and still. Even the old floorboards seemed to creak more softly, as if mourning too. But Sheryl had been right, it was a gift to have someone nearby to help me through those first few weeks. I hadn't been prepared for the fatigue that followed me like a shadow, nor the deep ache in my body from the fall and the stitches left behind by the C-section.

Still, even in the haze of pain and sleepless nights, there was a kind of joy I hadn't known was possible. The kind that wells up quietly when you're holding something so new, so impossibly perfect, that you almost forget the world outside. I would sit rocking her in the early hours, heavy-eyed and hurting, but full of wonder. Her tiny fingers curled around mine like she was anchoring me to something unshakable. And in a way, she was, pulling me back to life, one breath at a time.

There's a strange, holy stillness that comes with those first days of motherhood, when your body is broken but your spirit feels split wide open by love. Every cry, every sigh, every little flutter of her lashes against her cheek reminded me that life, even in its most fragile form, is powerful.

Lena and Andrew came to see Baby Andrea and me not long after we returned home. When I saw Lena holding her, something soft twinkled in her eyes, a light that made me certain she'd be a wonderful mother someday. She cradled Andrea with quiet reverence, her voice tender as she whispered to her, like she already loved her as her own.

Andrew was more hesitant, his movements careful, almost shy. But when he finally took Andrea into his arms, I saw the awe in his eyes, the way he breathed like he was holding something delicate. I caught the low murmur of his voice as he leaned close to her tiny ear. Words of protection. Of promise. Of love. And my heart swelled, nearly too full. What a wonder it is, I thought, how a baby so small can draw such deep tenderness from those around her, can bind people together in a love that feels sanctified.

Shay called every evening after work, never missing a night. His eyes lit up every time he saw Andrea on the screen, the corners of his smile softening as he spoke to her like she could understand every word. He promised he'd visit just as soon as he finished the report he was working on. I longed to see him more than I expected, longed to feel his presence, to lean into the comfort his voice offered through the phone.

But it would be two weeks before he made it. By then, I was ready to return to my little camper, to the quiet rhythm of just me and my daughter. Momma and Daddy didn't want me to go, but I needed to be home. Not just any home, the one I'd made for us.

The very day I arrived, Shay did too. He showed up that evening, standing on my steps with a bouquet of pale wildflowers in one hand and a tiny silver rattle in the other, engraved with Andrea's initials.

He stepped inside, and I took the flowers, burying my nose in their sweetness as I filled a vase with water. When I turned around, he was holding Andrea, looking down at her like she was the only thing that had ever mattered. The way his face softened, the way his arms adjusted instinctively to her every twitch, nearly brought me to my knees.

He would make some child a wonderful father one day, I knew that in my bones. And the thought settled inside me, bittersweet and sharp, because I knew my little girl would never know that kind of father in Jesse.

Andrea Grace began to fuss, her hungry cry filling the room. Shay gently handed her back to me, and I settled into the rocker to nurse her. She latched quickly, her cries fading as she fed, eyelids fluttering closed like a soft curtain.

Once she was milk-drunk and warm against my chest, I rose and laid her in the small crib beside my bed. I lingered there, watching the steady rise and fall of her breath. My heart was overflowing.

When I returned to the living room, a wave of dizziness took me by surprise. I stumbled, but before I could fall, Shay was there, his arms strong and steady around me, pulling me close.

"Are you okay?" he asked, voice low and concerned.

I nodded, but the truth was tangled in my throat. His warmth was so near, his breath brushing against my skin, and all I could do was look up at him. Our eyes locked, and before I knew it, his lips were on mine.

Hot and needy, but tender and attentive.

He pulled back slowly, like he wasn't sure if I'd let him go. And truth be told, I didn't want to.

I'd never been kissed like that.

It didn't just stir my body, it stirred something deeper. It moved mountains, calmed winds, and silenced storms. It terrified me.

He stood there holding me, neither of us ready to let go, like if we did, the world might tilt and spin off its axis. We stayed wrapped in that fragile stillness until the soft rustle of blankets from the crib reminded us that life, however small, was still calling.

"I better go," he said, his voice low, reluctant. "It's getting late, and you need to rest while you can."

"When will I see you again?" I asked, hating the desperation I heard in my own voice, even as I tried to hide it.

"I'll come by tomorrow evening," he promised.

With one more kiss, gentler this time, like a whispered vow, he slipped out the door. The click of it closing behind him felt louder than it should have, echoing through the small space like a sigh.

I crawled into bed and turned to the cradle beside me. Andrea lay there sleeping, tiny fists curled against her cheeks, her breath a rhythm I hadn't known my heart needed. I watched her for a long while, not ready to close my eyes.

I prayed her sleep would be peaceful, free of the weight the world so often lays on girls.

I felt only gratitude in my heart.

Gratitude that, after all I'd been through, the Lord still placed something so pure in my arms, so untouched by this broken world, so perfectly whole.

A child who was mine.

I got a beautiful surprise the following day.

There was a knock at the door, and for a moment my heart leapt. I half expected Shay, even though I knew he was off interviewing a local antique dealer about Depression-glass said to have belonged to a bootlegger's widow. Lost history, he'd told me, and the way objects remember.

But it wasn't Shay.

Mari stood in the doorway with a gift bag in her hands and that familiar soft smile, joy folded into gentleness. "I figured you might need a little something today," she said, stepping inside.

I opened the bag and drew out a folded baby blanket, pale cream with hand-stitched edges, the yarn worn buttery-soft. A faint scent of cedar clung to it, like woods after rain.

"My mother made that," Mari said quietly. "She gave it to me when I had my baby girl."

"I didn't know you had any children," I said, fingers lingering on the stitching.

"She only lived four months." Her voice caught; the words settled into the room like dust on old pine. "After that, I packed the blanket away. It's been asleep in the hope chest ever since."

Tears blurred my eyes.

"I want you to have it," she said. "Not just for Andrea, but for you. You've become like a daughter to me, Jenny. Watching your strength bloom has been one of the quiet blessings of my life."

I held the blanket close, the weight of memory and love stitched into every corner. "Thank you" felt far too small.

Mari nodded, eyes shining. "Some things aren't meant to stay buried. Sometimes love circles back around when we least expect it. Mama would've liked that blanket finally getting some use."

"Oh, Mari…" I wrapped her in a hug that tried to say what words couldn't.

When we parted, she wiped her eyes. "Now where's that baby? I've been dyin' to get my hands on that little sprout."

We settled on the couch, afternoon light spilling through the windows like warm honey. Mari cradled Andrea, humming a lullaby that felt older than memory, woman-made comfort stitched straight into the air.

Peace washed over me. My daughter would never have to wonder if she was loved; the circle of women around her made sure of that.

I found myself talking, about Mamaw's fading memory, about losing Papaw and trying to reconcile the man I adored with the secrets he may have carried. Then about Shay: the gentle return, the storm I hadn't noticed brewing until he kissed me, the fear of failing again now that someone else relied on me.

Mari listened, rocking Andrea. When she spoke, her words were slow and sure.

"Love never has been simple. Sometimes it cuts, sometimes it heals, and the hardest truths do both."

She met my eyes. "Your Papaw likely held love and sorrow in the same hands. Your Mamaw chose to stay, not because she was weak, but because she believed cracked things can still hold water. You don't have to live their story, but don't let fear write yours either. You've walked through fire and kept your heart intact. That's what real love needs, someone who holds on when it's easier to run."

Fear still murmured in my heart, but so did her truth. If briars and grief had shaped me once, maybe, just maybe, love and grace could shape me again.

Mari had to leave that evening for a gardening show in Chattanooga. She kissed Andrea's forehead and hugged me tight.

"I'll stop back through on my way home," she promised. "Don't forget, you were made for this."

After she left, I tucked the cream blanket around Andrea Grace and whispered a promise: one day I'd tell her about the woman she's named for, and about the tiny girl whose blanket now keeps her warm. Some stories deserve to be remembered, stitch by stitch.

After she left, the camper felt quiet again, but not empty. Her words and the scent of herbs lingered. I was just beginning to settle Andrea down for a nap when I heard another light knock at the door.

It was Shay.

I let him in, and the moment he stepped through the door, I felt the steadiness he carried settle into me.

"Let's go outside and talk while she naps," I whispered, grabbing the baby monitor off the counter.

We settled into the old patio set I'd bought secondhand. It had a little rust around the legs, one chair that leaned just slightly to the left, but it suited the space just fine. The evening was soft and golden, the last light of May casting long shadows across the grass. The air smelled of freshly cut hay, and a chorus of peepers echoed from the woods beyond the creek.

Shay told me about his day, how he'd driven out to interview the antique dealer. He described her shop as a maze of dust and stories, every shelf holding some forgotten thing that someone once loved. He made it all sound poetic, even funny, and I rested my head on his shoulder, letting his voice wash over me like a lullaby. I remembered Mari's words, her quiet encouragement to let love find me again, and without even realizing it, I let my heart crack open just a little wider.

I must've dozed off. Bone tired from so many nights of waking up every few hours, my body finally gave in.

"Come on," Shay said gently, brushing a strand of hair from my cheek. "Let's get you inside."

He helped me to my feet, steady and slow, like he had all the time in the world.

Once inside, I tried to fight the weight dragging down my eyelids, but Shay stopped me.

"Lie down," he said. "I'll stay a while, keep an ear out for her. You need rest."

Too tired to protest, I crawled under the covers and let sleep take me.

Sometime in the night, I stirred and blinked toward the soft glow of the kitchen light. Shay was sitting in the rocker, bottle in hand, feeding Andrea with the milk I'd pumped earlier. His voice was low, soothing, something between a hum and a prayer, as he rocked her with a tenderness that stirred something deep in me.

When he noticed me watching, he smiled.

"Go back to sleep," he whispered. "I've got her."

And I did, heart full, body light, wrapped in the kind of peace that only comes when you know someone else is holding your world in their arms and treating it like something sacred.

I awoke around four in the morning to her soft little whimpers, hungry again. The room was dim and still, the kind of quiet that only exists in the hours before dawn. I gently lifted her from her cradle and brought her into the bed beside me to nurse.

As she latched on, I felt Shay behind me—warm, solid, steady. Poor thing must've been worn out, too. I nestled back against him, and without a word, he pressed a slow, tender kiss to the back of my neck. Then his arm slid around me, gathering us both in like we belonged there.

In that moment, it felt like we fit just right, like somehow, he was the missing piece that might hold us together for good.

The next day, when he had to leave to head back to work, I could see the sadness in his eyes. "I don't want to leave you," he said, "either of you."

"I know," I whispered, resting my head against his chest as he wrapped me in his arms.

There was something about the way he held me, gentle, sure, that made me feel softer than I'd ever known. Not small. Not weak. Just… real. Like the woman I was always meant to be, stripped of all the armor I'd carried for too long. With him, I didn't have to be hard. I didn't have to brace myself for disappointment or brace myself to survive. I could be vulnerable, and I trusted, down to my bones, that he wouldn't use that against me.

That's when I knew I was falling in love.

But this time, it was different. It wasn't the breathless kind of love that comes quick and wild, the kind that crashes in and burns itself out. It wasn't just hunger or heat, though Lord knows I found him devastatingly handsome.

There was something about him that stopped me still. The way his eyes softened when he looked at me, like he saw every scar and didn't flinch. The roughness of his jaw against my cheek, the quiet power in his hands when he held the baby, like strength and tenderness had struck some rare accord inside him. Even the lines around his mouth, etched there by years of stories and silence, seemed carved for smiling. He was the kind of man who didn't need to say much to make you feel safe.

And while desire stirred in me, warm and undeniable, what I felt ran deeper than anything I'd known before.

No, this was something quieter. Steadier. Not like fire or lightning, but like the hush of dusk settling over a mountain, the way the light fades but leaves everything glowing. Love that didn't demand attention, but stayed, rooted deep, like something time couldn't touch.

It was home.

# Chapter 31

*Journal Entry– June, 2015*

*The raspberries are starting to come in. I saw them from the window this morning, bright as blood against the green. Harlan used to pick them for me, back when we still danced in the kitchen and laughed like we were young. I keep losin' things.*

*Yesterday it was my thimble, but I found it in the butter dish. Last week it was the kettle, burned clean through before I even knew it was on. But it's not just the little things. It's the names, too. The dates. The way the porch light used to flicker when Harlan came home late. I remember that flicker more than his face some days.*

*There are whole years now that feel soft at the edges, like old photographs left in the sun too long. I try to hold onto them, but they slip right through, like water through a cracked jar. I can feel the holes.*

*Sometimes I walk into a room and I'm not sure why I'm there. Stand still, try to remember what I was looking for. Other times, I find myself cryin' and I don't even know why. There's a hollow feeling I can't explain, like I've lost someone, but the name won't come. And then it does. Harlan.*

*And then I think maybe it's me. Maybe I'm the one who's gone. Just not all at once.*

*I reckon the Lord is letting me fade a little at a time, so it don't feel so sharp. But it still scares me. What if I forget the people I love before I go? What if*

*they have to grieve me twice?*
*If this gets found someday, I hope they'll know I was trying to stay. I was*
*trying real hard.*

*-Ruth*

We all noticed Mamaw forgetting more and more. Little things at first, where she set her glasses, what day it was, whether she'd already eaten breakfast. But then the memories started slipping faster, like leaves pulled loose by a hard wind. Daddy worried over her, quiet and constant, until Momma finally said, "Bring her home." And that's what they did.

That fall, after Andrea was born, they brought her to their house to stay. Fixed up Sheryl's old bedroom with all her favorite things—her blue quilt, the framed picture of her and Papaw on their wedding day, the lace doily she always kept on the dresser. Tried to make it feel familiar, soft, safe. Something her hands would still recognize, even if her mind couldn't always follow.

Some days, she was mostly herself. She'd hum old hymns while folding towels or ask how the garden was doing, like nothing had changed. But other days... she'd sit staring out the window for hours, lips moving without sound, eyes clouded over with something none of us could reach.

Winter had come, and Mamaw was having one of her hard days, so Momma was tied up taking care of her. To help, Sheryl and I went back to Mamaw's house to start sorting through her things, deciding what to keep and what to box up. We moved from room to room slowly, like we were walking through someone else's memories.

The first time I stepped into her house without her in it, something in me clenched. It was too quiet, not peaceful, just hollow. Like the walls had exhaled and forgotten how to breathe. I paused in the hallway, struck by a strange stillness. A framed photo of Mamaw and Papaw hung crooked on the wall, the edge of the glass catching the light in a way that made it look like the image was crying. I reached to straighten it, then let my hand fall. Something told me to leave it as it was.

I stepped into her bedroom and ran my fingers along the edge of the vanity. "She used to sit right here," I said, voice low. "Brushing her hair. Writing thank-you cards. I remember she had a little box of mints she kept in the drawer… said sugar helped her think."

Sheryl opened the closet, sifting through scarves. "I remember that. She kept everything in its place. Like she was afraid if she lost one thread, the whole thing would unravel."

My hand hovered over the drawer of the vanity, hesitating. It was pushed in all the way—flush, centered, like it had been closed carefully. Intentionally. A ripple of unease passed through me. Something about the air felt off, like a storm that hadn't broken yet. I almost left it alone. Almost walked away. But something in me, a whisper, a knowing, reached forward and pulled.

That's when I found the letter.

Tucked deep in the drawer of her vanity. Folded up neat like it had been waiting. Waiting for someone to find it or maybe praying no one ever would.

There was just one word written at the top.

**Ruth.**

In my soul, I knew this letter held secrets before I ever opened it. It carried a weight no piece of paper had any right to.

The air changed when I unfolded it, like something terrible had just been unburied.

And when I read the first line, my heart stopped.

*My Dear Ruthie,*

*There's no good way to say what I've done. No words holy enough to wash the blood from my hands. You deserve the truth, even if it rots everything we ever built.*

*It was over a year. I let it go on that long. With the girl in the woods...Andrea. She was younger than she had any business being near a man like me, but she was sweet in that lonely, searching way. She made me feel seen. That's no excuse, just the truth.*

*We met out by the lake, or whenever I was fixing fences on the ridge. She'd come up like a ghost, always barefoot, always grinning like she knew a secret. I should've sent her away the first time. I didn't.*

*You were always at church or off helping somebody, God's work. And I was out there doing the Devil's.*

*She came to the house that night. Right to our front porch, like she belonged there. You were gone, sitting with Miss Ella while she passed. You remember that week? You were gone a lot, doing good. And I was about to ruin it all.*

*She told me she was pregnant. Said I had to leave you, marry her, raise the baby right. She meant it, Ruthie. Said if I didn't tell you, she would. Said she'd stand on the steps of the church Sunday morning and spill it all.*

*Something in me snapped. I told her we couldn't talk there, not where others might see. I walked her out past the wood line, back to where the raspberry brambles had overgrown the path.*

*She was crying. I was shaking. She said, "If you loved me, you'd do right by your child." She was holding her belly like it was already ours.*

*I don't remember deciding to do it. I pushed her back, and she stumbled, caught her foot on a root, and went down hard. Her head struck a stone with a sound I still hear in my sleep.*

*She was still breathing, moaning, and trying to crawl away. But I didn't stop. I dropped to my knees. My hands were around her neck all at once, and I finished it. My thumbs pressed in, and I didn't let go until she stopped moving. Eyes wide. Mouth open. Like she was still trying to tell me something.*

*I sat there beside her for a long while. The moon was coming up. My hands wouldn't stop shaking. I didn't cry. Not then. I just felt hollow.*

*I covered her with brush and vines. Dug into the thicket, made sure no one would stumble on her. Then I drove her car to the edge of the county line and left it on the side of the road. Wiped the steering wheel, the door handle. All of it.*

*Then I went to the lake.*

*Where we used to meet.*

*And I drank.*

*I'm not sure how I made it home.*

*You came in early the next morning. You kissed my cheek and said I smelled like whiskey. I told you I'd had a hard day. That was the truth, I guess.*

*I've lived with it since.*

*Her body's been found now, and we've heard the whispering.*

*I don't ask for forgiveness. I just wanted you to know. Not for my sake, but so you don't think she was just a girl gone wild. She was someone. She was scared. And I destroyed her.*

*If you hate me now, I'll understand.*

*I never deserved the life you gave me.*

*I just hope God will be more merciful than I've been.*

*-Harlan*

My hands shook so hard I nearly dropped it. The words blurred, not from the ink but from the tears welling up, spilling over before I even realized I was crying. A sound escaped me, low and broken, something between a gasp and a sob. "I held the letter tight, as if my arms could stop what my heart already knew. It was in me now. Burrowed deep.

I slid down the wall, knees giving out beneath me, and sat there on the floor, breathing like I'd been kicked. The letter crumpled in my fist, and I wanted to scream, wanted to tear it apart, to undo what I'd just learned. But you can't unread something like that. You can't unknow it.

Papaw. My Papaw.

The man who rocked me to sleep and snuck me spoonfuls of peanut butter when Mamaw wasn't looking. The man who taught me to fish and whittled me toy animals out of cedar. That man had killed a girl.

Not just any girl, a girl whose bones I found tangled in the thicket. A girl whose name had haunted me for half my life.

My breath came in short bursts. Grief. Rage. Horror. Shame. They all crashed together like waves in a storm. How could he? How could he look me in the eyes all those years and carry that weight without ever flinching?

And worst of all, did Mamaw know?

I rocked there for a long while, silent and shaking, until the room stopped spinning. I didn't know what to do next. Who to tell. Whether to tell. All I knew was the world wasn't the same anymore. Something inside me cracked wide open.

And nothing would ever fit back the way it was before.

I didn't hear the footsteps. Didn't register the door creak.

"Jenny?" Sheryl's voice cut through like a blade.

I looked up, and her face went white. "What happened?" She crossed the room in two strides, crouched beside me. "What is that?"

I couldn't speak. Just held the letter out with a trembling hand.

She took it gently, read the first few lines, then sat back against the wall like her spine had snapped. Her mouth opened, but no words came out at first. Just a breath. One long, shaking breath.

"Oh my God…" she whispered, hand going to her mouth.

And then the room filled with silence. Not the peaceful kind. The kind that presses in and steals the air from your lungs.

Sheryl looked at me, eyes shining. "He… He did it?"

I nodded. "It wasn't an accident. He… he meant to. He meant to kill her."

Sheryl clutched the paper like it might tear through her hand. "What do we do with this?" she asked, voice barely audible. "Do we… tell someone? Does Mamaw know?"

I shook my head. "I don't know. I honestly don't know, but she didn't even know Andrea. And now… she doesn't remember enough to understand this if she did."

Sheryl let her head fall back against the wall. "God, Jenny."

"I don't know what's worse," I whispered. "What he did… or the fact that we loved him anyway. That we still do. And now everything feels… ruined."

Sheryl reached over and took my hand. "It isn't ruined. It's just… broken wide open."

And we sat there, on the floor of Mamaw's old room, two grown women clinging to each other like little girls, trying to hold the pieces of the truth together before it swallowed us whole.

We were pulled back into the moment by the cry of my baby, now nearly a year old. I rose to my feet and walked over, looking down at her sitting in the playpen, red-faced and reaching. There she was, my daughter. The blood of my blood. The same blood that once flowed through Papaw Harlan's veins. And her namesake… Andrea Campbell's blood had been spilled by his hands. My mind spun, sick with the weight of it. What did this mean for her? For us?

*What were we going to do?*

I turned to face Sheryl and asked just that.

"What are we supposed to do with this?" My voice shook. "What now?"

She looked pale, like the air had gone out of her lungs. "We wait," she said quietly. "We wait until Mamaw's gone. She don't need to know this now, not at her age, not with her memory slipping the way it is. What good would it do but tear her apart?"

I stared at her, heart pounding. "So we just… keep it secret?"

"For now," Sheryl said, eyes glistening. "We let her have peace. She's lived through enough."

My hands clenched around the letter, knuckles white. "And what about Joyce? What about Andrea's mama, waking up every day not knowing what really happened to her daughter? What about Samantha, growing up in the shadow of a missing sister? You think they've had peace?"

Sheryl dropped her gaze.

"I get what you're saying," I went on, voice rising with every word. "But this ain't just about Mamaw. This is about Andrea. She was carrying a child, Sheryl. She died alone and scared and buried beneath the thicket like she was nothing. She deserves justice. Her family deserves the truth."

Sheryl wiped at her eyes, her voice barely above a whisper. "And what if the truth kills what little we have left?"

I stepped back, shaking my head. "Maybe it will. But silence already has. Look around, this family's been living under the weight of secrets for generations. Maybe it's time we broke the cycle. Maybe it's time somebody finally tells the truth."

Sheryl was quiet for a long time, just watching Baby Andrea settle back into sleep, her tiny chest rising and falling like nothing in the world had shifted. Then she finally spoke.

"Just give me a little time," she said softly. "Not forever, just a little while to think. To figure out how we tell it… without hurting Mamaw more than we have to." Her voice cracked. "She doesn't deserve to carry this so close to the end."

I hesitated, my jaw clenched, still holding the letter like it was burning through my skin.

"Please, Jen. Let's not do anything rash. Just a few days. We can pray on it. Think it through."

I gave a slow nod, even though it twisted something low in my gut. "Alright. We'll wait… for now."

We didn't speak after that. Just moved through the quiet like we were walking across ice, both afraid to make the next crack. We decided to call it quits on going through Mamaw's things for the day. Sheryl packed up the small box of sweaters, Mamaw's favorite books, and photo frames to take over to Momma and Daddy's.

I folded the letter back along its worn creases and slipped it into my bag, feeling its weight settle over me like dusk.

"Let me know when you get there," I said as she loaded the last box into her trunk.

She nodded, and we shared a look that held too much to put into words.

Then I headed home, alone with my thoughts, and the truth I could never unknow.

That night, I lay in bed staring at the ceiling, the letter folded on the nightstand like a coiled serpent. Sleep wouldn't come. My thoughts wouldn't quiet.

How long had Mamaw known?

Had she kept Papaw's secret for years, tucking it away in the quiet places where hard truths go to hide? Or had she only just found it, tucked away like a ghost he left behind for her to find? Maybe he'd written it as a deathbed confession she never saw at all. Maybe she'd read it and forgotten, the words slipping through her mind like water through a cracked jar.

I didn't know what haunted me more, the thought of her knowing and saying nothing, or of her never knowing at all.

And what were we supposed to do now? What would this truth do to our family once it was spoken aloud? It had lived buried under briars and red clay for decades, growing roots in the silence. Would dragging it into the light bring peace… or splinter what little we had left?

It was one thing to wonder if he might've done it, to hold the question at a distance, to tuck it away when it got too heavy. It was another thing entirely to *know.*

Knowing didn't just change the past. It rethreaded every memory, every gesture, every moment we thought we understood.

And once you *know*, you can't unknow. You either carry it, or you let it burn everything down.

I turned onto my side, facing the cradle where my daughter slept. She stirred, one tiny hand curling near her face.

Andrea.

A name heavy with blood and memory, given to my baby in hopes it might carry something new, life and hope instead of loss.

I pulled the covers tighter and shut my eyes, as if I could keep the questions at bay just a little longer.

But I knew sleep wouldn't save me from the truth.

Not this time.

# Chapter 32

*Journal Entry– September 21, 1958*

*The wind's turned, and you can feel fall creeping in by the way it hushes the trees. I pulled the quilts from the cedar chest today, like Mother told me to, aired them out in the sun while the leaves whispered down like old secrets. Harlan came by this afternoon. Said he had somethin' for me. He fidgeted like he does when he's nervous, hands in his pockets, eyes down. Then he pulled out a little ring—thin, simple, gold. No box. No grand speech. Just said, "If you'll have me, I'd like you to wear this."*
*It wasn't flashy. Wasn't big. But it fit, and it was real. Just like him. Just like us.*
*I said yes, of course.*
*And when I slipped that ring on, I didn't just feel chosen, I felt seen. Not for what I looked like, or how I spoke, but for the quiet parts of me nobody ever seemed to notice. The parts that cook biscuits from scratch, hum while hanging laundry, and cry at radio songs.*
*I reckon love ain't always loud. Sometimes it's steady, like creek water winding through the hills—soft, but sure. That's the kind of love I want to build with him, the kind that lasts.*

*-Ruth*

S heryl and I drew closer in our shared knowledge, like quiet conspirators bound by blood and burden. There was tension between us, sure, but we clung to each other anyway, afraid that letting go of the other might let everything else fall apart. It never felt like the right time to bring the truth forward. Christmas passed, then Mother's Day. Dates we didn't want to ruin. But the secret stayed heavy, a shadow cast over our babies as they grew. A veil of lies, of blood and silence, draped over their innocence.

I couldn't keep it to myself any longer.

I couldn't keep it from the man I had come to love, not just as a steady presence, but as a future. Shay had spent his every spare moment with Andrea and me. Sunday dinners, slow evening walks, grocery store runs, and the everyday quiet of folding laundry beside me. He never pushed me for anything I wasn't ready to give. Just held my hand when I needed it. Kissed me gently. Let me come to him at my own pace. And when he finally told me he loved me, loved us, it was by firelight, his voice soft and certain. I told him I loved him too, and I knew then what I had to do.

That same night, I unburdened my heart.

I told him about the letter. About Papaw. About the night I found it and the weight it carried. I laid it all bare. Ugly and gutting and true.

The words hit Shay like a blow. I saw it in the way his shoulders dropped, in the way his eyes lost their focus. He'd stopped pushing for the truth about the case months ago, not because he no longer cared, but because he saw what it did to me. The toll it took after that first dinner with my family. And because, as a journalist, he'd hit the same wall the police had. The case was old, cold, and frayed by time. He'd said it himself: unless something new surfaced, Andrea Campbell's story might never be solved.

But now… the truth was staring him in the face.

I was terrified he'd hate me for it, for what Papaw did, for how long I held it close. Like somehow the sins of my grandfather had seeped into me. Tainted me. And maybe, in a way, they had. Maybe I'd clung too long to keeping the peace.

He didn't yell. Didn't ask for more. He just stood there and said, "I need to go."

"I'm sorry," I whispered, but the words tasted hollow. Too late.

We had searched together, side by side, for justice. It had bound us. Changed us. And I had broken that trust. I wanted to explain, but as he walked away, each step felt like a mile. I knew I had to give him space. He deserved at least that.

*Would he forgive me?*

Weeks passed in silence. He went back home, and when I texted to check in, he replied that he was fine, just needed time to sit with the revelation.

The whole time the silence stretched, I was scared to breathe. I had expected the police to show up at our door any day, demanding the letter, but they never came. I kept the envelope tucked away in the top of my closet, but its presence felt louder with each passing day, like it had a heartbeat of its own.

When Baby Andrea's birthday neared, he finally called.

"I miss you both terribly," he said, voice hoarse with all the things we hadn't said. "I've carried the weight of this for a while now… and I think I understand why you didn't tell me right away."

"I should've told you sooner," I said. "I know that now. I was scared, and I didn't want to taint something good. But the truth matters. Andrea's family deserves it. Sheryl just… she asked me to wait, to let Mamaw have peace while she's still here."

"I get that," he said. "But you have to tell. You have to give the police the letter, Jenny."

"I will," I promised. "Just… give me a little more time. I need to talk to my family first. I don't want to blindside them, especially Mamaw."

"It's not my secret," he said gently. "Not my letter. Not my family. But I meant what I said, I love you, and I've realized something. If I want to be part of your life, I have to support you, even when it's hard. I'm sorry if I made you feel like you were alone in this."

"You don't owe me an apology," I said, choking up. "I'm the one who's sorry."

"I need to see you," he said softly. I could hear the desire in his voice.

"I need you too," I said, and I meant it. The weight of missing him had been lodged in me for so long, like an anchor I couldn't pull free.

"I wish I could come now," he said, regret clear in his tone. "But it'll be another week or so before I can make it down. Work's slammed."

"We can come to you," I offered, my voice lifting with hope.

"I don't want y'all to have to drive."

"It's okay," I said. "I'll tell Daddy I'm taking a few days off work. Momma can get a break from babysitting."

"You sure?"

"As I've ever been."

"I'll send the address," he said.

I knew he thought I'd wait until morning, but I didn't want to. I couldn't. I packed up mine and Andrea's things and headed out that night. He'd always been the one making the drive, but not this time. This time, I was the one coming home to him.

When we finally pulled up outside his little apartment on the edge of the city, I sat in the car a moment, taking it in. The building was old, square, and gray, more concrete than charm, stacked like forgotten shoeboxes under the hum of streetlights. Everything felt hard-edged and hurried. Not like home. Not like the slow curve of the backroads or the hush of the hills. Shay might've made his living chasing stories across pavement now, but he was cut from mountain cloth, born and raised in the backwoods of West Virginia, where men still split their own firewood and knew how to patch a roof. This place didn't suit him.

It wore him like a jacket two sizes too small.

I climbed out, Andrea bundled in my arms, and knocked on the door. My heart beat fast as I heard him on the other side.

When the door opened, there he stood in soft night pants and a faded t-shirt, hair tousled, eyes wide with surprise and something deeper, something full of longing. The dim light behind him painted shadows across his chest, and I swear he'd never looked more like home to me. Rugged. Handsome. Worn soft around the edges, like something well-loved.

He reached out, took Andrea from me without a word. He held her close, his eyes glassing over with the kind of sorrow you carry in silence. I knew then, he had missed us just as much as we'd missed him. With one arm still around Andrea, he pulled me into the fold, and the three of us stood there like a small, patched-together family. Then he kissed me—soft and slow, but full of everything he hadn't said. I felt the weight of the days apart, the pull of need just beneath the tenderness. It wasn't rushed, but it was deep, and it settled something in me that had been restless for far too long.

I stepped inside and looked around.

The apartment was clean, but sparse, just a couch, a small table with two chairs, bare walls. It didn't feel lived-in. It didn't feel like him. No plants, no pictures, no sign that anyone had ever curled up here to dream. No trace of the man I loved. It made me ache. For him. For what he'd been missing. For the life he'd kept at a distance to keep from being hurt.

This wasn't home.

But maybe we could be.

He went to the car and brought in our bags, along with Andrea's pack and play, which would double as her bed. I'd packed to spend a few days here, hoping to make up for the time we'd lost.

We called in takeout and settled in together. We ate and laughed, and with every passing minute, I began to feel whole again. The weight of secrecy was no longer pressing down on me like a low ceiling.

That night, after Andrea had drifted off to sleep, we lay side by side in his bed. He looked at me steadily, then reached across and tucked a loose strand of hair behind my ear. The longing in his eyes was quiet but unmistakable. I was ready, ready to give myself to him, fully, but on my terms and in my time. I leaned over and kissed him with the desperation I had felt for weeks. He kissed me back, his hands tracing the lines of my body—not hurried, not careless, but with purpose, with reverence. The need between us rose slowly, thick in the air like a summer storm building.

He laid me gently onto my back, kissing me deeply, our breaths turning shallow, fast. But then he pulled back. I followed, confused, until he eased me back down again with a softness that steadied me.

"Not now," he whispered. "Not like this. I want to take my time. I want to do this right. To treat you with the respect you deserve."

I felt equal parts frustrated and moved. "Do you not want me?" I whispered softly, that old wound of insecurity pressing in like a bruise.

"Oh, I want you more than you know," he said, pressing himself against me so I could feel the truth of it. "But you deserve more than this. I don't just want your body, I want your heart, your mind, your love. I want all of you for more than a moment. I want you forever."

The gravity of his words hit me like gospel. I'd never heard that before, not from any man. I'd only ever known the worth of my body, never the worth of my soul. But in that moment, with his words still hanging in the air and his arms wrapped around me, something long broken in me began to mend.

I let the promise of it all settle over me as we lay tangled together— gentle kisses, whispered dreams. No need to rush. No fear of being used up or left behind. And for the first time in my life, I felt truly seen. Truly wanted. Not for what I could give, but for who I was.

The next few days passed in blissful domesticity. Shay went to work, and I cooked for him in the evenings. We spent our afternoons exploring the city, him showing me his favorite spots, places that felt a little softer, a little slower than the concrete rush surrounding them. At night, we lie awake talking about our hopes, our wants, our dreams. He told me he didn't plan on staying in the city forever. He wanted a real home—one with a porch, a yard, and a little stream out back for his future children to play in.

I wanted those same things. And though I prayed he wanted them with me, neither of us was brave enough to say it aloud. Not yet.

Each night, he held me close, and I slept without fear. No nightmares. No tossing or turning. Just peaceful rest wrapped in the warmth of a man who loved me.

When it came time for me to return home, an ache settled into my being before I ever pulled out of the driveway.

"I'll be up to see you this weekend," he promised, kissing my cheek as he helped me into the truck.

"We can go shopping for Baby Girl's birthday," he added with a grin, knowing the day was quickly approaching.

"I can't wait. I already miss you," I told him, my voice soft.

"I love you," he said. And I carried those words all the way home like a prayer cloth folded into my pocket.

True to his word, Shay came that weekend, and every weekend after. No matter how tired he was, no matter the weather, he made the drive without complaint. And despite how much time we spent together, he was never possessive. Never selfish. He didn't try to tuck me away in some corner of his life. He wanted to belong in mine.

He spent time with Lena and Andrew, fitting in like he'd known them for years. He spent time with my family too, sitting at Sunday dinners, helping Daddy in the shed, carrying groceries in for Momma. He knew family was where you come from and what you build, something rooted deep and tended with care. His mother had loved him fiercely before she passed, and since then, he'd longed for that sense of belonging again.

His father had turned to the bottle in grief after Shay's mother passed, grief that hardened into silence more often than slurred words. Their relationship was strained, quiet in the way pain sometimes is when it's been left to settle too long. But Shay still called regularly to check on him, even when the conversations were short, even when they ended in more sighs than words. His dad had moved in with Shay's uncle, a bachelor named Thomas, who ran a small auto shop outside of Hawksbend. He said his Uncle Tom was rough around the edges, all grease-stained hands and blunt talk, but Shay spoke of him with respect. Said he'd taken them fishing after his mama died, and showed up when others didn't.

Shay had promised we'd visit soon; he wanted them to meet Andrea and me. "I want them to see what my life looks like now," he'd said. "Not just hear about it through a phone line." He told me he'd never brought a woman home before. That thought stirred something deep in me, something both weighty and tender.

I was going to meet the people who'd shaped the man I loved. The house where he scraped his knees, the porch where his mama taught him how to shell peas, the woods where he first learned to be quiet and listen. I wanted to see it all. And I hoped, in some small, quiet way, I'd belong with them too.

We made plans to go in the fall, when he could take time off work. But summer was just starting to settle in, softer than usual, like it was easing in on tiptoe. The fairgrounds had been set up for the yearly festival, something Shay said he'd gone to as a boy, long before he left West Virginia. He told me he wanted to take Andrea and me. I agreed, picturing funnel cakes, the Ferris wheel, and Andrea's wide-eyed wonder at it all.

The air at the fair was thick with kettle corn and dust coming from the tractor pull, the sky just starting to peach with sunset. Andrea squealed in delight as the carousel spun, her little hands reaching for the horses that danced in circles. Shay lifted her into one of the painted saddles, and I held tight to her waist. She bounced with joy, curls catching the wind, and for a moment, everything else—secrets, grief, shadows—felt far away.

Just joy. Just living in the blissful moment.

We met up with Sheryl, Luke, Lena-Grace, and Andrew by the corn dog stand, the air thick with the smell of grease and mustard and something sweet frying nearby. Lena-Grace threw her arms around Shay like he was an old friend, hugging him tight before pulling back with a grin. Andrew gave him a fist bump, casual and easy, like it was second nature.

I stood back for a moment, watching them together—laughing, teasing, standing shoulder to shoulder like they'd always been part of the same circle. And in that moment, the old heaviness had settled like silt, and something softer took its place. Lighter. Like the quiet click of a puzzle piece finding its fit, small but sure.

After the sun dipped low and the lights flickered to life, Shay tugged me gently toward the Ferris wheel.

"Ride with me?" he asked, his hand already reaching for mine.

I nodded and climbed into the cart. The world below grew smaller with every turn, noise and motion fading until it felt like we were the only two people left above the fairgrounds.

At the top, just as the wheel paused with us suspended at its peak, Shay reached into his coat pocket and pulled out a small velvet box. No speech. No fanfare. Just him, eyes steady, voice low.

"I don't need perfect," he said. "I just need you. You and Andrea. Will you marry me?"

Tears stung my eyes. For a second, I couldn't speak.

"I know it's sudden," he went on, voice shaking a little, "but I feel like

I've known you my whole life."

He was nervous, I could hear it, see it in the way he held his breath. But all I could do was nod, the yes catching in my throat before it ever found words.

When I finally spoke, it came out soft, but certain.

"Yes," I said. Then again, louder, truer.

"Yes."

When he slid the ring onto my finger, the tears came. It was a delicate vintage piece, not flashy but beautiful. It fit like it had always belonged there. Like something I'd known before.

Something that remembered me.

He kissed me then, high above the world, with the lights blurring beneath us like stars.

And for once, the future didn't feel like a question.

It felt like a promise.

After the fair, we headed to Momma and Daddy's to share the news. Daddy was outside on the porch, listening to the frogs croak, the kind of sound that settles into your bones if you've been raised on it.

Shay carried a sleeping Andrea inside and laid her gently on the couch.

"So… he asked?" Daddy said without looking up.

I smiled and held up my left hand.

He glanced down, nodding slowly. "I used to think a man needed to ask a father first. That was the way of it, back when I was coming up. But daughters got their own minds. And I trust you."

His words landed hard, steady, and true. I leaned into his side, and he slung an arm around my shoulder.

"You picked a good one," he added. "I can see it. In how he looks at you. In how you look back."

"I think so too," I said softly.

"I remember buying your momma that ring," he said after a pause. And suddenly, I understood why it had looked so familiar. It was the first ring Daddy had given Momma, the one she'd worn when she said her vows. He'd bought her a new one on their twentieth anniversary, but this one… this one had stood the test of time.

Just then, Shay and Momma stepped outside. She pulled me into a hug.

"Thank you, Momma," I said, holding out my hand to show her the ring.

"I always hoped one of you girls would have it," she said, her voice thick. "When Shay asked your daddy for your hand, I was glad to give it to him, to give to you. Luckily, he could return the one he'd already bought."

I turned to look at Shay, and he smiled at me in that quiet way of his, steady and sure.

As the night settled around us, I stood there on the porch feeling loved. The crickets sang, the porch light glowed softly behind us, and in that moment, I knew this was the start of something good. Something lasting. Something ours.

# Chapter 33



*Journal Entry– February 2, 1997*

*Snow's mostly melted, but the ground's still hard. The creek's whispering
again under the ice. Funny how even what's frozen carries a voice.
I believe the Lord brings things to light in His own time, but He expects us to
do our part, too. You can't build anything good on a lie, not even out of love.
I've watched families try, stacking silence like stones, thinking if they don't
speak it, it won't spread. But truth don't stay buried. It has roots, and it finds
its way up.
Sometimes it shows up in a child's eyes, asking questions you hoped they'd
never think to ask. Sometimes it comes in dreams, or in the ache you carry
when no one's looking.
But when it does come, you got two choices: keep hiding and let it rot
everything, or face it and let the healing begin.
Truth's sharp when it first comes out. Cuts deep. But it's like a blade the
Lord uses to carve away what's dying so something better can grow. That's
what I believe. And if it ever falls to one of mine to speak it, I hope they do,
with courage, and with grace.
Because what's said in love, even when it hurts, can be the very thing that
sets us free.*

*-Ruth*

The bridal shop smelled of starch and lavender, the kind of scent that clings to hymnals and Sunday dresses long after the benediction. Sheryl worried a row of lace sleeves, pretending the tremor in her fingers was excitement, not fear, while I slid hangers back and forth just to keep my breathing steady. We talked about hems and whether tulle would itch, about how Lena-Grace would surely sob through the whole ceremony, anything to keep from speaking Papaw Harlan's name. It hung between us like mist on a mountain holler until I finally whispered, "I'm telling the sheriff before I walk down that aisle. My vows need to be clean, my mind clear."

Sheryl's hand froze on the fabric; relief and dread stitched themselves into the same uneasy breath.

"We have to tell Momma and Daddy first," she murmured. "Let them decide what Mamaw should hear."

"I will after the ceremony. I want them to have one day that's just joy," I said.

She narrowed her eyes. "Is that why you're rushing the wedding?" I shook my head.

"Wait, Jenny, you're not pregnant, are you?"

I let out a startled laugh. "No, Sher, I'm not pregnant. We just… love each other. And we haven't yet…" Heat crept into my cheeks.

"What do you mean you haven't yet?" she echoed, one brow arched.

"Not all the way," I admitted. "He wants to wait, says I deserve the respect."

Her grin was wide and honest, easing the tightness in the room. "Well, that explains the hurry." We both laughed, soft and grateful.

"It doesn't hurt," I said, "but mostly it's Mamaw. I need her there while she still knows my name."

At that truth, the laughter faded. We never found a dress that afternoon, so we drove to the bakery instead, hoping to order a simple cake for the small ceremony. It smelled like sugar and warm flour, the kind of scent that should've felt comforting. But even sweetness can sit uneasy when your stomach's full of nerves.

The sun had started to dip as we stepped out of the bakery, the box of cake samples tucked under my arm. I was just about to say something, something light to lift the mood again, maybe a joke about lemon frosting or ribbon colors, when I caught sight of movement across the street, and everything in me stilled.

Lonnie.

He was across the street, holding the hand of a little girl no older than four. Her pigtails bounced as they walked, and she pointed excitedly at a balloon vendor near the courthouse square. Lonnie didn't smile, not really. Just nodded, distracted, like the weight of fatherhood had settled heavy on him and never let up.

My breath caught like a burr in my throat.  It felt like the world narrowed, the sound of traffic and voices dimming behind the thrum of blood in my ears.

There he was, living. Breathing. Raising a child.

The man who'd once stolen something from me that I hadn't even known could be taken. And now he was walking free, hand-in-hand with innocence.

And yet… something in his face looked hollow. Not haunted, exactly. Just worn out in the way that shame wears a man down from the inside. His shoulders slumped.

Some sins don't need fire to burn. They just need time.

Time, and a mirror. And sometimes the mirror is a child, someone who looks up at you with trust, not knowing who you were before.

I realized then that maybe I didn't need vengeance or justice after all. Maybe living with what he did, being reminded every day in the curve of his daughter's smile that some things couldn't be undone, was punishment enough.

The same way Papaw had carried his guilt like a buried fence post, rotting slow beneath the clay, unseen but shifting everything around it over time.

And if it wasn't brought up into the light, wasn't made new, it would surely fail, giving way when the weight grew too heavy. But if it was pulled out and replaced, set firm in good soil, then the fence could stand again. Not because the damage never happened, but because something stronger took its place.

That's grace, making the broken sturdy again.

A different kind of justice. One that doesn't always come with sirens or courtrooms, but with mercy. With rebuilding.

It's strange how the years peel you back. When you're young, you think justice comes like thunder—loud and sudden and righteous.

But I've learned it more often comes quietly, slowly as mildew creeping up the side of a house, until one day you see the rot plain as day and wonder how long it's been there.

The law doesn't always settle the score, but life does. God does.

He lets the weight of a man's choices press down on him 'til it bows the spine. And the only relief comes from laying it down at His feet, turning back to the Father, and begging for mercy.

I like to think Papaw did that before the end. That he whispered the Lord's name with a heart split open. I hope the same for Lonnie. I truly do.

Even if I never hear the words from his mouth. Even if no one else ever knows but him and God.

For too long, I wanted justice to answer to me. I wanted it wrapped in a neat box with a verdict I could point to. All it did was hollow me out.

Bitterness is a slow poison; it doesn't kill quickly. It curls around your ribs and settles in your marrow. It makes you think silence is strength and rage is righteousness.

Turns out, it isn't vengeance that saves you.

It's grace.

Grace, and the will to let go.

Days passed, and the memory of seeing Lonnie with his little girl stayed with me, not sharp anymore, just quiet. It lingered like a bruise you forget about until something brushes against it. I didn't speak of it to anyone, but it shaped the days that followed, softened the edges of my anger in ways I hadn't expected.

Life moved forward. Arrangements were made. Cakes were tasted and chosen, lemon with raspberry filling, sweet but not too rich. As the day drew near, chairs and tables were set out in Momma's backyard. Daddy built an arch near the spot where the creek whispered through the back of the property, right under the walnut tree where we'd spent so many summers catching lightning bugs.

I found my dress in a dusty corner of an antique store. It was vintage lace, soft ivory with delicate sleeves and tiny covered buttons down the back. The hem fell just to my ankles, and when I moved, it caught the air like it remembered another bride before me. It wasn't flashy. It was quiet and worn and lovely, just right.

I was a bundle of nerves. Laughing one minute, teary-eyed the next. I couldn't believe I was really about to marry my best friend—the man who never rushed me, who held space for all the mess I came with, and called it love.

The night before the wedding, sleep came slow and uneasy. I lay still, staring at the ceiling, listening to the creaks of the old house settling like it was holding its breath with me. At some point, without meaning to, I slipped under.

And I was back in the woods.

But not the way they used to be.

This time, the trees were hushed, holding more memory than menace. And in front of me, raspberry bushes lined the path, not wild and overgrown like they had been all my life, but arched, pulled back, and twined together above me, forming a chapel of thorns and bloom. Their canes bowed toward one another, heavy with fruit that bled red in the moonlight.

An altar, maybe. Or a warning.

Andrea stood just past the archway, barefoot in a pale dress, her hair dripping as if she'd risen straight from the river. But her eyes were clear this time, no longer clouded with shadow. And beside her stood a little girl.

Andrea Grace. She was older, but in my heart, I knew she was my child.

She held tight to Andrea's hand, her curls wild, her small bare feet rooted in the path like she belonged not just to this place, but to something far beyond it.

They watched me, quiet and still, until Andrea spoke.

*"She doesn't have to carry what I did."*

The words struck clean through me.

I tried to move, to go to them, but my feet sank into the earth like the soil didn't want to let me go.

Andrea looked at the child, then back at me.

*"You're the bridge, Jenny. Between what was buried and what's still growing."*

The little girl stepped forward, just enough for me to see she was holding something small in her other hand—a key, I thought. Brass and gleaming. She looked at me with a gaze too knowing for her age, and then she tugged gently at Andrea's fingers.

*"Say the truth,"* Andrea whispered. *"Plant it. Let her grow up in the light."*

Their voices rose together, soft at first, then circling the trees like wind: *Say the truth. Say the truth. Say the truth.*

And then it happened.

Without warning, their forms shifted, softened, until where they stood was no longer two girls, but a doe and her fawn. The mother turned to nudge the little one forward, and together they stepped beneath the raspberry arch and vanished into the trees.

For a long moment, all was still.

Then a breeze came low through the leaves, carrying a voice I didn't recognize but somehow understood:

*"This is the Kingdom of the Does. Where the wounded grow wild and the broken still bloom."*

I woke up choking back tears, the ghost of raspberries on my tongue, and the hush of hooves in my ears. The wedding was hours away, but the dream clung to me like dew on morning grass. I didn't need to wonder what it meant.

It was time to tell the truth.

The hills were still blue with dawn when I eased my truck into the sheriff's lot. A new metal placard over the door read **"Captain P. Serogia"**, tidy and unassuming, the way Pete had always been.

Inside, the office smelled of burnt coffee and floor wax. Pete sat behind the same battered desk I remembered from my high-school statement, only now the oak had been polished, and the man behind it had gone silver. He looked up, surprise creasing to warmth.

"Jenny Ann Thompson," he said, voice low-country soft. "Figured you'd be knee-deep in flowers by now. I wasn't supposed to be there till six, was I?"

"That's right, it's still at six." My throat felt tight. "But I need to hand off a burden first."

Something in my tone set him straight. He rose, gesturing to the little interview room off the bullpen, the same room where he'd questioned teenage me while rain hammered the old metal roof.

When the door clicked shut, the silence fell, and my heartbeat was loud in my ears.

I pulled the folded pages from my purse and laid them on the table. "Pete... this is a letter Papaw Harlan left. It's a confession. Andrea

Campbell." The words tasted like iron, but I got them out.

Pete didn't reach for the pages right away. He studied my face the way Daddy does when he thinks one of us is hurt. "You certain you want to do this today?"

"I can't stand in front of God and Shay with this still hidden. But I'm asking for one grace, Pete. Let me marry him this evening. Let Mamaw see me happy while she still knows my name. Tomorrow, you can log it. Question whoever you need."

Pete exhaled slowly, the breath of a man who's carried plenty of hard truths. "Your daddy ever tell you why we call the badge a shield?" he asked.

I shook my head.

"Not to hide behind," he said, tapping the letter, "but to hold the weight steady till folks can bear it." Then he slid the pages into a plain manila envelope, sealed it, and wrote the next day's date across the flap. "Consider it shielded till tomorrow."

Tears pricked, but I kept my voice even. "Thank you."

He rested a hand on my shoulder, steady, father-gentle. "Truth's a hard thing, Jenny, but it's never the wrong thing. Go get married. We'll walk the next mile together."

I stepped back into the morning light lighter than I'd felt in years, and I believed our vows might really take root in clean soil.

And the day moved forward, toward grace.

I turned up the drive just as the sun cleared the ridge, spilling gold over the hickory leaves. Shay was on the porch rail, cup of coffee in hand. When he saw me step out of the truck, our eyes met.

"You okay?" he called, voice low but sure.

I climbed the steps and pressed my forehead to his shoulder. "It's done," I whispered. "Pete's got the letter. He's keeping it quiet till tomorrow."

Shay set the cup aside and wrapped his arms around me, palms broad between my shoulders. For a heartbeat, we just breathed—coffee, morning grass, the faint scent of creek water drifting up from the holler.

"Feel lighter?" he asked.

"Like I can stand up straight again."

He brushed a curl from my cheek. "Then today we marry in the sunlight, Jenny Ann Thompson, clean and clear." He kissed my dirt-cool hands until the chill bled out of them. "Go on inside. Your mama's got hot biscuits and nerves in equal measure."

I laughed softly. Behind us, the arch waited, sanded smooth as a promise.

Inside, the house hummed with wedding bustle—pots rattling, Lena-Grace hunting ribbons, Andrew tying chair sashes in boy-scout knots. Momma spotted me, relief easing her brow, but before she could speak, Mamaw's voice floated down the hallway.

"Jenny-girl? You got a minute for an old woman?"

I found her in her bedroom rocker, sun falling through lace curtains onto the throw across her knees. Today her eyes were bright, cleared for the first time in weeks. In her lap sat a tiny velvet box, frayed at the corners. "Your Papaw bought this in '63," she said, fingers trembling but sure. "Said the blue stone looked like hope you could hold." She opened the lid. Inside lay a hairpin of lapis lazuli, deep as twilight, flecked with gold veins like threads of lightning.

"Mamaw, it's beautiful."

"It's wisdom and memory," she corrected, sliding the pin into my hair with surprising steadiness. "May it keep your mind when memory fades, and point you home when wisdom wanders."

I knelt to hug her, the pin cool against my scalp. She cupped my cheeks. "Walk that aisle, child, and don't look back. The Lord does the mending."

Tears blurred the room, but I saw her smile, and I carried it with me like a lamp into the hallway din.

By late afternoon, the backyard had turned into a chapel. White chairs flanked the aisle; Daddy's arch stood at the creek's bend, draped in wild fern and Queen Anne's lace. The water whispered its amen beneath.

Shay's Uncle Thomas tuned his fiddle near the porch steps; soft strains of "Amazing Grace" drifted over the lawn, threading through the willow branches like a prayer carried on the wind. Mari arrived first, carrying a clay pot of rosemary, "for remembrance," she said, placing it by the guest book with both hands like it was something sacred.

Andrew returned with a red-cheeked date in tow. He was a handsome young man, tall and neat in a navy button-down, with a smile that looked both proud and a little unsure. Andrew beamed beside him. Lena-Grace looped her arm through his and told him, loud enough for the holler to hear, that she loved him "come what may." He blushed all the way to his collar, and she kissed his cheek like she meant it.

Then, Lena found her own date—the lanky, dark-haired guitar player named Reed, whose hands moved like music even when the rest of him was still. He had a quiet way about him, the kind that makes you lean in when he finally speaks. He wore boots that had seen better days and a bolo tie that didn't match his shirt, but somehow it worked. Lena took a seat beside him, grinning like she already knew the whole night by heart.

Shay's father and brother sat in the second row of chairs, dressed in borrowed suits but earnest as sunrise. Daddy shook each hand, mountain-firm. Momma fussed over the boutonnières, pretending not to cry. Sheryl and Luke sat with both our girls, Alana holding Andrea Grace's hand as she wobbled to stand, her face lit with the kind of gentle pride children rarely know they're showing.

One by one, the others arrived: Pete and his wife, Mr. Ford and his family, old neighbors, church friends, familiar faces from the farmers' market and feed store, until the backyard filled with the people I loved most. Voices rose like birdsong, laughter tangled with wind chimes, and the air took on that soft golden hue that only comes when something holy is about to happen.

When the first rays of evening light spilled through the walnut leaves, just beginning to turn gold at the edges, bells strung on the porch rail rang sweet and clear. The guests rose, chairs creaking softly beneath them, dresses rustling like leaves in a shifting wind. A hush fell, the hush that lives between confession and covenant, between the letting go and the holding on. It was the kind of silence that feels full instead of empty, like the earth itself was pausing to listen.

I stood just beyond the arch, dress catching in the breeze, Mamaw's hairpin warm against my scalp like a blessing pressed into bone. The creek whispered its witness behind me.

And beneath the arch, with the water washing soft against the bank, the man I loved waited, not to rescue me, not to fix me, but to walk beside me.

We had come through fire and flood, secret and sorrow, and somehow, grace still held.

And now, in the light of all we'd survived, love waited to speak its vows.

# Chapter 34



*Journal Entry– March 17, 1982*

*Sometimes I think women carry a kind of quiet knowledge that men will never understand. It lives in our bones, passed down from our mothers and grandmothers, not in words but in glances, in sighs, in the way we know how to brace for pain before it ever comes. We learn early how to shrink ourselves, how to keep secrets in our pockets, how to dry our tears quickly so no one sees.*

*I think of my own mother, and hers before her, and I wonder how many wounds they buried just to keep their homes standing. I wonder how many nights they prayed through gritted teeth. There's a thread that connects us all. A thread woven with strength and sorrow, faith and fire. And I hope one day my granddaughters will feel it too, not just the weight of it, but the power. Even when the world tries to break us, we are not alone. We never were.*

*-Ruth*

The reception glowed soft and golden, string lights flickering like slow-moving fireflies across the backyard. The hush of early fall carried the scent of sweet tea, cut grass, and the faint smoke of hickory drifting from Daddy's grill. Laughter spilled across the tables in easy waves. Near the porch, Mamaw rocked in her favorite chair, hands folded loosely in her lap, eyes bright and lucid for the first time in days, catching every detail as if she meant to stitch it into memory.

It wasn't flashy. It wasn't grand but gleaming with the kind of love that doesn't need chandeliers or orchestras to prove itself.

As the sun slipped behind the ridge and the lanterns winked on one by one, Shay brushed a knuckle down my arm, a quiet signal only I seemed to notice.

"I've got something for you," he murmured.

We wandered to the edge of the yard where the lantern glow thinned into shadow. Fireflies stitched green sparks through the dusk. Shay reached into his pocket and drew out a small brass key, warm from his palm, tied with a ribbon the same dusty rose as my bouquet.

"This is yours now," he said, pressing it into my hand.

" A key?" My voice caught.

He smiled, the corners of his eyes creasing. "To our house."

My breath hitched. "What house?"

"Our house," he repeated, wrapping me in a slow, easy hug that smelled of cedar and wedding cake. "Out on Rebecca Lane in Wallens. I've been fixing it up the last couple of months, quietly. I wanted to surprise you."

I stepped back, blinking against sudden tears. "Shay… you did all that?"

He nodded, and the string lights behind him made a faint halo around his shoulders. For a second, I couldn't speak; the future felt so near I could taste it, honey-sweet and terrifying in equal measure. I looked down at the key, its weight a steady thrum in my palm.

"I want our first night to be in our own home," he said. "If you're ready."

A smile unfurled slow and certain across my face. "Let's go."

The farmhouse waited under a scatter of new stars, tucked between the river and a row of old maples that creaked softly in the breeze. Fireflies dotted the fence posts like votive candles. White clapboard gleamed pale in the moonlight, and a wide porch wrapped around the house as though it meant to hold us close.

I stepped onto the boards, fresh-paint scent still lingering, and slid the key home. The door eased open to warm pine floors, candlelight trembling on the walls, and the faintest hint of lavender drifting from somewhere deeper inside.

"It's three bedrooms, plenty of space to grow into," Shay said, voice colored with nerves and hope. "I haven't furnished everything yet, but I set up the bedroom, just the basics. Figured we could make the rest ours together."

In that moment, the empty rooms didn't feel unfinished; they felt expectant, like quiet pages waiting to be written on. And I realized home wasn't four walls filled, home was a key laid in my hand by someone who wanted to build a life with me, one room, one promise at a time.

Shay had placed tea lights around the living room and led me by the hand through the quiet hush of the house. The bedroom was modest—fresh white sheets, a sturdy oak bed, and a few scattered rose petals that looked like they'd been dropped by nervous fingers. A quilt was folded neatly at the end of the bed.

On the dresser sat a small wicker basket wrapped in cellophane and tied with twine. Inside were two champagne glasses, a pair of soft robes, and a box of dark chocolates nestled beside a handwritten note. For the first night of forever. Love, Lena & Andrew.

"I asked them to check the place earlier, light the candles, and just to be sure everything was right," Shay said with a grin. "Guess they went a little above and beyond."

The gesture caught in my throat. That kind of thoughtfulness, the kind that doesn't ask for praise, reminded me just how rare and precious true friends are.

"I didn't know what you'd like," Shay added, rubbing the back of his neck. "But I wanted it to feel like home."

I turned toward him, my voice soft. "It already does."

We didn't rush.  The night was slow and gentle, made of candle shadows, whispered thank yous, and a kind of reverence that made even the silence feel precious.

This wasn't the beginning of a fairy tale.

It was the beginning of something real.

We woke to birdsong and soft light seeping through gauzy curtains. The river murmured just beyond the window, steady and sure, like it had always been waiting for us to arrive.  Shay brewed coffee in a small percolator and brought it to me in a chipped mug that said Best Grandpa Ever. We laughed until we cried.

We didn't talk much that morning.  We didn't need to.  There was something sacred in the quiet, in the knowing that we had time now. A home. A life we could grow into.

But the world doesn't stop spinning just because you've found something good.

By late afternoon, the weight of what still needed saying had settled back on my shoulders.

"I'll take Andrea Grace to the park," Shay offered, brushing a kiss to my temple. "Take your time."

The house felt too still once he left.

Momma had made tea, the way she always did when the world felt unsteady. Daddy was in his chair, hands clasped over his stomach like he was bracing for bad weather.

"I need to tell y'all something," I said, my voice tight. "And I need you to listen all the way through before you say a word."

Momma nodded, but her fingers had already gone white around the handle of her cup.

I sat down at the kitchen table—the same one where Sheryl and I had broke beans, learned fractions, and cried over teenage heartbreaks. But this? This was heavier than all that. This would split something wide open.

I told them about the letter. About Shay and me, about what we'd found. All of it.

The silence that followed was a thunderclap.

Daddy looked like I'd kicked him. His face drained, lips parting, but no sound coming out. Momma blinked once, then again, like maybe she hadn't heard me right. "Jenny Ann… don't say things you can't take back."

"I wish I could take it back," I said, voice breaking. "But it's true. Pete will be calling."

Momma stood slowly. Moved to the sink. Turned the water on but didn't do anything with it.

Daddy rubbed his face with both hands and let out a sound that was part moan, part prayer. "Lord God," he whispered. "Daddy?"

I nodded. "The letter was real."

He sat back, stunned. "You remember when I said I saw those missing posters when I was little? When she disappeared? He would've already had two kids by then. Already had me."

Momma's voice was thin. "Why didn't Ruth say anything?"

"I don't want to think she knew," I said quietly. "Or maybe she did and buried it deep. But Papaw left the letter. Told it all. Said he was sorry. That he never meant to kill her, that it was a fight gone too far."

Momma swayed where she stood. Then she turned slowly and looked at me with eyes full of something I couldn't read at first. Maybe grief. Maybe shame. Maybe just the gut-deep knowledge that the people we love are never just one thing.

"I thought I knew who he was," she whispered.

"I did too."

Daddy stood, crossed the room, and wrapped his arms around Momma from behind. They stood like that for a long time, the faucet still running, like maybe it was washing loose the story the ground wouldn't keep.

"I needed you to know before it became public. I didn't want you to hear it from someone else," I said.

Momma turned and took my face in her hands. Her thumbs were trembling.

"Thank you," she said. "For carrying this. For telling us. For not running from the truth."

Her voice cracked. "He was a good man, but he also did something terrible. Both things can be true."

Daddy nodded. "And now the truth has to breathe. Even if it breaks our hearts wide open."

It was less than a week later that Pete called.

"We need you to come down to the station," he said, his voice calm but taut, like a rope pulled tight. "We'd like to get a DNA sample. Just to be sure. I'd ask Abe, but I know he's having a hard time just taking care of Mrs. Ruth."

Shay and I drove in silence, hands linked between us. The air outside the truck was crisp with autumn creeping in. Burnt orange drifted from the treetops like embers falling from a dying fire. I felt nineteen and ninety at the same time.

The swab itself was quick, cold cotton pressed to the inside of my cheek like a secret being collected. The nurse was kind, and Pete didn't say much, just nodded like a man carrying more weight than he wanted to. Shay stayed behind me the whole time, his palm steady on my back like a lighthouse beam.

"We'll run the sample in Knoxville," Pete said, sealing the envelope with care. "Could be six weeks, maybe a little more. It takes a while on these cold cases."

I nodded. "Okay."

I didn't ask what we both already knew, that if the child Andrea carried was related to me, then Papaw's letter wasn't a rumor or a fear.

It was the truth. Raw and irreversible.

Outside, the sunlight stung. I couldn't tell if the feeling clawing through me was grief or relief. Maybe both.

The days that followed blurred at the edges, too bright and too heavy all at once.

We painted the kitchen walls in soft eggshell. Andrea Grace learned to pull herself up on the window ledge. I kept fresh flowers on Mamaw's nightstand, even when she didn't know where she was. Some days she called me by Momma's name. Some days, she just stared past me and whispered hymns like prayers into the wallpaper.

And then, one ordinary afternoon, the phone rang.

Shay answered. Said nothing for a long time. Just nodded. When he handed the phone to me, his fingers brushed mine like a warning, like a curtain being drawn back.

Pete's voice was soft. "The DNA matched. There's no doubt."

My mouth went dry. "She was… she was Papaw Harlan's."

"I'm so sorry, Jenny."

He said other things, about reopening files, about procedures, and next steps—but I didn't hear most of them. I just stood in our little kitchen, one hand braced against the countertop, trying not to collapse under the weight of it all.

Shay came to me. Held me without asking if I was okay.

"I loved him," I said, barely above a whisper. "I loved the man who used to carry me on his shoulders and sing I'll Fly Away while we picked berries. And he did something unforgivable."

Shay's voice was low. "Love doesn't vanish just because it's tangled up with hurt. Sometimes they live side by side."

I nodded, but the feeling stayed lodged inside me, like a splinter buried too deep to pull free.

The sheriff held the press conference on a Tuesday morning, out on the courthouse steps beneath the flag that barely moved in the still air.

Reporters gathered with notepads and recorders; their camera lenses tilted toward the makeshift podium like vultures circling something finally dead.

I stood near the lemonade stand, close enough to hear, far enough not to be seen. Shay's hand anchored mine. Across the lawn sat Andrea's mama and sister, side by side but not touching. Grief had stiffened their posture, but I recognized something else there too, relief, raw and trembling, like a bird that had flown too long and finally found a perch. The kind of relief that doesn't come easily. The kind that only follows truth.

"We called this conference today," the sheriff began, his voice thick and deliberate, "to officially close the file on Andrea Kaye Campbell's case."

He paused, letting the words settle in. "The Campbell family has waited decades for answers. We now have them. Thanks to a letter uncovered after the passing of Harlan Thompson, and additional corroborating evidence provided willingly and transparently by members of his own family. We are confirming that Andrea's death was the result of a violent act and that Mr. Thompson was the one responsible."

A hush fell over the crowd, broken only by the soft click of a camera shutter. Somewhere behind me, someone gasped. I barely heard it. I'd already read the letter. I'd felt the weight of those words, handwritten and blurred in places, like even the page itself had grown tired of keeping secrets.

The sheriff continued, steady and solemn. "It's never easy to reckon with the sins of the past, but it is necessary. The Thompson family's decision to come forward, despite what it cost them, speaks to a kind of courage that doesn't erase what was done, but honors what is left. Their actions remind us that doing what's right is rarely painless, but always powerful."

He looked down for a moment, then added, "They chose truth over comfort. Accountability over silence. And in doing so, they helped shine a light that's been needed for a very long time."

Joyce Campbell stepped forward next, Samantha guiding her to the podium, hands trembling as she unfolded a piece of paper worn soft with re-reading. Her voice cracked, but did not falter.

"My daughter loved horses. She sang off-key. She whistled with her teeth just to make her sister laugh. She hated lima beans and loved snow days. She was ours."

She paused, holding the silence like a sacred thing. I said a silent prayer for her.

"Her name was Andrea Kaye Campbell. Say it. Say it when you speak of justice. Say it when you remember what it costs to bury a daughter and not know why. Say it when you see the stars and wonder who's listening."

Her hands fell to her sides, the paper still fluttering like a breath.

I wiped my eyes with the corner of my sleeve. It wasn't enough, not for what had been taken, but it was something. The truth had been spoken aloud, and that mattered.

Later, as the crowd drifted away and the heat pressed down like memory, I stood by the magnolia and whispered Andrea's name. Not for closure, but for honor. For peace. For every silent woman who never got the press conference, or the podium, or the ending.

Mamaw faded fast after that day, like some tether inside her had finally snapped.

One morning, just before dawn, Daddy called and said, "If you want to say goodbye, it should be today."

We gathered in the bedroom where she lay, her breaths thin and far between. The room smelled like eucalyptus and cedar and something older than both.

I took her hand in mine and whispered, "It's okay, Mamaw. You can rest."

Her eyes fluttered open one last time, blue and clear.

"Now we see through a glass, darkly…" she said faintly, smiling through the veil, "but then, face to face."

And then she was gone.

We buried her beside Papaw, under the oak tree. I knelt by the fresh earth, Andrea Grace in my lap, and let my tears fall without shame.

"Even when I couldn't hear them," I said softly, voice breaking, "your prayers still carried me. I know that now. I feel them everywhere."

Momma laid a hand on my shoulder. "You were her answered prayer, honey. Whether you knew it or not."

We stood there for a long while, until the light shifted gold and the breeze lifted the edge of Mamaw's funeral ribbon.  It floated like a benediction, like forgiveness on the wind.

I didn't know it yet, but that wind would carry me all the way to something new, something Mamaw had helped sow without ever seeing bloom.

But I would.

Because she believed I would.

Because she prayed it true.

# Chapter 35

*Journal Entry– April 5, 1962*

*Today, the redbuds bloomed along the ridge, bright as a promise. I stood on the porch this morning, barefoot in the cold, watching the fog rise off the pasture like breath from something sleeping. The air was sharp but sweet, and the world felt brand new. I believe there are days when the Lord reminds us what it means to begin again. This was one of them.*

*Abe was kicking in my belly—strong, steady. It made me laugh. I swear he already knows my voice. Harlan's been working hard on the fence line, trying to get everything right before the baby comes. He don't say much, but I see the way he looks at the cradle. Like he wants to be the kind of father he never had.*

*There's a peace in knowing the seasons turn, whether we're ready or not. A kind of grace in the waiting.*

*I don't know what this world will hand my children, but I pray they carry love like a lantern. That they walk through dark places and still shine. I pray they know that being tender isn't the same as being weak, and that even thorned things can bear sweetness, if you're patient enough to see it bloom.*

*Maybe that's what faith really is. Planting something in the dirt and believing it'll rise, not for yourself, but for the ones who'll come after. Like putting a tree in the ground knowing full well you'll never sit beneath its shade.*

*-Ruth*

I stepped out onto the porch barefoot, the old boards warm from the sun. The air had shifted sticky, swollen with the promise of summer. Raspberries grew wild along the riverbank, thorny and tangled but blooming all the same. I walked across the yard and picked one, dark red and overripe, and I let it rest on my tongue. I enjoyed the sweetness, one I hadn't tasted in years.

Earlier that week, the town square of Wallens filled with folding chairs, flower arrangements, and the low hum of a grieving community. A makeshift altar had been placed beneath the old sycamore that leaned like a sentinel near the war memorial. Andrea Campbell's name was stitched onto the white linen draped across the table, beside a photograph faded from time. It had taken decades for the mystery to finally be laid to rest, where folks could speak her name without shame or fear.

Reverend Lawson stood near the front, hand over his heart. Mrs. Campbell, stooped and silver-haired, rested a trembling hand in the bend of her daughter Samantha's arm. There were others from town who had helped search all those years ago, and those who had whispered stories when they thought no one was listening. And I stood with Shay, his arm strong around my waist, as the preacher read a passage about the lost being found. Then he opened the floor.

Shay stepped up, cleared his throat, and read his article, not as a journalist, but as a witness. His voice didn't waver, but I could see the way his jaw tightened on certain words, like sorrow chiseled from granite. Each line carried weight, like a stone skipping across the surface of still water—soft at first, then rippling outward until the whole town seemed to hold its breath. When he finished, silence fell.

One of Andrea's nieces came to me, hands shaking, eyes full of something deeper than grief, relief, maybe. "Thank you," she said, gripping my hand.  I nodded, unable to speak.  But inside, I felt something uncoil. The past had finally been given a place to rest.

After the service, a small reception was held in the fellowship hall of the old Baptist church. Dishes of cornbread, deviled eggs, and lemon pound cake lined the tables. I sat beside Andrea's aunt, Anna Truesdale, for a while, listening to her tell me about Andrea's laugh, how it used to carry through the hills like a bell. "She had a wild heart, that one," she said. "The kind the world don't always know how to keep safe."

I wore Mamaw Ruth's pearl earrings. They swung gently every time the wind stirred, and I could almost hear her humming just behind me. Her prayers, always a quilt stitched from mercy, had carried me even when I couldn't feel the stitches. It had taken me years to understand that kind of quiet strength, the sort that doesn't shout, but lingers.

A few days later, the mood shifted from mourning to matters of paper and property. At the lawyer's office, the waiting room smelled of dust and lemon polish.  The walls were lined with certificates and faded family photos that looked like they hadn't been updated in decades. The will was read with all the pomp of a grocery list, but I clung to every word. Sheryl and I received modest inheritances, not enough to change our lives, but enough to shape what came next.

"I want to put in a sunroom," Sheryl said as we stood in the parking lot beneath a sky full of low clouds.  She pressed her palm over her stomach, a soft smile playing at her lips. "Somewhere for the baby to nap. All that light pouring in."

"Baby?" I blinked.

She nodded.  "Spring baby.  Luke doesn't care either way, but I'm hoping for a boy."

A laugh slipped out of me, part joy, part disbelief. We were starting over, both of us. I thought of all the nights we'd cried ourselves to sleep under the same roof, both too stubborn to admit how much we'd needed each other. Maybe now, with a new generation on its way, we'd finally figure it out.

A few weeks later, she handed me paint swatches on the porch. "Come over next Tuesday," she said. "Help me choose. But if you try to make this kid's room banana-yellow, I'll revoke your auntie privileges."

Her teasing grin anchored us to something sure and mended; the sound of our laughter stitched shut an old seam.

Mari's retirement came like the last page of a well-thumbed chapter, worn at the edges, full of memory. She locked the doors of her Virginia greenhouse for the last time, apron wrinkled, hands still stained with soil. Behind her, the late-afternoon sun poured golden over the rows of rosemary and mint, casting long shadows that stretched like farewells.

Shay and I had driven up from Tennessee to help her pack: seed catalogs, dented watering cans, and clay pots etched with moss. When the last box was strapped down, I pressed the camper keys and title into her palm.

"You've earned your rest," I said. "Come home with us, be near family. And if you miss the smell of compost, you know where to find me."

She didn't answer right away. Just pulled me in, tight and trembling, and let the tears fall. We hugged beneath the hanging ferns, the hush between us crowded with everything words couldn't hold.

That hug was a hinge between seasons. Crossing back over the state line, Virginia pines gave way to Tennessee ridges, and the ache of goodbye softened into the promise ahead. The dream Mari and I once whispered over potting benches was about to flower on my own ground.

Dawn of the grand-opening day in Thompson Holler arrived warm and sweet, the sort of morning Mamaw called "an omen." My new greenhouse, perched on a cleared rise behind the farmhouse, carried Mari's legacy forward while growing into something more: a nonprofit sanctuary for women who needed the healing only soil could give.

Lena-Grace's hand-painted sign greeted everyone at the door:
**Grow where you are planted. Bloom when you're ready.**

Tiny daisies circled the words like shy confetti. I could already picture future snapshots of women holding their first seedlings beneath it.

Inside, air hung heavy with potting soil, lavender, sage, underscored by the faint perfume of raspberries from the patch out back. Rows of herbs waited in tin cans, each labeled in crooked handwriting. Voices drifted, soft, unsure at first, then warming like sun on glass.

Our inaugural orientation welcomed women whose stories, like mine, were thorny, untamed, yet stubbornly surviving. Introductions were hesitant, glances cautious, but laughter soon rose like birdsong. Someone tuned an old radio to gentle gospel. Lena-Grace passed out gloves and sweet tea, dabbing her eyes more than once.

There was grace in the dirt, in the rhythm of sowing and watering, in simply being seen. With every basil transplant and marigold seed. The Virginia greenhouse had closed its doors, but its spirit opened new ones here in Tennessee. Roots, once planted, never truly let go; they only look for fresh earth to keep on reaching.

Mamaw Ruth was with me in every row, in every stem that stood a little taller after being replanted. I thought of her garden back home, the rows never quite straight, the soil always full of rocks, but everything still grew.

At twilight, Andrea Grace and I walked barefoot along the riverside. The evening wrapped around us like a shawl, and the crickets sawed through the hush. She picked up stones and tried to skip them across the water, giggling when they plopped instead.

"I'm gonna get it to skip three times, Momma," she said, eyes full of determination.

"I believe you," I told her, watching her try again. This time it skipped once. We both cheered.

Shay's presence settled beside me like an exhale. He crouched to show Andrea Grace how to angle her wrist just right. Watching them, my daughter and the man who taught me love needed tending, not fixing.

He came to stand beside me, his presence settling like an exhale. He took my hand and didn't let go. We stood watching Andrea Grace until the moment stretched long and soft.

"I'm late," I whispered, leaning my head on his shoulder.

He turned, eyes wide, and laid his palm against my belly.

"I hope it's a girl," he said.

I smiled. "Me too."

Andrea Grace and I had brought an old metal bucket with us, the handle clinking with each step as we made our way to the bramble at the edge of the yard. The raspberries were thick this year—dark, heavy, and sun-warmed. We picked in silence at first, the quiet between us soft and easy.

Her little fingers reached for the low clusters, her dress brushing against the canes. "We're gonna make Mamaw's dumplins, right?" she asked, berry juice already staining her hands.

"Sure are," I said, dropping another plump one into the bucket. "She'd be proud of us."

When the bucket was nearly full, I stood back and looked over the patch. The wind rustled through the leaves like a whisper.

I plucked one last berry, held it to my lips, and tasted it slowly. No flinch. Just sweetness.

"Thank you," I whispered—to the bush, to the moment, to all the things that had brought us here.

Somewhere from the hush of the trees, I heard, "We bloom from what was buried. Even thorned things can bear sweetness. We are still growing."

The words settled in me like a seed, soft at first, then sure. I stood there a moment longer, letting the breeze pass through me, letting the weight of years and healing and memory fold into something whole. Because we are still growing, and growing things need tending. They need time. They need mercy.

Later that night, I sat with pen in hand and soft candlelight spilling across the page, trying to put words to the pain and beauty of it all. I think of all the roots Mamaw left behind, deep in this Appalachian soil. Roots I once tried to outrun, but now tend with care. There are plants growing in that greenhouse that I never knew the names of as a girl. There are stories growing, too.

I see it every time a woman presses her hands into the soil and feels herself becoming whole. Every time a seed takes root. Every time someone dares to bloom in a place they thought they'd never rise from. That's where Mamaw lives now, in the things we tend, in the things we grow.

Some folks might look back on my life and swear it reads like a ledger of grief, one hard entry after another, thick as kudzu on a fence line. They wouldn't be wrong. My days are strung with losses, buried bones, and nights too heavy to name. But sorrow from the outside looks different than sorrow carried in the bones. Heartbreak isn't a row of tombstones standing neat in the sun; it's a forge. Every blow, every flame, reshapes the metal until it rings clearer than before.

I used to think the fire meant to burn me down. Now I know it was tempering me, hardening the parts that needed to stand and softening the parts that needed to bend. Andrea's silence taught me to guard my own voice. Lonnie's cruelty taught me to heed the quiet warnings in a room. Papaw's hidden sins taught me that truth is compassion, even when it splinters the family tree. Carrying new life while the past clawed at my heels taught me how much endurance costs, and why it's worth the price.

None of that pain is a blessing by itself; God doesn't wrap tragedies up as gifts. The blessing is what can bloom in the scorch-print they leave behind: Sheryl still reaching for my hand on her darkest days, Mamaw's prayers lacing morning light, Shay loving without needing to make me smaller. Blessings are my children's laughter ricocheting off the rafters with heartbeats steady as church bells. Blessings are the raspberries that come back thicker every spring, no matter how hard winter tries to kill them.

So if my story sounds like sorrow stacked on sorrow, remember the other half: every wound became a door, every ghost a teacher, every darkness an invitation to strike a match. I am not the sum of the sad things that happened to me. I'm the woman who walked through them and kept walking, carrying both balm and blade in hands tempered by flame, shaped not just to endure, but to rise.

And if someone finds this journal years from now, I hope they feel not just the sorrow, but the rising. I hope they understand we didn't just survive. We loved through it. We built something from the dust. We found each other in the bramble.

And like Mamaw said, we stayed soft. We stayed rooted. And we bloomed anyway.

*Journal Entry– June 3, 2019*

*When you finally grasp how quickly time slips by, how brief and fragile this life really is, an ache settles deep in your bones. You begin to feel the weight of each moment, the hush that follows joy, the pause before goodbye. You start searching for ways to slow the clock, to savor every drop of time before it spills through your fingers. You hold tighter to the ones you love, knowing they can be taken in an instant.*

*Nothing is certain, except that everything is temporary. Loss becomes the only constant.*

*So we cling to hope, the hope that our souls are immortal, stitched from the same breath as the stars. That no distance, no years, no grave can separate us from the ones our spirit longs for. We are, each of us, bound to and a part of something greater, our Creator. And when the day comes when we, too, are called from this world of flesh and bone, we will find each other again. Whole. Eternal. Home.*

# Epilogue


*Many springs had come and gone—this one unfolding gently into June...*

The raspberry brambles stretched thick along the garden center's edge—still a little wild, still full of thorns, but now part of the place, claimed and tended. They arched like cathedral windows, tangled with memory and morning light. I moved slowly down the row, hose in hand, the sun warming my shoulders. The vines drank deep, their leaves trembling in the breeze like they remembered.

The greenhouse was already humming with life. Lavender swayed in the beds. Bees buzzed lazily at the lips of blooms. Somewhere near the back, a mockingbird trilled. We had added two new rows of hydrangeas that spring, soft blue and pale cream, planted beneath Mamaw Ruth's old trellis now painted sage green.

Andrea Grace stood at the checkout, clipboard in hand, hair pulled back in a red scarf. She had grown into a woman shaped by gentleness, her strength a gift from her mother who wrapped her in it daily, like a prayer. She kept her voice soft when instructing the volunteers, but firm when it mattered. She'd memorized the Latin names for half the greenhouse inventory, and I was sure she would run the place herself one day, better than I ever had.

Our youngest, Lettie Christine, had just started high school—a little wilder, a little louder, always tracking soil through the kitchen and forgetting to label her seedlings. She smelled of mulch and mint most days, her boots permanently caked in mud.  She spent more time singing along to the radio than pruning properly, but she had Mamaw's stubbornness and a sweetness that bloomed in unexpected ways.  I sometimes watched the two girls laughing among the raised beds and thought: this is the harvest.  Not just plants or plans, but people— growing, changing, becoming.

Just last week, I found Lettie out by the edge of the field, with my old bow in her hand.

"Found this in the shed," she'd said, holding it like it had been made for her.

I smiled but said nothing. Years ago, I might've used it to steady my breath, to remind myself of who I was.  Now, seeing Lettie with it— strong, wild-hearted, aiming toward something only she could see, it felt like a chapter had turned.

She released the arrow.  It flew wide, bounced off the hay, and she cackled like it was the best shot she'd ever made.

I hadn't felt the need to correct her.

Some things weren't about hitting the mark. Some things were about learning to pull the string, to let go.

I had stood at the edge of the field long after Lettie's arrow fell. There was something solemn in it, how the girl grinned and tried again, not needing perfection to know she was strong.

It reminded me of how we had all learned to keep on, not because the ghosts had left us, but because we'd stopped flinching at their presence. The past still knocked from time to time, soft as rain on a tin roof, but it no longer ruled the house.

I turned from the field, the breeze brushing my cheek like a memory. The garden center stretched wide before me, still familiar, still blooming in its own quiet way.

Out by the drive, the old metal sign still hung over the gate: ***Grow***

***where you are planted. Bloom when you're ready.*** The paint had faded a bit, but the words held.

Mari sat beneath the arbor near the roses, her white hair pulled into a bun, teaching a new volunteer how to prune without damaging the stem.

"Patience," she told the girl. "You're not just shaping the flower. You're telling it how to grow."

When Andrea Grace passed by, Mari winked. "My girl," she said with pride.

A shrill ring cut through the breeze. I smiled, wiped my hands on my old apron, and pulled the phone from my pocket.

"Hey, sweetheart."

"Quick interview in Tazewell ran long," Shay said, his voice as familiar as breath. "But I'm on my way. Tell Andrea not to lock me out like last time."

"She says you owe her sweet tea and a night off."

Shay chuckled. "I'll bring both."

I clicked off the call and tucked the phone away. I took a deep breath of soil, leaf, and sunlight before heading toward the back trail.

The trail wound gently through the heart of it all—the garden center nestled between our home on one side, and Momma and Daddy's cottage, we had built, tucked beneath the walnut trees. Dandelions freckled the path. Wren song echoed from the eaves. It wasn't just land. It was ours. Home.

Momma sat on the porch in her rocker, one of her afghans across her lap. The breeze lifted a strand of her hair, and for a flicker of a moment, she looked like the old photographs I'd seen of her mother, the one who left before I was ever born. It startled me, how much softness could live in a face that had known so much sorrow.

"You're early," she said as I stepped onto the porch.

"Just watering the brambles."

"They were blooming last time too, weren't they?"

I smiled and nodded. "They've come back strong."

Daddy stepped out from the house, broom in hand, and paused beside her.

She reached for his wrist without looking, her fingers curling over his like it was the most natural thing in the world.

He glanced down, gave her hand a gentle squeeze, and kept sweeping the porch, slow and steady.

There was a softness between them now that hadn't always been there, a quiet peace that settled like dust in sunlight, years in the making.

Later that afternoon, Luke and Sheryl pulled up in their truck with their teenage twin boys in tow, laughter tumbling out ahead of them like it couldn't wait to reach the porch. Alana pulled in behind them, beaming behind the wheel of her graduation gift, a shiny new car that still smelled like promise. Sunday afternoons brought the whole family home—feet up, lemonade poured, music playing low.

As twilight deepened, I paused beside the brambles, fingers brushing the leaves that had once drawn blood. The pain hadn't vanished, not entirely. What Papaw Harlan had done still clung to the corners of my memory, a shadow that softened but never fully disappeared.

Forgiveness had not come all at once. It had crept in slowly, like spring thaw, melting the hardened parts of my heart until what remained was love, not blind to the past, but bound to something deeper. There were still nights I woke remembering his voice, the way he laughed, the smell of his shirts hanging on the line. I had loved him.

And in that love, even knowing the truth, I had learned something about grace.

Over the years, the weight of his sin grew lighter, not because it mattered less, but because love outlived it. I remembered the good more than the evil now. I had to. Not out of denial, but out of obedience. Because Jesus had called me to. Because love, real love, wasn't a feeling.

It was a decision. A daily choice to extend mercy, even when it costs you.

I had clung to grief long enough. Now, I cling to redemption.

As night settled in, I returned to my office in the greenhouse, the world gone quiet but warm. The glass panes glowed faint gold, and the scent of rosemary hung in the air. I opened my journal to a fresh page and wrote:

*We are shaped by the ones who walked before us, their steps carving out quiet paths through the wilderness so we might find our footing. Their choices, their prayers, their mistakes, they all live in us, like rings in the trunk of an old tree. And now, it's our turn to tend the path ahead. To leave the world softer than we found it. Kinder. A place where love is the rule, not the rare exception. Where forgiveness is not earned, but offered. That's the hope we plant, even if we never see the harvest. That's the grace we pass on.*

I closed the book and reached for the folded card tucked behind the last page, a recipe written in Mamaw Ruth's hand, creased from years of unfolding, stained with time and berry juice.

**Mamaw Ruth's Raspberry Dumplins**
  4 cups fresh black raspberries
  ¼ teaspoon lemon juice
  4 ½ cups white sugar
  1 cup water
  ¼ tsp nutmeg
  2 cups all-purpose flour
  ½
  teaspoon baking soda
  ¼ teaspoon salt
  3 tablespoons shortening
  ¾ cup buttermilk
  **Directions:**

In a large pot, combine the raspberries, lemon juice, sugar, nutmeg, and water.  Bring to a boil, then reduce the heat to low, cover, and simmer for about 15 minutes. Stir occasionally, but gently so as not to crush the berries.

Meanwhile, in a medium bowl, stir together the flour, baking soda, and salt.  Cut in shortening using a pastry blender or fork until the pieces are no larger than peas. Stir in the buttermilk until the dough comes together. If too stiff, add a splash more buttermilk.

When the sauce is slightly above the level of the berries, drop dumpling dough in one tablespoon at a time. Cover and simmer for about 5 minutes. Flip dumplings over, cover again, and cook another 10 minutes. Let stand for 10 minutes before serving.

Best served warm, with someone you love close by.

# On Writing This Story

My goal in writing *The Secrets Raspberries Keep* was to create something deeply authentic, an Appalachian voice looking back on her past and reckoning with the moments that shaped her. I wanted the cadence of the narration to mirror thought itself: natural, unfiltered, sometimes fragmented, but always honest. A story that sounds like someone remembering and healing in real time.

I wanted to explore the weight of trauma, the secrets families bury, and the way silence ripples through generations. At its core, this is a story about womanhood and what it means to be a girl asked to carry too much, to endure quietly, and to bleed behind closed doors while the world looks away.

The story is also rooted in grief. In recent years, I lost all of my grandparents and watched old wounds rise, truths surface, and others disappear with the people who held them. Writing this book became a way to honor what was remembered and what was never said.

This book is an excavation and a reassembling of broken, sacred pieces. Its heartbeat is simple: ***we survive, and in surviving, we help others survive too.***

# About the Author

Amber Rochelle Gilpin is an Appalachian writer, artist, and educator from the Cumberland Gap region of East Tennessee, where she homesteads and raises her family. Her work is rooted in the landscapes, traditions, and generational stories of Appalachia, exploring themes of memory, resilience, faith, and the quiet strength found in rural life.

Once believing her voice was too small to challenge injustice, whether in the wider world or within her own community, Amber now writes to reclaim that voice. Appalachia is often reduced to a stereotype or dismissed entirely; her work seeks to complicate that narrative, revealing the depth, dignity, fierce loyalty, and enduring spirit that define the region.

She is the creator of *Milkglass and Memory*, a creative space where storytelling, art, and Appalachian heritage meet. Through both her writing and visual art, she honors the past while creating space for Appalachian voices to be heard, remembered, and rise.

You can find her work, art, and upcoming projects at:
www.milkglassandmemory.com